Taking the Leap

TAKING THE LEAP

A RIVER RAIN NOVEL

KRISTEN ASHLEY

Taking the Leap

A River Rain Novel

By Kristen Ashley

Copyright 2022 Kristen Ashley

ISBN: 978-1-952457-68-5

Published by Blue Box Press, an imprint of Evil Eye Concepts, Incorporated

BOOK DESCRIPTION

Taking the Leap
A River Rain Novel, Book 3
By Kristen Ashley

From *New York Times* bestselling author Kristen Ashley comes the
new book in her River Rain Series, *Taking the Leap*.

Alexandra Sharp has been crushing on her co-worker, John "Rix"
Hendrix for years. He's her perfect man, she knows it.

She's just not his perfect woman, and she knows that too.

Then Rix gives Alex a hint that maybe there's a spark between them
that, if she takes the leap, she might be able to fan into a flame. This
leads to a crash and burn, and that's all shy Alex needs to catch the
hint never to take the risk again.

However, with undeniable timing, Rix's ex, who broke his heart, and
Alex's family, who spent her lifetime breaking hers, rear their heads,

gearing up to offer more drama. With the help of some matchmaking friends, Rix and Alex decide to face the onslaught together…

As a fake couple.

ABOUT KRISTEN ASHLEY

Kristen Ashley is the *New York Times* bestselling author of over eighty romance novels including the *Rock Chick*, *Colorado Mountain*, *Dream Man*, *Chaos*, *Unfinished Heroes*, *The 'Burg*, *Magdalene*, *Fantasyland*, *The Three*, *Ghost and Reincarnation*, *The Rising*, *Dream Team* and *Honey* series along with several standalone novels. She's a hybrid author, publishing titles both independently and traditionally, her books have been translated in fourteen languages and she's sold over five million books.

Kristen's novel, *Law Man*, won the *RT Book Reviews* Reviewer's Choice Award for best Romantic Suspense, her independently published title *Hold On* was nominated for *RT Book Reviews* best Independent Contemporary Romance and her traditionally published title *Breathe* was nominated for best Contemporary Romance. Kristen's titles *Motorcycle Man*, *The Will*, and *Ride Steady* (which won the Reader's Choice award from *Romance Reviews*) all made the final rounds for Goodreads Choice Awards in the Romance category.

Kristen, born in Gary and raised in Brownsburg, Indiana, was a fourth-generation graduate of Purdue University. Since, she has lived in Denver, the West Country of England, and she now resides in Phoenix. She worked as a charity executive for eighteen years prior to beginning her independent publishing career. She now writes full-time.

Although romance is her genre, the prevailing themes running through all of Kristen's novels are friendship, family and a strong sisterhood. To this end, and as a way to thank her readers for their support, Kristen has created the Rock Chick Nation, a series of programs that are designed to give back to her readers and promote a strong female community.

The mission of the Rock Chick Nation is to live your best life, be true to your true self, recognize your beauty, and last but definitely not least, take your sister's back whether they're at your side as friends and family or if they're thousands of miles away and you don't know who they are.

The programs of the RC Nation include Rock Chick Rendezvous, weekends Kristen organizes full of parties and get-togethers to bring the sisterhood together, Rock Chick Recharges, evenings Kristen arranges for women who have been nominated to receive a special night, and Rock Chick Rewards, an ongoing program that raises funds for nonprofit women's organizations Kristen's readers nominate. Kristen's Rock Chick Rewards have donated hundreds of thousands of dollars to charity and this number continues to rise.

You can read more about Kristen, her titles and the Rock Chick Nation at KristenAshley.net.

ALSO BY KRISTEN ASHLEY

Rock Chick Series:

Rock Chick

Rock Chick Rescue

Rock Chick Redemption

Rock Chick Renegade

Rock Chick Revenge

Rock Chick Reckoning

Rock Chick Regret

Rock Chick Revolution

Rock Chick Reawakening

Rock Chick Reborn

The 'Burg Series:

For You

At Peace

Golden Trail

Games of the Heart

The Promise

Hold On

The Chaos Series:

Own the Wind

Fire Inside

Ride Steady

Walk Through Fire

Wild and Free

The Unfinished Hero Series:

Knight

Creed

Raid

Deacon

Sebring

Ghosts and Reincarnation Series:

Sommersgate House

Lacybourne Manor

Penmort Castle

Fairytale Come Alive

Lucky Stars

The Rising Series:

The Beginning of Everything

The Plan Commences

The Dawn of the End

The Rising

Mathilda, SuperWitch:

Mathilda's Book of Shadows

Mathilda The Rise of the Dark Lord

Wild West MC Series

Still Standing

Other Titles by Kristen Ashley:

Heaven and Hell

Play It Safe

Three Wishes

Complicated

Loose Ends

Fast Lane

AUTHOR'S NOTE AND ACKNOWLEDGEMENTS

A few years ago, I realized something.

In a great number of my books, the hero, or heroine, lives in the mountains.

I realized this as I was looking in the mountains around Prescott, trying to find a writing retreat.

I realized it as I viewed a number of properties, none of them right, but at every one, I felt something settle in me.

Perhaps it was the small-town girl needing that fix of what felt like home where the population wasn't as dense, and the pace wasn't as hectic. Maybe it was the small farm girl who needed bigger spaces around her to feel right.

Maybe I just really love the mountains.

But I found it, my retreat, and I knew it the minute I walked in. I hadn't even gotten through the first room, but that cabin was it.

It needed some work, so I had that done, and as things like that tend to do, it took forever (when it didn't really, I was just keen to be up in my mountain shack).

The day finally came when it was mine. With functional bathrooms where I wasn't in danger of falling through the floor and custom-made neon signs in the first room you walk into—one saying

Rock On! and one saying Chill Out—my life mantra and what I never wanted to forget to do when I got to that perfect little shack on Kit's Mountain.

Although my cat was uncertain (don't worry, she eventually came around), I knew during our first stay there that cabin was one of the best things I'd ever done in my life. There is a vibe there that's instant and unshakeable. I found a coffee mug in town to explain it, so I bought it. It says, Relax, You're at The Cabin. Being driven, hustling since I got my first job at a golf course at age thirteen, I needed that vibe and I needed it to be unshakeable.

I needed to remember that it's crucial sometimes to take a breath and be with the trees.

And since, I've written many books up there. They roll out of me like in the beginning when I first started writing. With nothing but the deer and the squirrels and the birds (and lots of bugs) as company, total quiet, sheer peace, creativity flows like magic. I'm Princess Aurora with all the little critters dancing around me in a world so tranquil and yet so alive, it's a constant source of inspiration and beauty.

This is no lie, once, I sensed movement out the sides of my eyes, turned that way, and a deer was pressing her nose up to my window, ears pricked with curiosity, watching me write.

Totally Aurora.

However, before I experienced all of that wonder, within days after the first time I spent time up there, I got a text from a friend telling me the Cellar Fire was raging not far from the cabin.

Suddenly, as a brand-new mountain girl, I needed to get educated very quickly about what it means when a wildfire is taking acres close to your home.

Daily…no, repeatedly for days, I checked the Incident Site to see what was happening with that fire. Where it was going. How much was contained. What the alert level was and if that meant I needed to prepare.

I wasn't even up there, so I was in no danger. But I kept thinking I should dash up and get the things that had meaning to me. I made a list in my head, not only for then, but for the future, if this should happen again. And I lamented the thought of losing that home that had stood since the '60s, had history and was already my sanctuary.

The percentage of the fire contained did not increase for days, and it's safe to say I was freaking out.

Until I got up one morning, checked, and it was to my stunned disbelief that the containment shot up exponentially.

I don't remember the exact number.

I do remember this was because the Hotshots had been deployed.

Not long later, the danger was over…and then the fire was out.

Now, it's all love and goodness in romance novels, but the truth of the matter is, for a novelist, you must weigh very important things. You'll have readers from every walk of life reading your novels, and although innumerable tales need to be told, responsible storytelling is, at least to me, important. You can't get everything right, and you won't, but you need to try and do your best.

When it comes to this book, I'm referring to two things.

One, I had to do my hero, Rix, justice.

And two, the fact this book is set in Prescott, which is not far from Yarnell, the location of the Yarnell Fire, in which nineteen souls were lost. Firefighters who were stuck when the winds changed, and in trying to save everything from the trees that point us to the heavens to those deer that press their noses to windows to the sanctuaries and safe havens of humans and so very much more, they lost their own lives.

This is a heart mark for anyone who lives around Prescott. If ever the conversation turns, the hush is heard when speaking of Prescott Fire Department's Granite Mountain Hotshots who lost their lives in that fire.

And as such, I really had to think about what I was doing with Rix, my hero in this book, who fictionally fought with those Hotshots to contain the Cellar Fire. Hotshots who not-fictionally-at-all saved my cabin and so, so very much more.

In other words, the Hotshots in Prescott are very real. The Cellar

Fire was very real. But the men and what happened to them during that fire in this book are fictionalized.

In the end, for a variety of reasons, I thought Rix's story was important to tell. However, I understand there may be sensitivity around such losses, or dramatizing such events, and as he shared his story with me, I did my utmost to handle it with care in giving it to my readers.

So here, I must say a few more things.

Thank you to firefighters everywhere, and I say that with a gravity mere words can't share. I hope I did the story of one of your fictional brethren justice.

And second, thank you to the fighters who saved my cabin, and those of my awesome neighbors, and those lives of the deer and boar and birds and all the vastness of the rest. So many people hear these stories of the men and women who fight these fires, perhaps not realizing it's not only marking that line so the places that are inhabited will be spared …but with each acre lost or saved, they're putting their lives on the line, preserving something precious.

And last, I need it known that I didn't enter into this story lightly. I tried to give it the weight it deserves.

As well as a happy ending.

As such, I must say thank you to one of my bestest besties in the world, Beth Bullard, OTR, who took all my many questions about how a man would recover and live his life as a double amputee and wrote a veritable term paper in response.

Beth, not only a tremendously experienced occupational therapist and former CEO of a rehab hospital, but also a writer herself, got it to the depths I needed it and shared information and articles and resources that helped me make Rix the rich character I fell so deeply in love with, I wanted to write a 50,000-word epilogue because I didn't want to say goodbye.

Beth made certain I built Rix into a man where, in her words there's "So much he can do…versus can't." That was in my head with every scene he was in, and that was the message I wanted my readers to take from this book.

Love you, Bethy, and thank you.

Thank you also to two men I'll probably never meet, AJ Montgomery and Army veteran Dan Nevins, for being inspirations. Just reading about both of these men was a privilege.

Thank you also to Donna Perry for cheerleading me through this book. It was fast and feverish, and it was fun having you at my side.

And as ever, and always, my posse at Blue Box Press, Liz Berry, Jillian Stein and MJ Rose, not to mention Asha Hossain and Kim Guidroz, and last Jenn Watson of Social Butterfly.

Writing for this imprint is like being handed the wings to soar if you just take the leap.

I took the leap.

And this book felt like soaring.

DEDICATION

This book is for those men and women
who turn to the hills to face the flames.
On behalf of the deer and the boar and the birds and the bugs
and the thousands of other creatures
and the thousands of trees
and all of the people.
Thank you.

PROLOGUE

SOMEONE LIKE ME

Alex

*I*t was happening.

He was flirting with me.

John "Rix" Hendrix, the coolest guy I'd ever met, the most interesting person I'd ever known, the most handsome man I'd ever seen, was flirting...

With...

Me.

And I was somehow managing to flirt back (kind of).

Okay, I might be relying on something from Moscow to do so (that something being their mules), but it was happening.

And I knew I wasn't making more of it than I should.

I knew that because Chloe and Judge were with us. We were out having drinks, celebrating the official beginning of our new Trail Blazer program (that day, Judge, Rix and I had signed on to new job titles with new responsibilities and new salaries with the expanded program—I got a promotion and a fifteen percent raise!—definitely worth sitting down to drinks with the man who terrified me most on this earth).

Chloe was giving Rix and me smug looks, but mostly me, and once, she'd even winked at me.

As an aside: Chloe Pierce, my boss Judge's girlfriend, was the coolest, most interesting, most gorgeous woman I'd ever met.

And even though (fortunately, so far, though maybe not now?) Rix had missed it, but although she hadn't said anything, I knew Chloe knew I was crushing on Rix...*big time*.

And I had been.

Crushing on Rix.

Big time.

She was happy for me.

I was happy for me!

Because Rix was *flirting with me*.

Me!

And the reason why this was crazy was not only because he was cool and interesting and handsome, and as yet, such a man had never shown any interest in me (no, the men who had shown interest in me lacked one or more of those qualities).

It was because I was, well...

Me.

First off, I was shy around cute guys (okay, I was just plain shy, but it got a lot worse around guys, and off-the-charts worse around cute ones).

Not to mention, I knew how to put on mascara, I just wasn't a big fan of wearing it (so, unless it was a super special occasion, or I was with my family, I didn't).

I had a little house up in the mountains (TBH, it was more like a big shack), but I was rarely in it because there were a lot better places to be (and my house was awesome, I just had a ton of interests and not a lot of them happened in my house).

I knew how to cook in a kitchen, but I cooked way better over a campfire (and in a hot coal pit).

There were Star Trek nerds, I was just a star nerd (that being, lying under them at night in the middle of nowhere and staring at them until I fell asleep).

I would rather snowshoe into a forest in the dead of winter, set up a tent and spend a couple of days in nature, reading by a headlamp at night cozied up in a one-woman sleeping bag in a one-person tent than sit by a fireside during a snowstorm with a mug of hot cocoa (though, that was nice too).

Many women didn't get me.

Men didn't either, and it was actually more men who didn't get me than it was women because I wasn't stereotypically womanly. Most women got there were lots of different kinds of women. Most men (in my experience) weren't that broad minded.

No, actually, it was more my family who didn't get me than anyone else.

My family didn't get me at all.

Which wasn't really surprising, seeing as I didn't get them either.

"Sexy as fuck," Rix was saying.

I came out of my musings to focus on his words.

Words he was aiming at me (me!).

Words of which one of them was "sexy."

A flutter assaulted my belly at hearing his gravelly voice utter that word (at me).

"What?" I whispered, like talking louder might break the spell of how close he was sitting, leaned in even closer, talking to me, but doing it with his attention centered right...on...*me*.

Yowza.

"That glass dome glamp sitch in Joshua Tree," he answered, reminding me what we'd been talking about. "Never thought I'd say those words, glamping is better than not camping at all, it just isn't my gig. But it was just that fuckin' awesome. Bedding down under the stars at night..."

Oh my God!

He was into sleeping under the stars just like me!

"Waking up with the sun..."

That wasn't as great as stars, but it was cool.

Something happened to his eyes which saw results in specific parts of my body before he finished.

"The shower that was top and sides all glass. Getting wet and clean with a near-on three-hundred-and-sixty-degree view of the Joshua trees and the desert. Only thing missing was I didn't take a woman with me."

He stopped speaking.

Shoot.

That meant it was my turn.

"You'll have to…" My voice was clogged due to the fact my mind was on Rix in a shower that was all glass. Rix…*wet* and *slick* and *slippery*…in a shower that was all glass. So I cleared my throat, and when I did, his lips hitched in a way that those specific parts of my body, already perked, became veritably *primed.* "Text me the deets for that. I, uh…don't usually glamp but…"

I let that trail off, not because I didn't have more to say, but because I'd lost the ability to speak.

This was because his eyes were watching my mouth while I was doing it.

"Text you," he murmured to my mouth, like that wasn't where his mind was going.

I also had a sense of where his mind was going.

As in, he didn't want to text me the info.

He wanted to personally show me the site.

With the glass shower.

That he would be using.

With me there.

Or, perhaps, in it with him.

Lord.

"Yeah," I forced out, and it did, indeed, sound forced.

No, that wasn't right.

It sounded breathy and strangled.

As you could probably deduce, I was generally no good at flirting (or chitchat, or mingling, or social situations on the whole, but definitely top of that heap was flirting).

However, with Rix, I was a mess and not only now. All the time.

I didn't think in the time I'd known him we'd ever had a single one-on-one conversation.

This was the first of those too.

His attention returned to my eyes. "Yours?"

"Uh...sorry?"

"Coolest place you ever spent the night," he reminded me of the subject we'd been discussing.

It had been my question, and it might have been the ballsiest question I'd ever asked any man, not just Rix.

"I go off route," I told him.

"You mean off trail?" he asked.

I nodded, but then shook my head, which meant I ended up making a circle, which made Rix's lips hitch again, this time just with amusement. And making him smile like that, I felt like throwing my arms out and arching my back, like I was breaking through the tape at the finish line, coming in first, winning the prize.

"That too," I made myself say. "But I meant off route. I'm a byway person, not a highway person. And I was on a byway, outside Ouray—"

"Colorado."

I nodded.

"One of the prettiest places on the planet," he stated my personal opinion.

"Yeah," I said softly.

He let that soft sound float between us for a second.

I felt weird about it, weird in a wonderful way, like the sound I'd made was pretty and the word was meaningful, and he was getting off on riding it and the feeling behind it, before he prompted, "You were on a byway..."

Good God.

He was.

He was paying complete attention to me.

Listening to every word I said.

So *this* was how it felt to be the center of Rix's attention.

I'd wondered for a very long time.

I'd been a lot of beautiful places (a lot, a lot), but none was as heavenly as that right there.

"I was on a byway," I repeated, "and I pulled into this diner. Cool place. Had a counter with a pie under glass at the end of it and everything. Sat next to an old-timer, we got to talking, and he told me about some hot springs not many people know about. I remembered the conversation, what he said. So, on a long weekend, I drove back up in the winter, snowshoed in where he said to go, and he was right on the money. It was exactly as he described. Trees and snow and this tuft of steam coming up from the spring. Pristine, not a footprint, no one around. Pitched my tent close to the rocks around the spring, barely had to use my sleeping bag they were so warm. Sat in the spring until my fingers wrinkled. Slept with my head out of the tent, gaiter pulled up over my nose, listening to the burbling of the water, staring through the evergreens up at the stars."

I stopped talking, and Rix didn't start. He didn't move. And somewhere in sharing this memory with him, I'd missed his eyes had slid back down to my lips.

When he continued not to move or say anything for a long time, I finished, "So that's the coolest place I've ever spent the night."

"Heaven," he murmured, not shifting his gaze.

A shiver trailed down my spine.

"Yeah," I whispered. "Heaven."

He still didn't move.

I started freaking out, my lips with his attention on them beginning to feel tingly, and not thinking, I caught the bottom one with my teeth.

When I did that, his gaze came up to my eyes, and he had such a cocky look in his own, knowing just how hot he was, knowing just what reaction he was causing in me, it was not only mesmerizing, it was akin to about twenty minutes of foreplay.

Great foreplay.

So great, I almost moaned.

I did whimper (slightly and horrifyingly, because he heard it, and I got another hitch of his lips, and not the amused hitch this time, the *other* one).

Holy crap.

I might orgasm…

From flirting!

I instantly stood.

He sat back as I did, his brows snapping together as he looked up at me.

"I'll be back!" I cried.

I was unnecessarily loud. Thus, I felt Judge and Chloe's startled attention come to me too.

But I raced away.

Straight to the bathroom.

I didn't have to use the bathroom.

I had to give myself a pep talk.

Because this was Rix, *finally*, Rix and me talking, *flirting*, and I couldn't muck this up like I did practically every interaction I'd had with him.

And we worked together at River Rain Outdoor stores, before Hale Wheeler swept in and offered Trail Blazer, new titles and pay raises. At River Rain, Rix and me were not in the same department, but now we were on the exact same team. So not only would I see him every day, I'd be working side by side with him…every day.

I was in luck, when, upon a panicked check, I saw the bathroom was empty. Therefore, as I tried to instill myself with some courage, I wouldn't have an audience of some pretty, mountain-fresh, tanned, boho goddess washing her hands or using the facilities (which would, as every shy girl knew, have the opposite result when it came to courage).

It was just me in the restroom.

Me and my insecurities.

I stared at my hazel eyes in the mirror (a tortoiseshell brown around the pupil, leading to a marbled green that filled out the rest of the iris, not the violet of my sister and mother, not the green of my father, just plain-Jane hazel (as my sister described it)).

Then I took in the big, fat, dark pigtails that contained my thick hair and fell either side of my neck, down my chest.

Prescott, Arizona, where we all lived, was not a bustling metropolis.

I'd been here a while.

So had Rix.

This meant I not only worked with him, but I saw him out and about.

He was who he was, *how* he was. Those wide shoulders. That dark hair, short at the sides, longer but spiky at the top, most of the time messy and sexy, but sometimes sleek (and sexy). The square jaw. Those thick eyebrows that traveled to the corners of his eyes.

And the brown eyes that said he had a thousand stories to tell, some you wouldn't like, others that would leave you breathless.

Being all he was, he was never out alone.

What I meant was, unless he was with his buds, he was always with a woman.

He had a type.

Tall. Slender. Leggy. Athletic.

I was not tall.

I hiked. I paddleboarded. I kayaked.

I also ate.

So I did not have a svelte bod.

And those women I saw him with, they might all be mountain-fresh, tanned, boho goddesses who could keep up with him on a trail run (something he still did, even after he tragically lost both legs below the knees while fighting a wildfire in his previous occupation as a firefighter—see? totally the coolest guy I knew). But they also wore flowy dresses or Daisy Dukes and billowy blouses with flat sandals with tons of straps and mascara and maybe a winged eyeliner if they were feeling feisty, accompanying all of this with funky-chic wide-brimmed felt fedoras.

I'd look like a moron in a fedora.

I could just imagine what my sister would say if she saw me in a boho fedora.

As I was wont to do, the instant a thought that included my sister hit my brain, I shoved it aside.

But when I did, I was stuck with me.

Staring at my round face with its rounder cheekbones which was, indeed, tan, I tried to see myself with broad, tanner, muscled Rix, and I couldn't even conjure the image.

"What am I thinking? I work with this guy," I mumbled to my reflection.

I had no business flirting with a co-worker.

That was stupid. Crazy.

Embarrassing.

Maybe I was wrong.

Maybe it wasn't even flirting.

(Though I didn't have a ton of experience, I did have some, and it *felt* like flirting, not to mention, Chloe knew I was crushing on him, and she'd winked at me.)

"But this is Rix," I kept mumbling.

And it was.

Rix.

My perfect man.

He camped. He hiked. He kayaked. He came to work in the morning after a trail run or a ride on his handcycle. He headed out to parts unknown on his days off with his tent in his truck, coming back to work practically shimmering with the rapture of spending time in nature.

I did not trail run or ride, but I definitely came in from the outdoors shimmering after spending time in nature (at least, I felt like I did).

I'd never asked, I'd been too shy, but I'd bet actual, real money Rix had often fallen asleep under the stars, and not just in a glass glamping dome among the Joshua trees.

I bet he knew how to cook an entire meal under the earth.

I bet he knew what an impending thunderstorm smelled like, that certain snakes were threats (if you're caught by surprise...or being stupid), but bats and coyotes and bears were usually not (unless you caught them by surprise, or you're being stupid), and that you never, ever drank water from nature unless you went through the process of treating it.

Was all that not worth the risk?

Worth the risk of being embarrassed should I not be reading the current situation right?

Worth the risk of feeling the thrill?

The thrill of finding someone, and being with them...

Someone who got me.

Someone like me.

It was.

It was totally worth it.

To have Rix's big hand (I'd noticed his hands—his *big, rough* hands —and I'd noticed them about seven hundred thousand times in the exactly two and one-eighth years we'd been working together) wrapped around mine as we picked our way across a natural stone bridge over a creek.

To zip our sleeping bags together and whisper (and do other things) to each other under the cover of night.

Yes, even someone to cozy up with by a fire with cocoa and read on snowy days when we weren't under a ceiling of sky.

But to have those moments, say, to look into his eyes over coffee in the morning, and know he felt like me.

He was like me.

Because he was the one soul on this planet who *got me.*

"It's *so* worth it," I whispered.

A toilet flushed.

I jumped.

Someone was in there?

Yes, someone was.

A pretty, mountain-fresh, tanned, boho goddess wearing a felt, wide-brimmed panama hat and a big smile came out of a stall and headed with that smile aimed at me to the sink next to mine.

"Just to say, sister, it *is,*" she declared. "If you're talking about that hunk of tall, dark and handsome who was up in your space out there, it is *so worth it*," she declared. "Especially if he looks like that, is as into you as that and has a kickass name like Rix."

"I'm a nature nerd," I blurted, why, I did not know.

She shrugged even as she rubbed soap into her hands. "I've read *The Shell Seekers* thirteen times, and if a dude is not down to read it, even if he might not like it, he's out. We all got our thang. And by the by, that guy didn't look like a banker to me." She turned off the tap, shook water off her hands and turned to the dryer, exclaiming, "Killer! They have an Airblade!"

She then stuck her hands into the Airblade.

I stood staring at her attractive, sinewy back and shoulder muscles exposed by her spaghetti-strapped, oversized, muted-but-dizzily-printed dress, and I did this so long, the Airblade had worked its magic, and she'd turned.

"What are you still doing in here?" she demanded. "Go get 'im, tigress."

"I work with him."

She tipped her head to the side the same time she hitched a hip and put a hand on it. "So?"

"That could get messy."

"A non-messy life *totally* sucks."

This might sound crazy, but I knew she was right.

I got into a zen state when I cleaned my house, and I dug it.

Nevertheless, when it was done, a part of me always missed the boots thrown by the door, the coffeepot upended in the drainer, the Oxo pouring canister filled with homemade granola left on the counter, the throw tossed wide over the couch, the book spread open and lying on its pages, the jacket thrown over the back of a chair. All the signs that said, "Someone lives here, and they're not here tidying, they're out, busy *living*."

Did that translate to relationships?

To romance?

"I'll tell you what, a guy was that into me, I'd be *all the way* down with getting messy," my new bathroom friend announced.

Had Rix been *that* into me?

"I'm shy," I whispered.

"No shit?" she asked. "Girl, I noticed you two a while ago. At first, I wanted to walk by and high-five you for the way you were playing that player. Then I realized, well, hell. This is no play. This bitch is scared out of her brain about this dude, and it's so cute, *I could just die.*"

I was back to staring, this time at her mountain-fresh face.

"He thought it was cute too," she proclaimed. "But he thought it was so cute, he was itching *to pounce.*"

Rix.

Pouncing.

Oh Lord.

Now I was in danger of a standing-up, Rix-nowhere-near-me, bathroom orgasm.

"Really?" I breathed.

"Hi, I'm Dani." She stuck her hand out.

I took it. "I'm Alex."

To that, she for some reason shared, "Your hair is *goals.* I'm about to go and do what no woman under seventy has done in twenty years. Schedule a perm. Only so I can plait thick, fat braids like yours. You could play tug of war with those bitches. They're glorious."

I couldn't stop my smile.

She let my hand go. "Now we know each other, I can tell you, I've had my fair share of experience with players."

She was seriously pretty (and sinewy and tan and could pull off a panama hat, even in a ladies washroom), so I bet she did.

She kept talking.

"And as such, being a self-proclaimed expert, I could regale you with many tales of my field experience, so I know that man is seriously into you."

"I know him, and I've seen him with other women. He'd be more into someone like, to be honest...*you.*"

She shook her head, came to me, hooked arms, and guided us to and through the door.

"This is what shy chicks don't get," she started. "Guys like that have had me, over and over again. If they wanted girls like me, they wouldn't throw us back."

She seemed very sage, however, it should be noted that was a sad thing to say, but she didn't seem sad at all in saying it.

Maybe she'd found one who didn't "throw her back."

"Are you with someone?" I asked.

She made a scoffing noise, complementing it with, "Hell no. Hark back to aforementioned field experience. But also, I'm not settling down. I don't have a hold on even half my own shit. I don't need to take on some guy's shit too."

I pulled on our arms before we climbed the steps that led back into the bar so we'd come to a stop, and considering what she heard in the bathroom before she came out, I shared, "I don't think I have to tell you that I'm leagues away from owning anywhere close to half my shit."

Dani grinned. "Okay, what I didn't say was, even if that's the case, if a big, broad, hot, seriously-into-me guy got up in my space, and we clicked, like, bones and hearts and souls and stars aligning *clicked*, and he wanted to be along for the ride as I figured it out, I would *not* say no."

Stars aligning.

"I'm twenty-eight," I told her. "And I've never had a long-term boyfriend."

She swayed back. "You a virgin?"

At this question, I started to pull away because it was in that moment it hit me how much I was baring to a complete stranger.

She held on tight.

Even so, I said, "We're getting kind of deep. I think you're cool, Dani, and I appreciate you cheering me on, but I just met you."

"That's fair," she replied. "We won't go there. And you're right, we don't know one another, so I may be wrong, but maybe you haven't had a long-term situation because you never took the risk. I mean, I got experience, and some of it tore me up." Her grin returned. "But that doesn't mean I haven't also had loads of fun."

I had no reply because I knew she was right, and it wasn't like I didn't want to admit it, it was just that I didn't know where to find the courage to go for it.

She got closer. "Nothing is permanent, Alex. Not peace. Not happiness. Not joy. People don't understand that. They want those feelings all the time. But they're just not to be had. Also not permanent?"

Her last sentence was a question, an indication she wanted to be sure I wanted her to continue imparting her wisdom on me.

Obviously, I nodded.

She continued, "Heartbreak. Or pain. Or fear."

Holy wow.

She was right again.

"Once you understand that," she started to sum up. "Once you get that everything comes and then it goes, you learn to take the leap."

When I had no reply, she kept going.

"You even learn how important it is to take it." Dani turned her head toward the stairs, looked back to me, and gave me a big, encouraging smile. "Leap, sister."

She then gave me an arm hug, let me go, and she and her panama hat floated up the stairs and into the bar.

I stared after her.

Then I remembered the way Rix looked when he stopped staring at my mouth, he gazed into my eyes, knew he had me, and he wanted that.

He wanted *me*.

"Leap," I said under my breath.

Still totally scared to death, I nevertheless lifted my chin, headed up the stairs and straight to our table.

Chloe, Judge, no Rix.

Did he take the opportunity of me leaving the table to hit the loo as well?

I was almost to my vacated chair when I noticed Chloe and Judge were not sitting close, murmuring to each other, like they had been when Rix and I were doing the same.

They were staring back where I came from, across the space, to the bar.

And they looked ticked.

Even Judge, who was the single most easy-going guy I'd ever met. His jaw was all tense and a muscle was flashing up his cheek.

Curious as to what was pissing even Judge off, I turned in the direction they were staring and stopped dead.

I'd walked right by him.

Rix.

He was at the bar with a blonde, mountain-fresh, tanned goddess. He was also in her space, listening to her with rapt attention.

I could almost hear the propellers lifting up my heart, making it soar, splutter and give out and then it was in a nose dive.

Free falling.

I'd been gone…what?

Ten minutes?

"I gotta go," I said, again loudly, and both Chloe's and Judge's heads swung my way.

If I wasn't entirely engrossed in the fact my heart had crashed at my feet, I would have stepped back because Chloe looked like she was about to spit fire.

Instead, I grabbed my army-green hobo bag and tossed the long strap over my shoulder.

Judge started to rise from his seat. "Are you okay to drive?"

Damn it.

I probably wasn't.

"I—" I began.

But Chloe was now up too. "We'll take you home, Alex."

"No, you guys stay…um…" I didn't know what else to say because I couldn't drive, and I didn't want to make them end their night, and I couldn't catch a thought in order to decide which of my friends to call to ask for a ride home.

It was then, my eyes, without my permission, strayed back to Rix.

My throat tightened.

But my attention was caught by something else.

And I saw Dani was now sitting behind Rix, eyes to me, and when she caught mine, she mouthed, *Asshole*, then she magnificently frowned.

I wanted to find that funny. I wanted to feel the bolster of female camaraderie.

I didn't do either.

"We're taking you home," Judge decreed. "I just had one beer, Alex, so I'm good to drive. And Chloe and me are ready to roll."

I bet they were, in their loved-up bliss, perfect for each other, all moved in together, building their family (of dogs, for now).

They were *the best couple ever.*

If you asked me a year ago—that a gal like Chloe would be it for Judge—I'd have said no.

But she was.

Top to toe, inside and out, she was sophisticated and a city girl and had traveled the world and was super rich, and she worshiped him and didn't hide it.

She was lucky, she got that back. But that was Judge. When he found the one for him, that would always have been what he'd give.

And he did.

But me?

I was going home alone.

Again.

Having a great day, getting a promotion and a raise, heading into a future working on an amazing program doing good things for kids, a program endowed by one of the richest men in the world, downing some drinks with good people, flirting with a gorgeous guy...and ending all of that crawling into bed alone.

Again.

Way to go, Alex.

Awesome celebration.

Yay me.

Ulk.

"You sure?" I asked Judge. "It's a ways out of your way."

"Absolutely," Judge answered, his tone flinty.

I nodded.

We headed out, me ducking my head as I trailed behind them.

"I'll talk to him later," I heard Judge mutter.

I then heard Chloe reply, "You are not saying a word to him."

"What?" Judge.

"We'll talk. Not now." Chloe.

We hit the door and then the cool air hit my face.

But for the first time in my life, heading outside didn't make me feel free.

No.

Instead, it cost me a lot...

But when I stepped outside, I just stopped myself from dissolving into tears.

CHAPTER 1

THE MORNING

Rix

*I*t was the morning after Judge, Chloe, and Alex all ditched him at the bar.

He'd gotten out of bed as usual, at five.

He'd gone out for a bike ride.

Came home, made and downed a smoothie, showered, and now he was in Scooter's drive-through, getting a coffee.

That entire morning, he'd not once thought about the woman he fucked the night before, then, after they were both done, minimal cuddle time and an exchange of numbers (hers, he wasn't going to use, his, he'd shifted a digit so he didn't have to deal with ghosting her, and yeah, that made him sound like a dick, but her place was a disaster, she had three cats, and it felt like he walked out of there with layer of fur on him and throat full of dander—woman, man, he didn't give a shit, you kept your house, especially if you had pets—all that was on top of the fact she wasn't that great of a fuck).

He'd left her in her bed to get his ass home and hadn't thought of her since.

Nope.

All he could think about was Alex, all alone in a hot springs in the winter somewhere outside Ouray, staying in that water until her fingers were wrinkled.

And he did this wondering if she'd been naked.

What was that about?

Although the woman had a great head of hair and an even better ass, both that any heterosexual or bi man breathing would notice, Alex had always been that mildly annoying co-worker who was that because, when she allowed herself to be visible at all, which wasn't often, she acted weird.

Worse, she had no clue how to deal with a person living with a disability, which, when this was made noticeable—and because she was weird, this was noticeable way more than it should be—was a lot more than mildly annoying.

But until last night, he'd never spotted what a cool color her eyes were.

Two-toned.

He'd never seen that on anyone.

More, until last night, she'd never given him the chance to do the work it shouldn't be his to do: show her he was a guy without legs, but bottom line, he was still just a guy.

Further, he'd never realized how she was a lot like him, active, outdoorsy, happier on the road to somewhere, a trail to nowhere in particular, or best of all, smack in the middle of nothing that was everything than she was being anywhere else.

He was taken out of this thought, and how aggravating it was they were finally getting to know one another, and then she pulled an Alex, started acting strange and ditched him, when the person behind him in the drive-through tooted their horn.

Rix felt his eyes narrow as he looked to his rearview mirror, because whoever it was needed to chill. He couldn't exactly get out of their way, driving off without his coffee.

When his gaze hit the mirror, he saw the hood of a bright yellow Jeep, and before he'd even looked to the windshield, his throat had constricted.

But he looked to the windshield, knowing what he would see.

She wasn't the only one with a bright yellow Jeep in Prescott, but she was the only one who would toot her horn at him in Scooters' drive-through.

Peri.

His ex.

As in, ex-they-lost-money-on-deposits-after-she-dumped-him-when-he-lost-his-legs-fiancée.

Shit.

She waved at him, her hand moving fast, a smile on her face under her Oakley Split Times.

Jesus.

Smiling and waving like she hadn't completely gutted him when he was at his absolute lowest.

He lifted his own hand and flicked a couple fingers out, thankful the Scooter's kid was leaning through the window with his coffee.

Rix took it, put it in his cupholder, and moved to his hand control to go for the accelerator, stupidly happy that he'd put his legs on that day, rather than doing what he normally would do when he went to work, using his chair.

His truck had been retrofitted with controls so he could use his hands to drive. But today, Peri in his rearview—and shit you not, that was apt—he was glad he'd put on his legs, even if she couldn't see them.

Though, the minute he started to pull away, she hit her horn again, three quick beeps.

Rix slowed and glanced at his mirror in time to see her sticking her head out the window, her long blonde hair falling to the side.

"Hang on a second, Rix!" she shouted.

"*Shit*," he hissed to himself.

He should just go. Except seeing her going somewhere in her Jeep when he was out in his truck, and a couple of times noticing her in a place where he was (so he'd usually then leave that place so he didn't have to deal with an uncomfortable conversation, like this one was undoubtedly gonna be), he hadn't seen her since it all went down, and the fact it went down at all, she didn't deserve his time.

He didn't go.

He pulled off to the side.

She didn't glide to the window and get her coffee, she pulled off beside him.

When she got out, something drove him to do the same.

No, not something.

He was on his legs. When they did whatever she was angling for them to do right then, he would stand in front of her and look down at her to remind her of the them they used to be.

The them she threw away.

Because one of the parts of them she said she loved, since she was nearly five ten, was that he was six two, and she'd had a lot of boyfriends before him, but she hadn't had a lot of opportunities to tip her head back when she kissed a man.

She got off on him being dominant in a number of ways, not just that one.

Until she didn't.

When she was at the back of her Jeep, she peered around to him, her body jolting.

Yeah.

There he was, standing.

Half of the them they used to be.

Not the man in the chair she'd left behind.

And she was the other half, unchanged, sunshiny and exuding energy.

She quickly recovered from her surprise at seeing him on his feet.

"I'd heard you got your prosthetics," she noted.

Yeah, with the help of some parallel bars, a righteous physical therapist, and family and friends who took his back, he'd first gotten up on those mothers nearly two fucking years ago.

"You heard right," he unnecessarily confirmed.

"Can you wait a second?" she asked. "I'm just gonna go grab my coffee."

Only Peri would think, with a line that was four cars deep, she could drive off, park and walk up to the window to deal with her order like the world revolved around her shit and how she wanted it to go.

But even with this thought, he jutted out his chin to agree.

She turned and strutted back to the coffee joint, and Rix watched as she tossed her bright smile to the driver of the car at the window and scooted her slender body between that car and the building to get to the window.

The driver was a woman. She appeared peeved.

A man would have a lot more patience with Peri. Rix knew that from experience.

It didn't take her long to pay, scuttle out of her position and lope to Rix with her hair swaying, coffee in hand.

Her manner was all Peri, confident that she was all she was. Tall, gorgeous, great figure, head-turning, attention-grabbing just from walking into a room…or across the tarmac at a coffee place.

He crossed his arms on his chest.

It wasn't intentional, but it was a good move, her eyes dropped there as she stopped a few feet away from him, and he saw her tanned cheeks get pink.

Score one for Rix, because she dug his height, she also dug his build, including his chest, which was a lot more developed now since he had to use it so much.

"Yo, Peri," he greeted.

Her gaze lifted to his face.

"Hey," she breathed.

He felt that in his dick, like he always did when she talked like that.

Then something bizarre happened.

In his head, he heard Alex saying *Yeah*, all husky and hot, and he felt *that* in his dick *and* his balls.

What was that?

"Listen, I…" Peri regained his attention. When she got it, he noted she seemed like she was struggling. She started again. "How're you doing?"

Uh…

What?

"How am I doing?" he asked.

"Yeah, things going good for you?"

Was she serious?

He hadn't stood face to face with her in two years. And the last time he was face to face with her, he wasn't standing. He was lying in their fucking bed, and she was ripping his heart out in order to take a shit on it.

And she waylays him at a coffee place to ask how he's doing?

"I'm on my way to work, that's how I'm doing. I'm also wondering why I had to pull over at Scooter's to tell you face to face how I'm doing. If you're curious, you got my number, you could text."

She winced like he'd been an asshole or something, when he hadn't been altogether friendly, but he hadn't been an asshole, then she stated, "I deserved that."

All right.

What?

"You deserved what?"

"You never used to talk to me like that."

"Talk to you like what?"

"Like you don't have time for me."

For shit's sake.

"Peri, no disrespect, but right now I actually *don't* have time for you seeing as, like I said, I'm on my way to work."

"We need to talk," she asserted.

They did?

"About what?" he inquired suspiciously.

"About us."

There it was.

The answer to his earlier question.

She was not serious.

This assertion came out of nowhere.

And with what she'd made of them, and the time that had elapsed in between, which was significant, he knew one thing.

It would go nowhere.

Rix took a calming breath before he reminded her, "Peri, there is no us."

"C'mon, honey, there'll always be an us," she said quietly.

Nope.

She was not serious.

And with her standing there, five feet away, her coming there in her Jeep, him in his truck, when they used to wake up beside each other and go to work together if their schedules synced, paying separate for coffee, when no way he'd let her pay for shit, a stark reminder of what became of them, all of this because of her decisions and actions, he was losing his hold on calm.

To move them along, he shared more history, and since it would no way adhere to what he was saying anyway, he didn't sugarcoat it.

"The memory is burned on my brain, about two days after I got home from the hospital, you spotting me as I transferred from chair to our bed, then you sitting down beside me in that bed and saying we weren't going to work. I also remember you relating to me how decent of a person you were, seeing that, even though I no longer had a job, not to mention, I had no freaking clue what I was going to end up doing to make a living since I'd been a firefighter since I was nineteen, and incidentally, I had no legs…"

She winced again.

He powered through it.

"…you were okay that you took the financial hit of canceling the reception place, the cake and the flowers. Though I ate it because I paid for the invites and the save the dates, which, and not only because we'd sent them, couldn't be returned. I was just lucky it was my friends who were going to be our photographer, caterer and DJ, considering the day I was supposed to marry you, I was in a hospital bed, and they were more worried about that than getting paid."

She studiously kept hold on his gaze, not looking down to his legs, when she stated, "That was so close to when it all happened, Rix. You have to understand. I was still adjusting."

Jesus, he couldn't believe his ears.

"*You* were adjusting?"

"It happened to us both," she shot back.

Okay.

He tried.

But now, calm was a memory.

"No, it did not." Rix waved a hand at his legs. "It happened *to me*."

She leaned in earnestly. "It happened to both of us, honey. That's what you didn't get. And we need to talk about it."

"The time to talk about it was before you gave up on me. Or, to give you some space, not long after. Not years later, Peri. But you dumped my ass *two days* after I got home from having both my legs amputated. From that point on, we didn't have anything to talk about anymore."

She lifted both hands, still holding her coffee in one, and pressed them toward him.

"We shouldn't be discussing this in Scooter's parking lot." She dropped her hands. "Come over. Any night this week you want. I'll make us dinner."

Dinner?

She wanted him to sit down to dinner with her?

The woman liked her weed, maybe she was high.

"I'm not coming over for dinner, Peri."

"Rix—"

He shook his head and cut her off. "No. You made your decision. It wasn't yesterday that happened. It was almost two years ago. We've moved on."

"Yes, *you've* moved on to screwing everything in Yavapai county."

Wait.

Was this shit because she was jealous?

"You don't get a say where I put my dick anymore, babe," he pointed out.

"That's not you."

"What's not me?"

A snap was hitting her voice. "You aren't that guy, Rix."

"You're wrong. Remember? That's why you left me. I'm an all-new guy, Peri."

She leaned back. "I see. So you have something to prove," she surmised. "Think on that and think on refusing to come over to have dinner and talk things through. Think on it while thinking on who you're proving that something to."

Yup.

No longer calm.

At all.

"Whoa." He uncrossed his arms to lift a hand, palm her way, not pressing. "Now I get it." He put that hand on his chest. "Sorry, we went our separate ways, I haven't been in the loop. Guess congratulations are in order that you got your degree in counseling since you fucked off and left me," he noted sarcastically. "We haven't had a full conversation since the day you moved out, but still, you understand my motivations and have a diagnosis about my behavior. Well-spotted, Dr. Poulsen."

She wrinkled her nose in irritation.

He'd used to think that was cute.

The fuck of it was, it was still cute.

"You know I hate it when you get snide like that," she retorted.

Rix gestured to her Jeep. "Feel free to be on your way."

She stared at him through her Oakleys.

He stared back through his Smiths.

And that was another reminder. Three years ago, he wouldn't know dick about sunglasses, except he needed them, and he'd buy what he liked. Now, after working outdoor retail since he could get back to a paid job, he did.

That wasn't a bad thing, his job hadn't sucked, he got a good discount, his salary had been decent, his insurance great, his firefighters' insurance covered his leg situation until the day he died, so that wasn't a worry, and he could add to his 401K.

It wasn't anything near what he loved doing.

He'd been doing what he loved doing.

And then that tree came down.

Their staring contest lasted far too long.

Though, when he was ready to end it, she did.

And she did this by whispering, "We're not done, Rix. We'll never be done," and as if it proved some point, she slapped the rear quarter panel of his truck (and it sucked, but he had to admit, him turning off to have this chat instead of driving off, like he should have done, definitely proved her point).

After she did that, she whirled, her hair flying, that familiar jump in her step that was one of the first things he noticed about her, how she even walked with an extra current of electricity, and she rounded her Jeep, got in, and pulled out.

In this time, Rix did not mess around.

He was in his truck and ready to roll too.

He was pissed he had to follow her to the stoplight.

He was relieved she went left, and he was going right, to hit downtown, where their new offices were.

With the new program, they needed more space. They were relocating from the local River Rain Outdoors store that also housed the national headquarters, which was on 69 between Prescott Valley and Prescott.

The new offices weren't ready to move in yet, but it was getting close, and after officially signing on the day before, Judge had planned for the three of them to meet up with their new finance guy at their new space to see how the renos were going and get the lay of the land.

He wanted to be excited about all this, like he'd been the last few months as he trained his replacement at the store and they started work on how they were going to merge River Rain's Kids and Trails program with Hale Wheeler's Camp Trail Blazer, then build more programs from there.

He wanted to be excited that he'd be making more money than he ever had in his life, that he had the kickass title Director of Programs (Judge was Executive Director, Alex was Director of Outreach, and their new guy, Kevin was CFO).

He wanted to be excited that his job would not be confined to one building in one town, but he'd be all over, not just the US but eventually the world.

And he wanted to be excited when he hit downtown and drove to the back of the building, the entire top floor their organization now occupied, and he found a parking spot that said, RIX HENDRIX, DIRECTOR OF PROGRAMS, TRAIL BLAZER, which he knew was the real reason Judge wanted them there that morning.

The signs were a surprise, they were awesome AF, and Judge, Alex and Kevin, as well as Rix, all had one.

But he wasn't excited.

His mind was filled with Peri's bullshit, the color of Alex's eyes, and what the fuck Alex's deal was that they were finally connecting, then she stands up in the middle of it and walks off, doing this before she ditches the bar (and him) altogether.

In other words, he wasn't in the greatest of moods when, carrying his coffee and thinking he should have probably gotten them all one (but he only knew Judge's order, though he wondered what Alex drank, and that was whacked too) he finished climbing the four floors to the top, something that put him right in Trail Blazer's new space.

It was a good find, being right off the square and having windows all around. Great views. Brick walls. Kickass columns cutting through the space.

It was gonna be fantastic working there.

In front of the elevator that was between the sets of stairs that came up on both sides at the back of the building, there was an area where a receptionist desk would be when they decided on furniture. A wide panel behind it made of rough but attractive wood that Rix knew would eventually have the Trail Blazer logo on it, once they'd decided what that would look like. And beyond that was a sea of open space that would soon hold furniture, office equipment and staff. All around the edges there were offices, with Judge and Kevin getting corner ones and Alex and Rix sandwiched between them, side by side.

The renos were done, they just needed the tech stuff to happen (and that was gonna happen imminently) and to fill the space with furniture.

And bodies.

His mood didn't get any better when he rounded the panel, saw the rest of them already there, standing outside what was going to be Alex's office (the one that would be between Judge and Rix's), and it was only Kevin who called, "Hey, man."

Alex, as usual, barely glanced at him, which answered the question that whatever breakthrough they had last night had more to do with her downing mules like they were Kool-Aid than them actually finding a connection.

But it was Judge that surprised him. His closest friend, and now boss, looked right at Rix and didn't hide he was pissed, and Rix knew him well enough to know who he was pissed at was Rix.

Rix glanced down at his watch.

He wasn't late so what the hell?

He returned his attention to Judge and lifted his brows.

Rix doubted Judge would get into it then, whatever it was, but he didn't get a chance when Kevin asked, "Did you see the signs for our parking spaces?"

He turned to Kevin. "Yeah, I saw 'em."

Kevin smiled.

It was forced, but Rix smiled back.

Kevin's smile faded because he knew Rix's wasn't real.

Rix had met Kevin first as a customer at River Rain stores, the local one that Rix managed until yesterday.

Kevin was a big-time trail runner and kayaker, so he was in the store a lot. They'd struck up a friendship, which meant he'd been out both running and kayaking with Kevin, also hiking. He'd further been in with Kevin, watching football or basketball in some bar or at one or the other's houses, shooting the shit, eating wings and drinking beer.

The guy was a CPA, had a Master's of Economics from Howard University, loved the outdoors but didn't so much like his job working as the top finance guy for a huge HVAC company that serviced Yavapai, Coconino, Gila and Mohave counties.

Rix and Judge were so tight, a friend of Rix's was a friend of Judge's, and Kevin was the first person who sprang to mind when they

were divvying up duties and deciding which positions needed to get
filled first.

They all agreed, since Wheeler was endowing the program with
half a billion dollars, a finance guy was kind of important.

They were at one with poaching him, and fortunately, Kevin was
at one with jumping ship and coming onboard Trail Blazer.

This wasn't a surprise, Kevin was heavy into the outdoors, he was
going to be making more money, even if they were a charity (Judge—
and Wheeler agreed—felt that salaries should be competitive in order
to find the right staff), and he was already a volunteer for Kids and
Trails.

The perfect fit.

"The signs aren't the only surprise." Judge spoke for the first time
since Rix had arrived. He also started to move across the expanse of
the space to a long foldout table. "The designer has narrowed it down
to three schemes that fit our budget for the furniture, and we got the
logo options, five of them, all of them Wheeler's already approved. We
need to make some decisions."

He'd made it to the table and was spreading out some big sheets of
paper that, even from where Rix stood, he saw had a bunch of pictures
of furniture on them, and some regular sheets that had logos printed
on them.

As they all made the move to approach, Rix decided he'd give it
another go, edged toward Alex, and greeted, "Hey."

Alex was not five ten.

Tops, she was five six.

To kiss her, he'd have to bend deep.

Or coax her into his lap.

Jesus.

He'd gotten laid last night, what was his deal with this shit about
Alex?

He didn't have a shot to figure that out.

Her brown and green eyes flicked up to him, and he saw she was
pissed too.

Okay.

What in *the* fuck?

He stopped, reaching a hand down to touch her forearm, and she jerked to a stop with him.

She didn't have her usual trouble looking at him then.

She glared right into his eyes.

Yes.

Glared.

She'd ditched *him*, what'd she have to be pissed about?

"I said 'hey,'" he noted, his voice rougher than normal, because he was ticked.

"Hey," she spit out like the taste of it sucked.

"What's up?" he asked.

She tipped her head woodenly toward the table. "We're deciding furniture and logos."

"I mean with you throwing attitude at me."

Her eyelids coasted slowly down and coasted up even slower.

This unfortunately gave Rix the opportunity to note that she had very long, thick eyelashes, she wore no mascara, maybe because she didn't need any, probably because she didn't wear makeup at all, and they weren't the auburn color of her hair.

They were dark, with auburn at the tips, something he could see in their sunshiny offices, but not last night in the dark bar.

Seriously interesting.

And gorgeous.

He'd never noticed that either.

"Sorry?" she asked.

This took him out of his thoughts about her lashes, but only landed him in the sitch that he had to admit, she had a great voice. He'd always thought that, even before, when it hit him only vaguely. It was almost…cultured, like, sophisticated, which was strange for her, since she was definitely not a city girl. It was also deep. Not exactly Kathleen Turner in *Body Heat*, or he didn't think it was until they were talking last night about glass showers and hot springs.

Then, it was totally *Body Heat*, but better, because she had no clue it was.

It was annoying to have this in his ears when he was ticked that she was ticked because she had no reason to be ticked.

If anything, he was the one who should be.

Which reminded him…

"I asked, what's up with your attitude?" he repeated.

"My attitude?"

"You're pissed at me."

"I'm not pissed at you."

He'd had just that kind of morning, he didn't do what he normally did, ignored or avoided her shit.

They were going to have to work together.

She was going to have to get over it.

So he called her on it.

"Listen, Alex, I'm used to you not knowing how to handle the fact I got no legs, I'm not used to you being cool with me, opening up, connecting, like you were last night. Though, gotta say, I shouldn't be surprised you were reminded you were uncomfortable being around a guy like me and got up in the middle of a conversation and ditched me. But now I wanna know how that translates to you being pissed at me when it should be the other way around, 'cept it's not because I'm used to your whole bullshit awkward act."

She stared up at him as he spoke, the color draining from her face, and the instant he finished speaking, she asked in a quiet voice, "Not knowing how to handle it that you don't have legs?"

"I'm not the only double amputee on earth, Alex. Maybe the only one you know, but I'm not the only one. And we're gonna be working a lot closer together. I suggest you get your shit together about it, because it's not cool."

She stood entirely unmoving, including her eyes, which didn't blink, as she continued to stare at him.

"What's the holdup?" Judge called.

Rix turned his head that way. "We'll be right there."

When he turned back, he saw Alex looking that way, and she said something else.

"I'm heading to River Rain."

Of course she was.

Dodging him rather than dealing with him.

Her normal MO.

Rix clenched his teeth.

"What's going on?" Judge asked.

But before Alex could pull an Alex, avoid getting anywhere near him as she made a hasty exit, probably (although there wasn't much around except that folding table) finding something to bump into along the way, which would have been cute, if the reason she so desperately wanted to get away wasn't so fucked up, she looked up at him.

And then, shocking the shit out of him, under her breath, for only him to hear, she decreed, "You aren't the only double amputee on the planet, John Hendrix, but you sure are the stupidest one."

After delivering that, she was not awkward, and she didn't bump into shit.

Except him, because she far from avoided his person.

She crashed her shoulder right into his arm, doing this deliberately, so he swayed in a twist and his coffee sloshed in his other hand as she stormed past him and then through the space, her loose curls contained in her signature ponytail at the back of her head bouncing as she went.

Okay.

Again.

What in *the* fuck?

"Give us a minute, Kev," he heard Judge mutter as Rix stared after Alex, who shoved angrily on the bar on the door to the stairs and then disappeared behind it. "My office."

At Judge's last two words, Rix looked to his bud.

Or more accurately, watched Judge walk to the biggest office in the space, the one on the northwest corner.

Still clenching his teeth, Rix followed.

"Close the door," Judge ground out when Rix made it into the space.

Oh yeah, his friend was pissed.

Though, Rix reckoned he was a helluva lot angrier.

Rix closed the door, and for the second time that day (and it wasn't fucking eight-thirty in the morning, for shit's sake), he crossed his arms on his chest, even still holding his coffee.

It was a power maneuver, because, as previously noted, Rix was not unaware he was significantly developed in his upper body.

It was also a defensive maneuver, one his mother pointed out to him that he'd started using a lot, particularly during initial rehab after the amputations, and again when he went back to begin the painful and frustrating process of learning to use his prosthetics.

"We're all official now, work has started, we're not in our permanent offices yet, but this is happening, so you're going to have to get your shit tight about Alex," Judge demanded.

"I'm sorry?" Rix whispered.

"You need to be professional, and that means none of that shit you pulled last night, or whatever you did just now."

Rix didn't trust himself to speak, so he didn't.

"We have the means to do some pretty amazing things, Rix, so get it together," Judge finished.

"She just called me stupid," Rix pushed out, sounding just as furious as he actually was.

Although Judge looked surprised, he didn't look surprised about what Rix thought he should be surprised about, considering his response was, "In a sense, she's right."

Okay.

Not even eight-thirty and this was maybe the sixth time that day he couldn't believe his...*goddamned*...*ears*.

"So you're standing there, telling *me* that *I* gotta get my shit tight to work with some woman who has absolutely no clue how to behave around someone with a physical disability?" he asked. "Is that what you're saying to me?"

"No," Judge bit out. "I'm saying to you that you gotta get your head out of your ass and work with a woman who is so into you, she can barely see straight, and not turn on the charm and lead her ass on, only to dump her when something better catches your eye."

This time, Rix stood silent, still and unblinking.

"She's good at her job. *Really* good at it, Rix. But she doesn't need it, and she could get hired practically anywhere she wanted to go. Don't make us lose her. She's been by my side for a while now, we work great together. I need her. So pull your shit together, because I need you too."

On that, Judge made his way to the door, but stopped at Rix, who was just inside it.

"You know, I don't get it. I never will. But buddy, whatever you're working out, leave people like Alex out of it. She's way more vulnerable than you'll ever be, I don't give a shit you lost your legs. And if you open your eyes and see beyond you, you'd get that and stop acting like an asshole, and not only to Alex."

And with that, Judge walked out and back to where Kevin stood at the long table, not hiding he was watching.

Rix twisted away from them in order to stare out the windows toward the square, Judge's words slamming through his brain, along with a fuck ton of memories of run-ins with Alex Sharp.

Work with a woman who is so into you, she can barely see straight, and not turn on the charm and lead her ass on, only to dump her when something better catches your eye.

His life might have completely changed after what happened in that fire.

But he hadn't, not really.

Before Peri, hell, just last night, he was a man who got a lot of female attention.

He'd had women do some crazy shit to get his.

And he'd been around women who were shy who wanted it but had no idea how to go about getting it.

Alex was not creeped out about his legs, his chair, or his prosthetics.

She was a woman who wanted his attention, had no idea how to get it, and worse, had no idea what to do with it once she got it.

How the hell did he miss that?

Last night, he'd been flirting with her, lowkey, but he was doing it.

And he had to admit, when she responded…

No, the *way* she responded, all bashful and cute, he'd taken it out of lowkey mostly because he'd noticed her eyes, her voice was doing a number on him, and her hair was in those righteous pigtails that were so thick, straight up, his fingers itched to pull on one to see how close he could get her to him before she pulled away.

Then she'd gotten nervous, panicked and escaped.

Because the guy she was into was coming on to her, and she was Alex, she had no idea how to deal.

Christ.

Not only had he missed all that, he'd been a dick.

And not just a dick.

A colossal one.

"Well, hell," he whispered.

Judge was right, he had to get his shit tight.

And he had to smooth things over with Alex.

But right then, she was gone.

He'd come up with a plan to sort that and then he'd sort it.

They had a lot in common, and unfortunately, when he finally got his head out of his ass about her, it was at a time when he realized he wanted to fuck her.

But they worked together, he was fired up about this job, about working with Judge and Kevin, about doing the good they were going to do, he knew Alex was too, so he reckoned neither of them wanted to screw it up.

So they'd figure it out.

For now, there was nothing he could do, so he took a deep breath, turned, and walked out of Judge's office to go do something he had zero interest in and something else he only had slightly more interest in.

Look at and decide on furniture and logos.

CHAPTER 2

THE EVENING

Alex

$\mathcal{I}$ let myself into my place Friday evening, relieved beyond anything that it was the weekend, and I didn't need to expend any more effort trying to stay away from Rix.

Our bar celebration was Wednesday night.

He and I had our thing on Thursday morning, and fortunately, when the guys came back from the new offices, Rix didn't have the opportunity to approach me directly. Judge holed us into the conference rooms to finalize the furniture and logo situation (they'd needed me to be a tiebreaker on both, because Hale had also picked his top choices, and what stunk about that was that I'd voted with Rix and Kevin (the stinky part was the instant (both times!) I voted with Rix, he gave me a big smile (the first time) and a wink (the second), guess he was over it, bluh).

We also went through a bunch of other stuff about our hiring strategy and policies and procedures and shared assistants and interns, and you know, little stuff like the entire infrastructure that would support us going forth and building global programs that had wildly meandering arms including environmentalism and climate change, keeping kids active, getting them out of rural settings, and using lessons learned out of doors to build self-reliance and help guide errant kids back to themselves.

I had strong feelings about some of this (particularly that it was too much of it), but I'd been too shy to speak up, considering, in all of our other meetings about this stuff, Rix was there, clouding my brain with his sheer magnetism and blinding me with his good looks.

Not anymore.

(Okay, so maybe in the last two days I'd been clouded and blinded, but not as much as I used to be.)

Now I knew Rix wanted to talk to me, probably to smooth things over after he said something so incredibly offensive.

I mean, he thought I had a problem with him because he'd lost his legs?

How horrible is that?

Truly!

So, yes, until we sat together in the bar, we'd never had a real conversation, so he didn't know me.

But for heaven's sake.

I worked for the charitable arm of a huge retail store that took pains to reduce their carbon footprint as much as possible, collected money for conservation causes at the tills, and had a CEO who was one of the leading voices for environmental issues in the entire country. That charitable arm being working with kids to get them out in nature. Until recently, I organized the volunteers, and I, myself, had my own trails I worked with the kids, some of whom (both my volunteers and my kids) had varying disabilities.

And he thought I couldn't deal with a disabled person?

Sure, there were probably disability bigots in any field.

But...*me* in *mine*?

Honestly, when he'd said that to me, he might as well have slapped me across the face while doing it.

Though, it felt like he did, just hearing the words.

One could say I was o-v-e-r *over* my crush on Rix Hendrix.

Ugh.

He was a jerk.

This was good, since we had to work together, and I had no business crushing so bad on a co-worker that might play with me because he had no one else to flirt with but would never go there, not with me, and oh, by the by, he thought I was an intolerant loser.

Huh.

Okay, so, when he hit my desk around lunchtime that day and dialed up his naturally oozing charm to ask me to lunch, I had a *mild* rekindling of the belly flutters that would always get out of control when I was around him.

But luckily, Chloe showed up out of the blue and informed Rix she was "whisking me away" (her words), something she did in order to treat me to lunch at Farm Provisions for a "girlie personal celebration" (again, her words) of my recent promotion.

This was unnecessary, but I was happy for the excuse to say no to Rix.

Rix appeared unhappy, very much so.

Whatever.

Exacerbating this situation was the fact that I was getting calls from home.

Since Thursday, my sister called (twice), my mother called, and that day, my father called.

This happened.

Primarily it went like this:

Blake, my sister, remembered she had a sister and immediately grew concerned her lifetime of effort was seeping away, and as such, would get in touch with me in order to top up her endeavors to make certain I didn't start feeling less peculiar and inferior than she wanted me to feel (which was to say, she wanted me to feel these things a lot).

If, in a timely manner (she usually gave it an hour or two), I did not pick up or respond, my sister would call our mother to remind her she had another daughter and complain about my lack of attention to her desires.

My mother would then call to tell me to phone my sister.

When I avoided my mother, she'd call my father, and since he hated hearing from my mother (they'd been divorced when I was seven, and they were as acrimoniously divorced as they had been married), he'd call to demand I get in touch with my sister as well as contact my mother. He did this mostly so he wouldn't have to personally deal with one of Blake's tantrums, and he wouldn't have to deal with Mum at all.

They seemed oblivious to the fact that I got as far away from them as I could go and not end up in California (nothing against California, I just hated traffic, was an introvert so not big on being around huge populations of people, and it was damned expensive to live there, regardless of the fact I was a millionaire trust-fund baby—I had money, but I didn't want to spend it on a house I wouldn't be in very much).

Now, it was the weekend.

Now, it was time to decide whether to throw my tent in my Subaru and head out somewhere or spend time at home, maybe switching out the annual flowers in the pots scattered all over my deck (autumn was coming, it was time) and take a few day trips hiking or paddleboarding.

I was dumping my bag on the kitchen counter, contemplating this, as well as dinner, when my phone rang.

I dug it out of my hobo, looked at it, and even though the number was local, I didn't know it.

So I ignored it, tossed my phone on my bag, and went to my fridge to open it, stare in it and decide if I wanted beer, cider, or wine (along with deciding what I might cook to go with one of those, or if I wanted to drive back down the mountain to grab something at Wildflower).

I moved from fridge to cupboard and inspiration struck.

Spaghetti with turkey-meat red sauce.

Fast, yummy, and a good evening carbo load for the long hike I'd just decided to take the next morning.

I had a glass of red wine in hand, was letting the red sauce simmer (nothing to get excited about, it was a jar of Ragu, but I always spiced it up with Italian seasoning, minced garlic and red pepper flakes, and in order not to waste anything, rinsing the jar out with a big chug of water that had to cook down), when I turned and gave myself a moment to take in my space.

The shack was two floors, staggered since it was built into the mountain. It had five "rooms," even if two of those weren't strictly rooms.

Kitchen and living room were one long space on the bottom floor. There was a small powder room in the front corner tucked under the stairs, and in the back one, a small space for some storage that I'd converted into a pantry (because I wasn't home often, but when I was, I liked to cook). The upper floor was open to all of this. It was a loft bedroom with a gnarly pine paneled, slant ceiling. It was narrow but also long so it included a reading area off to the side. At the end of this was a small walk-in closet and the "master bath" (of a sort). The bathroom was tiny. It didn't even have a tub.

Big windows everywhere (including three sunlights) and two sliding glass doors to the deck that ran the whole front of the house, one set off the kitchen, one off the living room area.

Everything in the place, except sturdy pieces that would need to last a while, like couch and mattresses, was vintage or repurposed or antique, even the vases, lamps, kitchen stuff and knickknacks. It was hodgepodge, mismatched, but there was color and vibrancy that looked good, but also looked lived in and loved, so it managed to be calming.

Underneath all of this was one of the five reasons I bought the place.

FYI:

Reason one, those windows.

Reason two, that long deck.

Reason three, it was small so it didn't take long to clean.

Reason four, it sat on four and a half acres that were all mine.

Reason five, the entire bottom of the structure was all unfinished storage.

Perfect to house snowshoes and poles, skis, camping gear, my kayak, my two bikes (one road, one trail), and the humongous

Christmas tree and all the trimmings I put up for that holiday (because…*Christmas* but then there was *Christmas in the mountains* which was, like, a trillion times better than regular Christmas anywhere else).

So, yeah.

In about a thousand square feet of living space, I had it all.

All I needed.

Really, whenever I took a second to see what I'd created with this place, I wondered why I didn't spend more time there.

I was about to go out on the deck, kick back, and allow the sauce to simmer while I chilled with my wine when my phone rang again.

I walked to it, and saw it was the same number as had called before.

Really, it should be illegal, like it was in England, for marketing people to call, unless expressly given that permission. All the bogus calls that interrupt your day and useless voicemails you had to delete?

Maddening.

As I was annoying myself thinking on something I couldn't control, rather than simply ignoring it, something I attempted to do (obviously, I failed that attempt on a regular basis), my phone rang while it was still signaling the other call.

The new call was my sister.

I needed to take it. She'd only keep calling as well as activating the family to get her fix of belittling me at the same time pretending she was the "good sister" because she was the one who put effort in keeping in touch.

I'd learned it was best to get it over with.

Anyway, I had wine.

I was thousands of miles away from her in her (actually, in Mum's) upper west side apartment in New York City.

I'd survive.

I took the call. "Hey, Blake."

"Finally," she snapped.

Totally deck time.

I moved to the stove, put the lid on the Ragu and turned it way down, doing all this asking, "What's up?"

"I'm getting married," she announced.

I *just* stopped myself from moaning, *Oh, please no.*

The reasons were twofold why I had this reaction.

One, my sister wasn't going to be bridezilla.

She was going to be Queen Bride-idorah, Godzilla's most formidable foe, King Ghidorah's far more ruthless mate.

Two, she was marrying a man named Chad, who was so very A Chad, it was almost impossible not to be physically ill the minute you entered his sphere.

This was not like me. I saw the good in everybody (except, lately, Rix, for obvious reasons). My experience was, people were generally good, and everyone had flaws, including ourselves. It wasn't kind to expect other people to adjust or accept your flaws, and not accept or adjust to theirs. Further, it took very little effort to find the good in people, and see that, for the most part (except with Rix recently), the good outweighed the bad.

But Chad…

Well, Chad was a different story.

I was not close to my sister, but family was family, and I spent quite a bit of energy attempting to live and let live, not only with her, but with everyone.

However, Chad was just that much of a clueless, blank-eyed, forever-frat-boy pill, I couldn't quite stop myself from detesting him.

"To Chad?" I asked tentatively, sliding open the door in the kitchen space.

"Of course *to Chad*. Who else would I be marrying?" she snapped. "We've been together for three years."

"Right," I muttered, lowering myself onto the cushions of one of the woven rocker chairs on my deck at the same time sucking back a hearty sip of wine.

"Anyway, the wedding is happening in October."

I blinked at the plethora of pine trees in front of me.

"Sorry? October? Like, October next year? Or October, next month?"

"Next month," she sniffed. "Late in October."

My sister spoke a certain language to me, one in which I was fluent.

The translation of all of this was that she'd been engaged for a while, but she was only just now telling me.

That was okay by me, it meant I could avoid all the kowtowing involved when Bride-idorah was in wedding planning mode.

I started to take another fortifying but relieved sip of my wine.

"And Father says you need to be my maid of honor."

I choked on my wine.

It managed to go up my nose *and* down the wrong tube, and after I set it on the little round table beside me and pounded my chest a few times, I managed to get out, "What?"

"I know it's late notice, but the good news is, all the showers and stuff are already done, and I don't want a hen night because they're vulgar. So you don't have to plan anything. You just have to show up."

Another translation: one of her other friends had organized her shower, and possibly her hen night, and I wasn't invited, not only to the shower (obvs), but to ring out her singledom in style.

"I've ordered your bridesmaid gown," she informed me. "You're still a size sixteen, right?"

I fluctuated between a size twelve and fourteen.

I had never been a size sixteen.

My sister was my height and had my same build, and she was a size four.

So…yeah. There was that.

"No, I'm currently a size twelve."

"Then you'll have to find someone to do alterations. I've also ordered your shoes. The tracking says the dress will arrive next Tuesday, the shoes next Wednesday. So you have plenty of time to deal with that. You can PayPal to pay me back."

"Uh…Blake—"

"The wedding date is the twenty-seventh."

Not, *Can you make it?*

Not, *Let me send you pictures of the shoes and gown to see if you think you'll be comfortable wearing them.*

Not, *Would you do me the honor of standing up with me and making the memory of the day all the more special because you're a part of it?*

None of that for Blake.

Just a phone call a little shy of two months away from the day I was supposed to show up across the country to be there.

"The rehearsal is the day before, rehearsal dinner that night," she kept on. "It's not *formal*-formal, but it's New York. I should probably send you a dress and shoes for that too."

"Blake—"

"I will," she decided. "And you can PayPal me for those as well."

"Hey, listen—"

"Dad says you can stay with him."

Oh God.

I kept trying. "If I could—"

"Do you need him to send the plane?"

"Really, Blake, what I need is for you to—"

"I'll get Cathy to talk to him about that and arrange it."

Cathy?

"Who's Cathy?"

"Daddy got me a PA to deal with...*things* while the wedding planning was going on."

"You mean a wedding planner?"

"I have one of those too."

I nearly started laughing.

So Blake had no job (she had no problem living off her substantial trust fund, doing it rent-free in Mum's apartment in NYC, which was enormous and unused because Mum preferred her townhome in London and the country estate she'd inherited from her father in Somerset). Nevertheless, Blake had an assistant to help her deal while she was not exactly planning a wedding because she had a wedding planner.

It was a wonder I wasn't talking to Cathy.

Though, I wished I was.

"I'll get Cathy to send you an itinerary that includes a dress code for each event," Blake went on, providing me the somewhat terrifying hint that there were more "events" than just the big one and the dinner the night before. "*But don't buy a dress* for the rehearsal dinner. I'll take care of that."

I wanted to roll my eyes at the "dress code" comment, but I didn't because that was always a sure bullseye for Blake.

Like I'd said, I knew how to put on mascara, I even knew how to put on false eyelashes (though I couldn't do it in fifteen seconds flat, like Blake could—seriously, I'd seen her do it).

But even if I owned some of it (thanks, Mum...and Dad), I didn't dress in Chanel.

I could appreciate fashion, it was art, it was a form of self-expression, so of course I could.

It just wasn't my thing.

I wasn't like them.

I wasn't about appearances. I wasn't about every day in every way making the point (subtly, of course, any other manner would be crass) that I had more than pretty much everyone around me.

The thing was, I might not be as classically, and classily, beautiful as my sister...and, incidentally, my mother.

But I wasn't a slob.

I wasn't an embarrassment (though, to them I was).

I wasn't backward or gauche (maybe a wee bit awkward, but only because I was quiet, and even though I could find the good in most people, I liked my solitude, and when I was around others, I didn't like there to be a bunch of them).

In other words, I was just...

Me.

And I wanted to be strong in the fact that I was me and not let their many insinuations that they weren't thrilled with that get to me.

Sadly, I had not managed to arrive at the place I could do that.

And one of the things that always hit me where it hurt was Blake implying I had no style.

I had style.

It was just *my* style.

Blake kept speaking.

"Now, do you need a plus one?"

Her tone on that question was unpleasant.

Even cutting.

Because she knew the answer.

And that would be no.

Instantly, visions filled my head.

Visions of me wearing whatever confection of bridesmaid dress was winging its way to me, walking down the aisle, turning my head, and seeing Rix sitting in a pew, smiling the same big smile he'd shot my way when I'd voted for the same furniture he did.

Visions of sitting by my sister's side, being ignored, at the bridal table, looking out into the reception, and seeing Rix there, winking at me encouragingly.

Visions of how my sister and my parents would react when I arrived beside Rix as he walked, or wheeled, I didn't care which, with me when they first met him, seeing him in all his tanned, fit, ridiculously gorgeous glory.

I'd say things like, "This is Rix Hendrix. He works with me at Trail Blazer, Hale Wheeler's new charity. He's the Director of Programs because most of the work is based out of doors, and Rix has visited at least one state park or forest in every state of the union."

Or proudly announce, "He used to be a firefighter. He's saved countless lives of people and wildlife and innumerable dollars' worth of property. Gave his legs doing it, but he was down for an insanely short period of time before he was using a handcycle on the trails or hiking in his prosthetics."

They would not approve of him in the slightest.

But all three of them, for three different reasons, would admire him, even if they'd never admit to it.

Though, I would stand tall, Rix at my side.

Dancing with Rix, even if I was sitting in his lap while he was in his chair.

Being Rix's.

And Rix being mine.

"Alexandra," my sister snapped.

"Yes."

"Yes, you're there, wasting my time by not speaking? Or yes, you need a plus one?"

"Yes, I need a plus one," I blurted.

Silence.

Oh hell.

Now what had I done?

"You're...*seeing somebody?*"

Oh God.

I should tell her I'm bringing a girlfriend. Pretty much all of my friends would be down with a free trip to NYC and a stay in my father's fabulous brownstone, and Lord knew, he had the room to put up another person (and I didn't question this because, no way, other than me, he'd allow anyone else to stay at his pad—I was an introvert who disliked crowds, he was an extrovert who seemed only to put up with (barely) the entirety of humanity not including a few of his close friends who already lived in New York, so they wouldn't need a place to stay—so absolutely no cousins or friends or errant aunties were going to mess up his sanctuary with their presence).

I did not say this.

I said, "Yes, I'm seeing someone."

"Who?" she demanded.

"Someone from work," I lied.

"Is it...oh my God." Her voice turned breathy. "Are you dating Judge Oakley?" Before I could say no, she continued, "I thought he was hot and heavy with that girl, the daughter of Genny and Tom."

Like she knew Imogen Swan, America's Sweetheart, and Tom Pierce, one of the greatest tennis players in history.

Though, since she existed in circles that included (even if peripherally, the rich folk were an incestuous bunch in NYC) Jamie Oakley, Judge's dad, who I knew was an acquaintance of my dad's, and Jamie was pals with Tom, maybe she did.

"No, not Judge. He's definitely with Chloe."

"Hmm," she sniffed. "Then who?"

It never would get back to him, and later, to explain why he didn't show, and in his place I was bringing a friend, I could say he was busy, doing good work to save the children of the world, I announced. "Rix. John. John Hendrix. But he's called Rix."

"Rix?" Again the unpleasant tone. "What's he do?"

"Like I said, he works with me."

"What does he do, working with you?"

"He's the Director of Programs."

"Is that important?"

"Well, he and I are on the third line down from the top on the organizational chart."

A moment's pause, probably Blake trying to think if she'd ever heard the term "organizational chart" and if she remembered what it meant.

I would gauge both were a negatory when she asked next, "Where did he go to school?"

God.

We'd entered an interrogation zone because she thought I was making him up.

I was, kind of.

But I wasn't.

"He didn't go to school," I snapped. "He became a firefighter right out of high school and continued to do that, getting on the Hotshots team. Tragically, he had to stop doing what he loved when the wind turned, he got caught in a fire, a tree fell on him and damaged his lower legs to the point he had to have both of them amputated. So, even though he often uses his prosthetics, I hope your ceremony and reception are at places that are accessible, mostly because that's the law, but also so Rix can be comfortable."

This was greeted with more silence.

"Anyway, dinner is simmering, and I need to check on it," I carried on. "So it'd be great if you could get Cathy to fill me in on everything so Rix and I can make plans. And I hope it goes without saying, I'm honored to be in your wedding party." Gag. "But I completely understand if you want one of your friends to be your maid of honor. I know Mum and Dad have a certain sense of propriety, but it's *your* wedding and you should have things as you want them to be."

"It really doesn't matter," she stated. "My girls get it."

Whatever.

"Well then, good. I'm happy for you." Gag times a thousand. "And I'll see you next month. Don't hesitate to reach out if you need anything from me." That was gag times a million.

"It's in hand. See you next month. And I cannot wait to meet this…" a very ominous pause before she finished, "Rix."

Ugh.

"Bye, Blake. And congratulations."

"*Ciao.*"

And she was gone.

I took in a deep breath.

My phone rang again.

Dammit!

It was that local number that had now called three times.

Since I was over it, whoever it was that was calling, added to my sister, my mother, my father, the fact I'd have to figure out some good reason why my "boyfriend" couldn't show at something as important as my sister's wedding, and the bottom line, the truth being I didn't have any boyfriend at all, I had no one like that who could be a buffer for me and what was to come next month.

In other words, I was in the perfect mood to take a call from a telemarketer for the sole purpose of telling them to stop calling me.

This I did, starting the process by biting, "Hello?" into my phone.

A brief hesitation then, "Sounds like your weekend isn't starting off right," came at me in a gravelly voice I knew and loved and recently decided I hated that I loved it.

Rix.

Rix was calling me.

My first inclination was to clam up. I could feel my palms getting sweaty, my heartbeat picking up, and even if he wasn't right there, I felt heat hit my cheeks.

Not to mention, this surprise attack meant my belly experienced a super-powered flutter.

My second inclination was to remember walking out of the loo after Dani's pep talk, ready to do my best to flirt, catch Rix's pass, see where that might lead, only to see instead that he'd moved on from me and then the next time I saw him, he insulted me.

Gravely.

So I did not clam up.

I demanded, "How did you get my number?"

"How do you think I got your number?"

"Is that an answer as to how you got my number?"

"Judge. How else?"

Of course.

Judge, who would want his only two directors (so far) to get along.

"Okay, then how can I help you?" I asked.

"How can you help me?"

"You called me, Rix."

"I called because some shit went down this week that we should iron out, you're avoiding me, this isn't a situation that can be avoided since we work together, so I was going to ask if you wanted to meet for drinks so we can sort things out."

God, disaster, drinks with Rix. I knew that firsthand.

"Though, I'm not gonna do that considering you're acting like I ran over your puppy when we just had a couple of misunderstandings that you gotta grow up and find your way to get over," he concluded.

I stared at pine trees wondering how I could forget that the awesome guy I'd been crushing on for forever was actually a huge jerk.

Then, when my head did not explode like I thought it was going to, I asked, "Just find my way to get over?"

"We flirted a little at a bar, not on work hours, no big deal, Alex. It happens all the time."

Um.

Ouch.

He wasn't done.

"And then I misinterpreted your behavior toward me, and for that, you got my apologies. It was uncool. But I hope you can look at it from my perspective and see that it wasn't that huge of a leap."

Not that huge of a leap?

"Hello?" Rix called when I had to take some time and quiet to get over that new morsel dropped from his (perfectly formed, so much, I'd memorized them so I could see them in my head) lips.

"You accused me of being a bigot," I whispered.

"What?"

"You said I had a problem with you not having legs."

"I thought you did, but that isn't accusing you of being a bigot. Trust me, Alex, a lot of people do not know how to deal with me the way I am."

"I'm not those people."

"I'm sensing that bothers you, but with the way you acted around me, can you understand how that would be my take?"

Actually, him pointing it out, I could.

And that stunk.

Worse, the way I acted around him was because I was into him, and one thing I knew for certain...

We could not go there.

"Yes," I forced out.

"Okay then," he said quietly.

"Okay," I replied.

"So, you up to get a drink?"

Was he crazy?

"No."

"Alex—"

"I'm sorry I gave you that impression. You're right, it does bother me that I did. But I'm...like..." God! "...not good around people."

"All right."

"I mean, I like people. I'm just...you know...I like trees and dirt better than people."

Did I just say I liked trees and dirt better than people?

Rix was chuckling, and it felt it like he was doing it right against my nipple. Thus, I squirmed in my chair at that feeling, and the fact that, considering he was chuckling at all meant I did, indeed, say I liked trees and dirt better than people.

"I like trees and dirt better than a lot of people I know too," he declared.

"No," I asserted hastily. "It's not like I'm a misanthrope or something. It's that—"

"Misanthrope?"

"Someone who doesn't like people."

"I know what it means, babe, I've just never heard someone use it in a regular, everyday sentence before."

One, he called me "babe."

So yeah, nipples again tingling.

Two, he sounded teasy.

Which had something a little farther south tingling.

Time to shut up.

"Judge says you live up in Groom Creek," Rix noted.

"I do."

"So I bet you got a lot of trees and dirt around you."

More teasing.

Therefore, it sounded strangled when I said, "I do."

"Right then, give me your address, I'll grab a six pack and we can finish ironing things out among your trees and dirt."

Again, I saw him at a table at my sister's reception, winking at me.

Right on the heels of that, I envisioned him relaxed in the rocker chair beside me, in my space, on my mountain, chilling out...

With me.

It was a beautiful vision.

"Rix," I whispered, but I didn't know what else to say.

I needed to get along with him.

I needed to stop crushing on him.

I needed to get myself together so I could be around him.

I could not have him in my space, drinking beer, ironing things out, just being with him.

I had to figure out how to be his colleague, do the amazing things I hoped we'd soon be doing, and behave like a normal, rational human being around him.

Then leave that at work and live my life without him in it in any way, except on the job.

I simply wasn't sure how I was going to manage to do all that.

Though one thing I did know, he couldn't be on my deck with me at all, ever.

On that thought, it hit me.

I was currently staring at my trees and dirt, on the phone with Rix, but something had changed.

In a big way.

And I felt that change drift along my skin like the light, but warm touch of a hand.

"Rix?" I called.

I heard him clear his throat.

Then I heard him state, "You got a great voice, Alex."

I blinked at the trees and dirt.

Rapidly.

"So, your address?" he pushed.

"I've got plans tonight," I lied.

Another brief hesitation, before, "Right."

"But we're good. I mean, we're good if you're good, because I'm good."

God!

I needed this call to be over.

"I'm good," he said.

"So, I'll see you Monday at work."

"Yeah, you will."

"Thanks for, uh…calling. It's good that's…um, behind us."

"Yeah."

"'Bye, Rix."

Another brief hesitation, then, with a change in tone I utterly refused to define (it was lower, even slightly heated), he said, "Later, babe."

Again with the "babe."

Co-workers did not call co-workers "babe."

I didn't get the chance to do the impossible, figure out some way that wasn't offensive or combative to share that.

He was gone.

CHAPTER 3

THE MEETING

Alex

*I*t was Thursday of the next week.

And one could describe my attempts at keeping things collegial and chill with Rix as a bona fide, unconditional disaster.

In fact, my week overall wasn't going all that great.

Allow me to sum it up.

Monday came, new sun, new day, new week, I had new plants in the pots all over my deck and a steely determination to be cool around Rix.

This went up in smoke when, before I even left my house to go to work, I got a text.

From Rix.

(Oh yes, I'd programmed him in the phone. I was no fool. No way I'd be blindsided again!)

What kind of coffee drink do you like?

I could have lied, and when I saw him at the office, said I was driving when I got the text and that was why I didn't answer.

But there was a part of me that was so excited to get my very first text from Rix, and that part was strong.

So strong, that thought didn't even occur to me before I texted back with oodles of curiosity, *Why?*

Because I'm buying you a coffee, babe.

Another babe.

That was three.

Highly inappropriate, even infantilizing.

I said not one word about the "babe."

Instead, I texted, *Iced Chai.*

Once I sent that, I texted, *Mocha latte, iced or hot.*

And on its heels, I sent, *For just hot, flat white.*

Then I got nervous that I might be sounding like a goof.

So nervous my thumbs couldn't seem to stop tapping letters, and I therefore texted, *I assume you want to know what I want right now, rather than all that I like. So just to say, I tend to be a coffee explorer, since I like coffee. And caffeine on the whole. That means the list is kinda long. But if you're asking for right now, which you are, because it's chilly this morning, flat white.*

After I sent that, I realized that I was absolutely sounding like a dork in sending it, *all* of it, including the three before. As such, I watched in agony as Rix's three dots cycled and cycled and then they did it some more.

Until I got, *How much coffee have you already had?*

This would have been funny if it wasn't so mortifying.

Just one, I responded miserably.

Try to cycle down cuz you'll have another when you get to work. Later.

I decided I'd texted enough, so I let that lie.

It didn't lie for long.

Rix showed at my desk at River Rain (which wasn't going to be my desk at River Rain for very long, it'd be my desk at Trail Blazer since we were moving the next day, Judge's office furniture, mine, and some unused stuff they had sitting around was all going to the new offices for temporary use because the telephones and Internet were being hooked up that day and it was time to occupy Trail Blazer).

Rix set my flat white down while I valiantly attempted not to blush, he made no attempt whatsoever to hide he totally did not miss I failed at this endeavor, smiled a smile that I wanted to think was friendly, but instead it seemed sexy, this thought being exacerbated when he muttered under his breath so I almost couldn't hear it, "Only you could make a rambling coffee order adorable."

I sat frozen.

Rix winked at me and said in his normal voice, "Bottoms up, Alex."

With that, seeing as he was in his chair that day, he wheeled away.

Since there was a lot going on with packing for the move and tech hookups and such, I only had to deal with Rix in passing for the rest of Monday.

However, Tuesday morning, I was shoving stuff into my bag at home, preparing to head down the mountain to dig into the move, when my phone chimed.

OK, I have ten minutes, explain today's coffee order.

Yes.

Another text from Rix.

A startled laugh escaped from me because he was being funny.

I then texted back, *You don't have to buy me coffee.*

To which he texted, *I know I don't.*

Then I sent, *I'm just saying, we're good. We had a blip last week. But now we're great.*

We're great?

Damn.

Why did reading those two words texted by him make my breasts swell?

Good. Great. I mean, things are fine. You don't have to butter me up with coffee.

So coffee is a way to butter you up?

Oh God.

What was that?

Was it flirty?

Or was it just being funny and friendly?

Or was it just a kind of getting-to-know-you, valued co-worker, but in a jokey fashion?

Tell him what you want and stop texting, Alex! I admonished myself.

I did not stop texting.

Well, yeah. Kinda. Like I said, I like coffee.

You did say that, so maybe you'll tell me what kind you want this morning.

Time to get beyond this.

Iced Chai.

That's tea.

Oh my God!

Flirty?

Or jokey?

I'm feeling tea today, I replied.

Right. And then he sent, *That only took five minutes. I'd fill the other five by asking you what kind of donuts you like, but we got a lot to get accomplished today. I'm sure I'll enjoy your dissertation on that, but I'd prefer to sort out my office so I can start doing the shit I'm getting paid to do.*

He one hundred percent did not need my views on donuts then.

Therefore, I noted, *Good call.*

He sent a smirk emoji, which shared the impossible.

Rix could even make emojis sexy.

Right.

So *totally* failing on being appropriate and professional with Rix Hendrix.

Proving this fact, I spent ten minutes trying to figure out what emoji to use to counter his smirk before I gave up, sent nothing and just drove down to work.

Tuesday was about moving furniture and boxes, unpacking, setting up computers and a half an hour phone tutorial, so the day was busy and the only tortuous part of it was that Judge took the entire team out to lunch, Rix sat beside me, and his knee touched mine the whole time.

Because of that, I could barely concentrate, I had no clue how I even ordered and consumed my food. All I could think about was his knee touching mine. And it only got worse when I'd eventually glazed over, thinking about said knee, he'd elbowed me, I'd looked up at him, and the instant I did, an expression came over his face that I was relatively certain scorched off my eyebrows, it was so hot.

"What?" I'd asked quietly, mesmerized by the look on his face.

He took a second, and that second included his eyes (that, incidentally, looked from afar like they were brown, but up close, I noted they were actually caramel), dipped to my mouth before they returned to my eyes, and he asked, "You want dessert?"

I wanted to devour a vat of caramel.

I thought this, staring into his eyes.

I continued thinking it until Kevin offered, "We can get a menu so you can see what they have."

I tore my gaze off Rix's face, felt my own flame, and avoided looking directly at Kevin or Judge (even so, I still noted Kevin staring at me closely, and Judge's gaze pinging back and forth between Rix and me), and I belatedly noticed the waitress standing there.

"No dessert, thank you," I said to her, humiliatingly throatily.

"Jesus," Rix muttered, now staring at the table and shifting in his seat, which made his knee brush against mine.

I tilted both legs to the other side, something I should have done forty-five minutes earlier, I just couldn't concentrate enough to think of moving them.

I escaped the offices the minute I could that evening, coming home to a big box propped against my front door (which, by the by, was located at the side of the house).

My bridesmaid dress.

With trepidation, and fortified by a glass of hearty red, I opened the box to feel the only relief I felt that day.

The dress was a pretty blush silk with tulle overlay, floor-length skirt with a slit to just above the knee. It had a slender ribbon belt that tied in a bow at the front, and it was off the shoulder with to-the-elbow sheer sleeves. The entire thing was covered in rose-gold embroidery of leaves and flowers, with dimensional blooms drifting from it all over the gown, but these were very thick around the bottom of the skirt.

It was airy, romantic, would be fitted, but not tight, not at all revealing, I knew I'd be comfortable wearing that style, and it had the price tag still attached.

Which was one thousand, four hundred dollars.

The good news was, the company who made it had such skewed sizing, a size sixteen was actually more like a twelve, so it was a bit big, but a nip here, a tuck there, and it'd fit great.

The bad news (outside the price tag for a dress I would wear once) was there was so much embroidery and so many blooms tacked on, it would take a very skilled seamstress to make those nips and tucks, which would likely cost another small fortune.

But at least it wasn't a tent on me.

After trying it on, I took a selfie and texted it to my best girls, Katie and Gal.

Katie, who worked on a ranch north of town as a ranch hand, and who, when she wasn't in Lee jeans, musty old tees and trucker hats, was the girliest girl I'd ever met (outside my sister…and Chloe), gave her stamp of approval with, *OMG! It doesn't make me want to hurl!*

Gal, who operated her own dog training and daycare center, who further had a year-round tan because she was outside more than me, and who once set fire in a barrel in her backyard to a Christmas present her mother sent her (it was a sweater dress, and that was half about her mother being a constant pain in her behind, and half about the dress, an item of apparel she hadn't worn since she'd learned to successfully throw a tantrum in second grade), was less impressed.

Her text was, *I have to change my shirt because I just threw up all over myself.*

I decided not to share its cost. Gal's business did okay, but Katie was far from rolling in it. They knew my situation, but they'd be seriously ticked Blake spent fourteen hundred of my dollars.

Wednesday morning, I did not get a coffee text, which, stupid me, made me kick myself for telling Rix we were good, we were *great*, and he didn't have to buy me coffee.

Until I was elbow deep in reviewing the applications for the joint assistant we were all going to share before it was decided who she or he would work for directly. But for the now, Judge didn't need to be on the phone about logos, and Rix didn't need to be testing Wi-Fi when we'd been tasked to present Hale with the menu of the first programs we were going to roll out under the new masthead.

And Hale was expecting that presentation in a week, and we were still all feeling we needed to carry on Kids and Trails as well as Hale's Camp Trail Blazer (because Hale told us that was non-negotiable, CTB was there to stay) *and* add more to that (well, that's what we'd all been discussing, I didn't personally feel that way, and from the vibe I was sensing from everyone else, they were feeling the same way, but no one had pinpointed it).

So we needed someone to deal with furniture orders and buying letterhead and things like that so we could actually get down to the business of deciding what services we were going to provide.

I figured this person would eventually be Judge's assistant, and even though I was never that, I'd worked side by side with him for a long time, so I suspected I knew maybe better than Judge what he'd need, therefore my concentration was deep on the applications.

Until, that was, a pink box thudded on my desk.

I looked from the box to Rix, who had wheeled into my office.

He'd been on his prosthetics yesterday, helping with the move, and I was kinda surprised (and definitely impressed), regardless of how active I knew he was, how much he'd contributed.

I also wondered what went into the decision-making every morning between chair and prosthetics.

My guess?

After yesterday's activities, his legs needed a break.

"You get first pick before the boys land on those," he stated.

I shifted my attention to the box, which, upon opening it, I found was unsurprisingly, since it was a bakery box, filled with donuts.

I turned my attention back to him. "Are you going to buy treats every day?"

A slash of a belly-flutter-inducing smile. "Maybe."

I did not want to pick a donut in front of Rix. It was a thing. A stupid thing. A ludicrous thing. But I had an expensive bridesmaid gown that was size sixteen that mostly fit, and he had, as far as I could tell, not an ounce of fat on him, then there was the fact that he dated tall, slender blondes.

To delay, I asked, "Which one do you want?"

"I already had mine."

Unhelpful.

I studied my choices.

There was no healthy donut.

There was also no dainty donut.

Though, there were some that were fat and calorie bombs, like the chocolate-covered, custard-filled one that I wanted.

I picked a glazed.

The second I did, he asked, "Seriously?"

"What?" I asked back.

"Glazed?" he returned, sounding disappointed.

"There's nothing wrong with glazed."

"I asked your favorite coffee, and you gave me three answers, none of which was, 'black with a sugar.' A glazed is the donut version of black with a sugar."

"There are other donuts I like, I'm just feeling glazed right now," I retorted.

He stared at me, then he shouted, "Men, donuts!"

And as he predicted, Judge and Kevin came in and landed on that box.

Kevin nabbed the chocolate-covered, custard-filled one, which was a bummer, since I was hoping I could go to the box later and devour it when Rix wasn't around.

I barely had that thought before Rix's rich, rough laughter exploded in the room.

Everyone looked at him.

But he was staring at me.

"Glazed, my ass," he muttered, then he wheeled out.

He'd seen me staring longingly at Kevin biting into my preferred donut.

Fabulous.

Fortunately, the day was filled with interviews and frustrating meetings with the interior designer to select wall décor and brain-storm break areas and storage solutions and layout plans, now that we'd picked the furniture (and none of us were invested much in this, so I knew I wasn't the only one who found this a sadly necessary evil).

I came home that day to another box.

This one contained a pair of ballet pink, patent leather, pointed toe, four-inch heeled Jimmy Choo slide style pumps with a rhinestone strap spanning the vamp.

They cost a thousand dollars, and it was unlikely I'd wear them twice, but it was highly likely my feet would be in agony before even the ceremony was over.

For reasons that were not a mystery—considering my mother as well as my father—my sister did and said hateful things, she'd done this all her life.

But I did not hate her.

She was my sister.

Though, I was going to hate her wedding day.

I knew it already.

But there was nothing for it.

I was also going to have to wear those shoes, repeatedly, and for long periods of time, to break them in and get used to them before the wedding.

I hated being a hater.

But I knew I was going to hate that process too.

Incidentally, Katie's take on the shoes was, *I wish we shared the same size* and Gal's was, *Is this a wedding or the torture portion of an inquisition?*

An important aside: my friends were the greatest.

This all brought me to now, Thursday morning, no texts, no coffee, no donuts from Rix, but we were heading into a ten o'clock meeting at the folding table that was now in the center of the vast open space, and it had some chairs around it.

There, we were all going to pitch what we thought should be the focal programs of the abundantly funded Trail Blazer mutual aid organization.

And I was determined to speak my piece.

Hale Wheeler, *the* Hale Wheeler, son and heir of the sadly deceased brilliant tech maestro, Corey Szabo, and simply Hale Wheeler, tall, slim, broad, movie-star gorgeous, jet-setting billionaire was going to be sitting at that folding table with us next Thursday, and we had to have ourselves together, not shoving leaves and rocks down every kid on the planet's throat while shouting at them, "You need to behave at the same time care about the earth!"

And I had to speak that piece in front of Rix.

I'd spent the first two hours of that morning polishing the presentation I was going to give about how I felt we should refine our mission, specifically, concentrate on camps for all kinds of kids, not just ones who needed a few humans to demonstrate they gave a crap (but those kids too). At the same time, I'd silently pep-talked myself that I'd spoken with Rix, I'd flirted with Rix, I'd texted with Rix, and I'd selected a donut with Rix watching. Therefore, I could talk about something I knew, and it meant a lot to me, in front of Rix.

I fancied myself in the zone when I finally sat down at the table with the team, only to have my zone obliterated when Rix declared, "I think you all missed my unwritten memo about someone picking up coffee and/or donuts every day. And by someone, I mean, that someone is not always gonna be me."

Judge and Kevin burst out laughing.

But I felt my heart twist.

Of course, he didn't just buy *me* coffee and donuts.

He got them for everyone.

Of course.

What was I thinking?

"I'll grab tomorrow's," Judge offered. "Going to Wild Iris. Text me your orders before seven-thirty."

"I'll get Monday," Kevin said. "Hitting Bosa like Rix did yesterday. Same with the texts." He looked to me. "Alex, you have my number?"

"No," I mumbled.

"I'll email you," he said.

I nodded and chimed in, "I'll do Tuesday. I'll let you know where I'm going."

"And maybe I can free some funds up to create a makeshift break area, before the official one is put in place, so we can make our own coffees when we get here," Kevin suggested.

"Works for me," Judge agreed.

"Finally, we have at least one coherent plan," Rix muttered.

I reached to my can of watermelon-lime AHA, thinking I should probably have brought in a ten-pack so everyone could have one (though we didn't have a fridge yet), as Judge pointed out, "We've been kinda busy hashing out job roles and space, so we're sitting here to get down to the business of building a coherent plan, Rix."

Rix looked right at Judge and said, straight out, "I get it's important we have computers and phones and desks and a place to do our business, but that's getting finalized. And we've discussed this. Now, we got a half a billion dollars, and because we do, we got stars in our eyes. We could have twenty billion dollars, and we couldn't heal this earth. We couldn't take care of every kid that's been let down by the schools or their parents or the system. We know we have to rein it in, but we got more money than most startups probably ever had, so it feels like we can do anything, when we can't."

"Which is why I asked all of you to come to this meeting prepared to share where you think we should focus," Judge returned.

"Right, so gotta say, you've been doing this job, and I've been involved," Rix replied. "But I haven't been doing the job. I'm Director of Programs and I could dream up fifty programs to pitch to Wheeler, but I'd be winging it based on the fact I have absolutely no clue what some inner-city kid needs seeing as I was raised by two loving parents in the pines and scrub and rock of Flagstaff. I'm also a white guy who lost his legs two years ago, but I had an undeniably great run of it until that time."

Holy cow.

This exact point (*sans* the personal mentions of being raised in Flagstaff, and obviously the limb loss) was in my presentation!

Rix wasn't done.

"We need Wheeler to back off a week, maybe two, probably more, so Alex and I can fly to Cali, spend a good block of time there, hitting up Camp Trail Blazer, talking to the staff, the counselors, the kids, but also chasing up kids that went there and seeing where they are now. The ones that turned things around, but maybe mostly the ones who didn't. What worked? What did they like? What broke through for them? Or why wasn't there a breakthrough? What could make it more powerful? What could reach more kids?" He shoved his laptop forward on the table. "I got a full interview drafted. I also called Frank, the head guy at CTB who replaced Wheeler, and he's good with Alex and me being around, talking to the kids, going out on rides, doing whatever we need to do to get some pulse, even a weak one, of what we're facing down. He's shared he's also happy to reach out to some graduates, ones who pulled it together, also ones that might talk to us, even if they didn't, so we can strengthen that pulse."

I'd had similar thoughts, but I hadn't fleshed them out that thoroughly.

Oh…

And I absolutely did not have some cockamamie plan to fly *anywhere* with Rix.

When I stopped staring in shock at Rix, I noticed that Kevin, who I knew liked Rix, was regarding him in a new way. It wasn't like he didn't respect Rix before, but there was a different respect forming after Rix's speech, I could see it.

Judge was studying him even more closely.

He then shared, "I had much the same thought, and because I did, I sent out a questionnaire to our recruiting teachers for Kids and Trails. What worked for them about the program? How the kids in general reacted to the pitch to go on hikes with us? We always got feedback from kids, parents and teachers who were in our program, but for the teachers, I got deeper into that and pressed for input on how they might expand or enhance the program."

I was loving this, mostly because it seemed, in a way, we were all on the same page.

Judge wasn't finished, however.

"I also devised a questionnaire to send out to youth programs, administrators of juvenile detention centers, child support programs.

The needs are going to be vast, preliminary searches are pulling up thousands of departments and organizations, so first, I gotta narrow that down to manageable levels that will provide us with representative data. But if they share, that data is still going to be extensive. That said, the questionnaire is devised to focus on time with kids in nature and what that might look like and what that might mean to the kids they work with. Still, it's going to take a lot of sifting through, so if you're all down with it, I want you to feed back on the questionnaire, I'll finalize it, and I'm gonna task Krista with getting it out, compiling the data and pulling out trends."

Krista was the woman who Judge had called that morning to offer the job of assistant, a woman we'd all been impressed by and unanimously agreed on (a miracle).

A woman who thankfully accepted the position.

And I was looking forward to the day when I didn't have to weigh in on wall décor and storage solutions, but I agreed that it was way more important for Krista to amass this information for us and make it manageable.

Therefore, I said, "I'm down with it."

"I am too," Kevin put in. "I also feel that we need to get Alex and Rix out to California, ASAP."

Uh-oh.

I thought we'd glossed over that to talk data collection and mining.

I straightened in my chair.

"Definitely," Judge agreed.

Oh no!

"Wouldn't that be a waste of resources?" I suggested swiftly. "If we want a personal touch, it would be better if I went and interviewed some of the Kids and Trails teachers. Or some of the kids. Or hit up the directors of youth programs. Or visited a few detention centers. We have one here in Yavapai County. I've been there before. The staff is amazing, they'd let me come back."

"You've visited detention centers?"

This question came from Rix, and there was a timbre to it that was weird.

Nevertheless, I looked to him. "Yes."

"By yourself?"

"Well, yes and no. Judge didn't go with me, but there were teachers and officers there."

Rix looked slightly mollified by that, but it remained weird he needed to be mollified at all.

I turned my attention back to the table to see I had another lunch scenario going on, but this time, Kevin was staring at Rix, however, again, Judge was looking between us.

And oddly, his lips were twitching like he thought something was amusing.

Kevin then looked to me. "Every viewpoint is unique. Rix could go, and he'd get one thing, but if you went with him, you might get another. I don't think it's an if, I think it's a when we go out, we should do it in teams, so the team can bring back some kind of unified input that amalgamates as many viewpoints as we can get."

Although this made sense, I opened my mouth to refute it.

But said nothing because Judge asked Rix, "When's Frank say it's good for you two to go out there?"

Oh no!

"He's ready when we are, just wants a couple of days heads up so…" Rix turned to me. "You free Tuesday through Friday of next week? I think that'll give us enough time to get what we need."

Tuesday through…

Friday?

Four days on the road with Rix?

Before I could answer, Judge muttered, "Dad says he's down to help wherever he can, I'll see if his plane is free."

Okay.

Wait.

Me and Rix alone on a private plane?

Alone together?

Then working together for four days straight?

Catastrophe!

"I don't mean to put a wrench in the works." I *so* did. "But it's not environmentally conscious to use private planes, Judge."

"You're absolutely right, and we have a lot of money, though much of it we'll be investing to endow programs, so no matter it seems like crazy money, we still need to take care of it and be frugal with its use. It's weighing pros and cons, Alex, and for a single trip to Cali, where last minute flights will probably cost a whack, if Dad's plane is available, I'm seeing the pros outweigh the cons."

I wholeheartedly did not agree.

I didn't agree with both of us having to go either.

I just couldn't figure out how to communicate that since they were all very clever and therefore making their usual sense.

So I communicated something else to buy time.

"We may be able to give the director a heads up, but to make the most of our time out there, we have other interviews to set up too," I pointed out. "I'm not sure we can have it all pulled together by Tuesday."

"As invested as I am in setting up a coffeemaker in our temporary break area, I could hit Target and knock that out in less than an hour. The rest of the time between now and Tuesday, we could be working with Frank to sort our visit," Rix replied.

We could be working with Frank to sort *our* visit.

We.

Our.

Someone tell me this wasn't happening.

"Right, that's a thing," Judge decreed.

Oh my God.

It was happening.

"I'll send my draft questionnaire to you all," Judge went on. "Since Krista doesn't start until the Monday after next, you've got until Thursday to get your input to me, so she can hit the ground running with that when she's here. That gives you time to plan your schedule in California as well as feed back to me." He grinned. "I'll go out and get the coffeemaker."

I stared at Judge, feeling horror, but hoping I was hiding it.

I then looked to Kevin, who seemed strangely very intent on studying the top of the folding table.

Finally, I forced my eyes to Rix.

He did a little upward jerk of his chin to me, which was ridiculously masculine and equally ridiculously attractive.

Okay, it was safe to say I wasn't simply failing miserably at being collegial and chill around Rix.

I was in straight up panic mode because I was facing a lot of time having to be that with Rix (and undoubtedly failing).

With zero buffer.

In other words, I was screwed.

CHAPTER 4

THE PLOTTING

Judge

Entering his house from the garage, Judge was not greeted at the door to his mudroom by his and Chloe's two dogs.

This meant his woman was either cooking (something the dogs never missed), or out on the deck (something else the dogs never missed).

He didn't smell anything, and since Chloe didn't mess around when she cooked, so the house always smelled like a dream, he knew it was deck.

He headed there, walking up the steps then to the French doors off the living room.

He saw her outside. She was wearing a gray and white striped sundress, her long dark hair down in loose curls, white-framed sunglasses on her nose, a light, white wrap around her shoulders to hold back the early fall chill, and her long legs were stretched out with her bare feet perched high on the deck railing.

Her toenails were painted blood red.

Last, her elegant hand was swung out and rosé in a stylish wineglass was sparkling in the still bright sun.

Her fingernails were blood red as well.

She looked like she was chilling after traveling forward in time from a quick trip back to the fifties in order to bitch slap Ava Gardner.

She turned her head to look at him through the doors after the dogs went nuts when they clocked him, and he saw her lips curve up.

Incidentally, they were red too.

It was too bad they had neighbors, because those long legs, all that hair, that smile, he wanted to sit in his chair beside hers on the deck, pull her in that dress astride his lap and do things to her that didn't need an audience.

Instead, he opened the door, dealt with Zeke and Montana accosting him, and called, "Hey, baby."

"Allo, *chéri.*"

"Getting a beer, and I'll be out. You need a top up?"

She shook her head.

He jutted up his chin, went to the kitchen, dropped his messenger bag on the counter, grabbed a beer, and headed back out.

Before he sat in his chair, he bent and pressed his lips against hers.

He pulled back. "Good day?"

"An interesting one."

He couldn't see her eyes due to the sunglasses, but there was something about her voice he couldn't put his finger on.

But having a year under his belt with this woman, seeing her exclusively for nine months of that, and living with her the last two, Judge decided to take a load off before he asked, "What's up?"

"I talked with Dru today."

Dru was Judge's stepsister who was more like his sister-sister, only they didn't share blood and his father had never been able to officially adopt her because Dru's biological father was an asshole.

"She okay?"

"She was very interested to know that your dad's sending one of his planes out here for Rix and Alex's use tomorrow."

This was perplexing. Dru was always into knowing what her big brother was up to, including work.

But not that deeply into it.

She also knew Rix, and they were tight.

But he had a feeling that wasn't it either.

"Why was she very interested to know that?"

Chloe turned to the view and took her time having a sip of her wine.

When she was done with that, he felt his lips had tipped up because she was red-hot when she was being super cool.

"She has a loose acquaintance in New York who's getting married in October."

At this seeming change of subject, Judge settled back and took a long pull from his beer, because Chloe was telling her story, and clearly, she intended to take her time doing it.

Since she looked good and smelled good, and because she wasn't cooking, that meant either he was (when he wasn't) or they were going into town to grab a bite (which was what they were going to do), then later they'd come home and maybe watch some TV or read, but definitely in the end they'd go to bed and fuck, he felt she could take all the time she wanted.

"Yeah?" he prompted when she didn't speak.

"Yes. And apparently this friend keeps track of a variety of things, including the Elsa Exchange."

Suddenly, he wasn't a big fan of hanging and listening to Chloe's story, considering the Elsa Exchange was a YouTube gossip show with a massive following, and its sole commentator, Elsa Cohen, spent a lot of time keeping tabs, and sharing them, about Chloe's and Judge's families.

"What now, Coco?" he demanded.

She turned to him. "Did you know that Elsa found out Rix's name, and she named him, fully, and also repeatedly, when she also showed several pictures of him, with you, with your dad, with Dru? This when she was doing all that reporting on us after your mom passed."

He'd not spent a second watching the Elsa Exchange after Elsa had interviewed Corey Szabo's ex-wife and rocked Chloe's world, so he had no clue this had happened, though he did know their families were a favored topic of conversation.

Rix being pulled into that garbage, he liked this even less.

He felt his mouth get tight.

It went with the territory for Chloe. Her mom, Imogen Swan, and dad, Tom Pierce, were two of the most famous people on the planet (especially Genny, whose new hit program that had started streaming last month had put her back on top as Hollywood's darling). Not to mention, Chloe had grown up essentially a family member of Corey Szabo, who was also one of the most famous people on earth, and on top of that, prior to his death, had been one of the richest.

Then, after her mom and dad divorced, Genny reunited with a lost love, Duncan Holloway, who was famous in his own right for being self-made, wealthy and an outspoken environmental activist.

Duncan was also, incidentally, Judge's former boss.

Further, it came with the territory for Judge, whose father was born into brash Texas oil wealth, then went on to make his own considerable fortune, and as such, had been dogged by the gossips and paparazzi for decades.

Thus, when Chloe and Judge got together, and that was outed after Judge's mom essentially, albeit inadvertently, killed herself after taking a cocktail of vodka and valium, they'd somehow become the It Couple.

This meant attention for them.

And the person who seemed most fixated on them was Elsa Cohen.

It also meant attention for others, like Chloe's brother Matt, sister Sasha, and her soon-to-be stepbrothers, Sullivan and Gage. Lastly, it meant Dru.

As yet, Judge did not know it meant Rix.

"I'll take your look that could kill as a no," she drawled.

"What shit is she saying about Rix?"

"Nothing, apparently, outside the fact that he's gorgeous, he's a national hero, and he's a stalwart friend."

Judge could handle that.

He took a sip from his beer.

"Though, he's even more of a hero than we thought, considering he's posing as Alex's boyfriend when she stands up as maid of honor at her sister's wedding next month."

Judge nearly snorted beer.

He successfully swallowed, looked to his girl, and asked, "What?"

"This acquaintance of Dru's, she's Alex's sister. Her name is Blake, and, you should know, darling, Dru isn't Blake's biggest fan. She referred to her as a 'mean girl,' and I could tell by the way she talked about her the level of that is on the high end of the spectrum."

Possible insight into why Alex was so quiet and shy.

"Anyway," Chloe went on, "Blake is an avid watcher of Elsa, and she remembered Rix, including tales told of him being your best friend, so she was very keen to get Dru on the phone to discuss this Rix person after Blake's sister, that being *our* Alex, told her he was her boyfriend and would be her plus one at the wedding."

Well, shit.

"Things are weird between them," he reminded her of something he'd mentioned before. "He definitely gets where she's coming from now. He's making an effort. I'm just not sure what kind of effort he's making, because it's not inappropriate, buying her coffees when he's getting them for everyone, joking around with her. There's still something...*more* to it."

"Is that *more* him practicing to pretend to be her boyfriend next month in New York?" she queried hopefully.

Disappointingly, he had to dash her hopes.

"If Rix was gonna do that, he'd tell me."

"So what is that more?"

"That more is, last Thursday in our meeting, he found out she visited Yavapai's juvenile detention center, and I thought he was gonna go mildly apeshit...*at me* because I let her be around potentially dangerous youth."

"Hmm..." she hummed, now it was her lips that were tipped up, and she turned back to the view.

"Don't read anything into that, my beautiful but scheming match-maker," Judge warned. "Rix is a throwback."

Chloe looked to him again, an eyebrow arching above her glasses. "A throwback?"

"He takes you out, he pays for dinner. If he has to park far away, he drops his date at the door and he's the one who hoofs it. And he leaves her there to go get the car at the end of the night. Holding the door open. Pulling out a chair. If he's wearing his legs, he gives up his seat to a woman, no matter her age and if he doesn't know her. Offering his jacket if it's cold. Shit like that."

No lips tipped up, a full smile. "So, essentially, *you*, just rougher around the edges."

"Peri, his ex, never filled up her own gas tank."

"Again, you."

Judge shook his head. "If your job meant you had to be around potentially, but nowhere near possibly dangerous individuals, I would not go mildly apeshit."

"You totally would."

He grinned at her.

Because he would.

"But I'd not stand in the way of you doing your job," he noted.

"We *are* talking about how you behave with me, you being the love of my life, me being yours, doing this alluding to how Rix is behaving with Alex."

He caught her drift, but felt it important to remind her. "Like I said, I think he would let me in on that, baby, if it was going there."

"He would," she agreed. "This means Alex's mean girl sister did something mean which prompted Alex to grab on to the first guy she could think of when discussing her possible plus one, and for obvious reasons, that was Rix. A clever ploy, considering she has plenty of time to invent an excuse as to why he couldn't come."

"That sounds plausible."

"So obviously, Rix has to go to New York with her, pretending to be her boyfriend."

It was a long incredulous beat before Judge burst out laughing.

When he was done, though, he saw Chloe was not laughing.

Oh shit.

"Baby, don't get involved."

"I am absolutely, one hundred percent getting involved."

"Were you not at the Raven the other night?" he asked.

She pressed her lips together.

Now she caught his drift.

"He knows she's into him," Judge continued. "He's being gentler with her. He's putting the effort in to coax her out of her shell. They're co-workers, they need to get along, communicate, co-exist in a healthy and meaningful way on a team. But like I told you, and that night at the Raven proved, Alex is not his type."

"So if it was any female who went to this detention center, he'd react?" she inquired.

"Maybe, I don't know. Probably," Judge answered. "It isn't chauvinistic, or it isn't intentionally or maliciously so. It's just the way he was raised. What I'm saying is, if she were to go back, he wouldn't step in to stop it, but he wouldn't like it."

"For her or any woman?"

"Definitely her, because he sees Alex as vulnerable now. But probably any woman."

She looked back to the view on another "Hmm" and sip of wine.

"Chloe," he said her name in a warning tone.

"They were cute together."

They were, when they were flirting at the Raven.

Judge would never have called that, but seeing it, the tentative way Alex was connecting with Rix, because he was obviously her type, she was not his, but they had a ton in common, it had seemed awesome.

Natural even.

Especially since Rix was that guy. A protector. A provider.

Alex didn't need that, in all but the ways that, regardless of Rix's physical condition, he'd be able to give it.

A societal and emotional buffer.

Rix was outgoing, and since she wasn't, he'd move mountains to make sure she was comfortable, to stand between those situations and her, or represent for the both of them when that needed to happen.

Judge had never thought of it like that, but in those senses, it was a match made in heaven.

He had to admit they were also cute as fuck, cat and mousing it all over the offices the last few workdays while they'd been getting ready for their trip tomorrow.

Judge wanted to think it was just that Rix was a natural flirt, it was friendly and harmless.

But he'd worked with the guy for years now, and while doing it, Rix had worked alongside a number of women at the store, subordinates, and up in the corporate offices, women who were his superiors, and Judge had never seen him act like he'd been around Alex this past week.

He was friendly with all his co-workers, he'd joke around.

But he wasn't teasing or playful…which was also part of that *more* that Judge had been noticing.

Still more of it was that heated look they'd exchanged at their lunch last Tuesday.

That was definitely *more*.

It could be Rix was putting additional effort into it because Alex was a hard nut to crack. Even in the beginning with Judge, she was quiet, reticent, and only really bloomed when she was in her element with the program, dealing with the volunteers, teachers, and mostly the kids.

He liked her because she was dependable, crazy organized and excellent at what she did.

But it had taken a lot of flights together, traveling to take the kids on hikes or to meetings in schools that he finally broke through and got to know her a little better.

And that was only a *little* better.

He studied his woman's profile.

Then he said, "You hatch a plot, you might regret it."

"I also might not," she replied, then took another sip of wine, and he sensed she wasn't considering whether or not to hatch a plot, she was already plotting.

"This is my best friend we're talking about, doll," he said gently.

She looked to him again. "Indeed, so isn't it time he found someone to make him happy?"

"How do you know that will be Alex?" he asked.

"How do you know it won't be?" she returned.

"It's a risk. A big one."

She had an answer to that too.

"Life's a risk, *mon beau*. A big one." She leaned over the arm of her chair and caught his forearm. "Honey, he's downing every beddable female in a six county area. You told me he was not like that before the accident. You told me it was Peri and only Peri, he didn't even look at other women. You didn't know him before Peri, but you two have shared, and from what he's told you, you know he was a relationship guy. She shredded him when he was at his lowest point. I may be playing armchair psychologist, but I don't think it takes a degree to see this change of behavior has some impetus. It could be he's proving the man he is even if he's lost his legs. It could be he's living his best life because he had a near-death experience. It could be he's acting out some revenge against Peri. What it isn't, is the real Rix."

Judge had not thought of any of this before Chloe, but settling down, finding his one, he'd thought of it. Because Rix had found his one, and then he lost her.

He'd also talked to Chloe about it.

"I mean, for heaven's sake," she continued, "he had a quickie with the flight attendant on your dad's plane when we were flying to Texas for your mother's funeral. We all had our minds elsewhere back then, but that was incredibly inappropriate."

"It was," he muttered. Then he stated straight, "But Chloe, these are big issues to tackle, and they're Rix's to tackle. Anyone attempting something like that will need support. And I can speak from experience, having a good woman at your back when life punches you in the throat is the way to go."

She sent him a soft smile.

"But I'm not sure Alex has that in her," he finished.

"She's a Sharp of the Coddington-Sharps, isn't she?"

Of course she'd put that together.

He nodded.

"Her mother is in line for the British throne," she stated.

"*Way* back in line," he said by way of confirming.

"*Mon Dieu.*"

"Yup."

"She's money, Judge, *old* money. *Ancient* money," Chloe pointed out.

"I don't see—"

"And she lives in an essentially one-room house in the mountains. I've been there. It's charming, and very her, but the trust fund she undoubtedly has means she could probably buy the entire mountain and carve it out for a reflecting pool for her castle. She might not be skipping-through-the-office happy, but that's just not the woman she is. However, she's clearly content in her own way. She enjoys her job. She's spoken to me of her friends, and she's obviously fond of them. She's built an entire life outside the one she was born into. One that has claws so sharp, they bleed you dry before you're able to speak your first word. And they dig so deep, you can never get free. So you go through life, especially the women, as a bloodless automaton, or, as it seems her sister might be, a bloodthirsty vampire, but you do it doing what you're told, not rocking the boat, not stepping out of line, and *absolutely not* sullying the family name. Alex is beautiful and she's bright and she's left that all behind and is *living her own life.*"

This was no lie, Alex was all of that.

"And you think she can't take on big, bad, damaged John Hendrix?" Chloe concluded.

Shit.

Fuck.

"Leave me out of it," he surrendered.

Her smile lit her face, even wearing the sunglasses.

"I mean it," he pressed. "If the shit hits the fan, I wanna tell Rix I had nothing to do with it." It was his turn to lean into her. "This goes south, baby, I'm throwing you right under the bus."

"Have you met my glorious mother and her fabulous fiancé, who *I* made certain did not let the past interfere with their future?" she queried.

He sighed.

She kept smiling. "This is going to be *marvelous*."

"It's going to be hell."

"It is not," she stated haughtily. "You'll have fun, I promise."

"Did you miss me telling you to keep me out of it?"

"I won't *involve* you, of course. But that doesn't mean I won't keep you informed."

He sat back in the chair and looked to the sky.

He then felt her lips press against his jaw before she said into his ear, "Darling, I'm hungry. You need to feed me."

To make her pay for the hell she was imminently going to put him through, he made her wait for him to acquiesce to her demand.

He managed a whole five seconds before he was out of his chair, pulling her out of hers and holding her hand as they moved in to the house.

Incidentally, he opened the door for her.

The one to the house. The one to the garage.

And the one to his truck.

Before he drove her to town, fed her...and picked up the check.

CHAPTER 5

THE RIDE

Rix

*J*esus, he needed her to start talking.

It was Tuesday, mid-morning.

They were in their rental, on their way to Camp Trail Blazer, and Alex had probably spoken only fifty words to him since they'd strapped into the plane three hours ago.

Not unusual for Alex.

And he never in his life thought he'd want a woman to babble, but right then, he not only wanted a babbling woman, he *needed* one.

Especially if that one was Alex and her voice.

He looked down at the phone he held in his hand, and he knew he shouldn't do it, but he did.

He pulled up the text that had landed while they were up in the air.

It was the last of over a dozen he'd gotten from Peri since he'd seen her at Scooter's.

All of the previous ones were invites to drinks, dinner, anywhere he felt comfortable so they could talk, with a few scattered *Just thinking of you* thrown in.

He'd replied to none of them.

But the last one, the one that came in less than two hours ago, read, *Okay, with your silence, message received. But I can't, and won't, let us go without telling you what I wanted to tell you face to face. I love you. I loved you then, I love you now, I never stopped loving you, and I WILL never stop loving you. You're the best man I've ever known, Rix. You made me happy. I think we can have that again, if you give us a shot. But if you can't, I understand. Just know...you'll always be in my heart.*

He wanted to be pissed.

He wanted to remember how it felt. How his first thought when she told him they were over, was *Christ, this hurts worse than both my feet being crushed.*

He was not pissed.

All that was in his head was her words, *I think we can have that again.*

He didn't agree.

He didn't because Peri could have lost her legs. Or been diagnosed with cancer and had to have a double mastectomy. Or got diagnosed with MS and he'd have to watch her suffer over years.

And no doubt in his mind...

He would have stuck.

He would have because he'd loved her. He'd loved her smile. He'd loved that she read Crichton-style thrillers, even though they scared the shit out of her. He loved she could look at the flight of a bird and tell him if it was an eagle, hawk, falcon, owl, whatever. He loved it that she'd complain about her feet being cold, but even as active as she was, she was too lazy to go get a pair of socks.

Or maybe she knew Rix got off on doing stupid little shit like that for her.

Peri could take on the world.

But when she was feeling lazy, he'd get her some socks.

In the end, though, Peri couldn't take on the world.

Because she wasn't strong enough to take on a him that was not top to toe *him.*

But he wasn't angry about it.

He'd been that for a long time. He'd been that when they faced off in Scooter's parking lot.

Though for some reason, he couldn't find that now.

So he was just confused as to what he *did* feel, since it wasn't pissed, and it wasn't Rix taking a beat to consider it possible they could work shit out.

But the bottom line in that moment was, like he'd managed to do for a couple of years now, he didn't want to think of Peri at all.

He'd spent months after she'd left him giving her all of his headspace.

He didn't have the energy to give her more.

"What's on your mind?" he grunted into the cab of their rented SUV.

He felt Alex jerk beside him, like she forgot he was even there.

That almost made him laugh, it being so Alex, her being self-contained, if not at ease in the world, seeming at ease in her head, *her* world.

Case in point, she didn't chat with him on the plane because she was nervous around him.

She'd told him she was into a podcast, was close to the end, and asked if he'd be offended if she finished it up.

He had a book, and when you had a book, you were always good, so he'd told her to go for it.

They sat in seats beside each other in that plane that had a variety of options of where to sit, him with his book, her with her eyes closed or staring out the window, her ear buds in, perfectly cool each of them in their own thing.

Though her surprise at the reminder he was sitting beside her made him want to laugh, he didn't laugh.

He wasn't in the mood to laugh.

"What?" she asked.

"What're you thinking?" he asked in return, figuring she'd say something about their schedule, what she expected of CTB, thoughts about meeting Frank, or practically anything about their trip or their work.

She didn't say anything about any of that.

She asked, "How do you decide between chair and prosthetics?"

At her question, Rix went completely still.

But that didn't mean he didn't feel it.

The funny sensation in his gut and chest.

Fuck, it seemed he could even hear it.

Like a tear. The beginning of a fissure forming. Straggling upward, from gut to throat, a warning that soon, that break would fracture and he'd be laid wide open.

He felt it, but he didn't fight it.

There was tension there, on the surface and buried deep.

It was solid, like granite. Packed there, tight, with over two years of heavier and heavier stuff landing on it, and then Rix would bury it, making it unbreakable.

Unbearable.

But with her question, that fissure was forming.

And it was like he had to hold still, waiting, even hoping, that what he was experiencing was what he thought it was going to be.

Because he needed the goddamn release.

His entire concentration was devoted to that, so he was startled when Alex's next words came fast.

And tortured.

"God, I'm sorry. That was inappropriate. It's none of my business. I'm so, so sorry. It just came out."

"Alex—"

"Forget I asked, if you can. You probably can't. It was that rude. *God*. I'm *so* sorry."

"Okay, but lis—"

"I'm sure you've noticed, I can be socially awkward. It's that. It's not about your disability. It's not like I...*obsess* about it, or anything. I've had, like, *a bunch* of stuff on my mind since we left. I mean, just, like, thirty seconds ago, I was wondering if we could change the radio station. That was just what was in my head when you asked what was, well...in my head. And so, it just came out."

"Right, but—"

She cut him off again, still talking in a hurry.

"And it's not like I don't have a filter. It's just, there's a lot on my mind. Work stuff and, um…family stuff, and we'd been quiet awhile, so I think I was just surprised you asked a question and I blurted out what was on my mind. That explains it, but I'm still *so very sorry.*"

"Honey," he said gently, "stop it."

Utter silence in the cab.

Rix broke it.

"Every morning, I assess two things…my day and my pain. I still have pain, mostly due to getting used to my prosthetics. It's getting better, slowly, but it's there. So if the pain level is low, and the day is active, and I'll be facing things that are a bitch to maneuver in a chair, I'll wear my legs. If I'm going to need to be seriously mobile, and accessibility during my day isn't going to be an issue, I'll opt for my chair."

"Oh," she whispered.

"That said, I'm trying to be on my legs more, because they still don't feel natural. They never will. It takes a lot of effort to use them. I expend forty percent more energy just to walk, negotiate turns, sit, stand, do anything than you do. But I can get better on them, so I need to use them. I knew I'd be needing to get up the steps to the plane today, and meeting the kids, which is better to do on my legs. So I'm on my legs."

He finished his explanation, and he did it thinking about the rental they were in, which Jamie, Judge's dad, had waiting for them at the airstrip where they'd landed.

Primarily, telling Alex he couldn't drive it.

He'd just read Peri's text, but also he'd become so used to saying shit like that to people about certain things, he now took on the edginess that brought like it was second nature. It just piled onto the rest that he was always compressing inside, tighter and tighter, so it all could fit.

But he didn't process it.

He never processed it.

So when he shared with Alex he couldn't drive, he hadn't processed her response.

When they'd approached, the rental car guy had handed Rix the keys and asked for his license.

At first, they'd exchanged a glance, because Rix wasn't big on the dude assuming it'd be Rix driving, like Alex having tits meant she couldn't handle an SUV, and he could tell by what he read on her face, they shared that sentiment.

So they could get on with shit, unspoken, they agreed to let that go, but when Rix said what he had to say, Alex had just replied, "Oh, okay," then she dug in her bag to get her wallet, handed her license over and took the keys.

She didn't look at his legs.

She didn't shift uncomfortably.

She didn't shoot a pitying look to the rental car guy that warned, *Be cool, you might not be able to tell, but the chair will be appearing soon when they unload it from the plane. My friend can't drive because he's disabled.*

She just got on with it.

Like she didn't try to muscle in when he threw his chair in the back of the SUV. Or give him an assessing glance, like she thought him tossing the strap of his bag over his shoulder was going to take him off balance and send him crashing to the tarmac.

He just waited for her to throw her shit in, he'd thrown his in, including the chair, and they went to their separate sides of the car, got in and took off.

"And you can change the channel, just no pop," he finished, his voice not its usual. It was lower, contemplative.

"What's your, uh...favorite?"

They had Sirius so he said, "Classic Vinyl. Classic Rewind. Lithium. Alt Nation."

"Cool," she said softly, reaching out.

But he was reaching out too.

Their fingers touched and her hand shot back like his carried an electrical current.

Rix forgot everything else that was taking up space in his head as his lips twitched when he was reminded how into him she was.

In turn, it reminded him in a lot of ways of Rachel.

Rachel was a girl in high school who was seriously pretty, she was also obviously into him, but she was like Alex. Painfully shy.

He'd wanted to go there, but he couldn't figure out how.

So he'd talked to his dad about it, and when he'd told his father he thought she was pretty, but she wasn't giving him an in, his dad advised, "Son, it's simple. Just corner her and ask her out."

So that was what Rix did.

When he did, he thought she would faint.

Up until that time, that was the cutest thing he'd ever seen.

Their first few dates, though, had been a disaster.

Even so, he still really liked her.

His father had then encouraged he persevere.

But it was his mom who said, "Effort is rewarded."

He wasn't sure what she meant, not entirely.

But he found out.

They stayed together from their sophomore year in high school to her sophomore year at the University of Colorado.

They'd given each other their virginity.

She'd been the first woman he'd loved, something he told her, and she was the first woman whose love he'd earned.

But then he'd decided to become a firefighter, she'd decided to become a doctor, and a number of long, painful conversations brought them to the conclusion that his career, the length of her studies, and the physical distance between them were not going to be conducive to a long-term relationship.

That had been their end.

It had fucked them both up so much, they kept in such close touch after carrying through their decision, they ended up helping each other to get over the breakup, and found they'd been wrong.

Distance and separate career trajectories did not end their relationship. It became long-term.

They stopped being lovers, but they'd never lost each other as friends.

She'd taken a long weekend off to come down and boss everyone around who was on his treatment team after they'd taken his legs.

She was now married, had a kid and was in the midst of building a thriving practice as a neurologist.

Peri had looked like Rachel.

But Rix was sensing Alex had her substance.

The Eagles filled the cab, telling them to take it easy, and he suggested, "How about I'll be navigator, hey?"

"Yeah," she agreed.

"Eagles good?"

"Yeah," she repeated.

He sat back and shared, "No one asked that before."

"Sorry?"

He looked at her profile.

She had her pigtails again.

Shit.

"About my chair and legs," he explained.

She glanced at him, then back to the road, and reiterated, "I'm sorry I did."

"That's not the point I was making. What I'm trying to say is, your question took me by surprise. To be clear, it was a good surprise. It's annoying as hell, everyone dancing around shit I have to deal with every minute of every day."

"Yes," she said softly, "I can imagine."

Her voice normally?

Killer.

Her voice soft?

It hit his balls and drove right up to his throat.

He shifted in his seat, reminded himself this was Alex, his co-worker, a woman he had a lot in common with, which meant he knew they could be friends, therefore he had to keep his mind off his balls and on building that between them.

Because the Director of Programs worked closely with the

Director of Outreach, so they needed that.

But also, he liked her.

And the only reason wasn't because she'd never known him as anything other than the man he was now, and she was that into him. Far from it.

But that reason still felt fucking good.

"So it was a pleasant surprise, but I had to wrap my head around it," he finished.

"Okay, cool," she replied. "But..."

She stopped talking and didn't start again.

"But?" he prompted.

"I'm just, I mean, I know it's not my place, but people dance around it with you in mind. Like, I thought I offended you, and that's the last thing I want to do."

"I get that."

"I see it's still going to be annoying," she mumbled.

"Yup."

"And you can probably sense people are curious, or worried, and you want to say, 'Listen, I'm still Rix. If you want to know, ask. If I don't want to talk about it, I'll tell you.' But it stinks, because that puts you on the spot to put that out there, and that's not fair."

He stared at her profile and grunted, "Exactly."

He watched her nod then she said, "I don't know if people say this, but they should, and I've, um...well, I've wanted to say it to you for a long time. But what you did, I mean, what you used to do, it means a lot to me. The risk you took in doing it, the price you paid. If I didn't...if there weren't places that you protected for me to lose myself in. Whole vast spaces where I can let all that lives in me out, I, um..." She took a second before she finished, "I don't know what I'd do. So, thank you."

It took him a second to respond, and when he did, he did it quietly, because he was moved, and what she said meant a lot to him. "You're welcome, honey."

"Did that make you...uncomfortable?"

"Not even a little bit," he told her, then went on, "Alex, just be yourself, all right? Like you said, if I'm not down with what we're talking about or things you're saying, I'll steer us clear of them. Yeah?"

"Okay."

"And same goes for you, seeing as I'm right now going to ask about all that lives in you that needs vast space to let it out."

It took her a second to reply, and when she did, she sounded pleasantly surprised.

"I think you know what that means."

He gave her a break, took his gaze from her, and watched the landscape roll by as she navigated the winding, two-lane mountain road.

Then he said, "Yeah, babe, I know what that means." He took in a breath and let it out, noting, "We got our own way of living large, hey?"

"Yeah, Rix."

And...there.

Now he was seeing he might want her to talk, but he absolutely didn't need it.

Because when she said his name, it was impossible not to feel that pretty much everywhere.

But the origin came from his dick.

As much fun as he was having, coaxing her out from under her shell, it was just his luck that he'd know the woman for a long time, and only realize he wanted her in his bed when her office was next to his, they had to travel together, and he couldn't go there.

They lapsed into silence for the twenty minutes it took to arrive at Camp Trail Blazer.

Rix had researched it extensively on the Internet, so he wasn't surprised when he saw a lot of dirt, rock, straggling trees that were beating the odds in that dry heat, bunkhouses, stables, corralled horses, outbuildings with doors opened showing they housed ATVs, cabins dotted around for staff who lived on site, and an admin building.

It was no frills, but none of it was ugly. There was landscaping. Rock formations around the buildings filled with native plants. A wide, deep, manmade crater the bottom of which he could see was a big firepit that looked significantly out of use, which was good, considering the lingering drought conditions. Even that pit being that deep, and not much around to catch fire, shit happened.

Though, it was a good place to meet, talk, teach, whatever.

Only strange thing about the place was, even though it didn't seem abandoned, it was deserted. Not a kid or staff member in sight.

Which meant they were probably out on a ride, something they did a lot, maybe packing tents, maybe not, but everyone loading up on the back of a horse to hit the desert and learn some life lessons about nature, survival, teamwork and themselves.

As Alex drove up and parked, the screen door to the admin building opened, and the man Rix assumed was Frank strolled out.

Barrel chested, not all that tall, salt and pepper hair, face with skin that had seen a lot of sun.

Behind him emerged Hale Wheeler.

"Oh my God," Alex breathed, "Hale's here."

Rix sat straighter in his seat as Alex's excited tone hit his ears and Hale Wheeler's good looks hit his eyes.

Brilliant.

He threw open his door as Alex did, angled out when she did, but took his time walking around the SUV, watching as Alex approached Frank and Wheeler.

"Hey…Hale…a surprise," she burst out in a staccato beat, goofy, making sense but not, and last, fucking adorable.

He fought clenching his fists.

"Alex, hey," Wheeler greeted, offering his hand.

She arrived at Wheeler on a skip hop Rix had never seen her make, and a vision clouded Rix's brain that he couldn't reel in.

His fist connecting with Wheeler's face.

Okay.

What the fuck?

"Rix." Wheeler turned his attention to Rix.

"Yo," Rix said, arriving at the guy and lifting his hand.

He took pains not to squeeze as tight as he wanted to before he let go.

It nevertheless shitted him that Wheeler had a naturally strong, firm handshake.

"You probably could guess, this is Frank Rossi," Wheeler introduced his man.

More greeting and hand shaking.

"I should apologize for the surprise," Wheeler told them when all that was done. "But I was in LA when Judge called to postpone our meeting, still there this morning. Woke up and thought, what the hell? I'm damned proud of this place, I need a break from all that other shit that's sucking my time. I'll meet you two up here, horn in on showing you around."

"Awesome," Alex peeped.

Wheeler shot her a grin.

Pink hit her cheeks.

Rix's pink.

And oh yeah.

He'd never seen her blush in front of anybody, but him.

So it damn well was *his* fucking *pink*.

Rix felt his molars grind together.

He stopped doing that and said, "Yeah. Great. So let's get to it."

To that, Wheeler shot him a glance.

Rix turned to Frank. "As you know, man, we got a hefty schedule, and we've both been looking forward to seeing all you do here. So why don't we hit it?"

Frank nodded, the deep grooves around his eyes crinkling, because he was proud of the place too. "You got it, Rix."

Frank threw out an arm for them to head in a certain direction, that being toward the bunkhouses.

Wheeler stepped aside so they could precede him.

And then Rix scored his first point for the board.

Alex turned to him, shot him a massive, gorgeous smile the likes he'd never seen from her before, the likes he instantly felt in his dick, his chest, his throat and burned into his brain, and on another skip hop, this time *his* way, she all but took his hand as she got close to him and they walked side by side to the bunkhouses.

CHAPTER 6

THE RESORT

Rix

"We can never tell anyone about this…*ever.*"

Rix burst out laughing.

He and Alex were standing side by side in her room at the exclusive desert resort that Jamie had also booked for them.

Earlier, when they'd told Frank and Hale what their home base was for the two nights they'd be spending in the mountains for the CTB portion of their trip, this before they headed down to LA to talk to some CTB grads on Thursday, Frank's eyes had bugged out, Wheeler had looked shocked, and Rix had explained, "This trip is on Jamie."

To which Wheeler had relaxed and replied, "Ah."

And now they were standing in a room with wide-plank wood floors on top of which were thick rugs. There was a wall of floor-to-ceiling windows that had an unobstructed view of pristine desert, minimalist, modern-but-rustic décor, a king-sized bed, an entire sectional sofa seating area off to the side, and a balcony that spanned the considerable length of the room.

"I take it you didn't become accustomed to five-star lodging that included pool, fitness center, spa and a Michelin star restaurant when Duncan was footing the bill," he commented.

Alex meandered in and dumped her bag on the couch, eyes to the view. "Duncan didn't make us stay anywhere gross, but...no. Our budget didn't extend to something like this. Because if it's program money, it shouldn't."

He stuck his head into the bathroom and said, "We need to make a deal. I won't Instagram a picture of myself in the soaking tub if you won't."

He was still in the doorway of the bathroom, leaning in and checking it out, when she shoved in front of him, her shoulder brushing his chest, the fresh mint smell of her hair going up his nostrils, as she asked, "There's a soaking tub?"

Of course her hair smelled like mint.

"Yeah," he grunted.

"I don't have a tub at my place. I'm *so* climbing into that," she told the bathroom.

Christ Jesus.

He got away from her, adjusted the strap of his bag on his shoulder, and said, "Right, I'm gonna hit my room to dump my bag, then go back down and get my chair. We'll give it maybe half an hour to chill in our own space then meet in one of our rooms. Or would you prefer to meet down at the bar?"

She was now fully in the bathroom, calling out, "We'll walk down together. Thirty minutes is good. Text when you're ready."

"Gotcha," he muttered, got the hell out of there, did what he told her he was gonna do, heading down to the lobby where they'd left his chair with the concierge.

Though, once he got there, he was told that *of course* a bellman had already brought it up and it was safe in his room.

This pissed him off, because he didn't like anyone touching his chair, which was why he'd left it with them and told them he'd come back and get it.

Also, it sucked ten minutes of the thirty he'd given to Alex to have some settling-in time, and he was thinking he needed that to do what he did the minute he hit his room (which was right next to Alex's and the exact replica of hers).

He called Judge.

"Hey," his bud greeted. "How'd it go today?"

"The kids were out on some work detail when we arrived, so we got a pretty thorough tour of the facility. Not sure what the place was like before Wheeler got rich enough to buy his own country, and Frank shared he'd been generous in fortifying their budget so they could upgrade a few things, but right now, it's fuckin' impressive."

"No doubt," Judge murmured.

"Kids came back, and I gotta admit, I wasn't prepared for what hard cases they were. We're talking dead eyes and blank stares."

"Fucking hell. That bad?"

"Worse."

"Shit."

"Yeah," Rix agreed. "Alex, though. Totally unfazed, Judge."

And she had been.

He'd been on Kids and Trails hikes with her, but back then, he'd only absently noted her presence. Though, it didn't escape him she was good with the kids. Not overly animated and fake, but she took them seriously, she gave them time, her full attention, quiet encouragement, and they responded to it.

This was different.

She did not act like all the kids at CTB were either there because a court told them they had to be to gain a different perspective in an attempt to get their heads out of their asses and learn to get their shit together, or their parents sent them for that same purpose. Thus, she didn't act like they were "other." In other words, she had to crawl up their asses to get them to respond to her, or behave warily, because she didn't know what to make of them.

She stood beside him when they did the short spiel they'd prepared, and when she delivered her part, she was matter-of-fact and all over handing out eye contact. Then, when it was time to break off and sit with individual kids that Frank had identified for them to talk to, kids who had been there the longest and seemed to be responding to the program, kids who might give them some insights, Rix noted her interviews went on longer than his.

Maybe this was because he was intimidating.

Maybe it was because he didn't know what he was doing.

Maybe it was just because she did.

"She's had a lot of experience, Rix," Judge reminded him.

"Yeah. New benefit to this trip, I can watch her and learn. But with that, we got an issue."

"What's that?"

"I wanna fuck her."

Judge didn't respond to that.

Which was good, because Rix had more to say.

"Kevin's point is valid, same experience, different perspectives, more rounded feedback, but further, two of us here, we're covering more ground. That said, in future, this kind of travel happens, I gotta do it with you or Kevin. I can keep my shit tight with her, and I will, and I know I'm putting you on the spot as my boss who's also my best friend, but what I'm sharing is honest. Right now, until I get a lock on it, that's where I'm at."

"Give me a second to process this, buddy," Judge requested.

"While you do, you should know, it's not that."

"It's not what?"

"She's pretty, great hair, but she's not just a fuck. That's not what I'm talking about. She's letting me in, I like what I hear, what I see, who she is, and we gotta work closely together day to day. That means I need to get this under control, put it behind me."

"Rix—"

Rix spoke over him. "Making my case, she digs Wheeler. Maybe she just admires him. Maybe she wants to jump him. But I spent six hours today fighting the need to ask him to pull out his dick so we could compare, and as you know, it's likely I'd win."

Judge laughed, which Rix thought was whacked.

So he shared that.

"This shit is whacked, brother."

"Okay, man, as awesome as we both are, deeply professional and committed to the cause, it was always gonna come to this eventually now that we work together in a way where we're actually working *together*. So we gotta understand what zone we're in when some shit goes down. So I'm asking you, not as the Executive Director of Trail Blazer, as your friend, why do you feel you need to get this under control?"

This was the exact opposite response to what he was expecting.

Which made it no surprise Rix's reply was, "Say what?"

"Alex is great."

This time, Rix didn't say anything.

So Judge kept going.

"As your ED, I'm not going to encourage you to enter into a relationship with a colleague, but one thing we have managed to accomplish, we've set our policies and procedures and there's not a no-fraternization rule. You're not a dick, and you know what we're doing is important. Alex is not stupid, and she knows the same thing. But you're both adults. I trust you to be smart and have professional boundaries when those are expected. So if you dig her, and she digs you, why wouldn't you go there?"

"I didn't say I wanted a relationship, Judge. I said I want to fuck her."

"Those are mutually exclusive?"

"It's not time for a relationship, especially not a complicated one. I just started a new job, and Peri's up in my shit to get back together again."

From Judge, there was a loaded beat then an equally loaded, "Sorry?"

"I told you she ambushed me at Scooter's."

"Yes, but you didn't tell me that was about being up in your shit to get back together again."

"She's been texting ever since, including today," Rix shared. "Telling me she thinks we can be happy again, and she'll always love me."

No loaded beat before a very heavy, "That fucking bitch."

Shit, but he loved this guy.

Best friend you could have.

Loyal to the bone.

"It's not gonna happen," Rix assured. "But we had a history, and I gotta think on that, give it some time. But still, I already know I'm gonna sit down with her and put a line under it in a way I don't leave a dozen and a half texts from her hanging."

"She doesn't deserve that, Rix."

"Mom taught me, the thing that makes a good person is not that they treat people like they deserve. It's that, no matter how hard it might be, you treat people right."

"Your mom's wisdom can be inconvenient," Judge muttered.

Rix chuckled.

Judge spoke.

"Though, the part I still don't get is why all this can't go down while you see what being with Alex might mean."

"I sense your approval of her, and I get that, she's great. But I'm not ready to go there again with another woman."

Hesitantly, Judge said, "Sometimes, it's not about being ready, Rix."

"I don't have the luxury of flying by the seat of my pants with this kinda shit, Judge."

Carefully, Judge said, "Okay. How's that?"

"What if it doesn't work out, and we're starting things up at Trail Blazer, and right now, there's four of us who work together. Alex and me don't need to drag you and Kevin along for that ride."

"You're talking sense, but let's go back to the other thing you said."

They weren't going to go back to it, because he should never have said it.

Judge didn't need to know where Rix had no choice but to be.

He'd be in a chair or on prosthetics his whole life.

Raising kids with no legs.

Hopefully growing old, but with no legs.

His life and his future looked different than other people's.

And the woman in it would have to get that in a way Rix wasn't certain that woman existed.

He'd wanted a wife, he'd wanted a family.

But the idea that he could wake up with his house on fire, his family under that roof, and it'd be a struggle to save himself, no way could he look after them, was the kind of snag he had trouble seeing past.

And that was just one example of maybe a thousand of them.

"I gotta go. Get settled," he changed the subject. "Your dad left us a message that he's picking up the tab for restaurant and room service, and to make sure we knew he was serious about that and he wanted us to take him up on it, he made a reservation for us tonight." Rix looked at his watch. "I gotta get cleaned up. Me and Alex are meeting up in ten."

"Rix…"

When Judge said no more, Rix asked, "What?"

"You know you can talk to me about anything, right?"

Here was the shit.

He loved this guy, but it was still shit.

If Judge wanted to know, he needed to ask.

And for the man Judge was in Rix's life, maybe he even needed to push.

A little.

Sometimes.

When it mattered.

"I just told you I wanted to fuck our Director of Outreach, I think I know that," he hedged.

Judge laughed and said, "Right."

"Tell Chloe I said hey."

"Will do. Keep up the good work."

Rix shook his head, unzipped his bag, and replied, "Piss off."

Another laugh and then, "Later, man."

"Later, bud."

They disconnected. Rix pulled out a white shirt, a clean pair of jeans and his dop kit. He went to the bathroom, tugged off his tee, washed under his pits, reapplied antiperspirant, examined his stubble, which was getting out of control, but he didn't have time to do anything about it.

He wet his hands, ran them through his hair, then changed his jeans, shrugged on his shirt, slid a brown belt through the loops of his jeans, and blanked himself through the process of switching the running shoes off his fake feet to a pair of brown leather oxfords.

He then texted Alex to ask if she was ready before he pulled some other shit out of his bag and kit to put it where he'd need it later, primarily the book he was reading, his sleep shorts and his shampoo.

He got Alex's reply of *Coming over* about half a second before her knock sounded at the door.

He knew it was her, but looked through the peephole anyway, which turned out to be a good call.

Because she'd pulled the pigtails out, her hair was down, she'd done something to it so it didn't have braid kinks, but instead was a tumble of curls floating over her shoulders and down her chest.

He had not once in the time he'd known her seen her hair down.

And this was not the time for him to see it.

Because it was fucking *amazing*.

She'd also changed. She was wearing a cream, ribbed, fitted racer tank that exposed another something new to Rix.

She had amazing shoulders.

A Michelin star also meant she put on makeup. Not much. But he saw liner along her lashes, glimmer on her cheeks, and gloss on her lips.

She didn't look more fuckable than he was realizing she very much was.

But makeup-less, Kids and Trails tee and army pants Alex was fuck-her-hard-and-fast-in-a-tent-after-a-long-hike-so-they-could-move-on-and-grill-some-hotdogs-and-cuddle-under-the-stars Alex.

This Alex was take-her-to-his-bed-and-make-her-whisper-his-name-in-that-voice-of-hers-over-and-over-until-he-let-her-come Alex.

"Shit, fuck," he muttered, opened the door to her, and the rest didn't get better, because it did.

A sage green skirt with a deep waistband that clung to her waist and upper hips. A full skirt was attached to it, wrap-around style, the back hitting her ankles, the front edges gliding up at an angle to expose tan calves and a pair of light brown suede sandals that had a lot of straps, including ones that wound around her ankles, and a heel that wasn't high, but it wasn't short either.

She had a couple of gold medallions hanging down her chest, thin gold hoops in her ears and a slim clutch.

So Alexandra Sharp could clean up.

Really fucking well.

And she did it in a way that totally surprised him, but was also completely her.

"We got about forty-five before our booking. You wanna raid the mini-bar in here, or go down and hit the hotel bar?" he asked.

She opened her mouth to answer, but his phone rang.

When her eyes fell to his crotch, because his phone was in his back pocket and that was where the sound was coming from, he didn't want to dig it out, mostly because the call might be from Peri.

But he needed Alex not to be looking at his groin.

So he went for his phone.

It wasn't Peri.

It was Chloe.

He figured this was about one of two things (unless it was about both), her pushing him about Alex (because Rix was under no illusions, Judge told his woman everything), or her losing her shit about Peri (because Judge was loyal AF, but Chloe obliterated the loyalty scale to the point they hadn't created one to measure how deep her allegiance could go).

"Take it, we have time. I'll raid the mini-bar," Alex said, beginning to move into his room, so he stepped out of her way.

He hadn't brought aftershave or cologne.

But she'd put on perfume and holy goddamn fuck.

It smelled of musk and amber, it was woodsy, warm, but delicate and perfect for her because that was all her, but also, she could get that scent all over him, and he wouldn't mind wearing it, not only because it smelled of her.

Shit.

She headed toward the mini-bar.

He took the call from Chloe to get his mind off Alex.

"Yo," he greeted.

"Where are you?"

"In the only place that could be described as the middle of nowhere in California."

"California is a big state, Rix, there are numerous places like that."

"Well, I'm in one of them," he returned. "What's up?"

"Is Alex with you?"

Okay, Alex was not any part of either of the reasons he suspected Chloe would be calling.

The door shut behind him as he moved back into the room and asked, "Yeah, why?"

"And where are the two of you? At the hotel restaurant?"

When his eyes hit her, Alex was holding up a bottle of red wine in one hand, and a beer in the other.

He tipped his head to the beer.

She turned back to the cabinet, and he saw her tank entirely exposed her shoulder blades.

Her skin was smooth and tan.

Great.

"No, we're having a drink in my room. Again, *why?*"

"A drink in your room, excellent," she bizarrely decreed, then demanded, "Put me on speakerphone."

This was Chloe.

So…

No way in fuck.

"Chloe, tell me what you're calling about."

"It's important. Put me on speakerphone, I need to talk to you both."

"I'm not doing it until you tell me what this is about."

"It's about saving Alex."

At these words, his chest constricted and his eyes shot from Alex's shoulder blade to her profile.

"From what?" he growled.

"Her family."

It was at that, he realized he'd heard it, but missed it.

Earlier, Alex had said, *There's a lot on my mind. Work stuff and, um... family stuff...*

They then got into other things, so he hadn't asked about it.

And Chloe and Alex might not be tight, but they spent time together. They liked each other. Chloe was rabidly friendly and in your business, but somehow managed to be that way in a manner that was sweet and generous and thoughtful.

Yeah, it was crazy, but she had a knack with that shit.

He couldn't imagine Alex opening up easily with anyone.

But if there was someone she opened up to, it'd be Chloe.

"Going to speakerphone," he said, and hit it, moving forward just as Alex extended the beer bottle to him. "Chloe," he told her, taking the bottle.

Her brows inched together and she said, "Okay."

"Alex?" Chloe called.

"Hey, Chloe."

"Hello there, sorry to interrupt down time for you two, but obviously, time is of the essence. We have to plan."

Alex stared at the phone, clearly as confused as Rix was.

"Wine for you?" Rix asked her.

Alex's body jerked, she nodded and turned back to the mini-bar, but he moved closer and gently shifted her out of the way, setting his beer and the phone down to take over the drinks.

"Hello?" Chloe's voice came from his phone.

"We're here, but I don't think either of us know what you're talking about," Alex told her.

"The situation," Chloe stated.

"What situation?" Alex asked.

"For one, *your* situation," Chloe said.

"I...what's my situation?" Alex inquired.

"Coco," Rix grunted, popping the cork, "just spit it out."

"Well, it's good you two are hanging out, because you need to get a head start while you're out there together, practicing being boyfriend and girlfriend," Chloe announced.

Rix froze, but his ears still worked and he heard the gust of shocked air Alex let out, like someone had gut punched her.

"What?" Rix snarled at his phone.

"For when you go to New York for Blake's wedding," Chloe did and did not explain, the last part because it was an explanation, it was just that Rix didn't understand it.

"How do you know about that?" Alex asked in an agonized whisper.

Rix's gaze raced to her face.

Her pale face.

She was staring at his phone like it was going to grow arms and legs and chase her around the room.

"Know about what?" Rix prompted.

Her eyes darted to him, and her cheeks went scarlet.

"Well, obviously," Chloe's voice came at them, "considering Alex's sister Blake is...how to say this...*how she is*, Alex needs a fabulous plus one to shove in Blake's face and to get Blake off her back during the wedding. And for that to work, you two are going to have to sell it."

"I'm going with you to your sister's wedding?" he asked the woman who was in the room with him.

"Oh dear," Chloe murmured over the phone.

"I just...said that when she...asked because she was...well, she's Blake," Alex stammered in the room.

"And how is Blake?" he pressed.

"We're not all that close."

He watched her carefully as he turned fully to her and asked, "How huge of an understatement is that?"

"Um...colossal?" she asked back, like he could confirm her answer.

He kept watching her.

Chloe's voice came back to them. "Have I put my foot in it?"

"We got it from here," Rix said. "Later, Coco."

"Okay, but wai—"

That's all Chloe got out before he reached out and disconnected her.

He turned back to Alex.

She was staring at the door to the hall.

"Babe," he growled.

Her attention bounced back to him.

"What's going on?"

She shook her head. "Nothing."

"You got a situation with your sister?"

A one-shoulder shrug, a quick glance at the door again, then back to him, she said, "It's just…she's, well…we don't get along. We're very different. And when she asked if I was bringing someone to her wedding, she did it in a way she knew my answer. Because I'm not seeing anyone. But she's getting married. And it was her usual catty. I kind of wanted to…you know, maybe let the wind out of her sails a little bit. You sprang to mind, I, uh…" her gaze coasted from his to rest on the floor, "I don't know why. And um…when I told her I was bringing someone, she probably could tell I was lying, so she started quizzing me. I was kind of glad I picked someone I knew, instead of made someone up, so I didn't have to make *more* up." Her attention lifted, grazed his phone, and then came back to him. "I don't know how Chloe found out, but it's not a big deal. I just threw your name out there and then, later, I was going to explain you couldn't make it."

Rix stood there, staring at her.

"I'm maid of honor," she blurted.

Rix continued to stare at her.

"She sent me my dress and shoes. Combined, they cost twenty-four hundred dollars. I need to PayPal her."

"Holy fuck," he muttered.

"Yeah," she agreed.

"Why are you maid of honor if you two don't get along?"

"Because that's the way it's supposed to be."

"According to who?"

"Mom. Dad. Blake."

"I take it you declining isn't an option."

She shook her head.

"When's this happening?"

"October," she said slowly.

His brows knit. "Next month?"

She nodded.

"When'd you tell her I was coming with you?"

"The Friday before last."

"So, it's not like you told her that when she asked you to stand up for her and it'd be tough to get an out because by then, we'd have been seeing each other for a while, so two people together for a while, the sister's boyfriend would make a point of showing at a family wedding."

She swallowed, then shared, "She asked me to be her maid of honor then too."

Hang on a second.

"She asked you last Friday?"

She nodded again, but clarified, "Not asked. She told me I'd be her maid of honor."

"Is this a shotgun wedding?"

Another shake of her head. "No, that was just when she got around to telling me she was getting married. She's already had her shower, and I'm...well, she said she wasn't going to have one, but I get the sense I'm simply just not invited to her hen night."

That constriction in his chest hadn't lessened, but hearing this shit come out of her mouth, now there was a burning.

"Hen night?" he bit out.

"That means bachelorette party."

"And you're not invited."

She bit her lip.

"But you are expected to show in New York on top of paying over two grand for wedding shit."

She grimaced.

Yeah, his chest was burning.

Way down fucking deep.

"And she had her shower without you even knowing she was

getting married?"

"I'm kinda glad, Rix. Like I said, we're not close." She swayed, like she was going to take a step his way and thought better of it, then went on quickly, "Listen, I don't know how Chloe heard or what she thinks, but it isn't that big of a deal. I wasn't actually going to ask you to do it. I never expected you'd even know I brought you into it at all. But I'll just say we broke up, and I'll—"

"I'm going with you."

Her head went back on a powerful twitch. "Sorry?"

"We're gonna be fake boyfriend and girlfriend. I still have Peri's ring. Peri being my ex-fiancée. She returned it when she dumped me. You can wear it. We'll go whole hog, steal some of your sister's thunder, you show there already engaged. You can call it off whenever you feel like it. Or we can send them fake pictures of us living it up in Arizona for the next three years, I don't give a fuck."

Her eyes got huge.

Her glossy lips parted.

That top.

That skirt.

Her ankles.

Her curves.

All those curls in her hair.

That look on her face.

He wanted to kiss her.

And he was going to kiss her.

Because no way he could sell the fact that they'd decided to spend the rest of their lives together without him knowing how she tasted.

So he was going to know how she tasted.

He was going to memorize it.

She pulled her shit together, regrettably, and said, "Rix, you really don't have to do that."

"I know I don't. So, outside of behaving in bitchy ways, like cutting you out of her wedding shit, is she just a straight-out bitch to you, your sister?"

She pressed her lips together.

The sister was a bitch.

Alex that day, sitting with hard-faced, dead-eyed kids who'd been sent to the middle of nowhere to see if they could locate some thread of themselves to hold on to, unfazed, no fear, poised and attentive, eating shit from some woman who shared her blood.

There was "not close."

And there was *this* horseshit.

"Then I really do have to do it," he stated.

"My family is…they're…well, it's hard to explain."

It wasn't hard to explain. The look on her face, the fact she couldn't put it into words, the knowledge that Alex worked at a nonprofit and her sister sent her a dress and goddamned shoes that cost that much said it all.

"Are we friends?" he asked.

She rubbed her lips together a few seconds before she answered, "I think so."

"We're friends," he rumbled.

"Okay," she whispered.

Oh yeah.

He was gonna taste her.

Their preparation for this gig was gonna be thorough.

They were gonna sell the shit out of it.

"Friends look out for friends," he pointed out.

"This is asking a lot."

"Did you ask?"

Her eyes got huge again.

"How pissed is your sister gonna be when I actually show up?" he inquired.

Her gaze traveled him down and up, and that was when her eyes lit, and he could swear he saw a little dimple come and go in her right cheek.

All his life, he'd had women admire him. Hell, he'd lost both legs, and he still had it.

But never in his life had he felt it like he felt it when she said everything about how attractive she thought he was without saying one goddamn word.

Oh yeah.

They were gonna sell *the shit* out of this.

"I'll buy your ticket out there," she offered.

The hell she would.

He turned back to the wine, saying, "We got time to figure it out."

He then poured her a huge-ass glass.

When he turned to give it to her, he got her big eyes again as she took it.

Good.

That was what he was going for because he liked that look on her.

But she gave him a bonus.

She actually giggled.

It, too, was her. Quiet and it didn't last long.

But coming from Alex, it was a big deal.

He nabbed his beer and pointed the neck at her.

She lifted her glass to his bottle and caught his eyes.

"Here's to us, baby," he whispered. "And our long and happy life together."

More color hit her cheeks, but she didn't lose his gaze.

Nope.

That dimple came back.

And this time, as she touched her glass to his bottle, it stayed embedded in her sweet, round, glimmering cheek.

CHAPTER 7

THE ROCKS

Alex

I woke up before the alarm went off on my phone.

I was surprised I'd slept at all.

I curled up my legs, tugged at all the pillows I could reach, shoving some under my cheek, cuddling with others, and aimed my eyes at the windows, seeing desert for a short while before my vision blurred and my thoughts went to the night before.

After Rix and I toasted to our fake future together, we made a deal.

This trip was work, so even though, through spending time together, we'd naturally be getting to know one another better, in order to keep work boundaries, the "deep research" (Rix's words) would begin when we got back to Prescott.

It was a deal I was happy to make.

It took the pressure off.

Yes, the giddy, ohmigod-Rix-was-going-to-do-this! feel had abandoned me after my first sip of the massive glass of wine he'd poured me, and my anxiety instantly started spiraling.

But I could do work.

Which was what we did, over beer and wine in his room, then

steaks and wine in the restaurant, ending up at the bar, with more wine for me, and some bourbon on the rocks for Rix.

I was loose, but I wasn't drunk.

Though I was comfortable talking, because we were talking about CTB. We were talking about Frank and Hale and the kids. We were talking about the interviews, what we thought, what we'd learned, what surprised us, what didn't, and what was up next for our trip.

Rix had complimented me for how the kids connected with me, and when he expressed concern he didn't know how to reach them, I'd assured him that it was likely the kids didn't open to him as much because he was intimidating.

"You can imagine, for the majority of them, they're where they are because of parental issues," I'd told him. "And the truth of the matter is that the majority of that is absent or abusive fathers. So a big, built guy is already a natural threat. One who cares is something they may have little experience with. So you're overwhelming on two fronts, physically and emotionally."

I watched, and I'll admit I did it with fascination, as Rix took this in, sifted through it and had a myriad of reactions to it, being angry, interested, pensive and clearly cataloging it for future encounters.

We'd gone on to talk about Trail Blazer, going deep because Rix invited, "Say we don't have five hundred million, say we have five hundred billion, what would you do?"

That idea was so fantastic, but so awesome, and I had so much swirling in my head, I went crazy, giving it all to him.

He was right there with me the whole time, listening, and sharing his take, his thoughts, the things he'd like to see from Trail Blazer.

Then we went off on tangents, creating crazy schemes that would save the world (well, Rix didn't do so much of this, but the way he smiled a lot, chuckled a lot and often out-and-out laughed egged me on to do it).

It was fun.

I was having fun with Rix Hendrix.

Though, it wasn't all about CTB and Trail Blazer.

I'd learned the super cool story that his parents met in college in

Kansas, went on a couple of dates, didn't think it'd go anywhere, so that was the end of that. They'd then miraculously both ended up in Flagstaff, where they ran into each other again. Either taking the hint from the cosmos or being older and wiser and knowing more what they wanted, their couple status took hold that time, and now they'd been married for forty years.

Rix had been born and raised in Flagstaff, the second of two sons. His brother Joshua (and Rix shared, he was known only as Josh, like Rix was known only as Rix, which, of course meant Rix admitted he often called him Joshua), got married in the summer of last year. Seven months later, he and his wife Hailey gave Rix's parents their first grandkid, a girl, Kinsley (who heartmeltingly sounded like the apple of her uncle's eye). And on a recent phone conversation, Josh had shared with Rix that they were considering it was time to think about number two.

On my side of things, Rix had learned Blake was older than me (she was thirty, I was twenty-eight, which led to the knowledge that Rix was thirty-four, but next month, the week before we'd be going to NYC, he'd turn thirty-five). She was my only sibling. My parents were divorced, and didn't get along, before and after their marriage.

We dug no deeper than that.

However, I had filled him in with the details Cathy sent me about the wedding itinerary, which included an indication that Mum and Dad were one-upping each other, because Mum was hosting a brunch on the Thursday before the Friday rehearsal/rehearsal dinner. And therefore Dad was hosting a cocktail party on the Wednesday evening.

"This means," I shared with Rix, "Mum planned her brunch first, and then, not to be shown up, Dad decided to do a cocktail party, and ever since, they've been escalating hostilities. I know this because, for some reason, it's strongly encouraged for the women to wear a hat to brunch, and the cocktail party is formal."

"Well, shit," Rix muttered.

Shit was correct.

"But you don't have to show for those," I told him. "You can fly in on Friday or Saturday sometime. The wedding isn't until five."

"I'm in all the way, babe," had been his reply.

This was belly-fluttering, though it was also convenient, as it meant we didn't have to have a discussion about who would pay for his ticket. If he was in all the way, then he could fly on Dad's plane with me.

I didn't tell him that.

The more intimate, and frightening, details could come later.

During our "deep research."

The truth was, the night had been so fun, and surprisingly easy, when we walked together up to our rooms, and Rix walked me to my door, which was only one door down from his, but he still did it, and I looked up at him to say goodnight, part of me expected him to dip down and touch his lips to mine.

Because, yes, the night had seemed like a date.

Of course, the instant I had that thought, it flipped me out, so I dropped my keycard.

That meant instead of a touch of his lips on mine, I got a different touch.

His palm in my chest before he stated, "Don't go for it. I'm getting it. We got work to do, we both don't need concussions."

I fought a grimace, because I was *so* that girl who would bang heads with the guy as we both bent to retrieve something.

He nabbed my keycard, then handed it to me.

"'Night, Alex," he'd muttered.

"'Night," I'd replied, used the keycard, and without further incident, got into my room.

He didn't move from his spot in the hall until I was in and had flipped a light switch, and that was sweet, him being gentlemanly, waiting until I was safely inside.

I gave him a silly wave, which made his lips quirk.

And the door closed between us.

I alternately floated on air, and panicked, while getting ready for bed.

Once there, I'd tossed and turned, wondering how I was going to handle not only spending nearly six days pretending to be Rix's fiancée, but all that went into getting to know one another so we could convince my family I was.

I did this until eventually, I fell asleep.

Now, though, with Rix not there, the desert before me, and my morning plan to be up early so I could hit the trail our server at dinner had told us ran off the north side of the hotel, up a gentle grade, and in twenty minutes, you'd have a vista that included some rock formations that were definitely worth a short, forty-minute hike, I thought…this was doable.

Things had gone awry between us, but I'd been wrong.

Rix was not a jerk.

Rix was a good guy.

No, he was a *great* guy.

He cared a lot about what we were hoping to do at Trail Blazer, and he wanted to do it well, reaching as many as we could, making as much positive change as was possible.

He was also funny and he was interesting and he was a good listener and he clearly loved his family and he was going to do something really, amazingly sweet—pretend not just to be my boyfriend, but in order to make a bigger thing of it to be in Blake's face, he was going to be my fake future husband.

If he could be that awesome, I could do this.

I had no misconceptions that I was going to sail through this without a few clumsy moments.

But how hard would it be to get to know Rix, to share about myself, maybe to learn to hold his hand, accept a kiss on the cheek and perhaps a peck on the lips…or two.

And then we'd come back from New York, and we'd be friends, sharing funny stories about the look on my sister's face when she first saw Rix. Or how my father tried to figure out how to best a man who didn't live his life trying to make the point he was better than everyone else and didn't care in the slightest about something as inane as that, because he knew no one was better, people were just different.

Then later, someday when Rix found his real future wife, I could joke with her about Rix and my glorious but brief engagement, and it wouldn't destroy me that his love went to someone else, because I'd have him as my friend, and maybe her too.

Okay, that last part was probably pushing it.

On this thought, I reached out to my phone, canceled the alarm and got out of bed.

I brushed my teeth, made in-room coffee, got changed into some olive-green trekker shorts, an apricot V-necked tee, slathered on sunscreen, and quickly downed some caffeine while putting on my lightweight hiking boots. Then I grabbed my faded-camo bucket hat and sunglasses and headed out to the trail.

It was a gentle ascent, nice and winding around some steep rock that jutted up its sides, so eventually the resort was out of sight, and you felt you were alone in nature.

But once the end of the trail was in sight, so was something else.

Rix had had the same idea as me.

He was up on a bluff, wearing khaki, lightweight performance fabric hiking pants and a basil green tee.

And he didn't miss my approach, his cocky white smile aimed my way seemed to be gleaming in the sun.

But I'd stopped, because he was tanned and he was gorgeous and he needed a shave, but I liked his scruff, and he was smiling at me and he was out on the trail before six-thirty and I found that all so ludicrously attractive, I felt like weeping.

"Al, get up here," he ordered.

Al?

No one called me Al.

It was horrible.

But from Rix's lips, *I adored it.*

I got up there and saw why he was impatient for me to get there.

Not only were we in a spot that offered a spectacular vista, down below, there was an area made of sandy, waving, smooth, and in places, bulbous rock. It looked like the terrain of a different planet. I could see a studio in Hollywood wanting to film some *Galaxy Quest*-style movie there.

Film crews and actors crawling over that, maybe doing damage, I hoped they never did.

"Wow," I said.

"Yup. Pretty much the shit. Nice way to start the day, hey?"

I looked up at him with a small smile. "Hey."

He had shades on, but still, his mood was so good, it felt like he was twinkling at me.

As I was being bedazzled by his twinkle, he shifted my world on its axis.

He did this tossing an arm around my shoulders, adjusting our position so our backs were to the valley, and saying, "We can't waste this opportunity. Get in here. Pretend that you love me."

And he was extending his long arm out, his phone held in his hand in that way cool dudes held their phones for a group selfie, holding it horizontal, with his long fingers cupping the back.

But I was frozen stiff.

"Babe, shove in," he commanded, tightening his arm around my shoulders.

Okay.

Uh.

No.

This wasn't going to be doable.

He smelled of dust and man and sun, and my sports bra was buttery soft, comfortable and lined, but it wasn't padded, and that was currently a gigantic issue.

His phone arm went down and he called, "Alex."

I was still staring where the phone had been.

And then I wasn't, because his finger was under my chin and pushing it up.

My sunglasses hit his, and they stayed there even when his finger went from my chin so all of them could wrap around my upper arm.

"This is how you do it," he said gently, his hand trailing down my arm to get to my wrist.

He pulled it in front of him, tucked it around him.

He then said, "Leave it there, hold on."

I nodded mutely and did as told.

He retrieved his phone from wherever he'd put it and then ordered, "Cheek to my chest, Alexandra."

Oh God.

I nodded again.

Then I took a breath and laid my cheek to his chest.

Soft fabric, hard muscle underneath.

Beautiful.

"You're smack in vast, sweetheart," he murmured. "You can open up here. You can let it out. Close your eyes."

I closed my eyes.

"Do you feel it?" he asked.

It took a second (probably more like twenty), then I whispered, "I feel it, Rix."

"Okay, baby, open up and smile."

I opened my eyes, smelling dust, man and sun, feeling his strong arm tight around me, the power of his chest under my cheek, the warmth of the morning sun on my skin, the air fresh, but still all around us.

And in that moment, it was just Rix and me.

No one would ever have that moment.

No one, but us.

I was his, and he was mine.

For then.

So I smiled.

His phone clicked.

He didn't let me go immediately, and when he did, he turned into me so we were toe to toe, shifted his other shoulder to my side, and held up the phone in front of us.

"Our first picture fuckin' rocks, woman," he declared.

He was right.

It did.

My smile wasn't huge.

But it was content, and my dimple was out.

Rix wasn't smiling.

But there was no mistaking he was happy to be right where he was.

We actually kinda looked good together.

The phone fell away, and he muttered, "I'll text it to you. You can text it to your sister."

Right.

Pretend.

"Cool," I mumbled.

Even if it was pretend, nothing could dampen that moment for me, standing there with Rix.

We stared at the rocks, we took in the vista, and at the exact same second I was about to do it, Rix turned to me.

"Breakfast down in that sun room, or room service? And my vote is, room service. On one of our balconies. Our views are better. We get back, text me your order, I'll call it in. We can shower, get ready, by that time, they'll have the food up. We'll eat, and then we can hit the road."

"Sounds like a plan."

He did something with his hand, it moved up an inch, then fell, and I sensed he was going to touch me.

But he didn't.

Because we were pretend.

That produced a hint of melancholy.

But I shook it off and turned toward the trail.

Rix followed me.

———

I HAD A SHOWER AND WAS DRESSED AND VERY READY FOR BREAKFAST (IN other words, there was a rumble in my stomach).

I also had a text that just came in from Rix that said, *R&A Excursion 1, Operation Learnalot Nerve Center is my room. Breakfast on balcony T minus now.*

And I was thinking he really was funny.

I was also thinking I could love a guy that was that funny.

Then I stopped thinking and started to head out.

I had my door open and was about to step into the hall when my phone rang.

I expected it to be Rix, telling me to get my butt over there, because he was funny, but I was also noticing he could be impatient.

It wasn't Rix.

It was Chloe.

Considering what happened last night, I stepped back into my room, let go of the door and took the call.

"Hey, Chloe."

"Hello, Alex, is it too early?"

"No, Rix and I have already had a short hike and we're about to have breakfast on his balcony."

Chloe said nothing for a moment, and then she asked, "I do believe you two have a good deal to pack in before your sister's wedding, but…exactly how much practice are you getting?"

I wished.

"I'm in my room, he's in his, but I need to get over to his. That's where we're meeting and the food has arrived."

"Ah."

I didn't have a lot of time, so I got down to it.

"I took your call because I wanted to talk to you about last night."

"Yes, that's why I'm calling. We didn't quite finish, and to answer your as yet unasked question, Judge's sister Dru loosely knows your sister. And when you told Blake about Rix, you probably didn't know that Elsa Cohen has spoken of Rix, and your sister is somewhat of a fan of the Elsa Exchange. So knowing Dru knows him, she went fishing. I'm sorry to say, Dru isn't very fond of Blake, so she was concerned as to why Blake was calling about Rix, who Dru has become rather close to."

Damn.

Well, at least that explained that.

"Obviously, I jumped to conclusions," she went on. "I'm sorry if I made things awkward for you."

"We talked it through, and Rix is going to go with me to New York."

"Excellent," she purred.

"So I guess it's good you let the cat out of the bag, because Blake is going to hate me being with someone and she's *especially* going to hate that it's someone like Rix."

"Then I won't feel too badly I phoned, though I am glad that Rix cut me off, because I was going to discuss something else last night with the two of you, and given further time to contemplate, I think this should be between you and me."

"All right," I said warily.

"I'm not sure you've gotten to this point in learning of Rix, but he was once engaged."

Oh, we got to that point.

"Yes, he mentioned that."

"Obviously, considering he intended to make a family and spend the rest of his life with her, he loved her deeply."

A stitch pinched my insides.

I ignored it.

"Obviously," I mumbled.

"So of course, the blow she landed by ending things with him mere weeks after he had his accident, mere days after he came home after losing his legs, doing this *because* he lost his legs, was a heavy one."

When she finished speaking, I stood immobile, listening to the rushing in my ears, seeing my vision go white like static on an old TV screen.

I had no idea how long I experienced this before I heard Chloe calling my name.

I just knew it was long enough for me to identify the feeling I was feeling.

An emotion I had not felt in my entire life.

Rage.

"Are you there?" Chloe asked.

"Yes," I said, that one-syllable word harsh and trembling.

"I sense you feel much the same way Judge and I feel about Peri," she noted quietly.

"I sense you sense right," I forced through a throat that seemed dry and scratchy.

Chloe's tone was different on her next. No nonsense. Determined.

"Okay, Alex, it's no surprise to me that Rix is going to step up for you with your sister. He's that man. Very much so. As you'll soon learn. But as much of a bonus as that is, I hope you take no offense, this situation is not about you and your sister. Though I'll warn you, I don't know your sister, but her calling Dru, checking things out about you and Rix means she's sleuthing, and it's highly probable you understand why, so you two are going to have to be convincing."

I already knew that.

I still swallowed nervously.

"Alex?" she called.

"I'm here. I'm listening."

"Good. Now the important part of this is that Peri has recently approached Rix, and since then, has continued to try to reach out. She wants to get back together."

My neck tightened so tight, the very thought of moving it warned of agony.

"He doesn't want that, Alexandra," Chloe told me. "He loved her, but the kind of betrayal she treated him to…it's over. That's definite. He told Judge that, and Judge believes him."

I relaxed because I believed it too.

I mean, thank God he figured out before things got legal that the "for worse" part of marriage was not in the cards with this woman.

But it was still detestable how he figured that out.

"All right," I said.

"Though I think we both can agree that woman having the sheer audacity to kick him while he was down, and then when he's up. When he's back. After all the painful rehab. After psychologically dealing with the loss of two limbs. After learning to walk again. Run. Drive. Bike. Live. After he went through all that alone, she feels she's entitled to come back into his life, not standing by his side through the thin, thinking she can benefit from the thick of Rix. And on top of all of that, he now has an important new job with better pay, and the only direction from here is up. Well, that cannot happen."

The static and rushing started to return as I demanded, "Oh my God, do you think that's why she's back? Because he's working with Trail Blazer?"

"I've no idea how a woman like that thinks," Chloe sniffed. "Though, I know Rix is loving and devoted and now that the bad part is over, it could just be that it is over, and she wants the good stuff back."

My Lord.

That…

Bitch.

"Therefore," Chloe carried on, "she needs to see Rix with you. Moving on. Happy." A meaningful pause. "Are you understanding me?"

"I am absolutely, one hundred percent understanding you," I declared.

I wasn't sure, but I thought I heard her release a relieved breath before she said, "You leave it up to me how Peri sees you two together…repeatedly. But trust in me, I'll make that happen."

"Oh, I trust you."

"I know this is asking a lot from you. You don't tend—"

"He's marvelous."

"Pardon?"

I cleared my throat and said, "He's a really good man."

"Yes, I know."

"What you're asking might be the most important thing anyone has asked me to do."

Chloe made no reply.

"When he meets her," I began, "the woman that's for him, and he will, she needs to be perfect. Not a woman like that. So he has to be free, especially emotionally, to be open to having that kind of good in his life."

"Ummmmmmmm…" Chloe hummed, the sound lasting about ten seconds.

I took that as her not being certain I was up for the task, so when she quit making it, I told her, "It won't be easy, but I can promise to do my best. And that would be my *very* best, Chloe."

"Erm, okay, Alexandra."

"I need to get over to his room. The man Rix is, he's probably waiting on me to have breakfast."

"I can guarantee you, he is."

Again, I believed her.

Because that was the man Rix was.

And his fiancée *fucking left him* after he'd lost his legs.

My God, I hoped I was able to get a lock on it in my head before I saw her, because I honestly didn't know what I'd do if I didn't.

Fortunately, something occurred to me to take my mind from that, and quickly, I asked after it.

"I have to have my bridesmaid dress altered. It'll be complicated. It's a Marchesa and—"

"I'll handle it," she said. "Don't make plans Saturday. We'll probably have to go to Phoenix."

"Right."

"Alexandra?"

"Yes?"

"You're also a good woman."

Chloe Pierce was really neat. I knew a lot of women with a lot of money, a lot of beauty, a lot of style, and not one of them was like her.

So that coming from her meant a lot.

"Thanks," I whispered.

"See you Saturday."

"Yes. 'Bye."

"'Bye, Alex."

We rang off.

I stared at my phone.

Then I shoved it in my back pocket and marched out the door.

I realized I was pretty much hammering on Rix's when he opened it, asking, "Jesus, are the British coming?"

Ohmigod!

He was *so funny.*

And *so lovable.*

And *so marvelous.*

And his ex was *such a bitch.*

"That's a fallacy," I announced. "The colonists *were* British. So the call was that the *redcoats* were coming."

He stared at me.

Then he asked, "Is everything okay?"

No, it was not.

He was *astonishing.*

Miraculous.

Life.

And his ex was *a bitch.*

"I might have to go down to Phoenix with Chloe on Saturday to get my bridesmaid dress altered," I shared.

"Is that a dangerous mission? Are you wanted by the Phoenix police or something?" he inquired.

That got through, and I felt my lips twitch. "No."

"Is there a long story behind this that maybe you can share with me while I'm shoving food in my face?"

Yes.

He'd waited for me.

"No."

"So can I get on to shoving food in my face?"

"Yes."

He stepped aside. "Then get your ass in here."

I got my ass in there.

Our breakfast was set out on the table on the balcony, plate covers still on, the service trolley tucked to the side in the room.

I marched to the balcony and was utterly unsurprised when Rix noted, "Yours is to the left."

The left chair had its back to the windows, so that meant the view was the view. The right chair had its back to the railing, so the view was the shine off a big window.

I therefore went to the table, shifted my plate a little to make room, moved his plate by mine, then pulled his chair around, next to mine, so he had a view too.

After I did that, I adjusted my chair so it was in front of my plate, and I sat down.

He didn't.

He stood standing by the table, looking down at me.

"I don't hog good views," I declared, swept my plate cover off, and set it down with a clatter.

He lowered himself to the chair beside me.

I then swept his plate cover off and stacked it on mine.

"Al," he called when I was resting my napkin on my lap.

I looked up to him.

His eyes roamed my face before he asked, "You good?"

I'm here with you, so I'm fabulous.

For now.

But I'll take it.

"I'm famished."

And with that, I tucked into my food.

CHAPTER 8

THE BINDER

Rix

It was Sunday, Rix was heading up to Alex's place for dinner, at the same time trying to figure out how good, or how bad it was that he was keen to get there.

Something had changed with her.

Wednesday morning, she was different.

Not massively, but it was there.

She still alternated between being impressive with work, often a huge dork when she wasn't doing work shit or being quiet and peacefully in her own head.

But there was something between them that had...*settled*.

He couldn't say what it was exactly, because she wasn't completely comfortable with him, but within an hour, she'd gone from being entirely unable to fake a couple's selfie to making him sit beside her at breakfast.

And shit like that continued for the rest of the trip.

Not often, but it happened.

So, definitely.

Something had changed.

And Rix liked it.

Their trip had been fruitful. It'd also been enjoyable. And he couldn't get away from the fact that it sucked when they went their separate ways Friday evening when they got home, after they'd spent so much time together, and he dug the ease of being around her, got off on watching her work and how good she was at it, got off even more on getting to know her.

It sucked because he knew he had no shot of seeing her yesterday in order to officially begin their preparation to be fake engaged, because she and Chloe were heading down to Phoenix to do dress stuff.

Not to mention, Chloe, being Chloe, was taking Alex "in hand" and they were also shopping while they were down there in order that Alex would have appropriate outfits to wear for all the wedding shit that was happening. This apparently would take time, so they were spending the night at Genny and Duncan's condo in Phoenix.

Don't worry, Alex explained the itinerary, and I'm sorting you out too, had been the text he'd gotten from Chloe.

He didn't argue with her, even if he knew she'd bought Judge several suits that cost obscene amounts of money.

If she wanted to dress him, since he needed to represent for Alex, Chloe would make that work in ways he had no clue how to do, so he'd let that happen.

And Chloe was not Blake. Whatever she picked, she wouldn't make it bite him in the ass financially.

On a glance at his GPS that shared he was two minutes away, Rix told himself he was looking forward to having dinner at her place because they had a lot of ground to cover, and around six weeks to cover it in, so they needed to get stuck in.

But he was full of shit.

When the pin marked the spot on his truck computer and he saw her blue Subaru Crosstrek hybrid, he felt a warmth hit his gut.

And it stayed.

Her car was parked next to a roof that was level to a drive that butted the road that was just long enough to fit her car and his truck behind it.

From that roof, he knew her house was built down the incline and into the mountain, but even so, when he'd received her text yesterday, *Dinner tomorrow? Mine?* And he'd agreed, she'd said, *Sorry. It's not accessible. There are stairs. Will that be okay?* So he figured it'd be something like this.

And that was Alex.

Just straight up, out there, it was what was, and if they had to adjust plans, they would.

He'd told her he'd be on his legs so it was fine.

He didn't tell her he was curious as to where she lived, and that was why he was going to make it fine.

He parked, got out, headed to the side of the house where he saw the railing, and as he moved down her stairs, he further saw the pine needles on her property had meticulously been removed in an effort to make it defensible space.

Clearing ground cover was an aid to controlling wildfires.

"Fucking hell, this woman," he muttered, continuing down the steps.

There was a small deck landing that had some attractive pots filled with fall flowers arranged around the area. The landing was shrouded by close-growing pines at the side of the house on what was the second floor down, but there was a walkway that went around to the front where he could see a big deck sticking out.

Her welcome mat was woven sailor's knots.

Her door was glass panes, and he could see her through it, coming his way.

Guess you could hear cars parking from her living room.

She was in slash front pocket shorts in a gray-green. Wide V camel-colored tee showing lots of skin at her chest and her elegant collarbone.

No jewelry. No makeup. No shoes.

But hair down, so she didn't need anything else.

Watching her get close, it was coming clear why he was keen to get there.

She opened the door and looked up at him, no smile on her lips, but the dimple was rippling, there and gone and back again.

"Hey."

"Babe."

"You found it."

He looked to his feet, then to her, and lifted his brows.

When he did that, the dimple definitely popped, though only for about a nanosecond, before she flicked out her hand in an odd, hilarious, adorable way and stopped barring the door.

He walked in enough she could close the door.

But that was as far as he could make it before he had to stop dead.

Because her place was the...fucking...*shit.*

Big, slouchy, comfortable-looking couch that unquestionably would fit two. Bed up in the loft he could see had an iron footboard and some colorful, old-fashioned quilt folded at the bottom that looked like it was made up of stitched-together rosettes with a dripping, scalloped edge. Queen bed, so it'd fit two as well, but there'd need to be cuddling. Kickass farmhouse kitchen table with curve-back chairs. Wall of windows. Sunlights. Big deck with more pots with lots of flowers, also lots of seating options. Red cabinets in the kitchen that ran along the wall opposite him.

She had possessions. Books. A surprising (that she had one at all), but impressively large CD collection. Toss pillows. Warm-looking throws. The odd piece that was either bought while making a memory, taking an adventure, or she just thought it was pretty, lying around.

But it was small and contained, like her.

It was clean, and even neat, but not exactly tidy.

There was no massive, gourmet kitchen to wow you.

Not a single thing in the place looked like it was selected on a plan of setting the space.

Alex lived, and some of that life landed here.

That was it.

He fucking loved it.

"Cheeseburger eggrolls," she announced.

He looked down at her.

"Say again?" he asked.

"That's what we're having for dinner. Cheeseburger eggrolls. Made in the air fryer. And a quinoa salad. Brownies and ice cream for dessert."

"Sounds awesome."

"I use turkey meat, I shy away from beef. And we had steaks this week. I've met my quota."

"Works for me."

"First, the binder."

He did a slow blink.

The binder?

She strolled across the space, and he'd been busy with her hair, and her two-toned eyes, that dimple, her auburn-tipped lashes and getting her to talk comfortably with him in that husky voice, so he'd forgotten what a great ass she had.

Shit.

How had he forgotten about that ass?

By the time he lost sight of it, she was at the kitchen table, and sure enough, she was holding up a green three-ring binder.

The spine was thick.

"Can you come here, please?" she requested.

He walked across her space.

She must have had a candle or incense burning or something, because he smelled pinyon.

That made everything even better.

Jesus.

He stopped close to her, and she dropped the binder on the table with a plonk, and when she opened it, there was another plonk, so he looked to the table.

There were tabs, with paper between. He couldn't read them because her hand was in the way, and she was flipping.

Though, good or bad (he picked bad), she explained.

"All we need, but that's up for discussion. You might have addi-tional categories. Family." She flipped a tab. "Friends and Enemies." She flipped a tab. "Schooling." She flipped a tab. "Work experience." She flipped a tab. "Travel." Another flip. "Food." Another flip. "Enter-tainment, like movies, books, TV." And another flip. "Music, because obviously, that's its own category." Flip. "Hobbies and Favorite Activi-ties." One last flip. "Miscellaneous."

He felt her gaze so he turned his attention to her.

"Did I miss anything?" she asked.

"What the fuck is that?" he asked back.

She assumed a mystified expression that simultaneously made him want to take a picture so he wouldn't forget how cute it was, at the same time it made him want to kiss her.

"A life binder. I have sheets"—she looked to the binder, and with trepidation, he did too, to see pages flying as she flicked them off her thumb—"and so do you. My pages are white, yours are yellow. I fill in. You fill in. We study, passing it between us. Though, if you want your own binder, I'll make you one. And look, I've already started my part."

She flipped to what he knew was the "Entertainment" tab because he saw five precise columns with shit written under them. The headers were "Books," "Movies," "TV," "Other" and "Dislikes."

There was stuff written under those headings, but he didn't bother reading it.

He turned back to her. "Are you being serious?"

"You don't think it's a good idea?"

"Hello, Mr. Sharp." He looked down to the binder, reaching out a hand with fingers spread in order to use his fingertips to adjust it his way. "I'm marrying your daughter, and she enjoyed *The Queen's Gambit* and found Michelle Obama's *Becoming* moving and inspi-rational."

And yeah.

She'd written "moving" and "inspirational" with precise, bracketed arrows pointing to the words on the two lines under *Becoming*.

"Well, you wouldn't recite it like that," she mumbled.

He straightened away from that crazy binder, turned fully to her, looked into her eyes, and said quietly, "We'd known each other for a while. She annoyed me because I thought she didn't know how to handle the fact I'd lost my legs. But we found ourselves one night at a bar, talking about shit that mattered, and around the time I noticed she had the prettiest eyes I've ever seen, I realized it wasn't that. She was attracted to me and she's shy. She didn't know how to handle how she felt about me. You can imagine, for a guy like me, to meet a woman like your daughter, after life had made me a different man, knowing how attractive I was to her meant a lot. It took some work, she's no less shy, but I got in there. And a little while later, because she's all she is, I gave her my ring."

She was breathing heavily, and it was then he noticed her full tits.

But he wasn't about her full tits.

He was all about those eyes.

"Are you a different man?" she asked softly.

"I don't fight fires."

"You're fighting one for me."

His middle rolled back, and he felt winded.

He would be forever grateful that she let that slide and declared, "I still think we need the binder."

"I'm not recording my life in a binder."

"Okay, tell me, and I'll transcribe it."

"Sweetheart, I gotta know you stay away from beef...and why. I don't gotta know you liked *The Queen's Gambit*."

"Did *you* like *The Queen's Gambit*?"

"I haven't seen it."

Her eyes got huge.

Goddamn.

Fuck it.

It was time.

"We also gotta be comfortable with touching, and kissing, a lot."

Even bigger eyes.

"Uh...*why*?"

Her last word came out on a squeak.

Mm-hmm.

They were totally going to be kissing a lot.

"We're getting married," he reminded her.

"Yes. Of course. Cheek kisses and pecks on the lips. My family isn't about demonstration."

"Well, your fiancé is."

"Rix—"

"We gotta sell this."

"I know, but—"

"Babe, we're gonna be making out."

And even *bigger* eyes.

"I—"

"It's gotta be done."

"But—"

"And you know it."

She pressed her lips together.

She knew it.

"This isn't about what your family does or expects." He turned to the binder, closed it, and for good measure, shoved it so it slid several inches across her kickass table. He looked back to her. "It's about who *we* are…together. And I'm affectionate."

"I'm reserved."

He nodded. "You are, except around me."

"My family is going to think it's weird if I'm pawing at you."

He grinned. "I don't want you to paw at me," he totally fucking did, "and it's not like I'm gonna be grabbing your ass. But there are things you can't fake. And intimacy is one of them."

The squeak was back. "We're going to be intimate?"

They were.

How far that would go, he had to get his head straight about, because however that was, it had to be right in the end. It was going to be her call entirely, but whatever call she made, Rix had to make it so when it was done, there was not even a little bruise for her to feel, and he could walk away knowing that.

So yeah, he was nowhere near having his head straight about Alex.

"You know it's always up to you how far that goes."

Her shoulders slumped with relief.

"But we have to know each other in that way. What our touch feels like. What each other tastes like. You'll be safe. You'll like it. And it's always in your power to start or stop it."

She looked longingly and maybe a little desperately at the binder.

"Honey, give it up with the binder."

She turned to him. "I don't know if I can marry a man who hasn't watched *The Queen's Gambit*."

He let that settle in for a beat.

Then he burst out laughing.

And while he did it, not for practice, not pretend, it came natural when he swung his arm out, hooked her at the waist and pulled her into his body.

Oh yeah, she had big tits.

And she'd put on her perfume.

He finished laughing while holding her eyes and felt her hands where she'd rested them, not pushing, but not quite comfortable with it, on his chest.

"Feed me, and we'll watch that show," he said.

"It has seven episodes."

"Okay. We'll watch a couple tonight and we'll watch a couple when you come over to dinner at my place on Wednesday."

"It's a bingey type show."

"Right, then we'll hunker down and bust it out next Sunday."

"I'm not sure I can lie around for seven hours, watching TV."

He knew he couldn't do that, though he'd attempt it for her.

Okay.

Right.

Rix was worried as fuck that he was getting his head straight about Alex.

Even so, he dipped down, and the movement made her tip her head back.

They ended with their faces a couple inches apart.

He didn't shift.

She seemed frozen.

He took advantage.

"Tell me how you wanna watch that show. Two Friday? Two Saturday? Three Sunday?"

"That'll work," she breathed.

"My place, your place, my place."

"Okay."

"You know, you do have the prettiest eyes I've ever seen."

"Thanks," she whispered.

"Dress fitting go okay?"

"You might find we do need the binder, because I'll need to take a couple of weeks off to recover from surgery after selling a kidney."

He did not let her go, but he straightened.

That was when she pressed in at his chest, not to push him away, reassuringly.

"Rix—" she began, her tone conciliatory, proving, in the time they'd already spent together, that they had definitely gotten to know one another.

"That's fuckin' bullshit."

"It's a wedding. It comes with the territory."

"It's still fuckin' bullshit, and it pisses me off."

"I have the money."

"It doesn't matter, and it doesn't make it any less bullshit."

She said nothing, but she was watching him closely.

"I don't have a bad temper, babe, it's just how much that shit is bullshit."

"We've established it's bullshit, because I don't disagree. But there's nothing we can do about it, I can afford it, so I need to start making eggrolls because I'm worried you might be a little hangry."

"I'm not hangry."

"All right, but these eggrolls are really good, so you'll want to eat them."

She was going to have to learn that being rational, calm and then moving to assuage any blood sugar issues he might have going on was not the way to handle Rix on the rare occasion he was ticked.

Those efforts had to be tactile.

But now was not the time to share that info.

"Can I help with dinner?" he asked.

Her lips twitched, the dimple flirted with her cheek but decided not to make an appearance, and then she said, "Yeah."

He let her go.

She went to the fridge.

Rix looked to the binder.

Music, because obviously, that's its own category.

"I can fry turkey meat, you pick music," he said.

She turned to him, a jar of pickles in one hand, a packet of turkey in the other.

"Okay," she agreed.

She threw the meat on the counter, setting the pickles beside it.

He moved to the kitchen. "Where's your skillet?"

"Can you grab the mushrooms and onion out of the fridge? We need to sauté those first."

"Gotcha," he muttered and did that.

By the time he'd started cleaning mushrooms, Mumford and Sons was playing.

There it was.

They had something else in common, and he didn't learn it from a binder.

And yeah.

He was getting his head straight about Alex.

And it was worrying as fuck.

CHAPTER 9

THE GIRLS

Alex

"*L*ate show-ers are annoying," Katie complained, even though she was on the floor tussling with Murphy, the creamy Labrador whose dad was almost always late to pick him up from Gal's doggie daycare center.

It was Wednesday night, and me and my girls had met up at Gal's place before going out to grab dinner and a few drinks.

"Yeah, you look like you're being tortured," Gal stated, resting back on a carpeted slopey thing that the dogs raced over and climbed on, though it looked like two lounge chairs connected by a platform. And it doubled as that. Case in point, she was fully relaxed, her feet up on a stack of wooden boxes with big holes in them that the dogs took naps in.

I was balancing my behind on the exercise ball I'd rolled out of Gal's office that Gal used as a desk chair.

"We have food to eat and drinks to drink," Katie almost whined. "And none of that is *here*."

"All the restaurants in Prescott don't close in the next half an hour, Kate," Gal pointed out. "We'll be fine, and he'll be here soon."

Murphy play-growled as Katie tugged on the rope they were both pulling.

Katie play-growled back.

And Murphy liked that so much, he nearly let go so he could concentrate more on his tail wagging, but he recovered just in time and didn't lose hold on the rope.

"It's a ploy, you know. Dude's into you," Katie announced.

"Hardly," Gal scoffed.

Katie successfully pulled the knotted rope from Murphy and tossed it far across the gym-like space.

Murphy, ears flapping, tongue lolling, went after it.

"You are *so* in denial," Katie said, watching Murphy.

"He's got two jobs. He's a busy guy," Gal replied.

"He picks up his dog fifteen minutes after you're supposed to close so he can be sure to be alone when he chats with you for fifteen minutes after that," Katie noted.

"He's also a friendly guy," Gal asserted.

Murphy had returned, the tug of war was back on, but Katie was looking at Gal. "You do know I work *and* bunk with five guys. I'm around them twenty-four-freaking-seven, except for these sweet-reprieve girls' nights that don't come often enough. I know how men's minds work."

"If he liked me, he'd ask me out," Gal retorted. "Murphy's been coming here two days a week for six months."

"Girl, Dave is the dude version of Alex here." Katie jerked her head at me. "I mean, he's tall, lean, blond and gorgeous, rather than auburn and curvy and gorgeous, but he's also shy as hell. You're gonna have to make the first move."

I could tell by Gal's changing body language that she was getting ticked.

This happened between my two girls, but then again, it would.

Sunny, friendly, girlie, forthright Katie was going to rub up against world-weary, cynical, rabidly independent, forthright Gal.

It was just the way it was.

Though, sometimes it wasn't pretty.

Now seemed to be stacking up as one of those times.

So I grew alert.

"He's not shy," Gal said sharply.

"He's shy," Katie shot back. "Not all guys are King Swagger. Maybe he's been burned. Maybe he was gawky when he was young and he doesn't realize he's grown up to be a hottie. Maybe he's just an intro-vert"—another head jerk my way—"like Alex, and he needs you to take the bull by the horn." She grinned a sassy grin. "As the saying goes."

Gal had sat up through this, and when Katie was done, she snapped, "He's not shy, and he's not into me. He just runs behind a lot when the tours are on."

FYI: Dave, who for certain was into Gal, was semi new to town. He owned a small house and a large stable on the outskirts of Prescott Valley. During the summer, with tourists, or city-dwellers looking for something to do outside the Phoenix or Tucson heat, he did hiking and horse riding tours. Part-time in the summer, and full-time in the winter, he also drove a delivery van for UPS.

Oh, and he was totally a hottie.

I didn't know why Gal wasn't going there. But I was not someone who pushed. Gal was a big girl, and I figured she had her reasons.

Treat others as you want to be treated, and all that.

Katie, however...

"You're the ballsiest chick I know," Katie stated, "and you don't have the guts to ask a hot guy out."

Oh boy.

That was gauntlet thrown.

This statement was perhaps true, but still.

That glove was resting between them.

And Gal never ignored the glove.

Now was no different.

She plopped both Birkenstocked feet down on either side of the dog run and opened her mouth.

"Rix is coming with me, and he's going to pretend to be my fiancé for Blake's wedding."

Obviously, that was me.

Both of them looked at me.

No, both of them gawked at me.

Even cool-customer Gal.

These were my closest friends, as in, the two people I loved the fiercest in the whole world.

Perhaps the only people in my life that I'd loved fiercely.

So they knew of my crush on Rix. They knew I worked with him. They knew Rix had flirted with me, then left me hanging. They knew we'd had words, patched it up and had been on a work trip together.

They did not know about the upcoming ruse.

I launched into the update.

"It's a long story that involves me lying to Blake to say I had a boyfriend, and that boyfriend was Rix. Elsa Cohen, that gossip person on YouTube. Blake knowing Judge's sister, who knows Rix, and calling her to catch me out on a lie. And Chloe thinking Rix is the guy he actually is, and he'd said yes to doing this already. But when Chloe spilled the beans, he said yes to doing it. We're officially getting to know each other so we can pretend to be in love and looking forward to a long and happy future together. He came over on Sunday. We made my cheeseburger eggrolls and ended up outside on my deck, drinking beer and getting into a heated debate about which *Star Wars* movie was the best. He's an Episode Four guy and refused to be swayed, no matter how solid my case was for *The Empire Strikes Back*."

Neither of them said anything.

"Though," I muttered, "when our discussion veered off to who was more badass, Tango or Cash, we both agreed Cash. Then we watched *The Bastards of Baseball*, which is really good. Sweet and inspiring, but also sad."

Both of them remained silent.

"The wedding festivities include a formal cocktail party, a brunch, a semi-formal rehearsal dinner, and the big day, where I'll be in four-inch heels for hours. Rix has committed to all of it, though I'm not sure he understands I'll start bitching about my shoes at the one-hour mark, and he's all in to sell it. As such, we have a binge weekend planned to watch *The Queen's Gambit*, his house Friday, my house Saturday, finale at his house on Sunday. Things such as this will continue for the next month plus so we can get to know each other and successfully pull the wool over everyone's eyes." I drew in breath. "Oh…and he says we're going to have to get used to touching and kissing each other, therefore we'll be making out a lot."

Now Katie had her mouth hanging open, and Gal's eyebrows were to her hairline.

Gal recovered first.

"Wait, you crushed on him for years, when he discovered you were alive, he led you on and then blew you off at a bar, and now you're fake getting married?"

I nodded my head.

"How hot was the desert at Hale Wheeler's camp for wayward kids?" she inquired.

"We were in an air-conditioned, five-star resort when Rix decided we were going to pretend to be looking forward to a joyous future together," I told her.

"And he's saying you're going to have to make out…*a lot*?" Katie asked.

This was the part I wanted to talk about.

Though there was a part of that, a part that made it important that was never going to be theirs to know.

The Peri part.

"He's right," I told them. "You know Blake's going to look for any chink in my armor, Dad's going to be uber competitive, which means he's going to look for any chink in Rix's armor, and Mum's going to be judgy. We're going to have to be seamless and flawless, and I can't be freezing up every time he touches me at the same time telling everyone how thrilled I am I found my perfect man."

"This is…" Katie didn't finish.

So I did it for her. "Terrifying?"

"Really cool," Gal drawled.

Katie's head swung her way, and they exchanged a look that included Katie bugging her eyes at Gal.

This wasn't that she didn't think it was cool. Katie was all about adventure. She was an everyday-is-a-new-day type of girl. Leap now, look later.

This was because Gal was not that at all.

Gal turned back to me. "Obviously, your future husband will have the stamp of approval from your two best friends. Therefore, we'll need to meet with this paragon who swept you off your feet."

Okay…

This had suddenly taken an unexpected turn.

Katie's head now swung to me, and she breathed, "Ohmigod, *yes*. You can't really know a woman unless you know her friends."

"Totally," Gal declared.

I stared at them.

And then I told them something they had to know.

"You realize this whole deal is flipping me out."

"I'm flipped out too," Gal replied. "I mean, one second, this guy is blowing you off, the next he's volunteering to enter the lion's den with you."

"No, Gal," Katie stated urgently, reading Gal, probably correctly. "When we meet him, you can't be all"—she puffed out her chest—"*you must traverse the Girl Friend Ritual of Fire to go forth with my bestie.* You'll scare him off."

"If *I'm* going to scare him off, think of the mincemeat Helena is going to make of him when she gets him between her jaws," Gal retorted.

Oh, and as my two closest girls, they knew all about my family.

And straight up, what Gal said was the gods' honest truth.

Though, I suspected not only would Rix be able to charm Gal, if he couldn't, it wouldn't faze him. He didn't strike me as a guy who had to have everyone like him. I also suspected he'd find Mum curious in the way you observe a black widow spider from the opposite side of the glass.

"Can we get back to the whole we-have-to-make-out-a-lot thing?" I requested. "Which, I failed to tell you, he told me it was mine to start when I was ready and stop if it was getting too much. Which is cool of him, but *it's mine to start*."

A look came over Gal's face that I couldn't quite read, except I knew, for me, it was frightening.

Katie's eyes grew bright. "This is your golden opportunity to pounce on your big crush."

See?

Totally leaps before she looks.

"I'm not a pouncer, and remember, he's doing me a favor. This is all fake," I reminded her.

Gal was now studying me.

"You still can have fun while it lasts," Katie noted. "You're a super good kisser. He's getting the deal of the century with this."

I loved she thought that.

And as mentioned, I just loved my friends.

Though with that, she was kinda full of it.

"I'm not a super good kisser, Kate," I told her, though, obviously, I personally wouldn't know if this was true or not.

I'd never had any complaints.

But no one had given me an award either.

"Trent said you were the best he ever had."

"Trent was trying to get in my pants."

"And he succeeded," she fired back. "And remember, he didn't say that *to me*. He said it to Forrest when he didn't know I was standing behind him. If I remember correctly, he was full into locker room mode and he said"—she took on a gruff man voice—"'Bitch is hot in bed, but shit, the things she can do with her mouth. Don't need to fuck her with the way she kisses.' He was totally bummed when you broke up with him."

"He was supposed to help on a hike with the kids, got drunk the night before, and begged off because he was hung over," I replied. "Deal breaker."

"Yeah, gotta admit, that was uncool, and like, 'Dude, do you *not* know the chick you're dating?'" Katie agreed.

"Has Rix ever bagged on a hike, even when the man has lost both his legs?" Gal queried smoothly.

I looked to the floor and bounced on the ball, because no way Rix would ever do that.

Ever.

"Set up a night we can all have a few drinks," Gal ordered.

I lifted my gaze to her.

Or, I should say, I lifted my confused gaze to her.

"I don't understand why you think this is a thing. My family has never been out here. Thus, they've never met you two. I've mentioned you, but I can promise you, they have no interest in my friends, and don't even remember your names. It doesn't matter if Rix has your approval or not to fake being my fiancé for a few days."

"You don't think someone is going to ask, 'What do Alex's friends think of you?'" Gal queried.

"No. Though, if they do, he can just say, 'We get along great,'" I returned.

"We're meeting him, because we so totally have to. And you're making out with him...*a lot*...because you *so totally have to*," Katie decreed.

I did so totally have to, at least the second part.

Rix told me I would be starting it, and could stop it, and outside of holding me against him on Sunday (which felt *insanely* nice), he made it very obvious that we were just hanging for the rest of the night, and we weren't going to take it there.

That was what we did.

Then, at work the last three days, he was entirely appropriate, friendly and teasing, as was his way. He'd asked me out to lunch that day, but he'd also asked Kevin (Judge was down in Phoenix, doing something with Chloe). We had a full weekend of *Queen's Gambit* and getting-to-know-you. Even so, he wasn't pushing more time together in an effort to try to get some from the girl who needed him so she could deal with her own family since that'd be a nice side bene for him for having to play his part in this whole charade.

And I had my own agenda with all of this.

It was one thing to sell our great love to my family, but Rix had actually been in love, and undoubtedly slept with his ex, so she'd know possibly at a glance if we'd gone there. We weren't going to *go there*, but I had to stop acting like such a goof whenever he touched me.

The few times I'd had it, I liked his touch.

Too much.

That was the problem.

But this wasn't about me. It was about him. And I had to get over myself, because I had no idea when we'd be running into this horrible Peri woman, but when we did, I had to be ready.

I'd promised Chloe, of course.

But that wasn't it.

This was for Rix.

"Finally," Katie mumbled under her breath, letting Murphy win and pushing to her feet.

I turned my head to see sandy-blond, tan, tall, lean, keen Dave walking in, glancing at me and Katie, smiling and clapping at his dog, who was bounding toward him, then it was all about Gal.

Seriously, Kate was right, Gal had to be in denial.

Katie was blonde, sun-kissed, cowgirl cute.

I was what I was, but part of that was that I was female.

And Gal was tall, dark, slender, self-assured…

And clueless.

Because he didn't see cowgirl cute, and he didn't see me, he barely saw his adorable dog.

But he sure saw Gal.

"We won't bite, and it really will be good he meets us," Katie, suddenly close, said, taking my attention from watching Gal walk over to Dave. "Your family probably will never ask him about us, but you know if you met his buds, you could tell a lot about the guy he is. Same goes for you." She smiled a mega-watt smile. "And we're gonna make you look awesome."

I knew, because his best bud was Judge, and Judge (I was rearranging the order these days), was the second best guy I'd met.

In other words, she was right.

Gal was right.

It was just another layer to add to the characters we were going to play, and it wouldn't hurt.

It might be fun.

"I'll ask him," I said.

"Groovy," she replied. "I'm gonna start turning off lights so they'll get the hint. If I don't, they'll stand there and chat for the next hour."

That was an exaggeration, but shooting them a glance, Dave was clearly not intent on a quick pick-up, and Gal wasn't intent on getting either him or his dog out of the door.

I rolled my ball to where my bag was lying on the other side of the dog slide, grabbed my phone and texted Rix.

My friends say we should all go out for a drink.

I had the shoulder strap of my hobo crossed over me and was about to roll the ball back into Gal's office when my phone binged.

Just tell me when.

My hand tightened on the phone, because really, he was amazing, and really, Peri was *so stupid*, and really, truly, completely, I couldn't wait to play my part in letting her know how stupid she was.

We'll plan, I texted back.

The ball was back in the office. All the lights were out but the ones by the front door. Katie was leaning against the wall by said door, glaring at Dave and Gal, who were standing in the center of the space lit now only from the waning sun coming in the windows. Murphy was racing around them, and they were ignoring him, as well Katie's hint (they were so totally into each other, yeesh).

And my phone binged again.

Great. Six at mine Friday, but Saturday, do you want to hike Watershed before we kick back?

I so totally did.

With Rix?

I so totally, completely, *absolutely* did.

Morning or afternoon hike? I asked.

Lady's choice, he answered.

I like mornings.

Me too. Then, right on the heels of that, I received, *I didn't notice. You got a grill on that deck?*

Yes.

After Watershed, we'll hit Park Plaza for lunch and pick up some beer. We'll go to the store after that. You do sides, I'll grill meat.

Sounds great.

Up for a kayak Sunday?

Ohmigod!

Totally!

I loved kayaking!

You bet.

You got your own, or do you rent when you go? Cause I got an extra.

Hmm.

Was that extra kayak Peri's?

I didn't ask.

I texted, *I have my own.*

Course you do. My girl wouldn't rent a fucking kayak.

His girl.

My belly flipped.

See you tomorrow, babe, he said.

Yeah. Have a good night.

You too. Have fun with your girls.

Will do.

I thought that was the end of it.

But it wasn't.

Rix sent another text.

You get drunk, you call me, Alexandra. I'll come get you, them, I don't care. Take you all home. Even if it's late. Yeah?

Yep.

Peri was *so stupid*.

We won't get drunk, I assured him.

Shit happens. Call me.

Kate sometimes has to be up and working by four, so we won't get drunk.

What I'm saying is, you're free to let loose. Enjoy yourself. I got your back. So if you decided to do that CALL ME.

Okay.

Maybe it was me who was stupid for being involved in this, because eventually, I wouldn't even be able to pretend he was mine.

I'll call you.

Promise.

I promise.

Go have fun.

Later.

He sent the sunglasses emoji.

I grinned at my phone, inspiration struck, and I sent the blushing-smiley-face emoji.

To which he sent the heart-kiss emoji.

Yes.

The heart-kiss emoji.

Lord.

My belly melted, and I could feel my grin change.

Then I came back to the room.

Dave and Murphy were gone, all the lights were out, and Gal and Katie were standing at the opened front door, staring at me.

"Rix is down to meet for drinks with you guys," I shared.

"I bet he is," Gal drawled, a knowing look on her face.

Whatever.

Katie giggled, a happy look on her face.

Whatever.

"Let's go eat," I said.

Then I pushed through them and walked out the door.

CHAPTER 10

THE STORY

Alex

Friday night, I pulled up the side drive at Rix's place and parked behind his truck, which was under an overhang that came off the side of his house.

He had a place a few blocks northeast of downtown Prescott, super close to where our new office was, maybe only five blocks away.

I was not surprised to see it was a small crackerbox house, painted white with black trim, though the front door had a big window, around which it'd been painted barn red.

I was also not surprised to see the yard was exceptionally well taken care of and beautifully landscaped, with clusters of aspen trees, thick tufts of spiky ornamental grass around the front steps, and there were two large trees on either side that had to be at least forty years old. Their canopy was wide and covered the entire house, and as such, undoubtedly threw much-needed shade.

Though, they also served to make the whole space seem settled and safe, an oasis that had sat there for a long time, and hopefully would remain there a lot longer.

I grabbed the bottle of wine and the six-pack of Goose Island Stout, which Rix had told me was his favorite, and got out of my car.

I then walked up to the door, noting his porch décor was two deep-swayback, dark wicker bucket chairs, in which it would be impossible to sit in without slouching, so they looked amazingly comfortable. The table between them was a sawed-off log, upturned on the end.

Rix also had a string of lights that swooped across his porch, as well as trailed out above the front yard on a diagonal to a big tree on the corner of his property, then trailed back, forming a triangle.

It was simple.

And totally rad.

I could see on summer nights and winter mornings, sitting on that porch, sipping wine or coffee (respectively), keeping an eye on the quiet neighborhood and waving at neighbors as they drove past.

I hit the doorbell, but even so, I saw inside.

And at that, I was surprised.

Wood paneling on the side wall, in front of which was a light-blue twill couch flanked by somewhat large, square end tables. A coffee table before that, two armchairs facing it. Gleaming wood floors that looked like real oak. An attractive area rug under all of that which was in a traditional jagged edge Southwestern design in the colors of light blue, dark blue, white and peach.

At the end of this, there was a partial wall of brick, which included a fireplace, and above it, a large, mounted TV.

There was a wall of windows to the other side, which gave him a view of more grasses and the trunk of his shade tree.

At the back, to the side, beyond the partial wall, I saw a rectangular dining room table, four chairs, two on each side.

Beyond the partial wall, I couldn't see and didn't try, because Rix had rounded it and was walking toward me at the door.

My mind had been skirting around the thoughts that Rix's attractive, airy space had been put together by or with Peri.

But it skirted that no longer when I caught sight of him.

I'd never known him with legs, so I didn't know what his gait used to be like.

And there was definitely a hitch in his step, no escaping it, even if it was minimal.

However, I figured the sexy sway of those lean hips had always been there.

He'd changed from the crisp cargos and button-down he wore to work to very faded jeans and an equally faded tee that used to be navy blue, had a white insignia over the heart with some bars under it and beneath that, it said PRESCOTT FIRE/MEDICAL.

On the left arm, there was a yellow circle.

In it was the number 19.

Seeing that, a chill slid across the small of my back, like it always did at the reminder of the nineteen Granite Mountain Hotshot fire-fighters who died in the Yarnell Fire. Something I assumed in one way or another was what happened to anyone in Prescott or Prescott Valley who was reminded of those men who lost their lives in 2013, one of the worst losses of men in firefighter history, obviously not including 9/11.

During my crush days, I'd done my research through what I hoped were not telling or inappropriate questions to Judge. But Judge had offered up the information that that was before Rix's time as a Hotshot.

He'd become one right after that tragedy.

And then he'd had his own tragedy.

He opened the door and stood in it.

I stared up at him. "Hey."

His lips twitched. "Hey."

Okay, right, in this scenario, what would a fiancée do?

I had to break the seal on this, and I feared if I didn't now, it would be never.

So I got closer to him.

He didn't move.

I leaned even closer to him.

He bent his neck, holding my gaze.

My heart slid up and lodged firmly in my throat as I rolled up on my toes.

Something happened in his caramel eyes that triggered something happening between my legs, so although I was aiming at his mouth, in the end, I panicked and brushed mine softly against the side of his.

I got a nuance of the feel of his lips, the full, heady impact of the bristle of his whiskers (he'd come to work on Monday shaved, but he hadn't shaved since, yes, I was keeping track) and then I started moving away.

I didn't get far.

His hand came up and cupped me under my ear.

"Hey," he murmured this repeat.

Annnnnnd….

Ohmigod.

The sound of that *drove up* between my legs, like a phantom thrust.

He was still murmuring when he went on, "I feed you. I water you. You bring shit to my house again, baby, and I spank your ass."

I blinked.

Though I did it through another phantom thrust.

He let me go (though he didn't do that until after he'd glided his thumb soft as a whisper along the sensitive skin in front of my ear, *gah!*), tugged the bottle of wine out of my hand, the handle of the six-pack from the other, then he stepped back, reaching an arm long with the wine in his hand to indicate my welcome.

I walked in.

Being in his house was better than being outside, looking in.

It really was attractive and well-put-together, but not in a way it was scary. Like, you didn't want to touch anything or mess anything up.

You would definitely feel comfortable curling up on that couch with your feet under you or setting a drink on one of the plethora of options available.

I heard the door close and then Rix and his swaying hips were moving through the space.

"We're having baked chicken parm and couscous 'cause I'm not feeling a lot of effort. I'll wow you with my culinary skills tomorrow at the grill. We're chilling out tonight," he declared as he went.

I followed him.

We rounded the partial wall, and I met his kitchen.

It was another revelation. Mid-century feel. Light-wood cabinets with top edge, long finger cabinet pulls. Pear-colored tile with interesting white lines through it going from the stainless-steel countertops to the ceiling. Though, on the back wall, sandwiched between narrow upper cabinets and counter with the sink, was all windows. A short bar with two stools on the outside which faced the dining room table.

And there was a rolling stool off in a corner that had a high seat, much higher than his chair, which was probably what he used to cook when he wasn't on his legs, or used to rest on when he was giving his legs a break.

"Did you do all this work yourself?" I asked, glancing around.

"Nope," he said, tucking the beer and wine in the fridge, then turning to me. "My dad taught me, you don't know what you're doing, don't do it. I could YouTube how to install a kitchen sink, but this house is over fifty years old. There could be shit I don't know what I'm dealing with in the walls, under the floors. Lucky I have a bud who does know what he's doing who did it in exchange for me providing muscle when he had bulky materials being delivered and other shit he needed that a layman could do running a contracting business. Though, he did it in his spare time, so it took almost a year for this kitchen to get done. Six months each for the bathrooms."

He was grabbing a stemless wineglass from one of his cupboards.

There was already a bottle of rosé open on the countertop.

And Rix kept the information flowing.

"The living room was already paneled, though, and I put in the floors, after my bud gave the approval that what was underneath was good to go."

He poured, and I approached when he turned.

He handed the glass to me.

I had questions to ask that I was uncomfortable asking.

They were things I'd need to know, things I *should* know.

His life.

His history.

His heartbreak.

Sure, understanding he stubbornly stuck to the original *Star Wars* as his favorite in the franchise (I mean, he wouldn't even discuss *Rogue One*, which was lunacy) was important.

But there were much more important things.

And as his fiancée, I'd know those things.

So as my fingers curved round the glass, and I allowed the zap of energy I felt when they touched his to course giddily through me, I asked, "Was this before your fiancée, with her, or after?"

He looked dead in my eyes and shared, "The floors went in before. The rest, when I was with her."

"Did she live here with you?"

A curt nod and, "She moved in halfway through the kitchen reno." He turned to the fridge, and I noted with no small amount of satisfaction that he grabbed a Goose Island. "Then she moved out."

Right.

I'd pretty much used up my courage to dig into that situation, so I took a sip of wine and dropped the subject.

Rix popped open his beer.

"Chicken is already in the oven," he announced. "I'm gonna finish getting these carrots in the water. You're on couscous duty."

He said his last nabbing a box of Near East couscous that was on his counter.

I approached him again, taking the box.

"Pan beside the sink, baby, measuring cups are that cupboard there"—he titched his head toward a cupboard—"butter in the fridge unless you want olive oil, that's by the stove."

I nodded.

He turned back to a cutting board that had some sliced carrots on it. "Eating out back on the deck."

"'Kay," I mumbled, making a mental note not to bring up Peri again, because Rix wasn't a fan of talking about her.

What I did not make a mental note of was what that might mean.

We finished making dinner in silence that wasn't companionable, but it also wasn't entirely awkward.

We loaded up our plates in the kitchen, cutting up our chicken at the counter so we didn't have to do it in our laps, since Rix told me he didn't have a dining table out back.

Then we went to Rix's small-ish (actually, it seemed less small and more intimate) back deck, and by then, I was used to the revelations.

Still, it should be noted, his deck was fab.

"This," he muttered when he noted my appreciation, "is all mine."

He hadn't stained it brown or red, a cool and unusual choice.

The wood of the floor was stained gray, partial walls slanting down each side to provide privacy from the neighbors were stained black. Benches were built in, covered in white or black and white striped pads and pillows, making them look cozy. A hammock-weave club chair with cushions sat opposite a corner bench. Some small tables for drinks. And even black lanterns with battery-powered candles in them.

"Your place is awesome, Rix," I told him as he indicated I was to curl into the cozy bench seat with a jut of his chin.

I did that, putting my glass down on the small, round table in front of me and holding my plate.

He lowered himself into the chair and set his beer aside on his own table, stating, "Your place is better."

Really?

"You think so?" I asked.

"Yup," he said, scooping couscous on his fork.

"Because it's in the trees," I deduced.

"No, because the inside is kickass and very you," he contradicted.

I stared at him, feeling that compliment snuggle down deep.

He shoved couscous in his mouth.

"Well, you're wrong," I told him, spearing carrots. "This deck is everything, and your front porch isn't far behind."

"You dig what's not yours," he murmured.

No, I dug what was his.

What was him.

After downing my carrot, I tasted his chicken.

Succulent, the "parm" part was an oregano and garlic spiced panko/parmesan coating that was pressed into a thin layer of sour cream on top of the breasts. They'd then been roasted to juicy perfection.

I chewed and swallowed.

Delicious.

"We gotta get into the deep shit, babe. It's time."

My eyes lifted to his and the sharp-cheesy, juicy-chickeny taste turned to dust in my mouth.

"What deep shit?"

He didn't lead into it.

He just went for it.

No warning, he gave it to me.

A precious gift.

And a gaping wound.

"Cellar Fire. Team was good. We were good. We'd been warned the weather might turn, trained, always, to know that was a possibility. Had a rookie scout. The man was an experienced firefighter, but new to the Hotshots. Somehow, he'd accidentally turned off his radio. So when the wind shifted, he didn't get the call. Which meant he didn't give us the call."

I sat motionless.

Rix continued sharing.

"Still, we were good. We felt it, saw it, and we had an escape route. Fire came fast, though. Always does. Seemed like just a blink, we were in the thick of it. Saw the tree that had caught and knew it was gonna go down before it did. My buddy Rob was in front of me, and right under it. He didn't see it. Ran to him, pushed him clear, thought I was good, I'd have time. Turns out, I was about four inches short of time. To this day, not sure what happened. How it hit both at the same time. Had therapy with a social worker through rehab, she thinks maybe it's a block. Complete blank of maybe five, ten seconds. I remember seeing the tree. I remember running to Rob, pushing him.

Then nothing. And then I remember when it hit. Calves, ankles, heels."

Disturbing tingles shot up my own heels, ankles, and calves.

He took a breath.

I didn't speak.

Then Rix kept going.

"From the way it felt, knew it crushed my feet. That tree had to be heavy, because the boots we wear are no joke. So from the get-go, my feet were toast. Tree was also ablaze. Had my gear on, which protected me from the fire, but that tree was fucking heavy, and fucking hot. Rob tried to drag me clear. Adrenaline rush amped his strength, he pulled me, and that fuckin' tree came with me."

"Rix," I whispered, my entire body now tingling as what he endured came alive in my head.

"The entire team rushed back, crazy motherfuckers, felt like the whole world was on fire by then. But they got me out from under, carried me out of there. Damage was done, though. The whole thing probably lasted five minutes, but it felt like we were dealing with that tree for hours. Docs tried like fuck to save my feet. Multiple surgeries. Obviously, that miracle just wasn't gonna happen."

My plate held in front of me, I didn't take my eyes from him, his face neutral, his tone matter of fact.

And I didn't speak.

Though I knew one thing, it wasn't discussing Peri that put him in a mood.

It was knowing he was going to give this to me, and relive it while he did, that put him in a mood.

"Rob quit," he went on. "About a year later. Felt guilt he shouldn't feel that it was me, not him. If he'd been behind me instead of the other way around, I knew it would have been him, not me. He'd have seen that tree, like I did. He would have done exactly what I did. He's married, has three kids. So it fucking sucks it happened to me, but I'd rather it be the way it turned out. He lives in Florida now. No wild-fires in Florida. He runs a car detailing service, and on the weekends, to get his rush, he jumps out of planes or goes paragliding."

I remained silent.

Rix kept talking.

"Woke up once in the hospital, few days after they took my legs. Nic, Rob's wife, was sitting beside me, face red, eyes a fucking mess. It was quiet, you couldn't hear it at all, but still I knew she was sobbing. She didn't say any words. Just bent over, kissed the back of my hand where it was lying on the bed. Then she stared at it. Stared at my hand like it was some marvel or something. Like the face of the Madonna was forming on it. She looked back at me, got up and walked out, like I said, through all of that, not a word. I was groggy, head not in a good place, but later, thinking about it, I knew..."

He trailed off.

So I whispered, "It was that hand that saved her husband."

"Yeah," he said gruffly, looked to his plate, and forked into a piece of chicken.

God, he was even more amazing than I already knew he was.

In fact, I wasn't sure I could fully take that in, that was just how amazing he was.

"I don't know what to say, but I have questions," I said quietly.

"Shoot," he said to his plate.

I drew in breath.

"That rookie on the radio?"

A short nod. "Brian. He quit too. I don't know where he is. He dropped out, doesn't keep in touch with any of the guys." Rix looked to me. "You should know, this town...the department has great insurance. But I was injured on the job, so anything to do with my legs is covered for life. Hospital stay, rehab, prosthetics, chair, truck retrofit, OT stuff for the house, all covered. And when I wear out my legs, which happens about every three years, could be earlier for me 'cause I'm active, I'll get fitted for new ones. Or if I need extra to do different things, I'll get 'em. But this town, these people, they took a collection, raised so much money for me, Alex, I paid off my fucking house."

Tears hit my eyes.

"Lost my legs, got a house."

"Rix," his name broke in the middle.

"I'm good, sweetheart," he said.

"I hate that happened to you," I replied.

"Me too. But it did. And I'm good."

"I don't want to talk about anything deep anymore," I blurted.

"Okay, baby," he agreed gently, but his eyes on me were gentler.

"It's not that I'm weak," I stated quickly. "It's not that I can't listen to something horrible and painful and tragic that didn't even happen to me. It's just that I like you. You're a really amazing guy. And it upsets me a lot that something painful and tragic happened to you. And I need a bit to let that story settle. Okay?"

More gentle with his, "I said okay, honey."

I sniffed and stared at my plate.

As a number of thoughts tumbled through my head, I didn't know Rix was watching them tumbling until he ordered, "Don't be pissed at Brian, everyone makes rookie mistakes."

And yes, what my brain had tumbled to was that I was angry at fucking *Brian*.

I still was when I turned my attention back to Rix.

"*You* paid for his mistake," I spat.

"You think he isn't?"

Ugh!

Why was he being so benevolent and rational?

I stabbed a carrot so hard it broke apart.

So I stabbed the pieces.

They broke too.

"Al, it's already dead," Rix joked.

I gave up on the carrot, my plate entirely, and reached for my wine.

I downed half of what was left in my glass.

"There's my girl," Rix muttered, and as I lowered my wineglass, I saw his amused gaze on me.

"Stop being adjusted," I complained.

"You want me to get up and throw my deck furniture around?"

"Can I?" I asked.

"No," he answered, lips twitching.

"I don't have anything deep like that to share," I admitted.

"I'm glad, though your sister's a bitch, and that couldn't have been fun."

I rolled my eyes.

"Everybody has their damage, babe," he noted.

I then squinted my eyes at him and accused, "You're being adjusted again."

He grinned. "Sorry. Can't help it. That's just me."

"Though, my sister *is* very difficult to deal with," I sniffed, and turned back to my plate. "And we haven't gotten into *Chad*."

"Chad? Who's Chad?"

"Blake's fiancé."

"His name is *Chad?*"

Rix sounded like he was about to bust out laughing, at the same time hurl.

And yes, that was precisely where it was with Chad.

I nodded. "Think of everything that defines a *Chad* and then multiply that by a thousand," I said. "That's Blake's *Chad*."

He was smiling. "Well, fuck, baby."

"Exactly."

He started chuckling.

"Warning, if Chad manages to form a coherent thought outside wondering where his next drink or good time is going to come from, he's going to hate you," I told him.

He chewed some chicken, swallowed, and asked, "Why's that?"

"Because, and excuse me for being vulgar, but my guess is, the size of his penis is not all that much to write home about. However, the second he sees you, it'll shrink an inch he can't afford to lose."

At that, Rix didn't bust out laughing.

He roared with it.

Only minutes after he told his story, hearing that laughter, watching it, I knew it was the crowning achievement of my life until that point.

That feeling was addictive.

So I went for more.

"I'd ask you to tamp down your natural magnetism and virility for Chad's sake, but it's going to be too fun to watch him visibly not measure up, so you have my permission to open the floodgates."

His hilarity had quieted down, but it was not gone when he said, "Thanks for permission."

I swallowed some couscous and replied, "You're welcome."

He lifted his brows. "Natural magnetism?"

"Like you don't know," I mumbled.

"Virility?" he teased.

"Shut up, Rix," I ordered, fighting the heat coming to my cheeks.

"Okay, baby," he murmured, and shoveled couscous into his mouth, but his eyes didn't leave me.

We ate for a while without talking.

"Wanna hit Marino's for a sundae before we crash in front of the TV?" he asked.

I had a life canon.

I never said no to ice cream.

Therefore, I answered, "Totally."

"Yeah," he said softly, his gaze still stuck on me. "That's my girl."

That didn't warm my cheeks.

But it did warm everything else.

CHAPTER 11

THE REVEAL

Elsa Cohen

"The Elsa Exchange"
Celebrity News and Interviews
YouTube Channel

"Oh, my wonderful watchers, I'm so pleased to report that love clearly fills the air in the mountains of Arizona. Yes, it's true. After the surprising reunion of one Ms. Swan and one Mr. Holloway, which fed into the exceptional pairing of one Mr. Oakley and one Ms. Pierce, we have even *more* news of loved-up bliss heading out of the southwest."

Picture on screen of John "Rix" Hendrix in a faded navy firefighter's T-shirt and Alexandra Margaret Sharp in a pair of skinny jeans with distressing close to the frayed hems that hit a few inches above her ankles, a white, short-sleeved blouse up top that was knotted at the front and rolled at the wide sleeves. Alexandra also had a layered anklet on her left ankle above her sand-colored Rothy's slip-on sneakers. Further a layered necklace at her neck made of tiny wood beads and silver chains with some miniscule dangling pendants.

The couple was walking out of what appeared to be a casual restaurant, not holding hands, but they were close, Hendrix's hand on the small of Alexandra's back.

She had her eyes aimed to the sidewalk.

He had his head turned toward the road, stubbled, square jaw naturally jutting. He was walking on the street side, sheltering Alexandra on the inside.

Cut to another picture of the couple, same night, moments later, Hendrix standing in the street, holding the door, eyes aimed to Alexandra's derriere as she climbs into his truck.

Cut back to Elsa.

"You may remember the rugged, heroic, ex-firefighter, current do-gooder John Hendrix who stood by his best friend, an Elsa Exchange regular, the handsome Judge Oakley, during the terrible loss Judge suffered when his mother passed this past summer."

Photo on screen of Hendrix and Oakley standing with heads bent together, both wearing somber expressions and dark suits.

Cut back to Elsa.

"Well, when you're in the presence of greatness, you brush shoulders with greatness, so it probably should be no surprise this handsome specimen caught the eye of Alexandra Sharp. Yes, that's Alexandra *Sharp* of *the* Coddington-Sharps. And yes, I mean *those* Sharps whose name is synonymous with Rockefeller, Morgan, Astor and Carnegie. And yes, I mean *those* Coddingtons, as in, the Marquess of Norton, whose family seat in Somerset...a seat that once was a castle but eventually became a sprawling manor...a seat that was a favored place for King John, the real one, not the one of the Robin Hood legend, to sup when he was out west participating in one of his favored pastimes back in the early 1200s, hunting...*that* seat is Alexandra's family home."

Picture on screen of tall, large, boxy but understatedly elegant mansion with numerous chimneys made of mellow creamy-yellow stone, its grandeur rising above a nest of trees high on a green hill.

Cut back to Elsa.

"And yes, that would be *the* Alexandra Sharp, who might have to don the crown should some horrendously tragic event happen to wipe out forty or fifty members of the peerage before her, but nevertheless, the case remains, she stands in line for the British throne."

Photo on screen of a teenage Alexandra wearing a fluffy white gown of yards and yards of tulle, in full curtsy, head bowed, who, exactly, she's curtsying to is cropped from the picture. But whoever it was had a hand lifted Alexandra's way, it was wearing a white glove, and around the wrist, there were diamonds.

Cut back to Elsa.

"Though, Ms. Sharp likely isn't holding her breath for a residency at Buckingham Palace. And she doesn't need to, considering the amalgamated trust fund that found itself under her discretion on her twenty-first birthday. Funds that included entitlements from the Sharp and Coddington lines, not to mention what came to her through her paternal grandmother."

Picture on screen of a very young Alexandra wearing a lacy, little girl frock, walking next to an elegant, stately, rail thin woman in a heavily sequined gown with upswept dark gray hair that had a streak of white coming from the left temple, her look reminiscent of any elderly woman in a Disney cartoon.

Cut back to Elsa.

"Oh yes, our Ms. Sharp is also of the esteemed Bernhard line. We don't have an exact figure, my wonderful watchers, and it would be *très gauche* to share even if we did. However, those who know and have shared tell me Ms. Sharp doesn't have much to worry about, at least financially, while she's frolicking with her hearty beau under those big skies out west."

Elsa takes a delicate breath.

"Now, she might be as American as apple pie."

Long lens photo on screen of Alexandra in an orange kayak, mid-paddle, trailing Hendrix, who's gliding in front of her in a blue kayak.

Cut back to Elsa.

"But that peaches and cream skin tells its own tale."

Telephoto shot on screen of fresh-faced Alexandra standing close to and smiling up at Hendrix, who's grinning down at her. They're next to a truck bed with the orange and blue kayaks in it, beyond that, a stunning backdrop of blue lake and brown rock.

Cut back to Elsa.

"Yes, love is definitely in the mountain air, my wonderful watchers. And I, for one, am pleased as punch for Mr. Hendrix. A true American hero who lost his legs fighting a wildfire in those same mountains. He's finally getting the prize he paid dearly to earn, hooking himself to one of the oldest, status-topping families on *two* continents. Although, we mustn't fail to mention, we're still in a congratulatory phase for the upcoming nuptials of Alexandra's big sister, Blake, who will soon be marrying Chad Head, of the Hampton Heads."

After saying this, Elsa smirks.

Then a photo on screen of a heavily made-up, dark-haired, peaches-and-cream-skinned, violet-eyed woman wearing a high-necked, shoulderless, pleated, black cocktail dress standing next to a tall blond man with classical, angular features, wearing a suit. Both are smiling fixedly, straight into the camera.

Cut back to Elsa.

"But everyone knows about sibling rivalry, my wonderful watchers, and methinks it's quite obvious who won this round. Don't you agree?"

Picture on screen of Hendrix and Alexandra exiting what appears to be a liquor store. He's got the fingers of one hand curled into the handle of a six-pack of craft beer, his other hand is dangling down Alexandra's chest as she's tucked close in his arm. She has a narrow paper bag with the neck of a wine bottle cradled in one arm, the other curled around his waist.

Again, Alexandra's watching where her feet are going, thus Hendrix is clearly steering them, staring straight ahead. Something is amusing, however, as Alexandra's lips are curved, a dimple depressing her right cheek, and Hendrix is flashing a wide, white smile.

They're both wearing attractive hiking gear. They're both sporting healthy tans. They're both wearing sporty but stylish sunglasses. And as the sun shines down on them, they look young, hale, and happy.

Close in on Elsa.

"Well, my wonderful watchers, I'm feeling it's time for a vacation. And I know what part of the country is calling my name. Of course, nothing against the Hamptons, *we all know* how marvelous they are. But there's winning and then there's *winning*. And I think it's clear which Sharp sister won and where she was when she claimed victory. Now, until our next exchange, keep it positive. Elsa is signing off."

The branded Elsa wink and blowing of kiss.

Sign off.

Alex

I WAS IN MY BATHROOM, TRYING TO TAMP DOWN ON A MINOR FREAKOUT that showed telltale signs of burgeoning into a major one.

Chicken parm and sundaes at Marino's, then back to Rix's Friday night, after the devastation of him telling his story, and into the beginnings of *The Queen's Gambit*, all of this was a nuanced beginning for the sheer abundance of what was to come.

Saturday was hiking, during which we'd shared sporadic idle chitchat, but far more of Rix's patented teasing, and me finding I was beginning to have no issue shoveling that back at him. This mingled with a number of stops to take pictures that included selfies that neither of us mentioned (and at least on my part, even thought of) as pretend.

This segued into lunch that, somehow, some way, through some miracle, we naturally ordered meals we both wanted, and thus we shared.

Yes, *shared.*

Eating off of each other's plates and everything!

It didn't even occur to me at the time.

It didn't occur to me until now, which was one of the reasons for the minor freakout blossoming into something bigger.

Though, it did occur to me, last night, after grilling, eating and arguing about whether we were going to make a quick batch of chocolate chip cookies to munch on while watching TV, or cinnamon oatmeal cookies (Rix wanted oatmeal, Rix won), that finding our two corners on the couch, which was what we did Friday night, Rix had decided, was history.

My lip brush upon greeting him Friday was not repeated.

But last night, Rix waited until I settled in, managing this by hitting the bathroom while I was curling into my side of the couch.

When he'd come back out, he didn't sit opposite me.

He arranged himself around me, in doing so, needing to rearrange me.

Although, at the start, I'd played ragdoll, not knowing what to do or how to behave, in the end, that was all he did.

We cuddled. We watched TV. And sometimes, Rix leaned into me to reach to the plate of cookies on the coffee table.

And the next step in our campaign to get comfortable with each other had been taken.

At first, as mentioned, I'd semi-panicked.

However, it didn't take long for it to penetrate that Rix felt good, he smelled good, and bottom line, it felt amazing, lying snug up against him on my couch while watching TV.

So in the end, like everything else I was finding when it came to Rix, it wasn't hard at all.

This morning, we'd headed out early to get our kayaking in, already having the plan that we'd go our separate ways when we were done so we could shower and get some weekend things accomplished that all this togetherness was delaying us doing.

Therefore, I went home, had lunch, did some light housecleaning, changed the sheets on my bed, went through some mail and paid some bills, then took a shower.

Which led me to now.

The mushrooming freakout.

Because, for the finale to our TQG binge, I'd selected a creamy-beige colored dress with a delicate floral pattern, a drop waist made of a smocked elastic panel and long sleeves with elastic cuffs. It had a flirty skirt that hit a couple of inches above my knees.

I added turquoise and silver jewelry at neck, ears and fingers.

Then came the dusting of powder over my face, a brush of blush to accentuate the sun-kissed color already on my cheeks, and a faint sweep of highlighter, just because my world felt glittery, so I guessed somewhere in the depths of my brain I felt it needed to translate visibly.

A thin layer of liner on my eyes under a shimmer of shadow, just on the lids. A single coat of mascara that, nevertheless on my eyelashes, even I had to admit was a sensation.

I'd washed my hair, and fully styled it, something I hadn't done since I was back home last Christmas.

This meant more than tying it back in a ponytail or braiding it one way or the other.

Instead, I gave it volume, using product to define and separate my natural loose curls, and leaving it long.

Some nude-peach lip stain with gloss was a finishing touch.

And of course, my perfume, which was Bulgari, given to me originally by my father, but it was the perfect scent for me, so now I bought it for myself.

Last, a pair of high-ish-wedge-heeled, platform, cognac leather strapped sandals.

It was too much.

We were likely eating dinner on Rix's deck again and watching TV.

Probably cuddling (could I cuddle in a short-ish skirt? Or even...*should* I?).

Yes, it was too much.

Even if it felt like we were dating, we weren't.

Even if it hadn't occurred to me once, not since that text exchange at Gal's center, that this was pretend, it was.

I needed to clean my face.

And I needed to change.

Fortunately, I'd gotten this wild hair early, so I knew I had time to do both before I had to leave.

I walked out of the bathroom to go to the closet, my gaze going to my alarm clock on the nightstand just to be sure.

It was a fifteen-minute drive to Rix's house.

I was supposed to be there at six.

It was five after five.

Yes.

I had plenty of time.

I just made it to my closet to assess a new outfit when my phone rang in the bathroom.

I had it silence all calls except people I knew, so I headed back to the bathroom to check it, because it was rare when someone called, but it was usually important.

The call was Rix.

My stomach dropped.

Oh no.

He'd only phoned me once, to ask me out to drinks to iron things out during that blip we'd had.

Now, maybe something came up.

And because of that something, maybe he was canceling.

I told myself I didn't feel devastated by this as I nabbed my phone and took the call.

"Hey, everything okay?" I answered.

"Get your ass here. Now."

At his tone as well as his command, I stared at my pedestal sink.

"Alexandra?" he growled.

Oh boy.

He didn't call me Alexandra except on certain occasions, and those occasions were usually when he was being bossy.

And one could say he'd just been pretty freaking bossy.

"Is everything okay?" I asked hesitantly.

"Ass. Here. Now."

And then he hung up.

Well one thing I knew about that.

I was going to have to go with this outfit.

Because apparently, I didn't have time to change.

CHAPTER 12

THE DRAMA

Alex

I didn't take it as a good sign when I traversed the side path that led to his front steps that Rix was standing in his opened door, arms crossed on his massive chest, scowling at my approach.

On the drive there, belatedly, it occurred to me that an adjusted woman might be miffed at Rix's *Ass. Here. Now.* demand. A dramatic woman might be gearing up to throw a tantrum. And an enlightened woman would be justifiably outraged.

I hadn't settled on which one of those I was going to be (though, I'd tossed out drama, because I wasn't a tantrum-throwing person).

Nevertheless, I knew it was going to be one of them.

I was less certain when I saw how visibly ticked he was.

In fact, I wasn't even certain I wanted to finish walking up to his house.

What I *was* certain of was that I was not a child, and my future husband, fake or not, didn't get to speak to me like I was.

It was on this thought I stopped on his porch, and therefore could ignore his eyes sweeping the length of me before coming back to my face, seeming even angrier than he was before I got close (and it was good I could ignore this, or it would have been a hit to my ego, which wasn't very pronounced, but even I thought I looked cute in this dress), and I snapped, "What's going on?"

His heavy brows twitched, that was all the indication given that he wasn't a fan of my tone, but I read that indication, even before his rumbling-with-fury, normally-gravelly-but-now-it-was-a-veritable-quarry voice reverberated my way.

"You'll reconsider that attitude, no matter how hot it is, especially it coming from you when you're wearing that fucking dress and those goddamned shoes, when it hits you, like it hit me, that we work closely together. We spent nearly an entire goddamn week together. We've cooked together. We've cuddled in front of the TV together. We've even baked fucking cookies..." he seemed to lose it, bent slightly toward me, and snarled, "*together.*" He got a lock on it, and leaned back, finishing, "And nothing."

"Nothing?" I asked.

He spoke no further words.

He dropped his arms, turned and prowled into his house, and I knew this was also a nonverbal command to follow him.

I took a moment to consider seizing that opportunity to leave and come back when he'd calmed down from whatever had peeved him.

I didn't because I heard an impatient *"Alexandra"* barked from inside.

Oh no.

Unh-unh.

No way.

I stomped in after him.

"What?" I bit out, throwing the door closed behind me.

It didn't slam, but it didn't close gently.

Rix glowered at it, then glowered at me, then lifted his arm.

I noticed he had his TV remote in his hand.

So I looked to the TV.

On it was Elsa Cohen sitting in her signature mint-green velvet swivel chair, this particular episode, however, was paused.

She wasn't paused for long.

Rix hit go, the segment started playing, and as it did, I stared in horror, not only at all that was pouring forth, but that some of it was news so fresh, they had pictures of Rix and me from Friday…yesterday…and *that very morning*.

How…

Incredibly…

Creepy.

"Oh my God," I breathed.

When she was done, Rix paused her again, and slowly, cautiously, I turned my gaze to his.

"Needless to say," he started ominously, "I was surprised when I got the phone call from my mother not too long ago, who is, by the way, beside her-fuckin'-self I've finally found someone *worthy of me*, telling me our asses are up in Flagstaff next weekend so she can cook for you—"

"Oh my God," I repeated.

"—and I shouldn't worry about driving back in the same day. She wants us up there the whole weekend. She was so excited, she was making plans as she was talking to me. She's going to have Josh, Hailey and Kinsley over, for one. And she says we can sleep in my old room. Though, she did say she'd appreciate it if we didn't get up to anything, and warned that if we needed space to do our thing, she'd ask some friends if we can stay in their cabin so we could have privacy. If not, we have to sleep in the basement."

"*Oh my God*," I gasped.

It was like I made no noise.

Rix kept speaking.

"Goes without saying she just can't wait to meet you. She thinks you're very pretty and it's clear we're the perfect match and she really likes that white top you wore on Friday and wants to know where you bought it. She also wants to know if you've met the queen."

I closed my eyes.

"Fortunately," he went on, and I opened my eyes, "since I didn't know the answer to that question, or what the fuck she was talking about, or how the fuck she found out about us, Dad took the phone from her, so I didn't have to answer Mom's questions. But it's safe to say, if Mom was thrilled, Dad was fucking *ecstatic*."

This just kept getting worse.

Thus now, I was powerless to do anything but stare mutely at him.

"At the time, Mom was quiet about her feelings about the end of Peri and me, but I got where she was at. Though, later, she'd confide that she never really felt Peri was the one. Dad was, first, hurt, because he liked her and he liked her for me. Then, he got ticked. Now, he fuckin' *detests* her. So, seein' as I'm *so fuckin' happy* with a woman who *is made for me* and takes me as I am who also happens to be some fuckin' countess or some shit—"

Habitually, and unwisely, I cut in to share, "Marchioness, and Mum's that, since my grandfather died and the title went to her. I'm just an…erm…uh…" I swallowed as his angry expression deteriorated, which was kind of a miracle, just not the good kind, and I forced out, "lady."

He clamped his mouth shut, obviously now so furious, he no longer trusted himself to speak.

"I'm seeing I should have shared some things with you," I said quietly.

"Ya think?" he bit sarcastically. Then demanded, "You got nothing deep to give, Alex?"

"None of that matters," I told him the truth.

He swung an arm with finger pointed at the TV. "It matters to her and her fifty million fucking viewers, of which, my mother is one."

I shut up.

He crossed his arms on his chest, and I didn't know how it could be this way, further, I wasn't scared, still, it had to be said, if you didn't know him, that position was scary.

"I told you I used to be engaged," he noted.

I nodded.

"What I didn't tell you was, we were over when she couldn't deal with me losing my legs."

Oh dear.

We were here.

I never expected to be here.

But now I was.

Hell.

I took a deep breath and informed him carefully, "I feel at this juncture I should tell you that Chloe shared that."

The air in the room, already heavy, bore down suffocatingly.

Rix was the source of it and clearly immune to it because he talked through it.

"Well, she left about two minutes before I called your ass to get it down the mountain."

"Peri?" It came out on a squeak.

"Yeah, Peri," he confirmed.

Ulk.

Peri had just been there.

I shut up again.

"Now, Mom and Dad are fuckin' thrilled you're in my life. Peri, though, who's been in touch recently to see if we might find our way back to each other, we can just say that she wasn't feeling it all that much."

I wouldn't tell him, but still, I was kinda happy about that.

However, his reaction to Peri finding out about us had me concerned.

"Are you...is it...do you think—?" I stammered.

I was struggling.

Rix helped.

"Do I intend to give it a go with her?"

Another nod from me, this one glum along with terrified (Chloe said no, but she wasn't Rix, and he'd know).

"Babe, she dumped my ass when I lost my legs. So that would not be no. That would be *fuck no.*"

Right.

Like Chloe said.

Phew.

"Okay," I whispered.

"Still, she wore my ring. I loved her once. She says she still loves me. And recently, she's been back in touch. So, you know, I might have wanted to give her a heads up I got a woman in my life before she sees it along with fifty million other people."

"You don't have a woman in your life, Rix."

If the air in the room was suffocating before, it was afire now.

"I don't?" he asked in a deceptively even, calm voice.

"Well—" I began.

"If you say we're fake I'm gonna fuckin' lose…my… goddamned…*shit*."

I shut up again because first, it seemed like he was already doing that, and second, I was confused.

Because we *were* fake.

"So, yeah," he continued. "Twenty minutes ago, Peri stood where you're standing in a home we once shared, and I told her I was with someone else. Then I absorbed her justifiable, and I'll add, Alex, pretty extreme hurt that she's been texting now for weeks, and I didn't care enough for her and what we once were to give that to her in a personal way before a friend of hers phones her and tells her to watch that fuckin' cunt on YouTube."

He used the c-word.

He didn't shy away from cussing, far from it.

But he respected women (when he wasn't bossing them around, that "them" being me).

Oh boy.

"And that did not feel good, for her or for me," he continued. "But it can't be lost on you my parents went through watching their son lose his legs, lose his fiancée, lose his career, go through four different kinds of therapies in getting back up on feet again, just not his feet. So the fact that some pretty redhead with a cute dimple is out kayaking with him and making him smile is going to bring them insane amounts of relief."

No, that wasn't lost on me.

"Rix—" I started quietly.

"Baby," he whispered sinisterly, "don't say my name sweet like that right now. You. That dress. That hair. Those legs. The shoes. Your voice. You gotta know you can get away with a lot. But this…" He shook his head. "No."

Now I wasn't feeling dismayed that he'd been through all he'd just been through because I was procrastinating on my side of our getting-to-know-you business.

Now, I was slightly confused.

Though, the area between my legs knew precisely what was going on if the sudden dampness I felt there was anything to go on.

Then, he started walking toward me on an arc, which forced me, when I automatically started retreating, away from the door and into the room.

Actually no.

He wasn't walking.

He was *stalking*.

And my panties were not damp.

They were *moist*.

I kept moving, so did he, but he again started talking.

"We got a sitch here, sweetheart," he warned in that sinister tone.

"Rix—"

"Say my name one more time," he dared.

I wasn't quite certain what that meant, though from the flare in his eyes after I spoke his name, my female parts did, so I grew quiet about the time I ran into an armchair.

I shifted directions, so did he, herding me, and I had no choice but to head toward the couch.

Shit!

He continued talking.

"Now we're together for your family, *my* family, and fucking Peri."

I pressed my lips tight.

The backs of my legs hit his couch.

The front of Rix's body hit me.

Otherwise, he didn't touch me.

I didn't notice, though. I was concentrating on my nipples brushing his chest and panting.

He'd bent his neck and his face was close to mine.

"You get this, hey?" he asked softly.

"We can…we can…we can call it all off," I offered.

His brows snapped together, the room burst into flames (not literally, but it felt like it), and he growled, "We can?"

"No," I said swiftly, feeling that was the only safe answer.

"Yeah," he murmured, his eyes roaming my face, my hair, settling on my lips. "No. That dress. That hair. My mom I know is right now planning the weekend menu. Josh's probably already been ordered to clear his schedule. My phone rings, it'll be Hailey, because she'll be all over that Elsa bullshit." His face dipped closer. "In case you missed it, Alex honey, we just got in this for a lot longer fuckin' haul."

I was hearing his words.

I was even, in a way, processing them.

The problem with that was, I was watching his lips, from close, forming them.

And he had really beautiful lips.

So when he was done, this registered in some primal part of my brain that might be primal, but it was still polite, because I didn't interrupt.

But when he stopped, the coast was now clear.

And he was right there.

And my nipples were brushing his chest.

So, obviously, I jumped him.

Our lips crashed together, smushing against our teeth, Rix emitted a pained grunt, and my sanity returned.

It evacuated entirely when he suddenly had two handfuls of my ass, his fingers squeezing a message I didn't hesitate to respond to by hopping up.

I had my legs around his hips a nanosecond before I had my back to the couch and Rix's weight on me.

Ohmigod.

Heaven.

Though his body was on me, it was my tongue in his mouth.

He'd had a beer.

I tasted that.

But other than that, it was heat and strength and musk and *Rix*.

In other words, I couldn't get enough.

I'd never get enough.

But in that moment, I gave that effort my all.

This effort lasted so long, my hands were up his tee discovering the wonderland of the muscles of his back, and his hand was up my skirt and down my panties, skin-to-skin on my behind.

Abruptly, my body was jerked, he was seated, I was straddling his lap, his hand was still on my ass, but his other one had forced my mouth from his to the side of his neck.

His was on the side of mine as he growled, "Jesus, *fuck.*"

As those two words slithered down my spine, I realized I was panting.

I tried to stop doing that.

I failed when I felt the result of my kiss pressing between my legs.

Rix was hard.

And I'd made him that way.

My stomach did a somersault.

My brain panicked.

I began to move.

He clamped down with both hands.

He also whispered, "Please."

That was it.

That was all he said.

I stilled.

Slowly, gently, he slid his hand out of my panties, out from under my skirt, and wrapped that arm around my lower back, letting go of the pressure he had on my neck.

Slowly, mortified, I lifted my head.

Mortification fled at the molten caramel heat in his eyes.

Heat.

For me.

"You're a fuckin' great kisser, honey," he whispered, eyes to my lips.

Well, there you go.

Rumor verified.

"Thanks," I whispered back.

His gaze came to mine. "As awesome as that was, maybe we need to go a lot slower when it comes to that."

My mind thought that was probably a good idea.

Other parts of my body ardently disagreed.

However, I pressed my lips together and nodded.

"Though, to make things clear, I want that from you," he declared.

My heart skipped fifteen beats.

"You hear me?" he asked.

"I heard you, Rix," I answered.

"Your call. Always, baby. Hey?"

"Hey," I replied softly.

"Have you met the queen?"

Even if his eyes were maybe two inches away, I looked anywhere but at them and mumbled, "Ummmmmmm…"

His "Shit" was both amused and uncertain.

I looked right at him.

The time being nigh had passed.

So now it couldn't be avoided.

Thus, I stopped doing that.

"I have a thirty-five million dollar trust fund. I won't inherit anything of the Norton estate. Since Mum's an only child, that'll go to Blake, but more, her firstborn son, including the seat in the House of Lords. Though there are certain pieces of jewelry that have been earmarked for me. That said, I'm not allowed to sell them or bequeath them out of the family, and neither are my children. As you can tell from this, clinically, which is how my family operates, Blake and I have been fully informed of the arrangements. A hint of these, since Blake's inheriting Mum's flat in New York, I get Dad's brownstone. Blake gets the house in the Hamptons and the apartment in Paris. I get the 80-foot yacht in Miami and the compound on Mustique. My grandmother took a shine to me, that's Dad's mom, and left me her jewels, furs and gowns. All of them. And there are a lot of them. Blake was livid. Right now, for safe keeping, they're in a high security, temperature-controlled vault in Dad's brownstone."

I shut up.

"Go on," he encouraged gently.

I took a big breath.

And went on.

"Even before they got divorced, I spent almost all my summers in England."

"Why you call your mom 'mum.'"

I nodded. "That, and she wouldn't allow us to call her anything else."

"Okay."

"I liked it there. In England, it's a way of life to be outdoors. When it's nice weather, when it isn't. Folks hit the beaches. Bodies cover parks. People walk places. The footpaths are ancient. They're also public. It doesn't matter how rich you are, if you have a footpath going through your property, you can't stop anyone from using it."

"That's cool," he muttered.

"I know," I agreed. "I wandered a lot when I was out there. That's what they call it. Wandering. I like that too. That it's called wandering. There's obviously intent when you go out and do it, but it's also just doing it. Like, it's so peaceful. You're going nowhere, and you have all the time in the world to get there."

He started stroking my back.

His hand still at my neck started stroking my jaw.

Both felt nicer than I'd imagined they'd feel, and I'd had my fair share of daydreams about Rix and what it would feel like if he was mine, so that was saying something.

I kept talking.

"I honestly have no idea if my father and mother ever loved each other. Even their wedding pictures, earlier shots of them at parties or out on boats or on the beach, they're all posed. For Mum, not a hair out of place, lipstick always perfect. For Dad, it's like he thinks people won't take him seriously if he gets caught smiling, so he just doesn't do it very often. Dad being taken seriously is a big thing for him. He was taught he has to prove himself, because my grandfather had to prove himself, and my great grandfather, and so on. They came into vast wealth, and it wouldn't do for a man who's less than a man to inherit it."

"Right," Rix murmured when I paused.

"I guess the lack of affection might seem natural for Mum, given the stereotypical English reserve. But trust me, it's not. I spent a lot of time there and some English folk might not be overtly friendly, like Americans, or the Scots and Irish, but they're friendly and they're kind and loving. On his part, sometimes it felt like Dad actually forgot we existed. I know Blake felt it too. Her response was to act up. Dad's response was to teach us both a lesson for her transgressions. My response to that, and the fact that Mum and Dad fought a lot, like, a serious lot, was to try not to be seen, heard, or noticed at all."

He winced, and both hands stopped moving, his arm curving tight around my back, the other hand cupping my jaw.

Then he started to look pissed.

My hands were resting on his chest, but when I saw his shift in mood, I pressed in. "Don't be mad, Rix. I escaped."

"Okay, sweetheart," he lied, because I could tell he was still ticked.

"Anyway," I carried on in an effort to move us past that, "it wasn't just that. I wasn't like them. I never was. I felt it even before I knew what I was feeling. I think Grandmother Brooke was like me. She played golf and she'd drive herself places with her chauffer riding shotgun and give him the keys to take off when she got where she was going. But when he came back to get her, he'd get out, and she'd slide behind the wheel."

Rix's lips tipped up.

Yeah, that was Grandmother Brooke.

She was a character.

"And she'd snipe at Blake when she was lazing in front of the TV or taking too long to do her hair, 'The sun is shining, girl, by God, what's the matter with you?' She would buy me fancy dresses and make me wear them when she took me out to tea or to the opera, but whenever I pulled one on, she'd say, 'Never forget, when you're amongst the enemy, be sure you're wearing brilliant camouflage.' Then we'd go out for that tea or to the opera and she'd say things like, 'The key, my girl, is not what they think it is. They try to hide they're watching, but you know they are. Foolish waste of energy. It never fails to take someone off guard when they *know* you're watching.' And then she'd blatantly be up in everyone's business. I don't think she saw a performer sing a single note onstage. Her opera glasses were always turned to the audience."

Rix grinned.

I grinned too.

Then I stopped doing it and dropped my eyes past his lips.

"And I'll never forget, when she got sick and knew she was dying, she called me to her, told me what she was leaving me and demanded, 'The most important thing I'll ever say to you, Alexandra, is that not one single soul in history is remembered for toeing the goddamned line.'"

I drew in a breath at the memory, how frail she'd been, how I hated that when she was always incredibly slim, but still was filled to the brim with vim and vigor.

"That was when I knew," I told Rix's throat. "Not that I had to get out, I already knew that. I knew she *wanted* me to go. Maybe she worried that they'd yank my trust fund and I wouldn't have the means to go, so she gave me all she could so I would. And because she did, even though I never had to use what she gave me, I went."

"Was that hard?" Rix asked, and I lifted my gaze to him and shrugged.

"I thought it would be. I thought if I didn't start dating someone like Chad, or go to England and start dating an English Chad, and get involved on charity boards and mentor for debutante balls, they'd lose their minds. But I don't think in the first few months Dad even knew I'd gone."

"Fucking hell," Rix grunted, sounding like my words were a physical punch in the gut.

"It's better that way, trust me," I assured. "Blake still acts out, I think so Dad will remember she's around. Mostly, underneath those cries for attention, she does as expected. And the sad part is, she's going to marry a guy like Chad, who'll make her as happy as Mum and Dad were together. They'll create children. And she'll raise them to do the same as she does. What's expected. I know it's not the saddest thing in the world, but still. It's sad."

He looked like he had something to say, but he didn't say it.

When he didn't, I took in another breath, held his gaze and finished.

"I'm sorry I didn't tell you. It's weird, but it's almost embarrassing to be…well, *me*."

He had something to say to that.

"I don't get that, sweetheart."

"Not everyone has thirty-five million dollars, and I have to admit, if she doesn't lose interest in us, it won't be difficult for Elsa to find pictures of me hanging with a certain guy who is a lot closer to the throne than I am."

I knew he knew who I was talking about when his brows shot up. "No shit?"

"He's a cool guy," I muttered.

Rix started chuckling.

That surprised me, so I focused on him again. "I really am sorry."

He sat straighter on the couch, and he did it so he could wrap his arms around me, pulling me close to him, front to front.

If I didn't want to be awkwardly eyes to his chin, this kind of forced my forehead into the side of his neck.

One could say me straddling Rix and held tight to him would be the perfect catalyst for an epic freakout.

But the truth was, it was really comfortable.

When Rix didn't say anything, I did.

"I hesitate after all of that to share the obvious," I started. "But this wouldn't have happened if you let me fill out my part of the binder."

For the first time, I felt as well as heard him laughing.

Oh yes.

Being with Rix like this was perfectly comfortable.

"So, when we get married, am I gonna be a lord?" he teased.

It was me laughing then, and relaxing into him, because he was obviously over the drama.

"I don't think it works that way."

"Bummer," he muttered.

I felt his fingers resting on my waist dig in before he did what he seemed to be prone to doing.

He rocked my world.

"Gotta make sure you get, after that kiss, and pretty much everything that went before it, starting in Cali, that we're not fake."

I did not get that.

I stared at his strong throat, my relaxed body stringing tight.

"Seriously?" he asked, not missing my reaction, and this word sounded amused and annoyed.

I lifted my head to catch his gaze. "Rix—"

"No, we're not engaged. Obviously. And so you got what you need as we do this, I am not even close to ready for a relationship. I'm not looking for that. But I like spending time with you. I'm attracted to you. I want more from you, you in my space, me in yours, and physically. And I know you share those feelings with me. Though, if you wanna keep this fake, we gotta have a discussion, because straight up, Alex, I'm not in that place anymore."

I was stuck on one thing in all of that, even if all of that was huge.

"You're attracted to me?"

His eyes scanned my face before they came back to mine, and he said, firm at the same time gentle, "Stop it."

"I—"

"Chloe told you about Peri, that doesn't make me happy, but it's not a secret. Now you need to know that Judge warned me before we even had this deal you were into me. I missed it, but once he pointed it out, I realized it was pretty obvious."

Okay.

Uh.

Not good.

Judge had noticed.

And Rix knew.

I poised to spring off him, but his arms tightened again.

"Don't."

"Rix—"

"I want you."

I shut my mouth and stopped moving.

"We're young. You're gorgeous. You find me attractive. Isn't this what life's about? We enjoy it. We live it. We set my parents at ease for a little while. We put your family in their place. It gives me what I need to keep Peri from getting the wrong ideas. And while that happens, we have fun."

"We have fun," I parroted.

"Yeah. We have fun."

"Pretending to be a couple."

"No, being a couple that knows the stakes."

I edged back slightly, and he let me, then when I was as far away as he wished to allow, he stopped letting me.

That was when I spoke.

"And what are those?"

"That this, Alexandra," he gave me a squeeze, "is fun. Cooking together and TV and hiking and our mutual deep understanding that Kurt Russell is the shit. All of that, if you're down, will start to include me-spending-the-night, you-spending-the-night and all-you-can-get-up-to-in-the-night fun."

I shivered.

The fingertips of both his hands dug in, and his eyes got lazy.

It took effort, but I didn't get lost in his lazy eyes.

"So, friends with benefits," I noted.

"No," he refuted again, his voice warm now. Deeper. Coaxing. "A couple that enjoys each other and the time they spend together, doing it knowing in the end they'll still be friends. And that's important, Alexandra. This ends here, now, if you can't do that. And by that, I mean the fake couple part ends, the friend part remains. Always. I promise, I'll get it. Totally, honey. But I like you. You mean something to me. And I'm not losing you how I can have you. I'm just saying, I want more of you if you feel you're able to give it to me."

Rix threatening the end right now had me gripped with fear.

Okay, yes, he was saying there'd *be* an end.

He was planning on that.

But now, it would not *be* the end.

Not because of Blake's wedding (but yes, because Peri needed to get with the program, though I wasn't going to share the fullness of that mission, I was glad Rix was now on board, as it were).

No, because I couldn't let it end.

Because I liked him.

He meant something to me.

And I wanted more.

"I want more too," I admitted, trying to meet his eyes, not exactly succeeding, not exactly failing.

"So nothing changes, we go slow," and he finished with a steely, "except we're not fake."

I repeated that like I was rolling it around in my mouth, enjoying the taste. "We're not fake."

"Alex."

I focused on him.

"Seal the deal, honey."

The caramel was melting, so I knew what he was asking.

And we were a couple.

Rix and me, a couple.

Officially.

Not a normal one, but I'd never been normal, and I suspected neither had he.

But right now, that was what we were.

Something I never dreamed of being with Rix.

I had it.

It was temporary.

But I was going to hold on to it.

For as long as I could.

I pushed up and went in.

Like the first time, he let me kiss him.

Unlike the first time, when I eventually landed on my back with Rix on top of me, he started kissing me.

The getting to know you biz that evening had been pretty extreme.

The best part?

Rix thought I was a good kisser.

But I discovered he was better.

Judge

AROUND THE SAME TIME...

CHLOE WAS SITTING AT DUNCAN AND GENNY'S ISLAND, CHATTING TO her mom and Duncan while Duncan fried meatballs at the stove, and her mom prepared a salad, when Judge approached her.

She tipped her head back and smiled up at him.

He dropped his head, touched his mouth to hers, and then he didn't delay when he handed her his phone and earbuds.

Her brows slanted low over her eyes, but she took them, and her movements came quicker when she saw what was on the screen of his phone.

He watched as she watched that day's Elsa Exchange.

"Everything okay?" Duncan asked.

"I don't know," Judge answered.

"Oh my," Chloe whispered, her lips tipping up.

"I know that look," Genny said as she stared at her daughter.

Judge knew it too.

When the video was finished, Chloe took out the buds and handed them and the phone back to Judge.

Though "Interesting" was all she said.

"You have a hand in that?" he asked.

Her eyes narrowed on him. "Precisely which part are you referring to, darling?"

"Elsa Cohen knowing about Rix and Alex."

"Elsa Cohen?" Genny asked warily.

"Rix and Alex?" Duncan asked, shocked.

"I would not offer that woman a life preserver," Chloe snapped.

She would.

But he got what she was saying.

Judge relaxed.

Because she might have been meddling with Rix and Alex.

But she didn't do this.

"Mom and Duncan, you and I live here," she reminded him. "That means, for paparazzi, there's money to be made. The fact they stumbled on to Rix and Alex doesn't surprise me."

"Yeah," he muttered.

"What's going on?" Duncan demanded.

Chloe lost her mood and smiled happily at Duncan. "Oh, it's the sweetest thing in the world, Bowie."

Then she launched in.

Judge caught Genny watching him.

She lifted her brows.

He shook his head.

She sighed, but she did it on a small smile.

Then they all listened to Chloe's sharing.

Rix

Five and a half hours later...

"Hey," he called.

He knew it before he saw it.

But Alex lifted her head from his chest, trying to hide her hand dashing tears from her eyes.

"Babe, give it up. They soaked through my shirt round the time she went back to that school," he informed her.

Those eyes darted to his.

Tears in them, the green seemed more green, the brown almost amber.

So totally the prettiest eyes he'd ever seen.

"Tell me you liked it," she urged quietly.

The Queen's Gambit binge was over.

"I wasn't sure what your deal was with that show, but the last episode payoff was *massive*."

A huge smile split her face.

Rix pulled her up his chest and kissed it.

She tensed at first, then released and relaxed into him.

And his kiss.

He ended it and shared, "Tuesday, I'm grabbing El Gato and going to yours."

"Okay," she whispered.

"I'm spending the night."

Her eyes got big.

"We're not fucking."

Her brows dropped and she rubbed her lips together.

"Taking it slow."

She stopped rubbing her lips together and repeated, "Okay."

"Now, you need to go home, because you smell good and your hair's fuckin' fantastic and that dress has been doing a number on me all night so I want you in my bed tonight. If you don't go, I'm gonna see what it would take to get you to agree to stay."

She bit her lip.

He watched and muttered, "Right."

Then he did an ab curl, and in a couple more moves, they were both up.

His legs made it known it was time to remove his prosthetics.

He ignored that.

He also ignored the fact that in her bed on Tuesday, she'd see.

He never wore anything but pants and jeans.

So she'd not only see the prosthetics.

She'd see the stumps.

Yeah, he ignored that and walked her to the car.

He kissed her, closed mouth, and not for long, because if she started in, with the generosity of her little tongue, she wouldn't be going home.

Rix held the door while she folded in.

She gave him a cute wave and a little smile before she pulled out.

He watched her go.

He watched even after she was long gone.

And then he muttered, "You're a dick, Hendrix," to the dark street.

He knew he was.

Because he knew it.

He knew it was over even before his father mentioned the name Elsa Cohen.

He knew it when it was a physical feeling, watching her expertly lower herself into the cockpit of her kayak.

He knew it when she gave in on the oatmeal cookies.

He knew it when she got pissed at Brian.

He knew it when she texted about him meeting her friends.

He knew it when he saw that binder.

He even knew it when he heard someone coming, and then she rounded the rocks on that trail in Cali, the sun shining on her hair, making the red come out, the startled, bashful look on her pretty face.

He knew.

He definitely knew it now, *The Queen's Gambit* payoff.

The girl, quirky and bright and gifted, alone in the world.

Adrift.

No anchor.

But chess.

And then, suddenly, she realizes that she hasn't been alone for a long time.

That precisely because she was quirky and bright and gifted, she'd earned respect and a whole lot of love along the way.

Yeah, after that, he knew it for certain.

Still, he wasn't gonna do dick about it.

Because she was Alex.

And he was Rix.

And they might not have a lot of time together.

But he was going to give her everything he had to give.

Until it was over.

CHAPTER 13

THE PEP TALK

Alex

"Don't even start with me."

I stared at Gal on my phone, because she answered my FaceTime call like that.

Therefore, for obvious reasons, I asked, "What?"

"This play of calling me instead of Kate, because you know Kate is going to encourage you to go for it with Rix tonight, rather than backing off what the two of you agreed this weekend, and you think I won't. You think I'll talk you out of it. And you're grasping for reasons not to go for it."

I was rethinking how open I was with my girls and how much I loved them in my life.

At least I was rethinking that about Gal.

"Huh" was all I could say.

"Yeah," she agreed.

"So, that means you're not going to talk me out of being a couple with limits with Rix?"

There you go.

I was too open with my girls.

Last night in an epic Zoom session, I told them both all about it.

Including the fact I was having second thoughts about doing it.

Because, away from the mind-muddying presence of Rix, I wasn't certain it was that good of an idea.

"I'm going to tell you what you won't believe," Gal began. "And I know that, because I told you all this last night. But apparently, you refused to listen to me."

Ugh.

She kept going.

"So this time, bitch, listen up. You're amazing. You're sweet and kind and together. Your sister and mother might be classic English rose beauties, but you're a hundred times more attractive than they are, and not only because you have a fantastic personality, or any personality at all. You're just really freaking pretty. Also, there's nothing wrong with being an introvert, but you've got no reason to be shy. People like you. You're interesting. And in a world where everyone thinks their opinion on any little thing is important, someone being quiet and listening more than they jabber is a cool change."

I said nothing, and not only because I was listening.

Gal took that as her cue to carry on.

"So I'm going to tell you that if I see all this, Rix Hendrix is gonna see it. And obviously, he sees it. The man has been fucking everything that moves for a while now, and he wants to be a couple with you. Okay, it's a couple with limits, but he got nowhere near that with anyone else, so that's pretty freaking huge."

This was something to consider, all of it (and we could just say, since Sunday, I'd been considering it…frequently).

Because Rix had been a total manwhore.

I wasn't even very close to him before all this went down between us, and he was such a manwhore, I couldn't escape it.

It didn't feel good back then, but it wasn't my place for it to feel bad.

Now, if I understood what was happening, he was offering to give that up and just be mine (if only for a time).

Which, yes, was huge.

"And you've been in town for a few years, Alex," Gal continued. "But I grew up here. She was older than me, but I knew Peri Poulson in school. Everyone knew her. She's pretty. She's bubbly. She's tall and looks like a *Sports Illustrated* model, and she knows it. But when the whispers started that she broke up with her fiancé, the firefighter who got critically injured in the Cellar Fire, not a one of us who knew her was surprised about that."

This was news.

"Really?" I asked.

"Absolutely," she answered. "And I'll add that even all the guys she constantly had eating out of her hand thought that was low, because it super freaking was. She lost respect. She lost friends. And she deserved to lose both."

She one hundred percent did.

"You didn't share any of this last night," I noted.

"Well I'm sharing it now because you fill your life, but babe, seriously, you take zero risks. You're one of the coolest chicks I know with the way you go get it. But then again, there are some things, important ones, where you don't. Now, think about what's happening with you and this guy, because he had happen to him what happened to him, then finds out his fiancée is a puddle, not a lake. She's about appearances. He no longer worked in the River Rain advertising spread vision of what she wanted her life to look like. He'd fuck her Insta, and I follow her. She's all about her IG, showing the world how perfect her life is up in the Arizona Mountains. But it's for certain they haven't invented a filter to disguise prosthetics."

I felt my heart squeeze.

"Holy wow, she's that shallow?" I asked.

"I know her, but I don't know her very well. Maybe she has some substance to her," Gal allowed. "Rix went through a ton of woman like they were water, but he's stuck into you. Which suggests he has a type, and some superficial bitch is not it. So I can't for the life of me think there was nothing to her. But when you know who she is, and you see her around town, you'll get me. Her water bottles match her outfits, that's all I'm saying."

She need say no more.

I *so* got it.

To express that, I said, "Okay."

"My point is, this guy is coming off that blow, which was by far not the only one he was sustaining at the time it landed. I get his twice bitten in the ass by life, a hundred times shy. But he's down to be with you. And he's honest with you about where he's at. My opinion, that right there is enough to give this a go, have fun while you can, and end shit when it starts to feel like it's gonna get messy."

She'd lost me.

"That right there? I don't—"

"He's not promising you anything to the point he's promised you, in the end, there won't *be* anything but the friendship you guys will go back to," she explained. "That's big. Guys go in knowing that's where they're at, but they sure as shit don't share that little nugget with you."

All right.

From that comment, now I was wondering how open Gal was about things in *her* life.

"You just need to keep your shit sharp to make sure you protect that friendship, because it sounds like he's going to," she advised.

When I didn't say anything, she went on.

But her tone was gentler when she did.

"You wanted this guy, Alex, now you have him. Don't waste this opportunity. Hell, you should do it for every wallflower who didn't get her shot at her secret crush. It's almost a moral imperative."

I smiled at that.

She caught the smile and continued, "I can tell you like being with him a lot. Give yourself that. Have fun. Get laid. Share life with somebody for a while. Just keep a good hold on those heartstrings. If they start pinging a chord that demands a duet, cut him loose."

From Dani at the Raven, to Katie (because last night, she was totally about talking me into going for it with Rix), to Gal, the message was all the same and coming in clear.

And Gal was right, I never took risks.

Not risks like that.

And if anyone was worth taking a romantic risk on, it was Rix.

I wasn't sure about the heartstrings thing. I liked Rix so much, I knew that well would just run deeper and deeper.

But even if people claimed it happened, no one ever actually died of heartbreak.

But before that, we'd have time.

And after it, we'd still have each other.

And just a month ago, I never even expected him to be my friend.

"I'm going to go for it," I decided with a little clutch in my stomach and a little leap of my heart.

This time, Gal smiled. "Right then. Nail him down on when he's invading girls' night. I'm free every night this week but Friday."

"Thanks, Gal," I said.

"You bet, sister. Anytime," she replied. "Later."

"Later, babe."

We rang off.

I poured myself a glass of wine and headed to the deck.

Rix would be arriving any minute. He'd told me as we'd walked together to our cars after work that he'd be there with food at six thirty.

That gave me only an hour to get home, changed, tidy up breakfast dishes, fret, then call Gal to talk me out of doing what she'd instead talked me into doing.

I wanted to be a modern girl who was at one with enjoying a man, his time, and eventually his body, with only loose strings attached.

But by the time I heard Rix's truck growl up, park and go quiet, I was back to fretting.

When I heard him coming down the steps, I called, "I'm out on the deck."

I had my head turned, therefore saw him round the corner of the house.

Again, he'd gone from nice but casual trousers and a button down for work to jeans and a tee, this one black with a little yellow circle over the heart that said WHISKEY ROW.

I watched him walk up.

To me.

On my deck.

Him.

Rix.

In all his glory.

My (not so) secret crush.

Here.

With me.

And mine.

For a time.

And suddenly…

I stopped fretting.

"Hey," I greeted.

"Hey."

He stopped beside my chair and looked down at me.

He did this a while.

So long, it started to get freaky.

We'd been cool at work. Krista had started the day before, and she didn't need to come into a situation with an in-your-face office romance.

And although I knew Judge knew we were "together" (and maybe now knew we were *together*-ish), I sensed Kevin also knew something was up.

But we didn't make it obvious (or make it a thing at all).

Unless anyone interpreted the sexy winks Rix sent my way when he caught my eye.

Or the sexier chin juts.

Though, last night, he did kiss me by my car before we both went home.

And the same tonight, before we parted ways.

So I kinda was thinking he'd kiss me now, no audience, not on work property.

And we were *together*(ish).

Maybe he expected me to get up and kiss him?

"Is everything okay?" I asked.

"If you're gonna let me down, do it now, do it easy, we'll eat, and then I'll take off," he said quietly.

I straightened in my rocker. "What are you talking about?"

"Your kiss was weird."

"Sorry?"

"At the car, an hour ago, your kiss was weird. You been giving me looks all day." He put the bag of food on a table, dropped the backpack he had draped over his shoulder to the deck, then bent to me, one hand in the back of my seat, one on the arm, our faces close. "I told you, I'd get it and I'd be down with it if you didn't wanna do this. You can say anything to me, honey. You can talk to me about anything. Including cutting me loose."

Was he that tuned to me?

"I'm not going to cut you loose, Rix."

"Like I said, I'll get it."

"I want more," I whispered.

He stared into my eyes, deep into them, and he did this for another long while.

Then his caramel melted, his hand went from the back of my seat to sift up into my hair from behind my ear, and I finally got his mouth.

And his tongue.

Yes, I so wanted more.

I got it.

We did not kiss.

We made out.

I had both my hands wrapped around his neck, he still only had one sifted into my hair, but he'd tangled his fingers in it, when he lifted his head.

"Tapas are gonna get cold," he muttered to my mouth.

"Can't have that," I muttered back.

His gaze lifted, and for a second, clear as day, I saw stark relief mixed with lazy after-makeout heat.

Before I could fully take that in, he slid his hand out of my hair, reclaimed the food, his backpack, and I had no choice but to get up because he also claimed me by tugging me from my chair.

I got up, and holding hands, we walked into my house.

I HAD ON A PAIR OF HONEY-COLORED PAPERBAG BOXERS AND A BLACK slim-fit, shelf-bra cami, and I was staring into the mirror over the sink in my bathroom.

I'd changed, brushed my teeth, washed my face and moisturized, and I had no excuse not to go out to where I'd left Rix, sitting on the side of my bed.

I was fretting again, because my sleep outfit was cute.

But I didn't look like a *Sports Illustrated* model.

This is Rix.

You've shared another great, chill, awesome night with him.

He's still here.

With you.

Yours.

For a time.

Stop fretting.

And take the leap.

I sucked in a breath so deep, I had to choke-cough twice before I recovered.

Then I walked out, got past the hallway created by my closet, and stopped dead.

This was because Rix's deeply muscled, impossibly-wide-shoulders-tapering-down-to-his-narrow-waist back was on display.

And he had a tattoo.

Rising from the small of his back, the wingspan reaching from shoulder blade to shoulder blade, flames dancing all around, was a Phoenix.

Okay, how was it a woman's heart could weep and her vagina gush *at the same time?*

I didn't know, but it was happening to me.

He was standing, wearing sleep shorts that ran long.

But when he sensed me, he turned.

Oh...

My.

Protruding pecs, anatomical-style muscle definition, a collarbone that made my mouth water, black chest hair that covered his pectorals in delicious swirls narrowing to a line that followed the indent that ran down the middle of his cut abs, getting seriously dense under his navel.

That hair under his navel done me in, and since it did, I couldn't even fully take in his bulging, veined biceps and sinewy forearms, the last I'd seen before, but not as parts of all the other glory.

In fact, I had to reach out and hold on to the wall.

"You done in the bathroom?" he asked.

I was so overwhelmed by his sheer male beauty, I didn't catch the tightness in his voice.

I also couldn't speak.

I nodded.

He moved my way, almost past me, but he stopped.

I twisted my neck and looked up at him.

He stared at me.

It took a second before I realized that was odd.

I took a wild stab at what it might be about.

"Did you bring your toothbrush?" I asked.

He lifted a hand.

I tore my eyes from his handsome face to see he had a toothbrush and toothpaste gripped in his fist.

He even held a toothbrush and toothpaste in a way that was reminiscent of the caveman who beat another caveman to death with his bare hands in order to claim that man's cavewoman, and then he lifted the arm of his victim that'd he'd ripped from the poor guy's body up in victory.

I nearly moaned.

I fought that urge and said, "You don't have to bring toothpaste next time. You can use mine."

His head tipped to the side in a gesture of confusion.

And he still didn't move.

I was about to say something else, but didn't, because his hand came up, and as I was learning was Rix's way, he claimed my ear, this time the front of it and some of my jaw, in order to drop his head and brush his lips against mine.

He let me go and carried on to the bathroom.

I gave myself a sec to enjoy the aftermath of the lip brush before I finished the short trek to my room, turned my Vornado vintage fan on low, because I was a white noise, snuggle in your covers girl (thus even turned the fan on in the winter), then I wondered if Rix was a white noise dude.

In the end, I decided I could just ask him when he returned. If he wasn't, it was simple enough to turn off.

I dumped some toss pillows on the floor, pulled back the coverlet, slid in, and felt my lips tip when I pulled back Rix's side too. I then rearranged the pillows from standing on their end to sleeping position.

I was sitting cross-legged in bed when Rix came out.

I managed to get beyond his chest this time, and although the sleep shorts were long, they didn't pass his knees.

Which were cupped into his prosthetics.

I'd never seen them before, and they were badass cool. They looked bionic.

I lifted my gaze to him, not quite noting that his gait was not fluid with a hitch, but was wooden, as he made his way around the bed.

Though I did notice his eyes were glued to me.

"You sleep with a fan?" I asked.

"What?" he asked back in a way that it seemed like he wasn't certain what language I was speaking.

I tossed a hand out to the fan that was sitting on a long dresser that sat against the wall to the closet.

"Fan? I do white noise. But if it'll bother you, I probably could do without it."

"Probably" was pushing it, but we were feeling our way with this.

I'd fall asleep.

Eventually.

He was stopped by his side of the bed and staring at the fan like it'd dropped from space.

Finally, his strange demeanor hit me.

"Rix?" I called.

His gaze crashed down on me.

No other way to describe it.

It *crashed on me*.

"I'm taking my legs off now," he announced.

I felt my brows knit and returned, "Well, yeah. I mean, you don't sleep in them, of course. Right?"

"Right," he whispered, the weight of his attention still heavy on me.

What was going on?

Was I supposed to do something?

"Am I missing something?" I asked carefully when he didn't move.

"Are you missing something," he muttered, not a question, and he didn't answer me, but somehow, I felt like these four words were meaningful to him.

I just couldn't figure out why.

"Rix, you're kinda freaking me out," I said softly.

"You're a fuckin' unicorn," he declared.

I blinked. "What?"

He again didn't answer.

He turned. I got the phoenix back. He sat, and I was treated to the spectacle of his muscles moving and flowing before I heard thud one then thud two.

He swung his arm long, grabbed the covers, and he was twisted and in bed with the covers up to his waist before...

Before...

Before I could see his legs.

God.

I was such an idiot.

Like, start to finish idiot.

Like, sure, he was tuned to me. We seemed pretty tuned to each other.

But this man walked up to my chair on the deck a few hours earlier, and knew he'd be right there.

With me.

Like this.

But with him exposed.

I was a total dufus.

He turned his head to me, and ordered softly, "Wanna turn out your light, baby?"

I sat there, staring at him.

His face.

His chest.

The dense hair under his belly button.

My pink sheet and white matelassé coverlet resting across his hips.

"Alexandra."

My eyes raced up to his face.

"Can you sleep with a fan?" I whispered.

"Yeah," he grunted.

"Good," I said.

He twisted and turned out his light.

He came back, his gaze narrowed on me, and he asked, "You sleep with a light on too?"

Him and me?

We were doing this.

For a while.

And in that exact moment, I decided for my part I was *doing this*.

Heartstrings be damned.

I was giving this magnificent man everything.

Everything I had.

When he was done, he could move on to a woman who could make him happy.

And that would be devastating.

And glorious.

Because I wanted that for him.

I *craved* that for him.

But in the meantime…

I pushed up to my knees, then adjusted until I was facing him.

"Babe—"

He cut himself off when I yanked my cami over my head, and I was naked up top.

His gaze instantly dropped to my chest.

My breasts were large, not exactly in proportion to my body.

I'd always been a tad self-conscious of them.

Now was no different.

It was going to get worse.

I undid the drawstring of my boxers.

"Baby," he whispered.

I pulled them down, fell to my hip, shoved them over my knees quick as I could, kicking them off.

They flew over the side of the bed.

That was a lot farther than I wanted them to be, but I couldn't go after them now.

Before I lost courage, I got back up on my knees facing him. That done, I found I'd tapped too deep into my reserves, so I couldn't stop myself from covering what I could of my breasts with one arm, holding the bulge of my belly that I was about ten thousand times more self-conscious about than my breasts in my other hand.

Rix was statute still, except his eyes were moving all over me.

I felt the heat creep and said, "I should probably lay off the oatmeal cookies."

His gaze ceased roaming to rest on mine.

And his hand came out, fingers wrapping around my wrist at my stomach, but that was it.

Except he murmured, "Come here, Alex."

I didn't move.

"Baby, come here. Now."

I swallowed, started to move, and he threw back the covers.

I looked.

I saw his thighs and knees, muscled, perfect, pristine, several inches of flesh below, then his limbs were neatly tucked away.

I kept moving, swinging a leg over his hips, and hiding my nudity by bending forward and resting my torso on him.

His chest hair was even better, skin to skin.

He wrapped both arms around me.

"Christ," he said to my face, "you're fuckin' something."

"Can I kiss you?" I asked.

His tone rocked straight to guttural when he answered, "Fuck yeah."

"Can we have sex?"

No sifting or tangling, his hand went up and gripped my hair, his other one went down and claimed my ass.

And it was grating this time when he repeated, "Fuck yeah."

I kissed him.

He kissed me.

He was right.

Fuck yeah.

My hands roamed.

His hands roamed more.

I got stubble burn on my cheeks, jaw and neck, and I loved it.

He likely had teeth marks on his neck and collarbone, he acted like he loved it, and I hoped he did, though I knew I loved giving them to him.

His nipples were peaked because I'd nibbled at them.

My nipples were peaked because he'd rolled and pinched them.

I was so ready, my wet had started gliding down my inner thigh, when I broke our most recent kiss and asked, "Condom?" at the same time he grunted, "Wallet."

He then gave me the hottest grin he'd ever given me, and this time, I let myself whimper.

Then I sat up.

He twisted at the waist to reach to his jeans on the floor.

I shimmied down his legs, fingers in the waistband of his shorts, and pulled down, stopping suddenly when I had them at his thighs.

Because his cock sprang free.

His *massive* cock.

Perfectly formed, purple, veined and distended.

Holy God.

I didn't think, not once, so there was no hope of thinking twice.

I gripped him at the base, went in, and swallowed as much as I could get.

I felt the bed move powerfully, and the room rumbled with his groan of, "Jesus, fuck, Alex."

Then his hand was again gripping my hair.

It was encouragement, but I didn't need it.

Rix's big dick nestled in those dark curls, tasting of him, filling my mouth, hard and silk, I could blow him for a lifetime.

I didn't have a lifetime, but I had now.

So I went for it, sucking and stroking and licking.

Eventually, I vaguely sensed his hands on me sending a message, and since he was strong, it was a powerful message. So like a kitten, mewing and resistant when the bowl of milk was being taken away, I got my last licks in before he hauled me up his chest.

Then he rolled me so he was on top.

"I like your cock," I breathed.

"No shit?" he asked, his voice rough with sex, but also amused, and honestly, that mix was the best I'd heard *in my life*.

"I'm gonna want more of that later," I warned him.

"You got it," he said.

And he kissed me.

I felt his hand working between us, then he flipped us again, so I was on top, but I felt the head of his cock was pressing inside.

He ran his fingers into my hair on either side of my head, gathering at the back, and he whispered, "Alex honey, you're gonna have to take me."

I understood him.

That long, wide shaft, I had to set the pace.

I held his gaze and inched down, feeling stretched...and *wow*.

So good.

"Yeah?" he grunted.

"Yes," I whispered, inching down some more.

A muscle flexed in his jaw.

"Yes?" I asked.

"You're tight," he growled.

"You're huge."

"No, you're tight."

"You're still huge."

"Babe—"

I inched down quite a bit more.

His chin jerked up, and I got a full view of his roped neck and the line of his jaw.

Holy *wow*.

On one surge, I slid him all the way in.

Oh *yes*.

He righted his head, his gaze on fire, and my vulva caught the blaze.

"Yeah?" he groaned.

"Yes," I confirmed urgently.

"Thank fuck," he rumbled, whipped us back around, jacked up his thigh right when he did the same with my knee, and he thrust.

Powerfully.

Wow.

And again.

Oh God.

Again.

God.

Again.

I dug into his lats with my nails in order to hold on, because if he was going to fuck me into the wall, and there seemed real danger of that, I was taking him with me.

"Rix," I breathed, my sex uncontrollably rippling around his thrusting cock.

"*Fuck,*" he bit, hooking the inside of his elbow behind my knee, jacking it up further, and driving deep.

Wow.

"*Rix,*" I panted.

"Baby," he whispered, kissed me, and this being Rix, tasting him, taking the weight of him, having him fill me so completely, retreat and fill me again…

I was done.

I cupped the back of his head in both hands, and moaned down his throat as my orgasm overwhelmed me.

His tongue curled into it, his mouth sucked at it, then his face was in my neck, and his cock was driving deeper.

Faster.

He grunted so hard, I felt it inside me as I trembled through the end of my orgasm and clutched him to me.

Another grunt.

Then he wrapped his hand beneath my jaw, pressed my head to the side, sunk his teeth into my neck, buried himself completely, and groaned into my flesh.

Wow.

I felt the tremors swell through him, absorbed them, still soaring, but alas, coming down.

I coasted my hands over his skin, wrapped a leg around the back of his thigh, and I knew he was coming down too when he curved my other leg around his ass.

Then he was lapping at where he bit me, nuzzling my neck, and finally, he lifted his head.

"Okay," I stated the minute his eyes caught mine, "I've been crushing on you for a long time, but that was *way* better than all my fantasies. Like, it was all my fantasies *rolled into one*. It was just that… scary…*amazing.*"

He stared down at me, body fixed.

As he did, I realized what I just said.

All of it.

Damn.

A new kind of heat crept in, and I tensed to untangle myself from him and do what, I didn't know, but whatever it was would be a form of escape.

Rix still had his hand wrapped around my jaw, though, and it tensed.

"You had fantasies about me?"

Oh my God.

This was humiliating.

"What kind of fantasies?"

"Ummmm…" I hummed to his hairline.

"Okay, Al, put this one away. I like her a lot, but right now, bring the other one back who took one look at my dick, latched on, and deep throated me."

My eyes fell to his.

He was grinning.

Teasing.

Being Rix.

I relaxed.

"Baby, you gotta know, it is so far from a turn-off it isn't fuckin' funny that you fantasized about me," he declared.

"I think my point was, that was good," I lamely explained.

"I think I got your point," he replied, still grinning. "Though I was there with you, so I know it was."

"Okay, good," I mumbled.

"So back to these fantasies."

My eyes slid to the side.

He kept going.

"Because I've been jacking off to you for a while…"

My eyes darted back.

"…and I got a good imagination, sweetheart. But you bearing down on me, *twice*, like a goddamned *champ* was not part of them."

"Rix."

He bent, touched his mouth to mine, but didn't go far away.

"That was amazing, honey," he whispered.

"Yeah," I agreed.

I watched the warmth twinkle in his gaze then he muttered, "Get rid of this condom."

He was semi-hard, but still, there was a lot of him, so it felt nice when he pulled out.

He rolled off, rolling me to my side at the same time hooking both of my knees with a hand and lifting them so I was slightly curled into myself.

Then he reached out, and the covers fell on me.

God, he was so sweet.

He rolled again, twisted, and he was sitting by the side of the bed.

I watched him bend, realized what he was doing, reached to touch my hand to the small of his back, and offered, "I can take care of—"

I stopped speaking when his shoulder dipped, and over the top of it, his gaze seared into me.

All righty then.

Rix was going to get up and dispose of the condom.

He turned away from me, put on his legs, which required him standing and sitting, twice, before he stood one last time and walked to the bathroom, did his thing, came out and walked right to my light.

This was when I got my first top to toe of Rix.

Yeah, he had great thighs, and I knew that even if they were now covered in sleeves, they were just that great.

I licked my lips.

The light went out.

I felt the bed depress when he sat on it, the thumps of him taking off his legs, then the mattress rocked, the covers swished, he settled and turned to me.

Then I was dragged the few inches that separated us, and I was plastered, front to front, to Rix.

"I clean up after we fuck," he decreed.

Okay, yes.

As suspected.

I'd messed up with the offer.

He kept speaking.

"Me, and I clean you too, when we decide I can go in ungloved."

"Okay."

"It's not a problem, putting on my legs. I do it all the time."

"Okay, Rix."

His tone was getting rougher, and I'd know it was with impatience when he demanded, "Don't be freaked I'm laying this out, Alex. This is life for me. You in it, it's the same for you."

"Of course."

"So we just got to be real."

"I can do that."

"No timidity. No hesitation. You got a question, you ask. You got something to give, you offer. But you gotta be up for it when I lay out how it's gonna be."

Erm.

Hang on a minute.

"Was I not up for it?"

"I'm just saying."

He was just saying, but the problem was, that was all he said.

So I requested specifics.

"What are you saying?"

"You're bashful."

Um.

Bashful?

I laid a hand in his oh-so-delightful chest (yes, I could say that, even in the dark, it was the chest hair, and the expanse, not to mention the solidity), and I used it to push up to an elbow.

"I'm *bashful*?"

He used his oblique to push up to his elbow.

"Yeah," he clipped. "You're bashful."

"Did you actually just use the word bashful?"

"Yeah, because that's what you are."

"*Bashful?*"

"Babe," he growled, and I'd heard him growl, and obviously he'd called me babe before, but I'd never heard the way that came out of him in either sense.

And when it did, I knew we were going to have to fuck again.

"You're not some chick who's shy," he continued. "Shy is not you. You're a dork, sure. A goof too. You can be a klutz. Shit comes out of your mouth that's fuckin' adorable. You got a dimple. The softest hair imaginable, and a lot of it. You're an amazing kisser, which probably should have been a heads up when you got to the point you wrapped your mouth around my cock, but...*fuck*. It didn't. You got great tits. A tight pussy. You know when to use your nails. And you get off on a solid fucking. That's not *shy* or *timid* or anything generic like that. It's cute and hot. It's *bashful*. Now stop givin' me shit, hey?"

Being all of that (even the first bits, though I kinda wanted him to explain the distinction between a dork and a goof), but also polite, I waited until he was finished before I asked, "How many condoms did you bring?"

He was silent.

Then I wasn't on my elbow anymore.

I was on Rix.

And his hands were all over me.

But all his lips said was, "Baby."

I planted my hands in his chest and arched up. "That doesn't answer my question, Rix."

"Got us covered," he muttered, his fingers trailing up my spine, my neck, into my hair, and my arch was a memory.

"Okay," I whispered.

Our mouths met.

And lucky me, I got what I'd told him I wanted earlier.

More.

With a bonus.

Because it was more *of everything.*

CHAPTER 14

THE FRIENDS

Rix

"Slip me out."

Curled on the floor between his knees, her hair everywhere, Alex kept sucking him off.

"Al, slip me out."

She kept at him.

Fuck.

He slid his hands out of her hair, grabbed her under her pits, pulled her up, and planted her astride his lap.

She held on to his shoulders, her two-toned eyes vague and so goddamn sexy, he beaded.

Which meant he didn't fuck around as he shoved a hand between them and positioned.

"Take it all?" he grunted.

"Please," she whispered.

His girl seriously liked his dick.

He caught her pussy with his cockhead, and grasping her hips, he pulled her down.

Her head dropped back.

His did too.

Christ, her sweet, tight, slick, goddamned gorgeous, fucking cunt.

He felt her mouth on his throat.

He dropped his chin and ordered, "Fall back."

She raised her head. "Rix."

"All the way back."

Her teeth swiped her lip.

His eyes watched.

Fuck.

"Lap dance, baby," he demanded.

She caught his gaze, then did as told, leaning all the way back, her fingers wrapping around his wrists to hold on, her abs and his hands doing the rest of the work.

And Rix worked her.

He used her hips to jack her on him, watching her tits bounce, her hair sway, his dick, glossy with her wet, sink in and out of her.

"Go after your clit."

No hesitation, she went.

Oh yeah.

That was his girl.

"Rix," she breathed.

Christ, his name like that scorched through his cock.

"Tit too," he grunted.

Her other hand went to her tit.

She made a noise that made him jack her harder into his dick.

Alex's head fell fully back, her body arched, and goddamn…

She was something.

"Baby, you're gonna have to—" He didn't finish with the word "come."

Because she came.

He jacked her faster to give her more, and then kept doing it until he got his, then he pulled her up so she was sitting on his cock.

She rubbed her nose on his neck and then rested her cheek on his shoulder and sighed into his skin, all this with her arms around him, stroking his back with one hand just under his lat.

"C'm'ere," he murmured.

No hesitation, she gave him her mouth.

He took it until she moved restless in his lap, and he felt her pussy get greedy again.

Since he needed some time before he could be ready for her, he pulled her off him and set her in his bed.

She started to curl up, but he ordered, "No. Spread."

Her eyes locked on him, the tip of her tongue slid out, touching her bottom lip, she did as told, and he didn't delay.

He reached for the damp cloth he now kept by the bed for this reason.

A tender, thorough clean then he tossed the cloth to the floor, twisted, positioned, and buried his face in her pussy.

His Alexandra's pussy.

Fucking hell.

Dark and wet and rich, like pudding.

Spreading her open further with his hands on the hinge of her hips, he shoved in deeper.

She hooked his back with a calf and lifted the other knee, her fingers cupping his head.

He took his time.

He made her come.

Then he pulled himself up and over her and took his time making her come again, and this time, he came with her.

He was still balls deep when she whispered in his ear, "We probably should get ready for work."

His Alexandra?

Just like him.

An early riser, ready to face the day with energy.

Rix lifted his head, cupped a hand under her jaw, ran his thumb along her lower lip and muttered, "You first, shower."

She nodded.

He bent and kissed her, then he rolled off her.

She rolled with him and over him, and didn't mess around finding his tee and yanking it over her head as she walked to the bathroom.

They were day five with together. Entering day three with fucking. Her place that first night, and then for various reasons, his place the next.

She had sweet curves, he did what he could to show he appreciated them, but she wasn't there in comfort level yet.

So she hid them away.

They'd get there.

Just like they shot as fast as Alexandra could manage it to no condoms when, on Wednesday morning, about an hour and a half after they showed at work, she had walked into his office, right to his desk, where she leaned a hip against the side of it.

His mind was on possibly working late someday, and fucking her on it.

Her mind maybe wasn't on the exact same thing, but it wasn't far.

"We're having lunch together today, a late one, fast food, because we have an appointment at two at the clinic," she'd announced.

His brows went up in surprise.

But that didn't mean he didn't smile.

"I'll drive," he said.

"Gotcha," she replied, gave him a wistful look he felt in his groin, mostly because it reminded him of the look she had on her face when he'd dragged her mouth off his cock the night before, and she walked out.

Nope.

The woman hadn't even let a day slip by before they were giving up samples and paying for rushed results.

All that, all good, and since she was on the pill, it was *all good*.

Now it was Thursday. They had drinks with her friends that night on the schedule, staying at her place. Friday she was packing heavy and coming down to his because they were leaving early to get up to Flagstaff.

And they already had a drill.

This drill played out as she walked out of the bathroom, hair a mess on top of her head because it apparently wasn't hair-washing day, body wrapped in a towel she had clutched at her chest in one hand. She shot him a small smile, minimal dimple, pawed through her bag with her free hand to grab what she needed and disappeared back in the bathroom.

Rix lazed in bed, her taste still on his tongue, so he was all good, until she was out, ready to face the day, and after a quick stop to give him a peck on the lips, she headed to the kitchen.

He went to the bathroom in his chair, swung himself onto the bench in the shower, did his thing, and met her dressed and ready on his feet when the coffee was made, and that day, he saw it was avocado toast for breakfast.

He liked her in his kitchen.

And that was not about coffee and avocado toast.

Through all this, Rix was one hundred present with Alex.

He did not allow himself to go there.

He did not allow himself to remember the look on Peri's face the first time she saw his truncated, bandaged legs.

He did not allow himself to remember the way she'd turned away in bed the first time he'd pulled himself into his chair to wheel himself into the shower in order to use it sitting down.

Rix did not think about the fact that he'd fucked Peri in the shower more than once, standing on his own two feet.

But he did think that he'd fuck Alex in the shower, his ass to the bench with her bouncing on his dick.

Alex was completely unfazed.

The first time he showed her his prosthetics, she'd barely looked, and not because she was avoiding them, because she was thirsty for his chest.

But when she did see all of him, with some of him being metal and hydraulics, she'd asked about her fan.

The second time, when he'd been naked, she'd licked her lips.

It wasn't about a fetish (it had seriously sucked, but he'd run into one of those).

It was because that was just who he was to her.

That was all she knew.

But even so, rewind a year and a half and it was Alex in his bed, and he didn't come home whole, he knew it would be the same.

To Alexandra, he was just who he was.

She was more worried her fan would bother him than she was seeing him legless.

"Can I ask you something?" she queried as he poured coffee, her question taking him out of his head.

"Shoot," he offered.

"Was the phoenix before or after?"

She had the creamer out so he nabbed it and dropped some in, asking, "Sorry?'

"On your back. Before or after."

He put the creamer down and looked at her.

"After."

Her head barely moved with her nod because she'd already figured that out, she was just confirming.

He grabbed his mug, leaned hips to the counter and took a sip as she slid the toast she'd made him his way (he saw she'd sprinkled everything bagel seasoning on it, which probably made something pretty fucking good even better).

"You got no tats, Al," he noted.

She shrugged and bit into her own toast.

"You don't like 'em?"

"Yours is beautiful."

He grinned, set his mug aside, moved, pinned her to the counter, and wrapped a pigtail apiece in his hands, holding them behind her ears, trying not to let it sink in how good those thick ropes felt in his fists, and how long it felt like he'd waited to be able to claim them.

It had only been weeks.

It seemed like decades.

"I like your bed," he murmured.

"Mm?" she hummed, gaze on his mouth.

"It's girlie," he said.

Her eyes skipped up to his. "Girlie?"

"I'm an invader, fucking the bashful damsel, who, once she gets it in her mouth, won't stop sucking my cock."

His pink hit her cheeks.

He dipped closer. "We need some mods in your bathroom, though, for me to be able to use your shower."

"Okay," she whispered.

She could also use some rails by her toilet, but until they assessed how long this might last, he wasn't gonna ask her to take it that far.

He used her pigtails to pull her up on her toes.

When he did, she made a little mew and that drove right up his ass, straight into his balls.

He'd always had a strong libido, but that morning he'd already fucked her twice, she'd come three times, and he was going to fuck her again.

With this in mind, Rix nipped her bottom lip, traced his tongue along it, and with his mouth still there, ordered, "Turn around and brace, sweetheart."

Her eyes went hooded, he let her pigtails go, and she did as he said.

He reached around, unbuttoned and unzipped her pants, yanked them down to her thighs along with her panties, and then he shoved his hand between her crack, in the end curling in.

Soaked.

She was ready for him, his Alex.

With relief, he released his hard cock, positioned, and with a helluva lot more relief, he drove in.

Alex bore down.

Christ.

Rix mounted her, wrapping an arm around her chest to haul her into him, his other hand he dove in and fingered her as he fucked her, watching her. Her flushed face, her slick lips she kept moistened with her little pink tongue, listening to her soft moans and hitches mingled with his deeper sounds of effort.

"Weekend after next is ours. Fuck you all day, both days," he growled into her ear.

"Yes," she breathed.

"Your man needs you to put more effort into it, baby," he commanded.

She bounced in, meeting his thrusts, and he could feel her attempting to grind into his hand.

His balls drew up.

God, his girl, at his command.

He'd never had a woman give over like Alex.

It was spectacular.

"Can't get enough of you," he told her.

"Me...either," she forced out between thrusts.

"You like my big dick," he teased.

"Ye...es." She was not teasing.

Yeah she did.

"Rix," she gasped.

God, fuck, his name in her mouth when he was moving inside...

"You gotta come, Alex."

Her hand found his between her legs, but not to direct him.

She pushed through to feel him fucking her.

Fuck.

She had to come.

Her neck arched, lips parted, her pussy clutching him.

She was coming.

He gave her that before he let go and jetted inside her.

He ended it with his forehead next to her ear, the scent of her in his nose, and he knew how big his orgasm was when it was only then he noticed her little hand gently massaging his balls.

His dick still buried, it felt *phenomenal.*

Then again, it'd feel like that even if he wasn't still buried.

He lifted his head and looked down at her. "Our fuck weekend, let you play too."

Her gaze slid up to him, and she did not hide in the slightest she dug that idea.

He grinned. "Alex Sharp. My little mountain fuck bunny."

She rolled her eyes and pushed up from the counter.

What she didn't do was contradict him.

Totally his fuck bunny.

Rix was chuckling when he pulled out, jacked up his pants, pulled up hers and spanned her hips to turn her to him.

He kissed her, deep, wet and short.

When he was done, he ordered, "Clean up."

"'Kay," she mumbled.

"How much shit your friends gonna give me tonight?"

She'd told him that she'd told them about their past fake relationship, as well as the fact it was no longer fake.

Her eyes climbed to the ceiling, and she let her head drop to one side.

Even though that was cute on her, what it meant was her friends were gonna give him a lot of shit.

"Fantastic," he muttered.

"Katie will love you," she offered.

That's batting five hundred.

"Gal's going to bust your balls."

He heaved a sigh.

She wrapped her hands around either side of his neck. "Don't worry. I'll be there to protect you."

"The damsel doesn't protect the invading marauder whose dick she falls in love with," he educated her.

"Oh?" she asked, her eyes lighting.

"Yeah. She becomes his sex slave, though."

She slid her hands down to his chest and gave him a playful push, which was totally ruined since her dimple was pronounced the whole way through it.

Playful or not, he moved back because they had to get their asses in gear to get to work.

She headed to the bathroom.

He did up his pants.

Then ate his toast.

"Got ten minutes?"

Rix looked from his laptop, where he was reading some of the early surveys coming in and taking notes, to Judge, who was standing at his office door.

"Sure," Rix answered, sliding his laptop aside.

But he felt his brows come together when Judge came in and shut the door.

He'd never had a closed-door meeting with Judge, impromptu or not.

Then his friend walked to the folding chair that was standing in for the guest chairs he was going to get in two to six more weeks when their office furniture started arriving.

Judge sat, looked at him and stated, "Friend zone."

Shit.

"What's up?"

"I'm asking Chloe to marry me this weekend."

This was not what he expected.

It wasn't unexpected, but it wasn't what he expected after Judge closed the door.

What it was, was awesome.

He felt his face split in a huge smile as he stood and rounded the desk, saying, "Jesus, man, congrats. Damn." He had his hand up in front of him, elbow cocked, Judge had gotten up too, his hand was the same, they clasped, slammed their chests together and pounded each other's backs. "So happy for you. Shit."

They separated, and neither of them took a seat.

"Asked Tom last week. Asked Genny this weekend. It's a go."

"You throwback fuck," Rix razzed, still smiling.

"Most stressful thing I've done in my life, finding a ring good enough for Chloe Pierce."

"You manage it?" Rix asked, resting his ass on the edge of his desk.

Judge remained standing. "Genny says it's perfect. Sasha too. Dru loved it. So I have high hopes."

Rix got serious. "She'd put a beer tab on her finger if it was from you, Judge."

"Yeah," Judge agreed. "So what's up with you and Alex?"

Goddamn shit.

Sneak attack.

Rix tensed.

"Things have changed," Judge observed.

Alex told her friends.

Rix had not shared with Judge.

"They have. We're not fake anymore. We're together."

His bud, content deep down with his woman, happy now with this upcoming increase in commitment level, got visibly happier.

"Don't get excited," Rix cautioned. "She knows the drill."

The happiness faltered as confusion set in.

"The drill?" Judge asked.

"It's still for her family. Then Elsa Cohen pulled her usual shit."

Judge nodded. "I saw that."

"Yeah, so did my mom. And Peri."

"Peri?"

"Yeah. Peri. So it's now for my family, who're happy I've found someone, and Peri, so she'll back off. But mostly, it's for us. Me and Alex. I dig her. She digs me. We dig doing the same things. So we're gonna enjoy each other."

"Enjoy each other," Judge murmured.

Rix started to feel annoyed.

"You just gonna repeat shit I say?" Rix asked.

"I'm doing it because you're not making any sense," Judge returned.

"We like each other. She's great to be around. We have the same interests. She's fucking unbelievable in bed—"

Judge looked incredulous. "You've fucked her?"

"Like I said, we're together."

"Like, *exclusive?*"

That last word caught Rix in the throat, and he immediately turned his head to the wall that separated his office from Alex's.

They hadn't made that official, he just assumed it was understood.

The image of his sweet little fuck bunny sucking some other guy's dick assaulted his brain, and his hands clenched.

"Rix," Judge clipped.

Rix came back to the room. "What?"

"What the fuck is going on?"

"Do I need to get a whiteboard and spell it out?" Rix asked sarcastically. "We…are…together. And yes, it's fucking exclusive."

Or it would be, officially, as soon as he could get five minutes to inform Alex of that.

"So what's the drill?"

"The drill?'

Judge now seemed to be seeking patience. "You mentioned she knew the drill."

"Right," Rix murmured. "It's exclusive, but she knows I'm not looking for a relationship."

Judge stood there, staring at him.

This went on so long, Rix bit out, "*What?*"

"Don't do this," Judge said quietly.

Rix felt that in his throat too.

"Not to her," Judge went on.

"It's gonna end okay, bud. We both know our friendship is where we're gonna land, and we're gonna guard that."

"Jesus, Rix," Judge said tersely. "What's the matter with you?"

Now Rix was getting ticked. "Nothing's the matter with me."

"I'm not being a dick asking that, I honest to God want to know."

"Nothing to know since nothing's the matter with me."

"We need to talk. Tonight," Judge declared.

"I'm meeting Al's friends tonight."

"You're meeting *Al's friends?*"

"Yes," Rix ground out. "Al's friends."

"Al?"

Rix didn't respond to that.

Judge moved on.

"Tomorrow night then."

"Tomorrow, Alex and I have plans."

"Christ. Okay. This weekend."

"We're going to visit my folks this weekend."

Judge's head jerked back. "You're shitting me."

Rix stood. "Bud, this is not a big fuckin' deal. We're both adults. We've talked this through. We both know where it's at. Back off."

"Where it's at is you have your head in your ass."

Unh-hunh.

Oh yeah.

He was ticked.

"No, where it's at is you have your nose in my business."

They faced off.

It was Judge who broke it and walked to the door.

He didn't walk through it though.

He turned and said, "None of them."

"None of what?" Rix bit off.

"None of the women you fucked your way through were so meaningless, they were worth you taking your shit out on their bodies. Because there's not a single woman on this fucking earth who is meaningless."

Rix stood completely still.

"None of them were Peri," Judge continued. "Though, I figure you revenge fucking your way through Yavapai County worked, since it clearly woke her shit up."

"You need to get the fuck away from me right now, Judge, and we need some space," Rix warned.

"You lost your legs, man, you didn't lose your life. I don't know what you're trying to prove, or who you're trying to prove it to, you, Peri, the world, or all of those. But it wasn't okay you worked your shit out with anyone who would let you bang them. And it is *really* not okay you do it with Alex."

"This is not about Peri," he growled.

"You're right, it's about you," Judge shot back.

"You done?" Rix demanded.

Judge just stared at him.

"You're done," Rix whispered.

"I love you, man," Judge said firmly. "And I'm here to help any way you need."

"Yeah?" Rix asked. "You are?"

"Yeah, I am."

"Really?" Rix pushed.

Judge's head ticked and some of his cocky, know-it-all attitude slid away.

"You don't know dick, bud," Rix told him. "And there's one reason why. But you do know what *that* is."

"Rix—"

"You know who knows?'

"Rix—"

"Alex, because she fuckin' *asks*."

Judge winced.

Then he clipped, "Goddamn it, Rix—"

"You're done, get out."

"Rix—"

"Get *the fuck* out, Judge. We need space."

They faced off again.

Judge ended it again, this time with a parting shot.

"I fucked up, but you're fucking up. Stop doing it before she gets hurt."

He delivered that, and he was out the door.

But Rix felt that the deepest in his throat.

So deep, it seemed like he was choking on it.

———

"SHE'S LOST HER MIND WITH THIS WHOLE *ROGUE ONE* BULLSHIT," GAL declared. "I mean, who wants sad, hopeless *Star Wars*?"

"Word, sister," Rix agreed.

"Ugh," Alex grunted.

Rix grinned at her.

"I don't understand, why am I the only one who likes Tango?" Katie asked.

"It's the suit," Gal told her. "I don't get it, but you're a sucker for a suit."

Alex leaned into him and whispered in his ear, "It's the Italian Stallion."

"I heard that," Katie snapped. "So I like dark and built. Uhhhhhhh…"

She then swooped her hand up in front of Rix to indicate him.

Rix burst out laughing.

Alex was smiling to her friend.

Rix liked her doing that, looking happy, so he hooked her around the neck and pulled her into his side.

She relaxed into him and stayed there.

The night seemed like it was going to be a success.

Rix was glad this wasn't some trial by fire.

He was more glad Alex's friends were so fucking great.

Best of all, it was clear she loved being with them.

He should have known.

But bottom line, that was what they were. Great. Watchful at first, but nice. Then they warmed to him and they were funny all together, Katie was sweet, Gal had an edge to her that was cool.

It was all good.

And he needed that after his scene with Judge that morning.

"I'm feeling a *Big Trouble in Little China* night coming on," Gal decreed.

"We're in," Alex blurted, speaking for him.

He liked that too.

And not because that was possibly the best Kurt Russell film in history.

Gal started to say something else, then she sat bolt upright in her chair, her eyes aimed over Rix's shoulder.

He turned his head.

And shit.

Peri was standing there, eyes locked to him and Alex, face pale.

"What—?" He felt Alex shift to look too.

But he caught her eyes on the way.

"Peri," he murmured.

Her attention raced to the door, and she tensed in his hold.

"Five minutes, baby," he said.

She looked back to him, pulling from his arm and advising, "Hurry, Rix. She just rushed out."

Damn it.

He moved his gaze through the women at the table, got up and moved quickly toward the door.

He caught Peri getting in her car.

He waylaid her closing the door by putting a hand to it.

"You don't have to do this," she said to her steering wheel.

"Give me five minutes."

She looked up to him.

"I'm not feeling five minutes," she snapped.

"My intention is not to hurt you, Peri. But you had to know I'd move on."

"No, I didn't," she sniped. "Because *you* were in love with *me*. Like *married* love. Like *rest of your life* love."

She had the balls to hand him that shit?

He shook his head. "Okay, this is not why I came out here. I came out here to see if you were okay. I came out here because I didn't want you to do what you're doing, getting in your car when you're emotional. And I came out here to repeat what I told you Sunday. I have someone in my life now. We mean something to each other, and we all live in the same town. We gotta get past this."

"You mean *I* gotta get past this."

Well...

Yeah.

He didn't say that.

Her attention darted to the bar and then back to him. "She good with you rushing after me?"

"She told me to hurry because you were leaving."

Her chin slid into her neck.

Yeah, Alex being all she was was a surprise.

Though he never thought Peri would benefit from it.

He gentled his tone. "She's good for me, Peri."

"I was good for you once," she said.

"Not when I most needed it."

She looked like he'd slapped her.

But seriously?

Did she not remember when she'd walked away?

She recovered quickly. "Fuck you, Rix."

Now, that shit wasn't right.

"Peri—"

"Let go of my door."

He wasn't going to do this either.

He let go of her door and stepped back.

She slammed it and started up the car.

But he was already walking back to the bar.

He heard her pull out and then he saw her drive at a crawl by his side with her window open.

Fantastic.

He stopped.

So did she.

"Tell your buddies at the station they can go fuck themselves," she hissed.

Say what?

"What does that mean?" he asked.

"Ask them, they know. Hint for you, I didn't show up tonight out of the blue."

Ah, shit.

He pulled in a breath that expanded his chest, and let it out.

She raced away, and he hoped she didn't hurt herself or anyone else, driving like that.

He returned to the bar and did a sweep of it.

And...goddamn.

Sure as shit, there was Erin, who used to date Dylan, one of his buds in the crew at the fire department.

They'd broken up, but when it had to do with someone wronging one of their own, the tentacles of that family spread wide and didn't break.

No surprise, since she orchestrated it, Erin hadn't missed what had gone down. And when he caught her eyes, she smiled huge at him.

Considering what she did was loyal, but uncool, he tipped his head to the side to acknowledge her smile and that was it.

Rix resumed his seat, and again no surprise, the fun-night-out vibe had vanished.

"You okay?" Alex asked.

"Yup," he answered, reaching two ways. One for his beer, the other for her.

He took a sip and installed her where she was before Peri showed.

"She okay?" she asked.

"Nope," he answered.

They were all quiet.

Great.

That was when Gal shocked the shit out of him.

"I hope this sopping wet blanket isn't messing up my hair," she joked.

Katie giggled.

Alex gave him more weight.

"So, you know, all good," Gal bizarrely declared in Rix's direction. "There was a drama, and it's over. But on the bright side, practice for you when Alex gets you to the Big Apple and Blake is on the bridezilla warpath."

"I keep having dreams of her growing to the size of a skyscraper, wearing a wedding gown, and laying waste to Manhattan because one of the boutonnieres drooped," Katie shared.

"If she's the size of a skyscraper, I wanna go to this wedding, because can you imagine the size of the cake?" Gal asked.

Those two busted a gut laughing, with Alex in her way joining in. She was quietly chuckling.

Right.

Wait.

That was it?

No filthy looks or lingering stares or any other bullshit because his ex showing interrupted their evening?

This was not his experience with Peri's friends. Even if the situation had been out of his control, like this one, they'd find a way to make their feelings known about it.

"So," Katie started when she'd quieted down, aiming this Rix's way, "we've never met them. Alex's family. I'm still having nightmares."

"Do you have a hat for this crazy tea?" Gal asked Alex.

"No," was Alex's fortunate reply.

"Bummer," Gal muttered. "I think you should wear one so huge, it takes up three seats."

"Helena would have a hissy fit," Katie noted.

"Helena can go jump in a lake. Who does tea? We're in America, for God's sake," Gal replied.

Rix grunted his agreement.

"See?" Gal pointed at him. "Rix agrees with me."

"I didn't disagree," Katie pointed out.

"Americans do tea," Alex put in.

"Not with hats. With ice and lots of sugar," Gal retorted.

Rix started laughing.

Katie did too.

And Alex did too.

Yeah.

He settled in with his girl and a sip of beer.

Because Alex's friends were the shit.

RIX DRILLED INTO HER.

"This is mine, hey?" he growled.

"Yes, Rix," she gasped into the bed.

He sensed she didn't get him.

He slid in, stayed in, and bent over her, his cock snug inside, her ass snug to his crotch since they were both on their knees.

"Pay attention, baby. I mean it. Exclusive. Mine."

She turned her head as best she could and looked at him.

Now she got him.

"Okay, honey," she whispered.

He slid out and back in.

"That's yours," he told her.

"Yes," she breathed.

Yes.

Rix took hold of her and fell to his back, taking her with him so she was on top, bent slightly forward, which was perfect.

It was the first time since they took his legs he positioned his partner into a reverse cowgirl.

He didn't notice.

He grabbed two handfuls of a sweet, round ass, one thumb tracing her crease, and ordered, "Bounce, sweetheart."

Alex bounced.

Rix squeezed and flirted with her hole.

She bounced faster.

She bounced until she took herself there.

And she bounced until she took him there.

He cleaned her up, and they passed out in her bed.

But in the middle of the night, Alex woke him up, slipping his dick in her mouth.

He grinned into the dark.

His little mountain fuck bunny.

Rix threaded his fingers in her hair, opened what was left of his legs.

And enjoyed it.

CHAPTER 15

THE TABLE

.

Judge

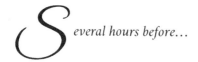

S everal hours before…

"You are not my sidekick anymore, *mon beau*," Chloe said before she clicked her tongue.

"I was never your sidekick," he replied on a sigh. "And you cannot say Rix didn't deserve someone getting up in his shit."

"My darling, beautiful man," she purred, "our job was to get them together, *et voilà*." To make her point, her eyes did not slide to Duncan and Genny, who were sitting at the table with them, mostly because her dad, Tom, was too. Nevertheless, her point was made. "It's then they do the rest."

"He needed Judge up in his shit," Tom entered the conversation.

"Yeah, he did," Duncan concurred.

Since her dad was up from Phoenix, Chloe's family was over for dinner. But when Judge got home from work, he was still stinging from his convo with his friend.

Chloe didn't miss it, and even if it might not have been good to share the full details with all of them, he was so pissed at Rix, he didn't care.

Chloe turned to her mom. "*Motherrrr*, explain to these men."

"Chloe's right," Genny decreed.

Judge stared at her in surprise.

Chloe was…Chloe.

Genny was mature and level-headed.

"Gen, she's not," Tom said to his ex-wife. Then to his daughter, "Sorry, honey, but you're not."

"She really isn't, baby," Duncan murmured to Genny.

"Okay," Genny started, "this is how it's going to go. Rix is going to tell himself that he can have this. And when it spooks him, though he won't be admitting that to himself, but deep down, he knows that's what it is, he'll think it'll be okay. They'll still be friends. He's going to keep doing that. And he's going to do it *while he's spending time with Alex.* Therefore, while they spend time together, they'll get to know one another and build what they're building. Then, one of two things will happen. He'll get his head straight, and all will be well. Or he'll lose her, and he'll stop at nothing to get her back. Then, as Chloe said, *et voilà.*"

"And what if his stubborn ass doesn't see the light?" Judge inquired.

Genny looked right at him, her expression gentle. "Then, Judge, I love Rix. He's a good man. Loyal friend. Funny. He feels like a member of the family. It's clear he's struggling with some things after what happened to him, and that breaks my heart. But he's neither stupid nor a fool. If he's that stubborn that he lets a good woman slip through his fingers, he not only deserves to lose her, she might be better off."

Judge shut his mouth.

Chloe smirked, but she also reached under the table to squeeze his knee.

"And then *that* will be when you get in his shit," Genny concluded.

"Mm-hmm," Chloe agreed.

"Wanna talk about the heavy he laid on you?" Duncan asked, and Judge gave him his attention.

He didn't want to.

But he did.

"I let him down," Judge admitted.

Chloe exchanged a glance with her mother, but said nothing.

Then again, months ago, she'd told him to ask.

Express interest.

She'd explained he'd never know what life was like for his friend, but he should communicate to Rix that he gave a shit.

He'd not done that.

Duncan nor Tom refuted him that Judge had let Rix down.

There you go.

He'd let Rix down.

But Rix had dropped everything to go to Texas with him when Judge's mother died.

And then Rix, with Chloe, Dru, and Judge's dad, had stayed glued to his side as he processed the addiction and dysfunction and fucked-up history that had been his relationship with his mom.

Now, Rix had lost his legs, and Judge had stood up for him to help him get a job in Duncan's store.

Other than that?

He'd been there.

But it was obvious he hadn't been there like Rix needed.

"Does he keep in touch with the men at the station?" Duncan asked.

"He talks about them, so I know he hasn't cut them out. But I don't think he stops in. And it's usually occasions that he goes to, not out to grab drink or something. Graduations. Weddings. Shit like that."

"Do they reach out?" Genny asked.

"I have no idea," Judge muttered.

And shit yeah.

He'd let Rix down.

Chloe gave up on his knee and took his hand.

Tom remarked, "It's never too late to be a good friend."

Judge gave Tom a nod, but said, "Rix is right, we need space. What happened today was ugly. We both gotta give that time to settle, put it behind us and move on."

Chloe's hand squeezed his.

"Then give him space, Judge," Tom said. "But also, when the time is right, stop doing it. My take, you've been doing that for a while, and he isn't real happy about it."

It hadn't taken him long to realize why Chloe was as incredible as she was.

And now, all of it was sitting at his table.

Judge nodded again.

"I need more wine, Mom, you need more wine?" Chloe asked, he knew, because she knew he wasn't enjoying this conversation.

And pure Chloe, she allowed it long enough he got what he needed.

Then she put an end to it.

"I could use more wine," Genny answered.

That was when three chairs pushed back.

"*Notre chevaliers*," Chloe murmured.

"Hmm," Genny hummed smugly into the last few sips of her glass.

The men decided nonverbally who'd go get the wine.

Then Judge went and grabbed another bottle.

CHAPTER 16

THE VISIT

Alex

I sat next to Rix as he drove us up to Flagstaff, trying to hold on to how I'd been feeling, happy to chat while I watched the scenery sliding by.

But we were nearly in Flag.

Which meant closer to meeting his parents.

Which meant I was getting nervous.

The drive had started out fun.

It wasn't the first time I'd been in his truck with Rix driving, but this time, I asked him to show me how the hand controls worked.

He did, and it was cool, something I told him.

I also told him it was even cooler how good he was at it.

"Gotta admit, babe, it isn't second nature yet. I still instinctively wanna use my feet."

I got that.

But it made sense he couldn't after he explained that, no matter how state-of-the-art his legs were, the loss of the touch factor, that sensitivity, made it not safe for him to use his feet.

And we'd had that discussion too, about how state-of-the-art his

legs were, how much he could do on them, but how they had limita-
tions. We'd talked about this last night on his deck, both of us on the
cushion on his bench seat, me between those legs, my back to his
chest, his arms around me, both of us staring at the stars, my favorite
place to be—and now that included being under them with Rix.

While we were discussing his driving, he shared, "I've read up on a
lot of shit, including what they're doing with bionics, and I don't
know. When you're like me, you don't want your hopes up about this
kinda thing, but they're making some serious advances. Less than
twenty years ago, we didn't have a fully functional artificial heart.
Now we do. Cochlear implants. Prostheses with sensory feedback. It's
some serious cool shit."

"Your legs as they are are pretty awesome, though," I told him.

His head ticked, then he grinned. "Good insurance, and a mom
having a mouth on her, I got top of the line."

Regardless of his grin and the outcome, that upset me. "They tried
to short you?"

"Insurance will do what they can to pay as little as they can for
what you need."

"But your mom stepped in?"

"You know that famous scene with Shirley MacLaine at the
hospital in *Terms of Endearment*?"

Sensing what was coming, I started laughing. "Yes."

"Child's play."

I kept laughing.

But I was happy for him.

Not that his mom had to step up. Not that she had to go through
that, or he did.

But that he had someone who did that for him.

We talked more about his legs, his rehab, how awesome his physical and occupational therapists were.

And why, recently, he seemed to be using his legs with greater
frequency.

"I need to get more used to 'em, babe. They're life. Gotta admit,
I've been a little lazy with that. But also, I met this chick. Beautiful

eyes, great head of hair, tight pussy. She's active, and I need to keep up with her."

That made my belly flutter, my clit tingle, my cheeks get warm, and again, I laughed.

I'd also leaned across to him and kissed his bristly jaw.

After I did that, I didn't pull fully away before I stroked it.

"Shoulda shaved," he muttered as I did.

I stopped stroking but still didn't pull away. "Your mom likes you clean-shaven?"

"She likes me, she doesn't care about my beard." He glanced at me. "Do you like a man shaved?"

I sat back and looked at the road, saying, "I like you."

He reached out and trailed a finger down my upper arm then put his hand back to the wheel.

So yeah, all good.

But we were now on the outskirts of Flagstaff, and very close to me meeting people who thought I was "perfect" for Rix.

Therefore, obviously, I needed to be perfect for Rix.

The problem with that was, I was a long way from perfect.

"Babe," Rix called.

"Yes?" I answered the landscape.

"What's on your mind?"

A lot was on my mind.

I'd only met the parents of one boyfriend, for one.

For another, that was because I'd only had one longish term boyfriend (and that term lasted only four months before we broke up, so that wasn't long-term at all).

And that boyfriend's parents weren't real keen on me. It was clear they thought me strange, removed, too reserved and not easy to be around.

Rix had experience with women. He'd been engaged. I suspected his parents met a lot more girlfriends than just Peri.

And now I'd seen Peri.

Sports Illustrated supermodel she was.

One hundred percent.

I didn't know why I didn't want to share any of this with Rix.

I just didn't.

So I lied, "Nothing."

Rix made no reply at first.

Then he said, "We never talked about it."

I turned to look at him. "Talked about what?"

"That thing with Peri the other night."

"Rix—"

"You told me to go, but were you okay with me going?"

I was confused. "Going?"

"Out to talk to her."

I was still confused.

"Well, yeah. Like you said, I told you to go."

"Baby, I don't want you to think on that, let it fester, get the wrong idea. I didn't go after her because of her. I went after her because Peri can be about drama, and drama behind a wheel is not a good thing. And because that had to be rough for her, and how she found out about us wasn't cool. Though, most of it was because it isn't her right to throw a drama. I don't need to deal with her pitching one whenever she sees me or us, and you definitely don't need to deal with it. She has to settle into the fact you and me are something, we're going to run into each other, and that's just what it is."

You and me are something.

"But I wouldn't have gone if you weren't okay with it," he finished.

"I was okay with it, Rix."

"You should know, she wasn't there as a coincidence."

Oh God.

Did Chloe—?

"Erin, the ex of one of my buddies at the department saw us, she also probably saw that Elsa Cohen thing. I called Dylan, her old boyfriend, yesterday. And he admitted Erin phoned him and they hatched a plot to get word to Peri I was there, alone, looking like I needed company."

Okay, I was not a Peri fan.

But that was harsh.

I mean, of course, I suspected Chloe of conniving much the same thing.

But the whole "looking like he needed company" was below the belt.

"Yikes," I mumbled.

"Unh-hunh," he agreed.

"Outside the fact she's gorgeous, I really don't have an issue with it, Rix. I haven't actually even thought about it."

"What does her being gorgeous have to do with it?"

I'd been looking at him.

Now I was staring at him.

Then I pointed out, "She's really gorgeous."

Another glance at me and then, "Yes, she's a good-looking woman."

"A *very* good-looking woman."

Rix stared at the road.

I stared at the road.

When he spoke again, it was soft. "You know I thought you had a problem with me being disabled."

I had no idea why he was bringing that up, but I confirmed, "Yes. I know."

"It annoyed me."

"I know that too."

"Because of that, I didn't see you."

I said nothing.

"I see you now, sweetheart."

I turned my head to look out the side window.

"Fuck, baby, look at me," he growled.

I turned to him. "I know you're into me, Rix."

"Are you paying attention?" he asked.

"Yes, which is how I know you're into me."

"I went after Peri because she can be about drama."

"You said."

"And after I got back, I was shocked as shit, because you and your friends knew what that was, it wasn't about me, or you, it was about Peri, and they just moved past it."

"I was there, Rix," I reminded him.

"Peri's friends wouldn't do that."

"Okay."

"Like attracts like."

Oh.

I shut my mouth.

I'd caught his point, but he kept going.

"Another example, obviously that shit with me going after her isn't festering for you. Peri let shit fester. I never knew when something I said or did or something that happened the week before or three months before would rear up and bite me in the ass."

Ulk.

That had to be no fun.

"That stinks," I muttered.

"Yeah. It was really no fun," he agreed.

I had to say, I was beginning to feel a whole heck of a lot better about where Rix was at with Peri.

Rix wasn't done.

"I'm willing to do the work to get you past whatever shit whoever in your life put in your head that you're not all that. But you're all that, Alexandra. I get that it'll take time, this isn't a telling thing, it's a showing thing. But you gotta pay attention as that goes down and let it sink in. Straight up, there isn't a soul on this planet who is beautiful outside who isn't beautiful inside. You can't be truly beautiful unless you got that in you. But you are both."

"Okay, honey," I whispered, my heart hammering in my chest.

"Okay," he grunted.

"It wasn't that," I told him.

"What?"

"You're tuned to me. You knew something was on my mind. And it isn't Peri. It's that I'm nervous about meeting your parents."

He reached out, took my hand, brought it to his thigh, and left it there before he returned to the steering wheel.

"They're good people. Friendly. And they already dig you," he assured.

"I've never really had a serious relationship."

That bought me another quick glance. "No shit?"

"No shit."

"Bashful," he murmured, but there was a nuance to that word that was almost a purr, so I felt that word trail across the small of my back.

I ignored the sensation at my back and said, "Something like that. Outside of guys in high school, which don't count, because that wasn't anything real, I've only met one boyfriend's parents. And they weren't that fond of me."

Another glance, this time with brows furrowed. "Why the fuck not?"

He wasn't dim, but that was a silly question.

"Because I'm not chatty and animated? Bubbly and googly-eyed?"

Brow furrow gone, now he was amused.

"Googly-eyed?"

"You know what I mean," I huffed, moving my stare out the windshield.

"My mom would puke at googly-eyed."

That was good.

"My dad talks enough, he won't even notice you don't do it much. Then again, he talks so much, you won't get a chance to do it."

Well, that was a relief.

"All right."

He squeezed my hand on his thigh and released it.

"Babe, chill. It's gonna be good."

"Okay."

"Really."

"I hear you."

"We'll just say, they both like Kurt Russell. Why do you think I'm a fan?"

That made a surprised laugh escape me.

"Well then, we have common ground," I joked.

He wasn't joking, his voice was low when he replied, "You totally do."

Mm.

"And they have good taste," I added.

"Yup, and *I* totally do."

Oh my.

"You're really going to have to stop being so awesome or we're going to have to take a side trip somewhere private so I can blow you to show my appreciation," I warned.

"Fuckin' hell, now I gotta fight wood before I see my parents."

"Now you know how I feel when you're being awesome."

"Make no mistake, beautiful, I pretty much am fighting wood anytime I look at you," pause, then, "or think of you."

I rolled my eyes. "Don't exaggerate."

He moved my hand.

Oh my.

He moved it again, to *my* thigh.

"Let's get there safe so I don't have to explain a hard-on to paramedics," he suggested.

At that, I busted out laughing.

I also felt tons better.

And such was Rix's magic, I continued to feel this way after we hit Flagstaff proper, then eventually entered an older, established neighborhood that sat among a ton of trees, the lots very large, most of the landscaping entirely natural, so it was really beautiful.

Rix pulled into a long, windy, paved drive at the end of which had a lovely large home built of wood and stone, with green trim and a matching garage door.

I was good through that too.

Through him parking alongside a big, white Range Rover.

Through me jumping out after he did.

It all fell apart when the front door opened and people piled out.

The rundown:

Rix's mom?

Ex-*Sports Illustrated* supermodel.

Rix's dad?

Rix, thirty-some years ago.

Rix's brother?

Rix, except with some of his mom's more refined features, not his dad's fully rugged ones.

Rix's sister-in-law?

Totally cover material.

Seeing Hailey's easy-breezy chic in dark jeans, a cream, double-pocket shirt, a fantastic belt and high-heeled booties, I mentally scanned my outfit.

Nice jeans with purposeful fading. Ivory shell with lace trim. Long, pink cardigan. Rosy-taupe, suede, low-heeled booties with a smart leather tote in almost the same shade. Drop necklace ending in a marbly, polished, pink-and-brown stone and a gold tassel. And it was the plain truth, I had on kickass shades.

I still didn't stand a chance.

This vanished from my mind as I was suddenly colliding with Rix's side, my shoulder slamming into him and remaining wedged there as he clamped on to me.

What on...?

I didn't ask.

His entire family was heading our way, and each and every one of them had a reaction to Rix claiming me almost violently.

Head jerks. Stutter steps. Widened eyes.

Rix moved us forward in our nearly fused-together state, and we all met in the middle.

His dad got there first.

"Son," he greeted hesitantly.

"Dad. Mom. Josh. Hails," Rix grunted.

I looked up at him, now shocked by his ominous tone.

His arm tightened, and I feared he might dislocate my shoulder.

He also kept talking.

"This is Alexandra. She's shy. She doesn't talk much. She can get uncomfortable around people she doesn't know, until she's comfortable around them. So be cool with her."

The last was voiced almost like a threat.

"You want to, I don't know, give them hugs or something first, honey?" I suggested. "That is, before you go into detail about the consequences of your family not being nice to me when you just told me in the truck how nice your family will be because they're nice."

He looked down at me. "I just don't want you uncomfortable."

"I'm not sure this was the way to go," I remarked.

"We lay it out in my family," he explained.

"I'm getting that," I replied.

"You were worried in the truck," he reminded me.

"I don't know, but I might be more worried now," I returned.

He scowled at me.

I rolled my eyes and turned to his family, sticking up my hand at random to whoever wanted to take it, and stated, "Hi, I'm Alex, and it probably comes as no surprise your son-slash-brother is overprotective. I'd appreciate it if you could just ignore his intro and stick with mine."

No one said a word.

No one moved.

Then Hailey snorted.

Which caused Mr. Hendrix to guffaw.

That led to Josh chuckling.

And Mrs. Hendrix moved forward, taking my hand.

"Alex, so nice to meet you," she said, not gushy or anything, just real.

"You too. Rix has talked a lot about you," I told her.

"Lord help me, I don't want to know what he said," she replied.

"It's all good," I promised.

"You can let her go, son, we won't release the hounds," his dad promised.

Reluctantly, Rix let me go.

He gave and received hugs (and through this, I got to watch a heartwarming Hendrix Show when his dad's hug went on a long time, his hug with his brother ended in a long, loving moment of eye contact, and Rix not only kissed the side of his mom's head, he did the same with Hailey).

I got introductions (his dad, whose first name was Garrison, told me to call him Gare, his mom, with whom I shared a name, though mine was my middle one, told me to call her Mags).

Then Josh asked his brother, "Do you want to go in first? Do a walkthrough? Make sure we haven't laid any traps?"

"Fuck off," Rix muttered, claiming me again, but a lot less aggressively.

"Language," Mags snapped.

"Where's Kins?" Rix ignored his mom to ask Josh as we moved to the house.

"Napping."

Rix then turned his attention to his mother and promptly communicated he wasn't over it.

"You couldn't have had just the two of you to start? You had to call Joshua and Hails here?"

"Rix!" I chided.

"What?" he asked me as we shuffled into his family's home, still attached. "It's a valid question. Your friends didn't trial-by-fire me. My family doesn't need to pull that shit with you."

"John Hendrix," his mother clipped. "*Language*."

"Mom, I'm thirty-four years old, give it up," Rix returned.

"Ohmigod," I breathed as it dawned on me. "You're the baby boy who gets away with everything."

Rix was unfazed by this. "Well, yeah."

"And...*yeah*," Josh confirmed. "And I have a million and five stories to illustrate that."

"Like you were the perfect son," Rix scoffed.

"I had to put the effort into not getting caught," Josh returned. "You didn't give a shit you got caught because you knew you could get away with anything."

We were all heading toward the kitchen, but Mags had already made it there, and she was addressing the ceiling.

"Lord God, you have my devotion. You've given me great bounty. I'm grateful, so I don't ask much. But can you please send a message down to my sons that they are to respect their mother in her own home by cleaning up their mouths? I'll accept a lightning bolt."

Hailey laughed softly.

I caught her eyes as I did the same.

"Sweetheart, they're boys," for some reason Gare pointed out the obvious.

"And this is why they don't respect their mother," Mags shot back. "You and that tired excuse of 'they're boys.'" She turned to me and Hailey, who was standing beside me. "Foul mouths? It is what it is. They're boys. Totaled car? No big deal. They're boys. Eight hundred dollars for hockey skates, *times two*? We must. They're boys. Girl's panties in *my* laundry that *were not mine*? It comes with the territory. *They're boys.*"

"Those panties had nothing to do with me," Rix said, too fast.

"Horseshit," Josh returned. "For fuck's sake, Rix, cut that crap. My wife is standing right there."

Hailey stuck her arm through mine and announced, "I feel like day drinking." She looked down at me. "Do you feel like day drinking?"

It was barely nine o'clock.

"Mimosas!" Mags nearly shouted.

"Let's do it," Hailey agreed, pulling me toward Mags and away from Rix.

I looked back at him.

He was glowering at Hailey's back like he feared she was about to rush me into a windowless van, and then I'd disappear.

When his eyes came to me, I mouthed *I'm okay.*

He jerked up his chin.

Hailey pulled me to a massive kitchen island from under which Mags was unearthing champagne from a wine fridge while Hailey let me go and went to the fridge-fridge to extract a plethora of fruit juices.

"Okay, this is the plan," Mags started. "We're ignoring them for at least half an hour. Maybe forty-five minutes. I think my blood pressure will even out by then. In the meantime, Elsa had some pix of you on her show today. Do you really know Harry?"

Damn.

I knew it.

Elsa wasn't done with us.

And she'd gone searching.

I shot Rix a warning, *don't intervene* look.

He scowled again but kept his mouth shut.

Then I answered his mother. "Yes."

"Good Lord," she breathed. "Is he as sweet as he seems?"

"Yes."

"That...is...*the*...coolest," Hailey declared.

"All right, let's get serious," Mags ordered. "Cranberry? Orange? Or pomegranate?"

"Pomegranate for me," I put in my order.

"Me too!" Hailey cried excitedly, like that meant we were blood sisters reunited.

I was seeing I was going to like Hailey.

I shot her a smile.

She returned it.

"Me as well," Mags stated. "Hails, put the others back. Alex, do me a favor, honey, and go grab the glasses. They're over there."

I went to where she indicated and grabbed the glasses.

I glanced at Rix while Mags mixed, and saw he was in a man huddle with his brother and father, but his gaze was on me.

I let my lips tip up.

He winked.

Okay.

There we were.

Boyfriend Bear Rix was standing down.

It was all good.

"He's been on them all day," Hailey said, so low, I knew I wasn't supposed to hear her.

"Mm," Mags replied in a way that it was both agreement, and a warning not to talk about it.

We were out back at the dining table on their deck.

We'd just had a dinner of marinated chicken breasts that Gare had grilled, corn on the cob and a pasta salad that Mags had already given me the recipe for.

The women were drinking wine, enjoying a cool evening post-food.

The men were in the yard, for no reason it seemed except they were men, and they felt more comfortable among trees, standing in the grass.

Rix had dark-haired, blue-eyed, adorable Kinsley curled in one of his arms. She was pretty much asleep, her chubby cheek on his shoulder and her dimpled hand on his neck.

They'd also pretty much been inseparable since she woke up, except for when she took another nap.

He'd even fed her.

All five times that had to happen.

Not so by the way…

It…

Was…

Insanely…

Beautiful.

"Did you know Rix before?" I asked Hailey.

Both women swung eyes to me.

"Pardon?" Hailey asked in return.

I clarified my question. "Before Rix lost his legs, did you know him?"

This question seemed to shock both of them for some reason, but Hailey recovered first.

"Josh and I were supposed to get married around the ti—"

Mags made a noise that was part clearing her throat, the rest was definitely a *shut up.*

But what Hailey said made me sad. "You had to postpone?"

"Rix was, um…Josh's best man. And Josh wouldn't…" she paused and finished, "So, yes."

Then she said no more.

But she didn't need to say more.

Even though that had to add to the heartbreak they were all experiencing, and it had to be a lot of work in reorganizing, in that moment I loved Josh with all my heart that he wouldn't get married without his brother.

"Well, I'm glad it finally happened," I told her. "And yes, he's up on them more. He told me he was being lazy, but he's barely using his chair at all these days."

Both women stared at me.

It was Hailey who asked, "He told you he was being lazy?"

I nodded. "But thinking about it, I think it was that his work at the store was more physical. In the office, there isn't that much needing to get around. He's far from lazy. Since I knew him, and he was just back into life after rehab when I met him, he's been fit and active."

"The pictures on the Elsa Exchange, he seemed to be very active," Mags murmured.

"Yes, he is," I verified. "He's up even before me if there's a hike to be taken, and I'm an avid hiker."

"Oh," Mags said softly. Then she asked, "Is there pain?"

"Sorry?"

"Being up so often on them, is he in pain?'

I shook my head but said, "I don't think so, but you know he wouldn't tell me. He doesn't complain. He just gets on with it."

Though, I made a mental note to ask him.

"Right, but he tells you other things. Like he's been being lazy," Mags remarked.

I looked her in the eye and said, "Yes." When she didn't look away, as kindly as I could, I finished, "Because I ask."

That was when she looked away.

Hailey was studying her wineglass.

Me?

I was getting angry.

"He talks about it. He likes to talk about it. It's his life," I pointed out.

Both women looked back to me.

"Okay, maybe he doesn't *like* to talk about it," I allowed. "But he has

no problem doing it, and it *is* his life. Anyone wants to share important things about their life with people they love."

"People they love," Mags parroted.

"Yes," I stated.

Mags and Hailey exchanged a glance.

After it was over, Hailey began smiling at her wineglass.

"You understand, there isn't a manual about this kind of thing,
how to deal with it on our end, when something like that happens to
someone you love," Mags told the yard, precisely where the men were
standing in it.

"No, I don't understand," I said quietly, and she turned back to me.
"I'm not a mom. I wasn't around when it happened to him. I'm lucky.
He'd been through the grueling part when I met him. I just get him
now. Rix, awesome guy, funny guy, handsome guy, active guy, who
also happens to have lost his legs."

"I see you took to heart Rix telling you we lay it out," Mags noted.

I shifted in my seat, thinking, even if everything I said was true
and honest, although the day had gone really well, I liked these people
and they seemed to like me, I'd just blown it.

"No, Alex, he's right. We do. And I needed to hear that," Mags
assured me.

"He told me you got him his legs," I mentioned.

"Assholes were trying to foist some junk on him," Mags groused,
and Hailey snorted again, this time into her wine, doing this no doubt
because Mags just cursed (and yes, that theme had continued, seeing
as both Hendrix brothers, and occasionally their father, did not shy
away from swear words).

Hailey recovered and told me, "Seriously, Alex, *the worst*. Nickle
and diming every freaking thing. It was disgusting."

"I'll tell you, I was never a proponent of socialized medicine,
until that happened to my boy," Mags declared. "We had to fight
tooth and nail for every little thing. Staff, awesome. Every one of
them, angels. The suits, an army of Satan. And we saw it. Some folks
going home early, far too soon, needing help and support and care,
but shuffled out the door because their insurance ran out or they

couldn't afford it. Then other folks getting top of the line everything."

"It was gross," Hailey piped in.

"It was. *Gross*," Mags firmly agreed, turning back to the yard.

"I'm sorry," I mumbled.

"Don't be sorry," Mags ordered, eyes to her son. "Life tests us. We all get different ones. This is one of his. And look at him. There's nothing to be sorry for. When it comes to my son, all I feel is pride."

"Oh my God, I'm gonna cry," Hailey whispered.

But I was studying my wineglass.

"Alex?"

I swallowed, sniffed, blinked a couple of times and looked at Mags.

Her face grew soft.

"He's the most wonderful man I've ever met," I blurted.

Her response was immediate.

"I'm not surprised."

Then she grinned at me.

I returned it.

RIX WAS SHOWING.

Not telling.

He was doing that lying in bed with me with his head on my midriff, drawing randomly on my stomach, sometimes kissing it, sometimes nipping it, once running the tip of his tongue around my belly button.

Mags and Gare's friends' cabin being occupied, we were in the basement.

Considering the fact that the basement room was the guest bedroom, complete with full bath, and one end of it opened out to a secluded patio that was cut into the earth, I wondered why we'd ever sleep in his bedroom, which clearly and hilariously had not changed since he left it.

Yes.

Ice hockey and lacrosse trophies.

Yes.

Rage Against the Machine and Limp Bizkit posters.

"His mother took posters with the girls on them down," Gare whispered to me.

I bet she did.

And yes.

An entire wall made of dark corkboard with push-pinned pieces of life: movie stubs, concert tickets, lift tickets, strips of photo booth pictures, bumper stickers, and a carefully spread and tacked Nirvana tee.

"Can we all stop standing in here now?" Rix had asked, and I had to admit, all of us standing in there *was* a little weird.

Almost as weird as that room being preserved like it was.

"It's like a shrine to you," I replied.

"Of course it is," Mags said breezily. "Josh has one too. Kinsley naps in there, her father all around her." She aimed a steady look at me, as if I'd dare contradict her (which I would not). "The grandbabies Rix gives me will do the same in this room."

"That's sweet," I commented, and it was (in a weird way). "And it's never too early to start appreciating Rage Against the Machine."

At that point, Rix hooked his arm around my neck, and leading me out of the room, said to Josh, "I win."

To which Hailey snapped, "For the last time, there is nothing wrong with N Sync!"

Everyone laughed.

Though, Hailey didn't.

Now was now. Josh and his family off home. We were doing brunch at their place tomorrow, and I was interested to see the house Hailey made with Rix's brother.

I was a lot more like Mags than she was. Mags wasn't shy, she was forthright and funny, but also down to earth. Hailey was a bit higher strung, not in a bad sense. She was just more openly emotional.

But Hailey was a doll, and the way she was, with Josh, they'd probably made a lovely, albeit, I suspected, a lot more feminine home.

Rix's mom and dad's house was very attractive.

But it wasn't lost on me that, if Mags ever had the urge, living with three men, she'd given it up long ago.

Mags and Gare's space was welcoming, lived in, sturdy and no nonsense.

I felt very comfortable there.

Best of all was how laidback and mellow Rix was in the house where he grew up.

He was definitely *home*, and I loved watching him in that element.

With his family.

"You're cute with Kinsley," I said softly, tracing the wing of his phoenix on his back.

He kissed my stomach then shifted so he could turn to look up at me, and now he was resting his head right on my tummy.

"I'm not cute with her. I'm communicating to her I'm the man who will rip the head off anyone who messes with her."

"Oh, is that what you were doing when you were shoving fruit in her mouth and babytalking her?"

"Yup. That was what I was doing."

"Not sure how I missed that," I mumbled.

"Get with the program," he returned. "And I don't babytalk. She and I have our own language."

"That includes you only saying things to her like, 'Look what a good girl you are,' and 'Is there a more beautiful girl in the world? Don't answer that. No. There isn't.'"

He lifted his brows. "Did I lie in any of that?"

I shook my head, because no, he didn't.

"No, I did not," he muttered, his hand finding mine, then his fingers threading through my own.

I watched his long fingers curl over the back of my hand, my feeling-lazy self starting to feel even lazier, and whispered, "They were worried about you being on your legs all day. Your mom is concerned about pain."

He stroked the back of my hand with his thumb and asked, "They talked to you about that?"

I didn't correct him that I talked to them about it.

I said, "Yes."

"No pain, sweetheart."

"Okay," I whispered.

He caught my gaze. "So you can stop worrying about it too."

I twitched my nose at him.

He brought our hands to his mouth and kissed mine.

I shared, "Your family is great."

"You have anybody?"

I felt my brows draw together. "Sorry?"

"There was your Grandmother Brooke, but she passed. Did you have anybody else?"

"I wasn't lonely."

"That isn't what I asked."

I pressed my lips together.

Rix watched.

Then he murmured, "Right."

"I have people now," I reminded him.

"Yeah you do," he replied.

Yes, I did.

I lifted his hand to my mouth and kissed his knuckles.

Rix turned his head and kissed my stomach again.

Then he didn't move. He moved me. Letting my hand go. Grasping my hips. Yanking me around. Tugging my panties off. Tossing my legs over his shoulders.

He dipped in.

My head pressed into the bed, I wrapped a calf around his head, the other heel I dug into the small of his back.

He finished me off fingering me while kissing me.

I finished him off by swallowing.

He pulled his sleep pants up while I put my panties on and tugged down my nightie.

He tucked us together, his thigh between my legs.

I would have no way of knowing that, except with me, he hadn't spent the night with a single woman since Peri.

But under no circumstances would he even part a woman's legs with his own.

I was blissfully unaware of this.

I was just blissful.

I would get more blissful with Rix.

This would last for a while.

But it wouldn't last.

Things like that never did.

CHAPTER 17

THE SHIFTING

Rix

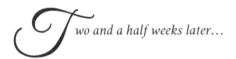wo and a half weeks later…

RIX WAS PACKING THEIR GEAR IN THE BACK OF HIS TRUCK.

He and Alex had taken a couple of days off.

They were heading north to a hot springs outside Ouray.

She had single-person gear.

He'd had double-person gear.

But the day before, even if it was a waste of money, since his stuff· was in excellent shape, he'd listed it all on Craig's List and gone to River Rain to buy a new two-person tent and sleeping bag.

He'd bought top of the line.

His old ones, he'd slept in with Peri. Fucked Peri in.

Alex wasn't getting anywhere near them.

He was shoving a cooler in the back seat of his cab when he heard the car pull up.

It was a red Evoque.

Chloe.

Fuck.

He knew what had her there, catching him at that hour in the morning.

Yesterday, he'd doubled up on what he'd been doing back and forth between the two of them for weeks.

He'd ignored a text from Chloe, and turned down an invite to dinner from Judge.

She pulled right into his drive, blocking him in, and got out.

It wasn't yet six-thirty in the morning.

She looked like she'd stepped out of a magazine spread.

"I hope you appreciate the effort," she said instead of hello. "I am *never* up this early if I can help it."

"Hey there, Coco. Good to see you too," he replied.

She halted a few feet away and ordered, "Stop it, Rix, and I mean that in more than one way."

Well, goddamn.

"Chlo—"

"He's asked you to lunch three times. Over to the house for dinner four times. And I've sent you five texts, and not a single one of them you deigned to respond to."

"Judge and me need space."

"He gave you space. Now, he misses his friend."

Rix clenched his teeth.

"He loves you. And once, just *once*, he was brutally honest with you. That's what you want, and you're punishing him for it?"

"He said shit that was not okay."

"Like what, Rix?"

"That's between him and me." He lifted a hand and shook his head. "I get it. I know he gave it all to you." He dropped his hand. "I'm glad he's got you. You listened to his side and you got his back. It's the way it should be. But that doesn't mean there's not another side."

"Okay, then talk to him about it."

Rix shook his head again.

"You work together," she bit out. Then she went in for the kill. "And this is hurting him."

"I'll get over it and I'll talk to him about it. That time is just not now."

She glanced at his truck then back to him. "And what is it time for now?"

"You're here, catching me at this hour in the morning, you know what this is the time for. He's my boss too, and I had to ask for the time off."

"*He* did indeed tell me you were off with Alexandra for a long weekend."

"Yup," Rix confirmed.

She said nothing.

This lasted too long.

But this was Chloe, and as much as he needed space from Judge, Chloe was something else.

They'd been brother-and-sister-in-arms once, flanking Judge who was waging war with his own emotions.

You share that kind of shit with someone, the bond goes deep.

More, she was the woman who was making his best friend happy.

So Rix would cut off another limb before he'd even come close to disrespecting her.

Her gaze was warm, her tone concerned, when she said, "I hope you know what you're doing, Rix."

"I do," he replied.

She let the perfect beat pass before she whispered, "With all of it."

Then she turned, strutted back to her Evoque, climbed in and took off.

Rix finished packing up, made sure everything was secure, and headed up to Groom Creek.

He'd been looking forward to this.

Preparing the food in the morning and putting it on hot stones so they'd have a kickass meal at night.

Sitting under the stars, sipping bourbon, getting steadily drunk and not caring because they only had to stumble mere feet into a tent.

Going into Ouray and killing time.

Fucking in a hot spring.

Spending four days, just him and his woman.

But now, he was in a shit mood because it was one thing to be pissed at Judge, specifically about that shit he'd said about Rix using women, but he also seriously wasn't a fan of him being in Rix and Alex's business.

It was another to have Chloe up in his face about it.

He made it to Alex's place, parked behind her car, and to let off some steam, he jogged down the steps.

He saw her gear inside, piled by the door.

She was in the kitchen.

He didn't bother with the key she'd given him.

When she knew he was coming, she always had the door unlocked for him.

He walked in.

"Yo," he called.

"Hey," she replied, standing in her kitchen. "I was going to make us a thermos, but instead let's stop by Wild Iris or Scooter's and java up for the road."

"Whatever you want," he replied.

She turned.

After she did, he expected her to get her ass over to him, give him a proper greeting, which he'd return by letting her little tongue dance in his mouth while he was feeling her up and/or squeezing her ass.

She stood in the kitchen.

When she didn't approach, he asked, "There a reason why you're over there and not over here with your tongue down my throat?"

"What's wrong?"

Yeah.

He was tuned to her, and that tuning only grew more proficient with time spent together.

And they'd spent a lot of time together, nearly a month in one or the other's bed practically every night, last night being a rare exception because she was with her girls.

They'd invited him, like they had the three times before. But this time, he'd declined, thinking she needed alone time with her friends, and maybe just some time alone. Especially on the cusp of them spending four days together.

With the kiss she'd given him after he'd explained that, he knew he'd called it correctly.

The women had decided on a night in at Alex's place, which put him down the mountain, in his.

But all that together time meant he could tell by the lilt of her voice or the flit of her gaze if something was up.

And fuck it all, she was the same with him.

"Nothing, kiss me then I'll load this shit and we'll hit up Scooter's."

"Rix."

And he read that too.

It said, *You're full of it. Spill.*

"Babe."

She finally started walking toward him, but she did it saying, "Honey, what's going on? It's not even seven in the morning. What's happened?"

"Chloe stopped by," he gritted.

Alex also stopped, too far from him.

"She's done with you freezing out Judge," she declared.

He felt his blood start to heat. "She tell you?"

"No, though it's impossible to miss you're freezing out Judge, and frankly, I'm surprised Chloe let it go on this long."

He and Alex had had brief chats about his sitch with Judge.

Very brief.

No details.

Obviously.

She hadn't pushed.

He knew looking at her, she was now in the mood to push.

Fuck.

"We got four days to look forward to, let's just go," he prompted.

"You should pop over, talk to him, make it real quick."

"I'll text him tonight."

"You guys are best friends."

"He's not going anywhere."

"Just make the effort. The effort will say it all. Tell him we're heading out of town, but you'll hash it all out when you get back."

"Alex, drop it."

"Rix—"

"*Drop it!*" he thundered.

He regretted it the instant it came out.

He was not a man who often raised his voice, and he was proud of that.

And he had never raised it at her.

Not once.

Fuck, since they had their misunderstanding in the beginning, he'd never really even been pissed at her.

That said, he was stunned immobile at her response.

She didn't move.

Didn't even flinch.

Calm as could be, she asked, "Are you done with that?"

Rix stared at her.

"I'm not going until you talk to Judge," she declared. "Go over. Phone him. I don't care which, Rix. But connect with him."

"He's old-fashioned," Rix bit off.

"Sorry?"

"He's a goddamn throwback," Rix said.

"I don't know what you mean."

"He got up in my shit about all the women I slept with between you and Peri."

She looked surprised. "He did?"

"He did."

"Why?"

Because he thinks you're one of them, which is not fucking okay.

"Essentially, he said I used them to prove something."

"Hmm."

What the fuck?

"Hmm?" he mimicked.

"That's an interesting take. Did you?"

"Did I bury my shit in a couple dozen pussies?" he asked.

"I take that as a no."

"It's a fuck no," he clipped.

"You had a lot of sex, Rix."

"Sorry, baby, the days where your legs were trapped shut by a bunch of crinolines or whatever-the-fuck ended a long goddamn time ago."

"Crinolines?"

He knew she found that amusing.

He was not feeling amused.

He shared that by saying, "Babe."

"Right," she whispered, still amused.

Christ.

"Women like sex," he pointed out.

"Yes, I wholeheartedly agree. We do," she concurred.

"Many women understand the concept of a hookup."

"Yes," she agreed again.

"And I hooked up with those women."

"Okay."

"I made no promises. I led no one on. If I wanted to get laid, I got laid with women who also wanted to get laid."

"All right."

He stared at her.

Alex stared right back.

Shit.

Fuck.

He looked to the ceiling and muttered, "I buried my shit in pussy."

"Mm," she hummed.

He looked back to her. "You're a pain in my ass."

Her brows went up. "I am? How?"

"'Cause now I gotta go smooth things over with Judge and tell that asshole he was right."

She finally came all the way to him, cupping her hand on his jaw and pressing close.

He slid his arms around her.

"Yes, you do," she murmured.

"And I blame you."

"I'll shoulder that blame."

Fuck, she was amazing.

He dipped his head.

She took his invitation and kissed him, her little tongue playing in his mouth while he squeezed her ass.

He broke it, and she asked, "You want me to come with you?"

"Yeah, you can keep Chloe occupied. She kept her claws sheathed earlier, but if she senses a threat, I'm not counting on that continuing."

"She loves you," Alex said.

She did.

"Yeah," he grunted. He then looked down at her pile of gear and back to her. "We'll go do this, come back and pack your gear, then we'll head out."

"Does that translate to, we'll go do this, come back, and you'll bury your new shit in my pussy, and then we'll go?"

Totally tuned to him.

"Absolutely."

Her dimple popped.

He dipped his head, and this time, it was Rix who kissed her.

———

HE HAD HIS ASS TO THE RAILING OF JUDGE'S DECK, HIS EYES TO THE glass doors, seeing Alex and Chloe at the kitchen bar, sipping coffee.

"You got the day off, I gotta get to work, man," Judge prompted.

Rix looked at him.

"It had been days since I was home after rehab, she didn't even look at them."

Judge didn't move or speak.

"I told myself I was being hypersensitive. It was an adjustment. We both had to adjust. I could barely look at my legs. It was no surprise she couldn't." He blew out a breath. "I wasn't hypersensitive. She handed me back my ring and was fully moved out in forty-eight hours."

"Buddy," Judge whispered.

"I loved her."

"I know."

Rix kept solid eye contact. "I don't love her anymore, Judge."

"Okay."

"But she gutted me."

"I know that too."

"I haven't processed it. The shit I did after. I've just acknowledged it to myself. I could go over faces, orgasms, but I did not prey on the weak."

"I was outta line with that," Judge conceded.

"Not entirely. I lost two limbs. I was using my dick to prove I was a man. I don't know to who, probably mostly me."

Judge, being the guy he was, didn't reply.

"It might have started about Peri, but it's not about Peri. And I gotta say, it's done with Peri. I've let it go with her. I did that a long time ago. Everyone else has to too."

"Because you're with Alex."

"She's a lot more together than you think, Judge."

"I don't think she's not together," Judge returned.

"I think there are ways you don't," Rix shot back. "But if everyone keeps up with the Peri shit, she's gonna absorb that in ways it just isn't there, and that can't happen."

He saw that penetrate in his friend before Judge replied, "I hear you."

"I've moved on."

"Good."

Rix glanced at the windows.

The women were on bar stools.

Chloe had her back to them.

Alex was facing him, but looking at Chloe, a small smile on her face.

He looked back to Judge, and it wasn't that he thought Alex could hear that he lowered his voice.

"I'm hers and she's mine, and I have no idea how long that's going to last. But we both need you at our backs with that."

A brief nod. "Okay, Rix."

"She's had no one in her life, Judge."

Judge slow blinked. "Come again?"

"Her grandma. Who's dead. That. Is. *It*."

"Fucking hell," Judge whispered.

"She likes you. She really likes Chloe. I'm gonna take care of her, Judge, and you fuckin' know that. But you have to too. What we got is ours. This isn't a dig and it isn't a fuck you, it's just the truth. It's none of your business. And how that plays out is ours too. In the meantime, from now until whenever, I wanna give her you. Chloe. And know, whatever is up for us, we'll both keep you."

Judge looked annoyed before he said, "Jesus, man, of course."

Rix relaxed.

Then he got into the next.

"I was outta line too, landing that shit on you about not being there for me. You were there for me."

Judge shook his head. "I danced around things, Rix."

"Alex had a conversation with Mom and Hailey. Pretty much told them to stop dancing too. Now Mom calls and texts and sends me bioengineering articles she's read, and I thought it was kickass, Alex laid it out for them like that. But Mom expects me to text a term paper to her after I read these articles, and I got a life, a job and a woman. I don't have time to read all that shit."

Judge was grinning.

"You know Mags, so you know I'm not lying," Rix muttered.

"Send the articles to Coco. She'll read them and do bullet points for you," Judge offered, and Judge's woman loved Rix as much as Rix loved her.

He knew that was the truth.

That said…

"Alex reads them. She and Mom discuss them. She gives me highlights."

Judge watched him closely.

Rix read it.

"I'm happy, brother. For now."

"Just for now?"

He shrugged. "Bottom line, that's all we got."

Judge kept watching him closely.

But Judge had to get to work, and Rix had four days off, his woman with him and a truck full of gear.

So it was time to move on.

"We good?" he asked.

"Always," Judge answered.

Rix pushed from the railing, they clasped hands, bumped chests, pounded backs, let each other go and moved into the house.

The women watched them.

Of course, Alex did it silently.

And Chloe did it speaking.

"I'm considering moving out of my career in fashion and into studying anthropology, for I find it fascinating how men cannot simply show affection without putting some regressed Neanderthal spin on it. See friend. Drop club. Stop dragging woman by her hair. Bump chests. Pound backs. Grunt about meeting up later to smoke those leaves that make the world spin while scratching parts of our anatomy. Pick up club. Grab hair. Hit the cave."

"What does anthropology say about you still putting on lipstick?" Rix returned.

Chloe smirked and murmured, "Touché, *mon ami.*"

"That's why they like each other so much. He doesn't take her shit. And she doesn't take his," Judge explained to Alex.

Alex just smiled at Judge.

Rix claimed her with an arm around her neck, tugging her from the stool. "You. Woman. Come. We go. Build fire. Camp."

Alex started laughing.

Right then.

That morning had not been fun and games.

But Alex pressed to his side laughing?

Now, it was all good.

THIS WAS ALL BAD.

"Fucking shit."

"Who is that?" Alex asked, her eyes to his house.

They'd been to hers.

They'd fucked quick on her couch.

They'd packed her gear.

But they were nearly to town when she announced, "Damn. I forgot the lanterns. Did you pack some?"

Since that was on her list to pack because she had newer LED ones, he did not.

They were closer to his house than hers, so they were swinging by.

And their timing sucked.

It was barely nine o'clock and this entire day *sucked*.

Because it started with Chloe shaking his shit, Alex doing it, and then having to face it...and Judge.

And now there was someone he did not want to see at his door.

"Brian," he answered.

Alex could be an adorable dork. She had times she could be awkward (which were also adorable).

For the most part, though, she was with it and extremely chill.

On learning who was on his porch, the feel that slapped him from her side of the cab was not chill.

He pulled up in his drive, but not under the overhang, ordering, "Babe, stay in the truck."

"Not on your fucking life," she replied.

And she was out before he came to a full stop.

"Goddammit," he muttered, cutting the ignition, throwing open his door and angling out after her.

She didn't charge Brian.

No.

She waited for Rix to round the truck and then she came right to his side.

Right to his side.

Something moved in him.

Throat to groin.

That fissure was shifting.

It happened, not ever as strong as the first time back in Cali.

But in moments with Alex, it happened.

This time, though, for whatever reason, the feeling was not welcome.

That sensation was so unexpected, so huge, for a second, he could do nothing but lock down on it.

"Hey...uh, hey, Rix," Brian called.

He turned to the man. "Hey, Bri."

Rix using his nickname, Brian's bearing shifted.

Relief.

Brian walked to them, his gaze darting to Alex.

Rix gave him the body language, so when Rix lifted his hand up to his chest, Brian clasped it. They held. But there was no chest bump or back pounding.

He let the guy go and stepped back.

Brian looked up at Rix.

"I went to that place you work. The new one. A woman there told me you were out of town. I'm only in town for a while, so I thought, what the hell? Stop by. See if you left yet." He glanced to the truck. "Looks like you're on your way."

"Forgot the lanterns," Rix told him.

Brian nodded and looked to Alex.

He also looked her up and down and visibly approved.

Watching him do it, Rix remembered that about the guy, the way he'd look over a woman, that way not being cool, this time, doing it to Alex, it was seriously not cool, but it was something Rix thought was about Brian being young.

Guess it wasn't.

He ground his teeth.

Then he introduced, "Right, Brian, this is my woman, Alex. Al, this is Brian. An old bud from the crew."

"Brian," she said, not cold, but not warm either.

Brian instantly knew she knew, his demeanor changed again, and he dipped his chin to her. "Alex." He then looked back to Rix. "You always got the best ones."

"Not always."

Brian flinched.

Memories were serving, and his latest one reminded him that Brian hadn't exited the scene until Peri had done it.

Brian shook that off and said, "Listen, I know you're out of here, but if you're back in time, I leave Monday. Maybe we can go get a beer or something."

"We aren't back until Monday night," Rix shared.

"Too bad," Brian muttered.

He then said nothing else, and did nothing else, like ending this scenario and leaving.

God damn it.

"Okay, I know what you need, man," Rix told him. "And I wish I could give it to you." He sucked in a breath. "I just can't."

The color ran out of Brian's face.

"Honest as fuck, I want that for you," Rix said. "But you fucked up. And you fucking up meant I lost my legs."

Brian's face bleached out.

"People fuck up," Rix went on. "You are far from the first to do it, Bri. And there have been much worse consequences. I know you'd go back to that day and do things differently. I know, 'cause you're like me, it haunts you. But shit like this happens. And it happened to me, because of you."

Brian gulped down a swallow, then nodded.

Then Rix gave it to him.

"I know that's gotta be torture for you, but think about this shit, man. You're coming to me to make it easier, and unless I work really hard at it, it never gets easy for me."

"You're right," Brian forced out, the words rough. He cleared his throat. "This was a bad idea."

He dipped his chin at Alex again and made a move to head to the car at the curb.

"I do want that for you," Rix said.

Brian stopped and returned his attention to Rix.

"It doesn't make me feel the slightest bit better you live with it. Different than me, but you do. I know you do. And that's no balm, Bri."

"I didn't think... I never thought that, Rix. That you'd think that. You're not that guy."

"I got my house." He jerked his head to his house. "I got a great job, pays more, honestly, than I ever thought I'd make." He took Alex's hand. "Got a beautiful woman."

"Right, yeah," Brian whispered.

"Shit happens. Bad shit happens. Seriously bad shit happens. Life goes on. We gotta do our best to do no harm and live it," Rix finished.

"I..." Brian shook his head. "Rix, man, thanks for your time. I shouldn't have... Anyway. You gave it, your time, and that's always been you."

Rix jutted his chin.

"Alex, nice to meet you," he said to Alex.

Again, all she said was, "Brian."

Brian took that hint and moved to his car.

Alex moved in closer to Rix.

Rix started to look down at her to see where she was at, but stopped when Brian called, "Rix?"

Alex's fingers closed so tight around his, there was pain.

He didn't wince or make a move to shift her hold.

He looked to the man he used to razz at the firehouse. The man who, the last time Rix saw him, was sitting in Rix's living room, trying hard not to look at Rix's legs, also trying hard not to throw up all over himself, after he dropped on Rix a five-hundred-dollar bottle of scotch.

Rix still had it.

But he hadn't opened it.

"Yeah, bud?" Rix called back.

"You happy?"

He felt that emotion.

He released her hand as his arm automatically moved to curl around Alex's neck at the thought of it.

But for some fucking reason, he couldn't say it.

"Look at me," he said instead.

Brian looked back and forth between Alex and Rix.

And then he genuinely smiled, gave them a short wave, got in his car and motored.

Rix looked down at Alex. "Ready to roll, baby?"

"My key to your place is in my bag in the truck, can you let me in your house?"

"Need to hit the head?"

"Please let me in your house, Rix."

He studied her.

Then he led her to the side door and into the kitchen.

She did not head to the bathroom.

She went out on the deck.

He went out with her.

She stood on the deck, staring at his back yard.

"Babe?"

It was his voice that flipped a switch for her.

Movements agitated, she turned to the pillows on his bench, nabbed a couple and, twisting at the waist to give it her all, she hurled them into his yard. Back to the pillows, off they flew. Then she went after the cushions. All the bench cushions, flung. The ones on the chair. Gone.

Then she stood at the foot of his deck and glared at them.

He got what she was feeling. He *really* did. It was still fucking adorable how she expressed it.

Rix didn't tease her to get her out of it.

Because his throat was closed and that tear in his torso was trembling.

"I'll put them back in a second," she snapped.

"Okay, sweetheart."

"You were good with him," she told the yard.

"Yeah."

"What the fuck was he thinking?" she asked the yard.

"I don't know, baby. If I fucked up like he did, there might come a time when I was driven to do the same. But you gotta understand, it's not just me, Alex. There were ten of us out there. I caught it, but the fullness of what he lives with is he knows. He knows that fire could have taken us all."

She made a "huh" noise that wasn't the normal "huh," but the sound you make to let out emotion you're holding so you won't cry.

"We can hit the road tomorrow," he offered.

She turned to him then and snarled, "We're going to Ouray."

"All right, honey," he murmured.

"You were good with him," she repeated.

He didn't have a reply.

"You're just good," she declared.

That fissure shifted, stronger, shuddering.

"Best man I've ever met in my life," she concluded.

She then stormed into the yard to retrieve the cushions.

Rix gave it a second to get a lock on it.

Then he followed in order to help.

THE PINES WERE DARK ARROWS, POINTING STRAIGHT TO THE STARS.

Rix was on his back, his pack shoved under his head, his fingers playing with Alex's hair.

Alex didn't need a pack. Her pillow was his chest.

They were lying on a blanket, wrapped in another one, out by a hot spring, staring at the heavens, when she remarked, "I gotta know."

"Know what, baby?"

"The difference between a goof and a dork."

Where did that come from?

"What?" he asked.

"You said I was a dork and a goof too. What's the difference?"

He'd never called her either fucking word.

"When did I say that?" he demanded.

"After the first time we had sex."

Oh yeah.

Right.

He had called her those because she was giving him shit about her being bashful.

He had no idea what the difference was, so he made something up.

"A dork is someone who does goofy shit. A goof is someone who says dorky shit."

He heard her soft laughter.

"Though, I should probably call you Lady Goof," he noted.

"Bluh," she replied.

He grinned at the stars.

She turned, pushed up and rested her arm and side with the bonus of one tit on his chest so she could look at his face.

Since it was a better view, he looked at hers.

"How'd you meet Judge?" she asked.

Since he'd lost purchase on her hair, he shoved a hand up her thermal and wrapped his fingers around the soft, warm skin covering her ribcage.

Offer him a thousand dollars, he couldn't tell you which he liked better.

Though, he was leaning toward her hair.

"Fourth of July," he answered. "I don't know, four years back, maybe five. River Rain does a thing for the parade. FD does one too. We got in a friendly competition that, no matter what Judge might tell you, was all his. He totally started it."

He could see the smile on her face, and he heard it in her voice when she asked, "What competition?"

"You toss candy to the kids. It got to be about who could toss the most candy. Swear, they had someone take off and hit a Walgreens to refill their load."

"So they won," she deduced.

"Only because they cheated," he informed her.

Her lips remained tipped up.

Rix gave up the goodness of her skin and bones to pull his hand out of her shirt so he could press his thumb against her dimple.

When he did, he got a reward, since she rested both tits on his chest, which meant her face was closer to his.

Now stroking her cheek and jaw, he picked up the story.

"After the parade, Judge and I got to talking. Could tell right away he was good people. The guys were getting together for burgers and dogs at a bud's house who had a pool. We were all on call. People do stupid shit all the time, but holidays, that jacks up in a huge way. But we were going to enjoy the holiday as long as we could. Asked Judge if he wanted to come. He was relatively new to Prescott back then, didn't know a lot of people, so he accepted. Miraculously, we didn't get a call out. That meant all night, he and me talked. It was weird. Like brothers reunited. We just got on and it seemed we were tight from the minute we met. I had close buds on the crew, but Judge and I went from calling shit to each other during a parade to being best buds in a blink."

And Peri, he didn't share, had hated it.

Rix making a friend that close, them going out for runs, hikes, on bro camping trips, it pissed her off.

She'd liked Judge because you couldn't not like the man.

But she'd been jealous of him.

Fuck, how he had he been so blind about her?

"I love your relationship with him," Alex said softly, and Rix was grateful she brought him back to her, but he wasn't surprised the words she uttered to bring him back.

"I love it too," he stated the obvious.

Her felt her dimple return.

"So...Lady Sharp," he teased.

She rolled her eyes to the heavens.

He kept at her.

"Babe, seriously, where's that fluffy white dress you wore in that one picture? Totally gotta fuck you in that."

She committed a miracle by shoving at him without moving even half an inch away from him.

Something that made him grin.

But it faded before he asked, "Probably not weird, it being your life."

"Okay, yes, there were polo matches," she admitted.

His grin came back.

Alex kept talking.

"And there were *events* with fancy dresses. And some of them were fluffy."

His grin got bigger.

She kept going.

"But mostly, my life was Dad's brownstone. Reading in a corner of the library. When I was old enough, escaping out to the city. Making certain I got in a dorm my freshman and sophomore years at Columbia so I could get out of the house. By the end, Dad was used to me being gone, so when I came back, because, obviously, juniors and seniors didn't stay in dorms."

"Obviously," he concurred with mock gravity.

And again, he felt her lips twitch.

"So I came home and pretty much had my own life. He had his. And once I graduated, I took off."

"Columbia?" he asked.

"Yes," she answered.

"Impressive."

"With my last name, Rix, I could go anywhere. Harvard. Princeton. Oxford. Cambridge. It isn't that impressive."

He moved his hand to cup her behind her ear.

"Your last name didn't get a degree at Columbia," he stated resolutely. "You did."

"Yeah," she whispered.

"What'd you study?"

"Nonprofit management."

That was his girl.

"'Course you did," he murmured.

She pushed up and touched her lips to his.

She settled back and asked, "You okay?"

"Gonna take my babe into the tent and fuck her in a minute. Zenned out from sitting in the springs. Only bad part is we gotta leave tomorrow."

"Yeah," she repeated.

And she sounded disappointed that they had to leave.

But there was something else in that word.

He shot her the same question. "You okay?"

"I'm great."

"Something's up," he pushed.

She gave it a beat before she said, "You seemed…" She was looking for words, he knew it when she found them. "Not as agile tonight."

"I get pain," he muttered.

She tensed. "I thought you—"

"Baby, you know," he started gently. "I told you, it takes effort to walk normal. It just takes effort. All the time. It's part of my life. I don't think about it. But sometimes it catches up to me. Don't know why. I've had way more active days than this. Whole weekends. There's no rhyme or reason for it. It's just what it is, and it's gonna be a part of my life for the rest of it in one way or another."

"Okay," she replied, but she didn't sound like she was happy with that word.

"Some people get head pain, Al. They can manage it, but it happens, and sometimes the pain defeats the management. But they live with it. Some people got diabetes, and they deal with it, but they accidentally miss a shot, or for some reason, shit spikes, and they got problems. And they live with it. It's like that. It just is what it is. And you live with it."

She reached to stroke his jaw this time and repeated in a tone he liked better, "Okay."

"And the hot springs helped," he shared.

"Okay, honey," she said again.

Time to move on.

"Now, about these fantasies of yours…"

"Ohmigod," she muttered, annoyed, and he grinned.

"Any of them involve fucking by a hot springs? I mean, we fucked in them, and we fucked in the tent, in close proximity to them. But now I'm talking right *by* them. Is that a fantasy?"

"I'm never telling you my fantasies, Rix," she declared.

"Why?" he asked.

"Because when you fulfill them, I get to have a little secret."

At that, he swept his arms around her, pulled her up and rolled her on the blanket so he was on top.

"Which ones I fulfill?" he asked.

"Not telling," she teased.

"Totally doing you in the hot springs was one," he guessed.

"Maybe," she hedged.

That meant yes.

Fuck yeah.

He put his mouth to hers and opened her legs with a hand.

His hips fell through.

"What other ones you got?"

"Rix," she breathed as he slid a finger up the inseam of her jeans.

Her hands were moving on him with a purpose.

But she didn't spill.

She lifted her head and kissed him.

Well…

To hell with it.

She got to have a secret.

And he got to have Alex.

In the end, it was a win-win.

So, under the stars, by the hot springs outside Ouray, Rix set about winning.

For the both of them.

And fulfilled another of Alex's fantasies.

RIX LAY IN THE DARK.

In the tent.

Listening.

There were bears out there.

Cats.

He had a lightweight portable camp chair that folded so small, it could fit in his pocket. He used it when he was camping to get his legs on.

But it wasn't easy, and it didn't go as quick.

So, like he had the last two nights, he lay, Alexandra snuggled up to him in their sleeping bag dead to the world, and he listened.

The reason he wasn't as agile.

He was exhausted.

Because what had been happening happened that night.

He didn't fall asleep until he couldn't stay awake anymore.

And in a couple of hours, he had to get up.

Because it was a new day with Alex, and they didn't have a future together.

So while he had her he wasn't missing anything.

CHAPTER 18

THE BOTTLE

Rix

hree days later…

"REALLY, THAT'S A FANTASTIC CHOICE. I'M NOT JUST SAYING THAT. IT'S one of a kind. Totally unique. We don't usually stock these in the store, but the owner loves this designer. She just can't turn her pieces down. You see why. It's that special. Though, you need to understand, even with your trade-in, that'll still be another eight thousand dollars."

It was his birthday.

Rix was on his lunch hour.

And he had a lot of shit to get done.

The surveys were coming in and Krista was compiling then.

The furniture was arriving.

Judge and Kevin had taken a trip to Chicago, which was a big Kids and Trails town, to talk to some students, parents and teachers. Their feedback reports were in his email inbox.

Shit was heating up. They needed to get down to it. Alex and him had taken some time off, and they'd be taking more next week to go to her sister's wedding.

He didn't want to pitch up to work late from lunch.

And this was errand one of two, both important, essential.

But it meant he'd probably have to hit a drive through for food, which sucked.

"And that's with a firefighter's discount," the associate said.

Well.

Hell.

He looked at her. "I'm not a firefighter anymore."

"Yes you are," she said softly.

He felt his neck get tight.

He ignored it and looked back down at what he was holding, pinched between his thumb and finger.

"I can talk to my manager, maybe get you an extra ten percent," she said.

With what he was holding, he could see that eight grand, with the discount.

The stone was big.

But it didn't protrude.

It was embedded in platinum with a constellation of other diamonds around it. So many, they wound nearly all the way around the band.

One big star in the middle, dozens of others twinkling around.

It was thick.

The weight was hefty.

But self-contained.

It wouldn't catch on anything.

It was also striking. Feminine. Unusual.

Alex.

"I'll take it," he decided, shoving the box with Peri's ring that was sitting on the glass in front of them toward the associate and handing her the one in his fingers.

"I'll give you the ten percent and deal with my manager later," she said.

"Obliged," he grunted.

She nodded, smiled, and told him, "It's gorgeous. She'll love it."

She would.

It was all her, an endless circle of Alex.

Also, even if people in her family's sphere could afford something ten times more expensive, that ring made a statement.

Peri's ring hadn't been chump change.

She'd picked it.

He remembered his mom's mouth pinching when they were discussing it, and how he'd gone five K over what he thought he could afford in order to get it for her.

"It's her engagement ring, Mom," he'd said.

"She isn't getting an engagement ring, she's getting a husband. She's entering into a marriage. That lasts a while. In other words, Rix, she has time. She can upgrade."

He'd gone for it anyway, because it made Peri happy.

And it had been a whack he'd dumped on that ring.

Alex's was a fuckuva lot better.

That said, this ring would be returned before the 30-day return period ended.

But in the time Alex had it, it'd make her happy.

———

HE DIDN'T SAY ANYTHING DURING THE FITTINGS.

He waited until he and Chloe were walking out of the tailor's shop toward their vehicles, Chloe babbling.

"They took forever to get here, and it'll be a push, but he promised they'd be ready by the time you leave next Tuesday. I haven't used him yet, but I have it on good authority he's exceptionally skilled."

"Woman, stop."

She stopped two ways.

Talking, and halting, as he did the same.

"I can read labels, Coco," he told her.

She didn't even bother to look guilty. "I know you can, Rix."

He jabbed a finger at the door to the tailor. "I just got fitted for a sports jacket, five shirts, two suits and a goddamn *tuxedo*."

"I do believe I was there, advising the tailor as this happened," she drawled.

"And you're charging me two grand for what's gotta be at least ten grand worth of shit," he concluded.

"This is how it works," she began as if she was talking to someone with a learning disability.

Rix sucked in breath in an effort to suck in patience.

"I am now an unwitting celebrity," she continued. "*You* are now an unwitting celebrity. And *you* have to represent. And for Alex, you *will*."

Shit.

Fuck.

For Alex, he would.

"I have a charity I run," Chloe carried on. "And through the benevolent hand of God, the natural order of things has twisted, and now department stores, boutiques and *designers* wish to curry favor with *me*. I do not deny them that opportunity. So, I made a few calls and told them who I was dressing. They know in the next week you're going to be photographed, copiously, and you'll be doing it being all you are. Young, handsome and vital, with a beautiful woman at your side who hails from two of the most aristocratic bloodlines in two countries. They were falling all over themselves to send me free clothes, Rix. I accepted and selected what would suit you the best, and that was difficult, as you're like Judge. A dream to dress. I wanted to put you in *everything*."

He scowled at her.

She got back on target.

"*En fin*, it didn't cost me a penny, but the time to make some phone calls."

Well.

Shit.

Rix said nothing.

"That two thousand dollars," she sniffed, "is your donation to Fabulous Foot Forward to compensate me for my time, my styling skills and having to put up with this conversation. Because I knew you'd hassle me if you thought I was covering you. Though, since that cat is out of the bag, I'll note now, the amount of your donation is negotiable."

"I just dropped eight grand on an upgrade of an engagement ring after Peri's trade-in, since Alex isn't gonna wear Peri's ring."

Her hair swayed as her head jerked.

"*Fake* ring, Coco," he reminded her.

"Right," she whispered.

"By the way"—he took her left hand and gave it a squeeze before releasing it—"congratulations. I don't know whether to threaten you to make him happy, or I'll kill you, or to threaten him to do the same thing."

"You're ridiculously wonderful," she purred.

"Are we done?" he asked. "I have to get back to work."

"We are."

He bent and kissed her cheek then he got in his truck.

And it didn't occur to him from start to finish of all that, she didn't say happy birthday.

"I'M JUST RUNNING A LITTLE LATE, HONEY," ALEX SPOKE TO HIM FROM his dash.

"It's a birthday, baby. They happen every year. You don't have to put much effort into it."

Rix had learned something new.

A wash-and-go woman was where it was at.

That didn't mean when Alex put some effort in, he didn't appreciate it.

He really fucking did.

He just wanted to make sure she knew who she was was what he wanted.

"Five, ten minutes, tops. I've already called the restaurant. They know we're going to be late."

"It's okay, take your time. I'm a couple minutes out. See you in a few."

"See you, honey."

They hung up.

After those couple of minutes of driving, he saw the globe string lights he'd draped off the side roof of her house as it slanted down the mountain. She had decent lighting, but that way, it was attractive, and every step was illuminated for her.

She could also far more easily see her house and the turn-off from a greater distance, which was something needed with as dark as it got up in those mountains at night without a streetlight for miles.

While he was setting that up for her, he'd gone wild, done her deck, zigzagging the strings from overhang to trees.

It looked the fucking bomb.

She'd loved it.

Since she was a deck girl, he'd loved giving it to her.

His headlights flashed on her Subaru, and he parked behind it, knifed out, went to the steps, and he could tell by what he could see, down Alex's mountain off the front of the house, the deck lighting was on along with the lights at the steps.

She was outside a lot, and he was there with her. On his deck. Hers. As much of their weekends as she could manage.

Maybe she was late because she'd had a glass of wine under her trees, and she hadn't turned off the lights.

This didn't upset him.

He'd wished he'd come earlier.

He hit the door.

Opened it.

Walked in.

"*Surprise!*"

Streamers streamed from the loft, confetti rained down, and people jumped out of the pantry and powder room, not to mention where they'd been hiding on the deck.

There was a tall stand covered in cupcakes on Alex's kitchen table, food all around it. More food on her coffee table. Steel tubs filled with ice and bottles and cans on her kitchen counters.

There was more out on the deck, he could see, including two half kegs.

The reason for all of this was she was there. Chloe. Judge. Katie. Gal. Kevin. Genny. Duncan. Chloe's sister, Sasha. Her father, Tom. Tom's girlfriend, Paloma. Rix's mom and dad. Some of his friends from the store…

And the entire fire crew with wives and girlfriends…

Were all there.

Shit.

Alex got to him first.

She was wearing a black slip dress with some meshy, see-through thing over it that had red and yellow shit stitched in, and that overdress ran longer than the one under it. High-heeled red sandals with lots of straps.

He loved his woman wash and go, but it was a fantastic fucking birthday present, her in those heels.

And wearing that smile.

"Okay?" she asked softly.

It was not.

"Yeah," he replied, forcing his mouth to smile.

Her head cocked.

She read the smile.

To distract her, Rix swept her in his arm and kissed her.

Hoots and hollers and from close a back slap.

He then heard his buddy Jarrod from the crew say, "Jesus, man, let us get a few beers in before we have to give you two the room."

Rix broke the kiss, and since he'd lifted his hand to her jaw during it, he swept her lip.

Only then did he turn to Jarrod.

"Fuck off, asshole."

Jarrod smiled huge and came in for a man hug.

Rix let Alex go and gave it to him.

And he felt it open further.

That thing in his chest.

It started oozing.

Infected.

He didn't have time to do an emergency patch job and stitch it together.

He was dragged into his own party.

HE WAS SITTING ON ALEX'S DECK RAILING, IGNORING HIS MOM AND dad's looks, Judge's, Chloe's.

Alex's.

For the first time since he got to the party, he had a second to get his shit tight.

So he was taking it when Gal moseyed up to him.

She swung up beside him and knocked their knees.

"So, the skinny," she began.

Ah hell.

She laid it on him.

"She didn't want your fire buds here. Or your store buds. But mostly your fire buds. You know. She's Alex. She wanted something quiet. You, her, Judge and Chloe, me and Kate. But more, she wanted that for you. Judge insisted. Said it was time. She enlisted Chloe, who sided with Alex, both of them saying you'd decide when it was time. Judge would not stand down. Said you were making strides, they needed to facilitate that. He enlisted Duncan and Chloe's dad. And to put some gusto into it, from afar, Judge's dad, and to push their case, *your* dad. Alex's next play was to draft your mom, who sided with the dudes. So your fire buds are here."

"Right," he muttered.

"So if you're pissed, it's all Judge's fault."

He shot her his first real smile of the night.

She smiled back and explained, "Your brother and sister-in-law couldn't make it. Too far, both of them had to be back for work tomorrow so they'd be getting home late, and they didn't want to leave your niece with a babysitter that long."

He nodded.

"A lot went into this, Rix, and I'm not talking cupcakes and hauling kegs."

He was getting that.

"Yeah," he whispered.

She studied him.

As she did, her neck arched sideways.

Too far.

Then she looked from him into the house.

Alex's house.

The house of a woman who did not like to be around a lot of people.

Filled with people who loved Rix.

Then Gal said to the house, her voice soft and pained. "I trust you, Rix. Do it fast. But do it right. We'll take it from there."

With that, she hopped down and walked away.

She didn't look back.

ALEX WAS TIDYING UP.

Everyone was gone.

"Babe," he called from where he was standing halfway to the door.

Alex looked up at him.

She was tweaked.

He wasn't surprised.

But seeing that, that wound opened more, too far, and he nearly flinched at the pain.

He tossed the box to her, sending it sailing across the divide between them.

Her hands came up quickly, and she caught it.

Then she stared at it.

"The ring," he explained.

Her eyes darted to him. "Peri's ring?"

He shook his head. "Traded it for another one. I got thirty days to return it. All good."

"Rix—"

"I gotta get going."

Her shoulders shot forward and back, like she'd suddenly been shoved.

And that wound tore open even more.

"Wh-what?"

He was moving to the door. "Dinner. Tomorrow. My place."

"It's your birthday. I haven't given you your present."

He stopped at the door. "Dinner. Tomorrow. Six. My place."

And with Alex standing across the room in her kitchen, staring at him, those fucking gorgeous eyes of hers haunted, he walked out.

Do it fast. But do it right.

It might not be fast.

But he hoped like fuck, when it happened tomorrow night, he did it right.

IT WAS A WEAK MOVE, WORKING FROM HOME.

But he needed that time to pull himself together.

She came in the side door at six-oh-seven, and he was not together.

When he saw her, his eyes immediately fell to her hand.

She wasn't wearing the ring.

All day, he wondered if she opened the box.

Looked at it.

Liked it.

Tried it on.

But of course she wasn't wearing it.

Because it was very real.

And totally fake.

"Hey," he greeted.

She walked to the end of the bar and stopped.

"Hey," she said softly, putting her hand on the bar.

He'd prepared.

It was sitting there.

She didn't notice it, but her hand was resting right by it.

Her hand that close, the rip sliced up his throat, filling it with the putrid bile that lived in him.

It tasted like shit.

"Before…" His jaw jerked to the side.

When it did, her frame locked.

He pulled it together.

"Before we talk, that bottle. It's for your dad."

Like she was in a dream state, or a nightmare, her gaze floated down at the bottle of scotch on the counter.

The five-hundred-dollar one he'd dug through his cupboards to find.

"For putting us up. A host's gift," he explained.

Even more slowly, her eyes came back to him. "That's a very nice gift, Rix."

Of course she knew how expensive that bottle was.

She was royal.

And he wasn't thinking bloodlines.

"Yeah," he grunted.

"It's unnecessary."

"You need to pack it, I might forget."

She lifted a hand, wrapped her fingers around the neck of the bottle.

He watched, watched her touch it, and pus seethed from his wound.

He had to ask.

So goddamned weak.

"Did you try the ring on?"

"Yes," she whispered.

"I don't know if they can size it before we leave."

"It fits."

It fits.

Do it fast. But do it right.

"It's important I don't lose you," he said gently.

She said nothing.

"We need to shift, baby," he told her.

She stared at him with those two-toned eyes.

Those amber tipped lashes.

Breathing softly from her mouth, pretty pink lips parted.

"We'll have dinner tonight, me and you. And I'll meet you at the airstrip on Tuesday. But between now and then, to get our shit together, move into our new space before we have to pretend, I think we need some time apart."

Alex remained silent.

"You're one of my best friends, baby, and—"

"Don't call me that," she said quietly.

"Al—"

"I'm not that," she said.

"Okay," he agreed.

"Not even in New York. When we're pretending. Don't do that."

"Okay," he repeated.

"Okay," she whispered.

They stared at each other.

Then it was Rix whispering.

"I can't lose you."

She nodded, fast.

They were coming.

He could see them.

Fuck.

Fuck.

Shit.

She lifted her chin to hold the tears at bay, and her husky voice was ragged when she said, "I'm sorry, Rix. We-we'll have dinner some other time. Wh-when we get back. Right now, I'm not hungry."

And, her fingers around the neck of that fucking bottle of scotch, she took it with her when she raced away.

—————

She was in before him at the office the next day.

He looked right to her the minute he could.

She was closed tight.

First time ever, even before they became them, she was closed so tightly away from him, he couldn't get even an infinitesimal bead on where she was at.

That meant he knew where she was at.

That tear inside became a slash.

He jerked up his chin at her.

No awkward wave.

No fluttering dimple.

She tipped her chin back and looked again to her laptop.

Rix hit his office, unsure how he made it there without a trail of slime following him.

He was wide open.

Gaping.

Leaking.

He'd barely sat when she was in his office.

"I won't take long," she said, coming right to his desk.

The folding chair was still there.

But his desk was new.

Real wood.

Big.

Important.

He'd wanted to fuck her on it.

He still wanted to fuck her on it.

He didn't know how he kept his seat without rushing her, herding her into his truck, taking her somewhere he'd never let her leave.

But he managed it.

It was a miracle.

She reached out, and he looked to her hand.

When she retracted it, on that big, important desk, she'd left behind the little gray velvet box.

"I'm going to call," she said.

His gaze sliced up to hers.

"Tell them you couldn't make it," she went on. "It'll be okay." That came fast because he was opening his mouth. "Honest. I'll figure something out. Something believable. They won't…it doesn't matter. I just thought on it a lot last night and you're right. I can't lose you. We can't lose each other. So we need time apart so we can make it to that space. In the meantime, I can't ask you…to pretend."

"I'm in this, I told you I was. I promised you that," he replied.

"You're out, Rix."

Christ.

Now he was bleeding.

"It's okay," she whispered. "I'll be okay."

Her face got soft.

And…

Hemorrhage.

"I promise," she said.

And then she walked out.

———

ALEX LEFT THE OFFICE AT LUNCH.

She didn't come back.

When Rix asked after her, watching him closely, Krista told him she was going to work from home.

For the rest of the day, Rix avoided her and Kevin, and he really avoided Judge.

And he got hunkered down to work.

He didn't get shit done.

———

WHEN RIX GOT HOME THAT NIGHT, IT WAS SITTING ON THE KITCHEN counter where he'd put it for her the night before.

Brian's guilt bottle of scotch.

Next to it...
The key to Rix's house.
Alex's key to his house.
There was also a note.

R-

> *It's too much. It's okay. It would seem weird giving it to Dad now anyway.*
> *We'll do something when I escape from New York.*
> *x-A*

Escape from New York.
She was making a joke.
An in joke.
Their joke.
Escape from New York.
And with that, Rix couldn't hold it in anymore.

What he'd spent years packing in exploded a half second before he seized that bottle by the neck, slid that fucking key off his counter and shoved it in his pocket.

Then he walked all that shit to his truck.

He tossed the bottle on the passenger seat, hauled himself in, leaned across to open the glove compartment, and saw the ring was still where he'd put it.

He then started his truck up, backed out, and drove up the goddamn mountain.

CHAPTER 19

THE EXPLOSION

Rix

He hammered on Alex's door.

But he didn't fucking wait for her to open it.

He let himself in, looking right, thinking she'd be on her deck.

She wasn't.

"Rix, what—?"

He looked left and up.

She was in her loft.

"Not even fucking face to face, Al?" he demanded, shoving his hand in his pocket, pulling out the key and then flipping it onto her coffee table.

It clinked and fell to the floor.

He then walked to her kitchen table and slammed down the bottle.

He turned back to her, again looking up.

"Your dad's gonna expect something from me. And you're gonna give him that *fucking bottle.*"

"Rix—"

"Fucking *shut up,*" he snarled.

The fingers of both her hands curled around the railing in front of her.

Rix pulled the velvet box out of his other pocket and slapped it on the table.

Then he went back to Alex.

"You've already told them we're engaged. They're gonna expect you to be wearing my ring."

"Really, Rix—"

"*You're gonna wear my fucking ring, Alex!*" he roared.

She fell silent, standing above him, holding on.

"I can't lose you," he bit off.

She nodded, quickly.

"I'm not gonna fucking lose you," he declared.

"You won't lose me, Rix," she called gently.

Rix.

Alex's *Rix.*

"There's too many stairs in this house, we can't live here," he announced.

Her head jerked.

"We can't live here," he repeated. "It's not safe."

He felt it then, drifting down to him.

Lapping at him.

Washing it away.

"You love it here. It's you. I love being with you here. I love sitting with you out on your deck. But it's not safe," he said it again.

Alex stared down at him.

He couldn't see the colors of her eyes.

He could only see…

He turned, grabbed the bottle, and with all his strength, sent it sailing.

Five hundred dollars shattered against her wall, shards flying, liquid splashing everywhere.

And he bellowed, "*It's not safe!*"

When he focused on her again, Alex was racing to him.

"Don't get near me, baby," he warned, holding up a hand to her.

A few feet from the bottom of the stairs, she stuttered to a halt.

"I can't keep you safe," he told her.

"Rix, honey, take a breath."

"They come in the night, what the fuck am I gonna do?" he asked.

"Who? Who comes?"

"It starts," he said. "It could be anything. We forgot a candle burning or some shit goes wrong with the wiring on the microwave. And we have babies. We have our Kinsley. We have three of her. What do I do?"

"Rix, honey"—those words were a naked sob—"please, take—"

"I can't lose you."

An audible emotional hiccup before, "You won't lose me."

"I can't protect you."

"You can. You do."

"*I can't fucking protect you!*" he thundered.

She said nothing.

"God. Christ. Fuck! *Christ!*" he bit off, beginning to pace, yanking his hand through his hair. He turned on her. "We're not having a gun in our home."

Surprised confusion hit her features, but she said gently, "Okay."

"People think they're fucking safe with guns, it's lunacy. No fucking guns."

"Okay."

"And no fucking stairs."

She nodded, again fast. "Okay."

"Fucking come in my house when I'm not there, drop that *fucking* bottle on me and *my* key? What the fuck, Al?"

"We, um…broke up."

"I didn't return *your* key," he pointed out.

Placatingly, she replied, "Yes, honey. I realize that now."

"Jesus."

He started pacing, less agitated, but still pacing.

Then something important occurred to him, and he rounded on her.

"I'll call you 'baby' whenever the fuck I want."

"Right," she mumbled.

"That's who you are to me, and you fucking know it."

She nodded, not as fast.

Rix wasn't a fan of that.

"You fucking are," he growled.

"Okay, Rix."

"Christ," he bit, and began pacing again, and there was silence while he did it.

Alex broke it.

"Can I…I sense there's something about that bottle."

He stopped and looked at her. "Brian gave me that bottle."

She turned her attention to the remains splattered across her floor, revulsion on her face and in her two words. "I see."

"Yeah, so, you know, perfect fucking present for your fucking dad."

Her gaze shot back to him, and now he saw surprised humor.

"I'm not joking. He deserves five-hundred-dollars' worth of guilt," Rix decreed. "Or he did. Now it's toast."

"You have a point," she murmured.

"Don't be goddamned cute," he growled.

She pressed her lips together.

"Pull that shit with leaving it at my house," he grumbled. "Now what am I gonna give your dad?"

"Um…nothing?" she suggested.

"Babe, have you met my mom?"

"Uh, yes."

"She drilled it into me. Someone lets you stay at their house, you give them a gift."

"We didn't give your mom and dad a gift."

His brows snapped together. "We were staying at *my* house. They'd lose their shit, we did something whacked like that when I came home for a visit."

"Of course. I see the difference," she mumbled.

Jesus.

He drew in a big breath.

Then he shared, "Judge was right. You gotta be less protective of me. I'm a big boy. It's time I start acting like it. I gotta get my head outta my goddamn ass. I miss my friends. They miss me. This shit I'm pulling is bullshit. Judge knows how to push me. When he does, don't push back. Let him do it."

She knew exactly what he was talking about.

"Okay," she agreed.

"Still, this is your house. If you're not comfortable with having a big party, you don't have a big fucking party."

"Okay," she said again.

Even so, he demanded, "Are you hearing me, Alexandra?"

"I'm right here, Rix. So, yes, I'm hearing you."

"You aren't, because you let me pull shit with you the last couple of days that was not on. Then you dropped that fucking bottle off and *my key*."

"I—"

"You know what we are. We can barely be apart from one another."

"No, we can't," she whispered.

"I get you need alone time. Time with your girls. I need time like that too. That's not what I mean."

There were tears in her eyes again, these a fuckuva lot different, when she replied, "I know what you mean."

"I'm struggling," he admitted.

She made her own admission. "I missed it."

"You can't possibly get it."

"You're right. I still missed it."

Rix shut up.

Alex gave it a few beats.

Then she asked carefully, "Who's coming?"

"What?"

"You said earlier, 'when they come in the night.' Who's coming?"

"Intruders," he grunted.

He watched her pull in a big breath.

Then she stated, "I am not making light of your concerns, honey, but home invasions don't happen that often."

"That isn't the point."

"I know," she whispered.

"So you give me those eyes and those lashes. And Peri's pulling her shit. And Brian shows his face. And I don't think about it. It's there. I know it's there. But I can't fucking think about it. So I bury it. I bury it with all the other shit I won't let myself think about. And so you know where I'm at, I started shoveling when that fucking tree fell on me."

Her eyes widened, then tender understanding filled them, and she asked softly, "Like what are you burying?"

"The new shit?"

She nodded encouragingly.

"Brian shows, and I realize I'm happy. I'm fucking happy. My feet and calves are incinerated or rotting somewhere, I don't know. I didn't ask what they did with them."

Alex cringed.

Rix understood that.

"And still, I'm standing there, you right at my side, and I'm happy. And I don't wanna blame him. My dad taught me, no matter the situation, always be the bigger man. Even if it costs you, eventually you'll get that back, a hundred-fold. And I cannot be the bigger man for him. I cannot sugarcoat it. But still, I do. And he leaves seeing me standing with you, having it all, knowing I'm good. I'm happy. More than happy, I got it all. And he's good. He leaves and I gave him what he needed. But he's left me with new shit I have to deal with."

"What shit?" she prompted when he stopped talking.

"Shit I don't know what to do with. Like, go back and Brian doesn't fuck up. Where does that leave me?"

She'd been with him, but that made her full-on perplexed.

"I don't know what you mean."

"You're on my back deck, so cute, tossing cushions around 'cause you're so pissed Brian did what he did, then he shows, expecting me to make him feel better. And I'm watching you throw a hissy fit, using everything I got not to think about how I didn't want to be anywhere but there."

Now she gave him surprised confusion.

"I'm sorry, *what?*" she asked.

"With you, throwing pillows off my deck. I didn't want to be anywhere else, but there with you."

Now, completely mystified.

Jesus.

She was even cute totally lost.

"Babe," he said patiently. "Think about it. If that tree didn't fall on me, I'd be married to Peri. We might have a kid. Josh and Hailey's wedding was supposed to happen just a couple of months before Peri and mine, and they already have a kid. Think about that. I'd be married to fucking *Peri*."

"Um..."

Still confused, though now a little freaked.

"Judge would not need to get me a job at River Rain," he went on.

She stared at him.

"Alex, honey, I would probably never have met you."

Her body pulsed.

There it was.

"Yeah," he said.

"Oh," she said.

"Maybe on a hike with the kids or something. But I'd *then* be thinking how I got my shit in the sling of being married to a selfish, self-absorbed woman, and possibly allowing her to be the mother of my kid. I would not be thinking about the cute trail guide with all the hair and the great ass wondering what she'd think of my big dick."

The dimple flirted with her cheek.

"Though, I hate to say this, especially to you, and remember, this is me trapped in an imaginary marriage with Peri, but even so, it's gospel truth, if I got a good look at your ass, I might be thinking it."

The dimple fully popped.

"So what? Now I'm supposed to be happy that tree fell on me?" he asked.

And another pulse went through her.

"You get me," he stated.

"I don't have an answer for all of that, sweetheart," she confessed.

"I know," he returned. "I don't either. It's one of those things in life.

Something fucking sucks and something fucking awesome happens because of it. It makes no goddamn sense. But there it is."

"Something fucking awesome?" she asked.

"Babe," he growled. "Seriously?"

She did the lip pressing and big eyes thing at the same time.

Christ.

She stopped doing those and asked, "Are you done shouting and pacing?"

"I think so," he answered.

She hesitated.

Then she moved.

And she hit him like a bullet.

He rocked back on a foot and wrapped his arms around her.

"Al—"

Her body hitched, and the sob exploded.

Oh Christ.

Fuck, but he'd fucked this.

He tightened his arms, dropped his lips to her hair and whispered, "Baby."

She didn't reply, didn't take her face out of his chest, she held on and her frame shook with her emotion.

"I'm a dick," he muttered.

"I'm s-sorry," she sniveled into his chest. "This isn't about me. B-but th-he last f-few days…they h-hurt."

"I know, baby. I'm such a fucking asshole, pulling that shit on you."

"B-but, I p-promised."

"Promised what?"

"We'd end, and I'd b-be okay. W-we'd s-still be f-friends."

"That was fucked up, sweetheart, and we both knew it. C'mon." He gave her a squeeze. "We both knew it."

"I didn't know it."

God-fucking-dammit.

"I'm such a fucking dick," he bit off.

She tipped her head back, he lifted his and saw her face red, eyes swollen and wet.

Shit.

"You were dealing with stuff," she said.

"You don't jack your woman around when you're dealing with stuff."

"Probably not," she allowed.

"Christ, Alex, *definitely* not."

"Well, it's not little shit you were dealing with," she defended his treating her like shit.

"Babe, it could be the last few hours before the big meteor hits, I'm a dick to you, you call my ass on it, get me?"

She stared up at him.

Then she grabbed his head, brought his lips crashing down on hers, and her little tongue was dancing in his mouth.

The taste of her, even the tears on her lips, Rix couldn't hack it.

He crushed her against him, took over the kiss...

This lasted a second before she tore from his arms.

He was confused half a second before he saw her running to the stairs.

He chased after her.

He caught her halfway up, whirled her, threw her over his shoulder, and her surprised *"oof"* scored through his dick.

He hit the top, got across the space, and tossed her on her back on the bed.

She recovered from the bounce pulling off her sweater.

He stood beside the bed and ripped off his Henley.

She was pushing her jeans down her legs while he finished with his belt.

Her pants hit the floor when his dick sprang free.

He barely had his jeans over his ass before his hips jerked because she'd latched on to his dick and was pulling him by it.

"Baby," he growled.

He could tell by her face she wanted it in her mouth.

He wanted it somewhere else.

Fortunately, he was bigger and stronger than her.

She lost purchase when Rix twisted and landed on his ass in the bed.

Alex made a mew of protest.

He swung her to straddling him.

She instantly got with the program.

Their hands bumped when they both went to position him.

She pulled away first.

He pulled away when she bore down on him.

"God, fuck," he groaned, reaching up to tug the band out of her ponytail.

She moved on him.

Her hair tumbled down.

He took a fistful of it and pulled it back.

She moved faster on him.

He yanked the cup of her bra down and sucked in her tit.

She moaned, her pussy convulsed, and now she was milking him.

He left her tit out, went to her mouth, and encouraged, "Go, baby. Fuck me."

Alex wrapped her arms around him, eyes hot and wild, cunt hungry, and she fucked him.

Dazed and gorgeous, he nearly lost control when she breathed, "Rix."

"Right here, honey."

"You'll never lose me."

Then she arched deep and came in his lap.

Rix watched, got off on her beauty, grasped her hips and guided her to give him the same.

His neck was bent, face in her tits, her arms around his head, when he came down.

"I'm gonna clean up this time," she said quietly.

He tipped his head back to refute that, but she got there before him.

"If you leave my bed, I'll…"

She didn't finish.

He felt his lips quirk. "You'll what?"

"Be mad," she stated firmly, and totally lamely.

"Couldn't have that," he muttered.

"Huh," she huffed, pressed her lips to his, unfortunately giving him no tongue, then climbed off him.

He was still hard so he grunted at losing her.

But she quickly made her way to the bathroom.

He fell back and hitched up his jeans, tucking his cock in. He wasn't big on losing her, but he had to admit, the handling and scrape on his slick, sensitive dick after having her back felt fucking great.

He didn't bother doing up his jeans or even sitting up.

She came back, bra righted, and untangled her panties from her own jeans. She slid them up then climbed in bed with him.

Just his head raised, Rix watched all that.

He let it fall to the bed when she fell full body on him.

"We gotta practice your threats," he teased.

"You didn't move from my bed," she pointed out.

"Right."

He grinned.

He stopped grinning when he noticed her eyes were swollen.

He framed the side of her face and stroked under her eye with the pad of this thumb, and it was a groan when he said, "I'm sorry."

Alex pressed into his hand, then dropped her head and shoved her face in his neck.

Rix curled his arms around her and shared, "It always keeps coming, Alex."

"What does?"

He didn't answer.

He gave orders.

"You need to call me on it. You need to get in my face. You need to shake my shit. You need to make certain I don't fuck up again."

"Rix—"

"And that's not fair to you. That shouldn't be yours."

"But—"

"If I was whole, you wouldn't have to deal with that kinda shit."

Her body locked.

"From the beginning, I'm holding you back," he continued, "when we both knew we were in deep. That was some stupid shit."

"We need to go back to—"

"And it isn't on. I don't even wanna think about where your head was at the last coupla days. You threw a fucking surprise party for me, my folks came down, all my buds were here, and I walk out on you? *Fuck.*"

She lifted up and wrapped her fingers over his mouth.

"Would you shut up?" she demanded. "God, I don't even have a shot at busting your balls. You're too busy doing it for me."

She glared in his face.

It was pretty hilarious.

He didn't laugh.

When she seemed to ascertain it was safe to do it, she took her hand from his mouth and demanded, "How are you not whole?"

"Babe." It was a quiet admonition.

"Okay, yes, right. I'll rephrase. You're whole to me. You lost something, and I'm not negating that. It left you with baggage. I'm not saying that's not heavy. But Rix, honey, stop making up shit to make it worse. I don't get it, but I'm in this with you, and I get that you're carrying it. Don't add me. I'm not a weight to be carried, and frankly, honey, it doesn't feel good that you think of me that way."

"I shouldn't have done that to you," he pressed.

"We both agree. But it's over, right?"

"It's never over," he warned.

"I know. But this one is. *Right?*"

"I just don't want you to think you should let me shit on you because I got shit to deal with."

"Okay, lesson learned. What's next?"

He framed her face in both hands because he needed her to *get this.*

"Alex, I hurt you, and I am not down with that."

"Rix, if you had your feet, you'd hurt me. Okay, I'm not Queen Relationship, but I have friends. I've heard stories. I know people. When you spend time with someone you care about, no matter how careful you might try to be, it'll happen eventually. It happened. We both learned from it. I hope you let some things go. Now...*what's next?*"

What's next?

She was so...goddamned...*amazing.*

He rolled her so he was on top and growled, "I'm gonna fuck you again, that's what's next."

She looked to her hairline, and even if her hands went down his jeans to his ass, she bitched, "He thinks sex fixes everything."

"It wasn't me who bunny-hopped the stairs so my woman would chase me," he pointed out.

Her eyes snapped to his. "I didn't bunny-hop the stairs."

"Did you want me to chase you?"

"I wanted us to have make-up sex in my bed."

"So you wanted me to chase you."

"Yes," she snapped. "Yeesh. I wanted you to chase me. Or at least follow me. But I don't *bunny-hop.*"

"You are a total fuck bunny."

She pulled one hand out of his jeans to smack his ass. "Rix! I'm not a fuck bunny!"

"My dick swung free, and you latched on like it was a lead."

Both her hands went to his shoulders, she shoved back, arched her neck and cried, "Ugh!"

He took the opportunity she offered, dipped his head, nipped her neck, then licked it.

"Hello?"

Both of them froze.

"We're here! And we brought tequila!"

The first was Gal.

That last was Kate.

Alex righted her head, and Rix lifted his.

"She's not in the bathroom." Gal.

"She isn't on the deck." Katie.

"What's this all over the wall and floor?" Gal.

"Oh my God. Do you think she's okay?" Katie.

"I'm up here!" Alex called.

"Oh! Hey!" Katie called back.

He swung off her and the bed.

"With, uh…Rix," Alex continued sharing.

Silence from below.

Rix did up all but one button and didn't bother with the belt.

He had a point to make.

He walked to the railing.

Both of them stared up at him, mouths open.

"Hey," he greeted.

Neither said a word.

"We're kinda busy," he told them.

"*Rix!*" Alex hissed from behind him.

From the noises she was making, she was getting dressed.

A waste of effort.

Gal recovered first. "We can see."

"Oh my God. Holy hell. Your chest is…*whoa*," Katie said, staggering back a step, her hand fluttering up to her neck.

Alex came up beside him. "Hey, guys."

"So he finally figured out he's falling for you," Gal remarked.

"Uh…" Alex said.

"Yes," Rix said.

He felt her gaze shoot to him.

Gal grinned.

"*Whoa!*" Katie shouted happily.

"We'll just take our tequila and go," Gal said.

"You can leave the tequila," Rix replied.

Gal lifted her hand to her forehead and flicked out a salute.

She also put the full paper bag she was holding on the coffee table.

Rix seriously liked that woman.

She approached Kate and grabbed her arm. "Let's go."

"I wanna stare at his chest some more," Katie protested.

"No. Let's go."

"Okay, I *need* to stare at his chest some more." She put her hands in prayer position in front of her. "*Pleeeeeease.*"

She said this as Gal dragged her to the door.

Before they used it, Gal sent them another grin.

Katie blew them a kiss.

The door closed.

Rix turned to Alex. "Why the fuck did you get dressed?"

"You're falling for me?"

"Babe."

He was sure that said it all.

She didn't move.

He did.

Dropping a shoulder, he hefted her up.

"Rix!"

She slapped his back.

He bumped her, and she went up then down on her bed.

He bent and went for her jeans, grumbling, "Waste of fuckin' time."

She slapped at his hands. "Oh my God. You're annoying. Let me do it."

She unzipped.

He yanked them down her legs.

Then he landed on her.

"Teamwork," he said.

"I'm falling for you too," she announced.

She didn't have to say it.

He'd seen it earlier, coming down at him.

Felt it, washing over him.

He'd known how big it was.

So big and strong, it carried it all away.

It might be gone.

It might come back.

But for then, for the first time in too long of a time, he'd lost the heavy.

And he could think about what was next.

"I know," he said.

She rolled her eyes.

Rix smiled at her.

And then he kissed her.

LATE THAT NIGHT, HE LEFT ALEX ASLEEP IN BED.

He put on his legs, jeans, Henley, and walked down the stairs.

As quietly as he could, he cleaned up the glass and the whisky.

One good thing about artificial feet, you cut them on glass, they didn't hurt or bleed.

Once he'd wiped shit down and it was all good, he pulled his phone out of his back pocket and went out on the deck.

Another good thing?

Your feet didn't get cold.

The phone rang, and it was a shit thing to do, calling this late, but he knew the last couple of days, Judge worried.

He needed to end that for his friend.

He'd definitely worried.

Three rings and a sleepy, "Rix? You good?"

"I'm falling in love with her, man."

Zero hesitation and…

"Yeah," Judge replied.

"I keep throwing obstacles in her path."

"Yeah."

"She just keeps vaulting over them."

Sleep gone, humor in its place, and another, "Yeah."

"I need to ask you, man. Don't let me fuck this up."

"Rix, you are without a doubt the single best man I know. You won't fuck this up."

Rix shut his eyes.

"You with her now?" Judge asked.

He opened his eyes. "She's upstairs, asleep."

"Go to her. I'll see you tomorrow."

"Yeah, thanks, later."

"Hang on…" Silence and then, "Chloe says she loves you."

Rix's chest heaved.

Then he pushed out, "Tell her she's got that back."

"Will do. Later."

"Later."

They hung up.

Rix went inside.

He made sure everything was locked up.

He went upstairs, got undressed, sat on the side of the bed and took off his legs.

Careful, he swung under the covers and curled into Alex.

"Okay?" she mumbled.

"Yeah, go back to sleep."

She pressed close.

Rix pressed in, pushing his thigh between her legs.

She hooked hers on the outside of it.

If he tried real hard, he could feel his calf resting on the sheet, instead of his knee resting there, half a calf and then…nothing.

He didn't try hard.

He focused on Alex's soft skin hugging his thigh.

And he fell asleep.

CHAPTER 20

THE FAMILY

Rix

 *our days later...*

Rix was totally going to fuck this up.

He pressed go on his phone, put it to his ear, shoved the jacket of his four thousand dollar suit back (yeah, he and Alex looked it up, her laughing, him stunned speechless) and shoved his hand in his pocket while he looked out the back window.

Ferns and shrubbery and a fireplace built at the bottom of a tall statement wall made of shiny gray something and edged in what looked like chrome.

Built-in seating.

And a built-in fucking bookshelf.

In the back fucking yard.

There was a fire burning in the fireplace.

And there was nobody out there.

Suffice it to say, they'd made it to New York.

They'd arrived the evening before.

It was a quarter to eight the next night.

And Rix had not yet met a single member of her family.

But he wanted to kill them.

"Yo, how's it going?" Judge answered.

"Well, we showed up last night," he said.

"Yeah," Judge replied slowly.

"No one met the plane."

Silence.

"They didn't even send a car. Alex had to call Cathy, her sister's assistant. The rich people airport has a nice lounge. It still sucked we waited an hour and a half in it, after sitting on a five-hour flight, even though Cathy said she'd send a luxury Lyft, and it'd be there in ten minutes. Apparently, she also told Blake she was doing this, and Blake lost her shit and said no Lyft. Sharps didn't do Lyft. Send a limo. So we waited for a fucking limo. Which it's worth a repeat, took an hour and a half. And nobody told us this change of plans, or we would have ordered our own goddamned Lyft. But we kept thinking the goddamned Lyft would show and no one would respond to Alex's calls or texts asking what the fuck was going on."

"I'm thinking, although that shit is already not right, there's an 'and,'" Judge remarked warily when Rix took a second to calm his shit.

"There's an 'and,'" he confirmed. "*And* we get to her dad's place, he's not here. But the staff is expecting us, though they expected us a couple hours earlier. The mom isn't here either. Sister. Nobody. We're fuckin' starved at this point, and they say they were instructed to make us dinner, anything we want. Problem is, we were supposed to be there hours before to tell them what to make. They ask us what we'd like to eat, and they'll cook it for us. You wouldn't believe the options they rattled off, which would probably take six hours to make. They're practically barring the kitchen so we can't scrounge up some cheese and crackers or something. We ended up going out, and we got slices of pizza from some walkup place Alex digs. By the way, the pizza here is the shit. So far, that's the best thing that's happened."

"New York pizza *is* the shit, Rix. But it isn't the best thing about New York."

"I'll take your word for it," Rix lamely joked.

Judge didn't sound amused when he asked, "What else?"

"Nothing today except her dad, her mom, her sister, fucking Cathy, members of staff and other assistants calling, telling Alex they'd let us know where we're to be, when. We're up way fuckin' early, because of the time change, but also early here, so we can get ready to rumble. First we're meeting the mom for breakfast, even though we're staying with the dad. And mind, Judge, been in his house twenty-four hours, seen hide nor hair of the asshole."

"Shit."

"But, the mom cancels breakfast. Then we're on with Blake and the mom for brunch. That's canceled. Since Alex is free, and the dad somehow hears of it, he decides he wants us for lunch. We go to some fancy restaurant, wait half an hour, some skinny guy in a suit shows and apologizes profusely that Mr. Sharp won't be able to make it, but please, enjoy ourselves, he's picking up the tab. So obviously, I got the fucking lobster, times two, and that would be times two just for me. Also always wanted to taste Dom, and now I have."

Judge laughed.

Rix wanted to get there.

But he couldn't.

"Blake says she wants us early for the cocktail party, a family gathering, and she *so can't wait* to meet me. We're supposed to pitch up somewhere, *not* where the cocktail party is happening. Which isn't here. The dad hates anyone in his house except staff, family at a push and 'close friends,' which Alex knows as his mistresses. Of which she also knows that number is plural."

"Jesus," Judge muttered.

"Yeah, so Alex is an old hand at this and has since realized that, even with the upcoming festivities, it's going to be standard operating procedure. Since it is, she tells me we shouldn't hold our breath to learn deets on when and where this family cocktail hour is gonna happen. Good thing. Blake never shares. So I lied about the pizza. We had hours to kill, and I took her mind off shit in ways we both like. *That's* the best part of New York so far. Now our new limo has been outside, waiting for us for the last hour, we're supposed to be there already, and Alex's phone is blowing up with demands from her mom and sister to know where the fuck she is."

Again, silence from Judge, but this time Rix could feel his own fury mirroring back at him.

So he repeated, "Yeah. This means I escaped the vicinity of her phone so I wouldn't lose my goddamned mind, and I'm downstairs in what could double as a museum or a mausoleum, not sure which. It's so big, it could be both."

He took a breath.

And kept going.

"So we leave at noon on Sunday. That's eighty-eight hours from now. But I'm not sure I'll make it through the next ten minutes without committing a felony." He pulled in another breath and finished, "The dad's got some good art. Feeling it'll look better after it sails through a window."

"Blow them off, do your thing, enjoy New York," Judge advised.

"That's precisely my plan. But first, I got this cocktail shit to get through."

"Okay then, I was going to let it be a surprise, but now I'm going to tell you. Good news on that. Dad and Dru were invited to all this shit. They declined at first, except for the wedding. They've since sent word they'll be attending."

"Thank fuck," he muttered.

"Thank fuck, what?" Alex asked.

Rix turned.

And stopped dead.

Because from the time he escaped her phone ringing in their room, to now, his woman had become another woman.

A sleeveless dress with full skirt that hit her knees. It was made of, fuck, he didn't know what it was. He just knew it was gorgeous. Embroidery or something, blue flowers and little birds, hints of red, all this edged in black on a netting over nude fabric. That stuff covered her over her breasts, then it was sheer at her chest, with just a couple of little birds floating around, a thin line of flowers at the throat, which was prettier than any necklace. A slim, black satin ribbon for a belt.

Her hair was pulled back, up, but soft.

Her makeup was full, most he'd ever seen her wear, but still subdued and perfect.

Her cheeks were shiny.

There were diamond earrings dropping from her ears, made up of tiers of big flowers and leaves that nearly brushed her shoulders and probably cost more than his house.

And high heeled sandals that looked like they were made of thin, black satin ribbons that included a sexy-as-fuck ankle strap.

He could smell her and…

His whole body felt the sight of the fact she was wearing his ring.

First time he'd seen it since he bought it.

And it was on her left finger.

"Alex is here," he grunted to Judge. "She's ready. Gotta go."

"You got this."

"Yeah," he forced out.

"You got *her*, Rix."

That cleared it.

"Yeah," he said firmly.

"Call me, try to have fun. Later."

"Later."

She was in front of him.

"Thank fuck what?" she repeated.

He didn't answer.

He reached down and nabbed her left hand.

He pulled it between them, the back of it facing up.

And thumbed the ring.

It did fit.

Perfect.

"Honey," she whispered.

His eyes went to hers. "That was Judge. Jamie and Dru are gonna be there tonight."

She smiled. "That's good. Friends. People you know."

"You look beautiful."

Her face got soft, she swished her hips, but she said, "Camouflage."

His attention went to the side of her neck. "You bringing Brooke with us tonight?"

She lifted her free hand, touched her earring. "She'd want to know what's going on."

"I don't know the woman, but I can confirm she really wanted you the fuck out of here, baby. Those earrings could buy a fleet of cars. Maybe a fleet of planes."

"Blake will know they're Grandmother's, and she'll be furious."

"Awesome."

Her lips tipped up.

"Ready?" he asked.

Her fingers caught tight hold of his, and her eyes didn't leave his own, a message he did not miss in the slightest, as she replied, "Absolutely."

IT WAS OCTOBER IN NEW YORK.

It was fucking cold.

And this cocktail party was outside on a roof terrace.

But no worries, they had space heaters.

Everywhere.

It felt like July.

They hit it, and Alex immediately said, "Okay, be cool."

"New plan. I'm not gonna throw some art in the outdoor fireplace that's burning even though there's no one there to keep warm. I'm gonna kidnap the man, take him north, and drown him in an area of the ocean that used to be an ice cap."

She laughed softly.

He looked down at her. "I'm being serious."

She looked up at him, laughing less softly and with more hilarity.

His vision exploded.

So did hers, he knew, because after he recovered, he saw her hand up over her brow and she was blinking.

He scowled at the photographer.

"One more, maybe two," the man asked eagerly. "Sister of the bride and her handsome fiancé."

Rix opened his mouth to tell the guy to fuck off.

Alex pressed to his side, sliding her arm around his waist, and said, "Of course."

He wrapped his arm around her, got rid of the scowl, but on principal, refused to smile.

The guy didn't take two shots, he took maybe seven.

Then he lowered his camera from his face and stared at the back, cooing. "These are *wonderful*."

"I need a drink," Rix muttered.

Alex laughed again.

He spotted a bar, they made it a step in that direction, then in a cultured English accent…

"There you are."

A slim woman in a pale pink dress with black lace at the shoulders and waist, lustrous dark hair cut to hit the middle of her swan-like neck, hair that was arranged to be off the face and behind one ear so you could see the black diamonds dripping from it, was in their space.

Her eyes were a deep blue.

Her skin was perfect pale.

She looked a little like Elizabeth Taylor in her later years, without the curves.

Alex's mother, Helena.

"We've been waiting for you," she snapped at Alex. "Family pictures were to happen at seven-thirty sharp."

Um…no.

But yeah.

He was totally going to fuck this up.

Not even a hello for her daughter?

One she hadn't seen since last Christmas?

"Hey, hi, nice to meet you," Rix butted in, lifting his hand to her.

She jerked back, her eyes came up, they were peeved, they got a good look of him, and her face went slack.

For a moment.

Then she rearranged it and smiled, lifting her hand, not to his, but so he'd take hers.

"You must be John," she drawled.

"No, Rix," he said, not taking her fingers, grabbing her hand and giving it a firm shake.

He then let her go.

She looked like she'd been mauled.

He glanced at Alex, who had her head turned away.

"Babe," he called.

She turned back, but hadn't yet put away the dimple.

Fuck.

She found this funny.

Guess that was a good thing.

"Yes, right, hello, Mum." She leaned in and they both did this shit where they swayed side to side, not getting even close to hugging or planting kisses on each other's cheeks or even touching at all, then she was back. "Family pictures? I didn't know there were family pictures."

"Cathy sent you an itinerary. Didn't you read it?" Helena asked snippily.

"I did, but it didn't say family pictures," Alex replied.

Helena opened her mouth, but said nothing as her eyes turned into slits.

"That's because we're not fucking doing family fucking pictures. We don't need family fucking pictures at every fucking hoop we have to jump through in this fucking dog and pony show."

A good-looking, well-built man who was maybe a couple inches shorter than Rix, with a white streak through his graying hair at the left temple, wearing a suit that Rix, who knew nothing about this shit, still knew cost twice as much as his, shouldered in and grabbed Alex by the shoulders.

Rix crowded them.

But the guy just pulled her up, kissed her cheek, and murmured, "Hello, darling."

He let her go and stepped back as Alex murmured in return, "Hey, Dad."

Her father did a once-over of her and declared, "You look beautiful."

Okay, maybe the dad was all right.

"She needs a bracelet. Her wrists are bare," Helena decreed.

The mom, though…no.

"She doesn't need a fucking bracelet, Helena, she's wearing Bernhard at her ears," the dad, whose name Rix knew was Edward, bit off.

"Your mother isn't here anymore, Ned, so please kindly stop kissing her ass," Helena retorted, saccharine sweet.

Edward cut through his ex-wife with a look and turned back to his daughter. "Don't listen to her. You're perfect."

"She is," Rix put in.

The guy's eyes cut again, to Alex's side and up to Rix.

He looked Rix up and down, nodded, and offered his hand. "It's good to finally meet you, John."

Rix took his hand, made sure the grip was firm, saw the man register it, approve, though Rix couldn't give fewer fucks, and he replied, "It's Rix and good to meet you too."

"Rix, yes, Rix. I remember that. Rix," Edward repeated in that way Rix knew people did when they repeated names of people who meant nothing to them, but they didn't want to be caught out not remembering it should they need it in the future.

They let go of each other's hands, and Helena decreed, "The photographer has been waiting."

"Would you allow, perhaps, your daughter and future son-in-law to get themselves a drink?"

"The bar isn't going anywhere," Helena sniped.

"Neither is the photographer," Edward returned.

She tried to launch daggers from her eyes as Edward dismissed her and caught someone's attention.

A second didn't elapse before an employee showed, not a server, someone in charge.

"Darling?" Edward asked Alex what she wanted to drink.

"Champagne," Alex ordered.

Edward looked up at Rix.

"Beer."

"An ale or a stout or a porter," Alex put in quickly to the staff person.

That person curved off.

"Good. Hearty. I have some craft brews at home. We'll share some by the fire while you're here," Edward invited.

"Good Lord," Helena muttered. "Since when do you drink beer?"

"We've been divorced for twenty-one glorious years. You don't know what I drink," Edward shot back.

"Mum. Dad. Rix and I haven't had dinner. And, you know, maybe it'd be good if you two weren't at each other's throats the first time you meet my guy *and* at Blake's nuptial celebration cocktail party."

"She means you," Edward said to Helena.

"She means *you*," Helena said to Edward.

Rix bent to her ear and whispered, "That's a no, baby."

She turned her head his way and giggled.

Fucking giggled.

He looked into her eyes, which were twinkling.

Right.

Maybe New York *was* gonna be fun.

"Okay?" he asked unnecessarily.

Lifting her clasped hands to her chest, she leaned into him, front to front, and tipped her head back.

He put his hands to her waist, felt her skirt around his thighs, saw the full back of it poof out, it looked great, it felt sexy as fuck, but still, he gave all that up to brush his lips to hers.

"Hey ho! We're the only ones allowed not to keep our hands off each other."

They broke away but only so Alex could slide back to his side, and they both latched on to each other before they faced a younger version of Helena in a cream, figure-hugging dress of all lace, showing serious cleavage, sky high heels, her dark hair much longer than her mother's and falling in her face on one side.

Blake.

With her was a tall, slender, blond dude with what Rix reckoned was a fake tan, because he'd never seen skin that color.

Chad.

"You must be Rix, yes? Is it Rix?" Chad asked, offering his hand.

"Yeah, Rix," Rix confirmed, taking it. "And you're Chad."

"Whoa, buddy!" Chad exclaimed. "No need to cut down any trees here," he went on jovially, pulling his hand from Rix's and trying to hide he was flexing it.

Good Christ.

Rix hadn't even squeezed hard.

"Rix, lovely," Blake murmured, then he experienced the whole sway side to side thing without touching when she did that to him, though he didn't sway.

He was right.

It was weird.

When she moved away, she draped herself on Chad's arm. "Chad and I are *so glad* you could come."

"Thanks for having me," Rix returned.

Blake looked to Alex and her fake welcome washed from her face. "Alex."

"Hi, Blake."

"You're in Grandmother's flowers."

Rix pulled Alex closer.

"They go with the dress," Alex replied.

"Very pretty dress, babe," Chad said.

And Rix's eyes snapped to him.

Chad was giving Alex a down and up but he felt Rix's attention, the orange of his face remained, but there was pale under it, and he leaned a bit back.

A server showed with a tray on which was a glass of champagne and another of beer.

Rix took the champagne for Alex, gave it to her, and was going after the beer when Blake bitched, "The bride doesn't get served?"

"What do you want, darling?" Edward asked.

She had her eyes aimed at Alex's champagne.

And he'd have called it before she said, "Champagne," in a way that it was clear she expected Alex to give hers up.

Okay, the sister?

Hell no.

"I'll get you one from the bar," Rix offered.

Blake opened her mouth.

"*Rix!*"

He turned.

And he smiled when he saw a flame-haired beauty making her way through the crowd.

He let Alex go right before Dru threw herself in his arms.

"Sweetheart," he murmured.

"It's so good to see you!" she cried, holding tight.

He held tight too, until she popped back, clicked her teeth, bopped her head, and slapped his chest. "You! Always so dapper in a suit."

She was in green satin, on the bottom, some posh sweater material, top, skirt like Alex's, long sleeves.

"And you look gorgeous," he returned.

"Rix," a deep voice said.

He looked up.

Dru moved out of the way as he one hundred percent hand gripped, chest bumped and back pounded Judge's dad, Jamie Oakley.

"Jamie, man, hey," he greeted.

Jamie held on through his, "Good to see you," and then held on longer before they let go and stepped back.

"Of course, you're all friends." Helena smoothed her way in there.

Jamie and Dru gave polite salutations to all and congratulations to Blake and Chad and then Rix shouldered in, pulling Alex back to him.

"Jamie, Dru, this is my woman, Alex."

"Hey," Dru said, moving in for a quick but genuine hug. "So cool to meet you. Chloe *loves* you."

"Good to meet you too," Alex replied, returning the hug, also genuinely.

"Alex, we met when you were a little girl," Jamie came in for a genuine cheek kiss and moved back. "You probably don't remember."

"Sorry, I don't," she said quietly.

"You were usually off in England or at a park whenever I was at your dad's," Jamie noted. "Always busy."

Alex ducked into Rix's pit.

There was his shy girl.

He slid his arm around her.

"That's my Alexandra. Never once complained she was bored or had nothing to do," Edward announced proudly. "If she wasn't daydreaming by the lake in Central Park, she was reading about the Loch Ness monster in the library."

"She has more wellingtons at Norton than the queen has in Sandringham," Helena crowed.

Blake had a look like she could spit rocks.

Right.

Maybe there was a dynamic here that Alex hadn't cottoned on to.

"You were getting me champagne, Rix," Blake prompted snottily.

"He's not a servant," Edward hissed. "Chad, get your fiancée a drink, for Chrissakes."

Blake's eyes did the slit thing her mother's had done.

Chad took off, and honest as fuck, Rix would swear he was escaping.

Yup.

Definitely a dynamic Alex hadn't cottoned on to.

"Dad and I want you two to come over while you're in town," Dru said to Rix and Alex. "I know there are a lot of wedding things happening, but I talked to Chloe, and she told me when you're free. Maybe dinner tomorrow?"

"We're having a family dinner tomorrow," Blake put in.

"Like we had a family cocktail hour today?" Rix muttered for only Alex to hear.

She bumped him with her hip.

Edward turned on Blake.

"I think your sister, who took time away from a job that means something and flew five hours to be here for your wedding, only to arrive and find that the assistant *I'm* paying for didn't arrange for a transfer from the airport to her family home so she and her fiancé had to go out and find pizza for dinner, for God's sake, can perhaps take a little bit of *her* time, which is actually *worth* something, because someone, that someone being *Hale Wheeler*, pays her for it, in order to visit with friends while she's home. Don't you?" Edward asked irately.

Jamie cleared his throat.

"Ned. We're in company," Helena scolded under her breath.

"Of course, Daddy," Blake whispered.

Edward looked to Rix. "She's thirty, and she calls me Daddy."

Rix said nothing, because he didn't like any of these people, but the dude was harsh.

He also thought of Kinsley, and that he hoped, if he had girls, they called him whatever they wanted to call him, just as long as they did it with love, until the day he died.

"We're hogging you. You have guests." Alex turned pointedly to her dad. "All of you. Mingle. We'll catch up with you later."

"Darling, I want some father-daughter time with you," Edward declared. "Before you go back. And you," he turned to Rix. "We'll need a discussion."

Alex tensed.

"I'm here for it," Rix said.

"Good," Edward replied.

"Dear, you'll be at the brunch tomorrow?" Helena was pushing in to do the sway thing again with Alex, so he had to let her go.

She came right back to him. "Of course, Mum."

"Do you have a hat?" Helena asked.

"Lord God, with the damned hats," Edward complained.

"Chloe Pierce went shopping with me," Alex said fast, in order to cut her mom and dad off from resuming their act.

Helen's arched brows arched further at the mention of Chloe.

"You'll like what we picked," Alex finished.

"That *is* a pretty dress," she muttered, doing it only because she knew who Chloe was, who Chloe's parents were, who Chloe's godfather was, and who Chloe was going to be marrying.

Not that Alex was wearing it.

Yeah.

The mom was a wash.

With a cold smile to Rix that he took zero offense to, because he reckoned it was the only kind she had, she flitted away.

Edward was already gone.

Blake had disappeared.

Chad came up, holding two glasses of champagne and looking confused. "Where's Blake?"

"Don't know, man. Mingling," Rix told him.

He continued to look confused before he grinned, sipped from one glass, then the other, turned and wandered off like he was at a frat party.

Once Chad was gone, Rix looked down at his woman. "You don't look like any of them. Are you sure you're theirs?"

Her lips went up.

Dru giggled.

"If it's going to be trouble for you, Alex," Jamie chimed in, "we can do a lunch. Breakfast. We'd really just like to spend some time with Rix before he goes."

"Dinner tomorrow would be *amazing*," Alex said with relief.

"Excellent," Jamie replied. "Nothing fancy. Completely casual. Just family."

"I'll make my spaghetti," Dru decided.

Jamie hugged his daughter to his side. "Her spaghetti is delicious."

"So what are you wearing to the brunch?" Dru asked. With a visible return hug to her father, she separated from him, moving to form a two-person girl huddle with Alex. "I was invited, but I can't go. I have something on."

Rix didn't let Alex go and watched this carefully.

Alex gave him an *I'm all right* squeeze and shifted away.

So he released her.

He continued to watch until he saw Alex was all good.

He then turned to Jamie.

Jamie didn't miss this and raised his brows.

Rix gave a short shake of his head.

They made small talk until Dru suddenly said, "Incoming, so we're outgoing," and then, hooked to Alex, they took off, Dru muttering dramatically, "Blake's bridesmaids. *No bueno.*"

And before Rix could react, they were lost in the crowd.

He sensed them, like if there were birds anywhere near this place, they'd all immediately take flight, and locked eyes on a trio of three gorgeous women dressed to show bodies they were very proud of, staring off toward where Dru and Alex disappeared.

Though one of them was drinking up Rix.

He turned his shoulder to them and gave Jamie his attention.

"I talk to my son," Jamie declared. "I know."

Rix sucked in a breath.

"Full disclosure, Chloe and Dru talk even more frankly, and we've got our orders. Things have been rough going for you two, and we're to make sure you both don't get bitten to shit in this viper's den."

Straight up.

He loved this guy.

"Tell me," Rix demanded.

"Helena?"

Rix nodded.

Jamie shook his head.

"I don't know her. She spends more time in England than here. Though she's well-heeled and well-connected, she's not well liked."

"No surprise. The dad?"

"Honestly?"

Rix nodded again.

"I like Ned. Quite a lot. I was growing up in Texas while he was growing up here, but the lore of the Bernhard-Sharps is legendary. Both sides of that family, for generations, all the same. There was a man he was meant to be, and if as a boy he didn't show signs of being that man, he was made into that man by any means necessary. Ned became that man."

Another nod from Rix.

"That said, the last five years or so, he's mellowed. I think because Helena is mostly out of the country and not driving him insane, something she spends a great amount of time doing. And Blake began to have her own pursuits which stopped including doing everything she could, most of it not good, to get his attention. He was able to be who he is or just stop dropping out to escape their games or bolstering his defenses to withstand them and actually start enjoying his own life."

"And his youngest daughter?"

Jamie watched Rix closely as he said, "He talks about her. A lot. Even before Hale got involved with the work you do. And not just because our kids worked together. He's proud of her. I think he misses her. I think she was the only sanity he had in his life."

Jamie got closer and kept going.

"Rix, you should know, she's out here because of Ned. He found out she wasn't in the wedding party, and saw the guest list and that she hadn't RSVPed. He asked why. When Blake made some excuse about how her invitation must have been lost in the mail, he asked why she was getting an invitation rather than wearing a bridesmaid's dress. And since he's not only paying for her wedding, he, alone, controls both their trust funds—"

"Holy fuck."

That was news.

Jamie dipped his chin. "Yes, until they're thirty-five. He can cut them off. He can reinvest. He can donate. And he can invoke, that being invoke clauses that would mean one fund would absorb the other, like Alex would get Blake's. Or it would be absorbed back into the family estate. My guess is, he cited the clauses and Blake asked Alex to be in the wedding. But my sense is, the bottom line in all of that was that he wanted an excuse to see his youngest daughter."

"Did planes stop flying westward?" Rix asked. "He get banned from his own home, which we spent last night and most of today in and we haven't seen him at all? That is, when we weren't waiting at a restaurant to have lunch with him, but he didn't show."

"Ned's a complicated man, Rix. In New York, for the last century and a half, his family hasn't only been one of the most prominent, they're also one of the most important. He employs a lot of people. He wields a great deal of influence. He takes both seriously, and as far as I can see, he handles them fairly. But that amount of responsibility takes time to manage. I'm not saying this in his defense. I just think, in his own way, he loves his girl. I always thought that, but when pictures started surfacing of her and you, and he knew I knew you, he was the one who told me a lot of this."

"He feel you out about me?"

"Absolutely."

"So that's why I got friendly Ned, we're buddies. Because you talked me up."

One side of Jamie's mouth lifted.

"No, I told him you were what you are. Loyal as hell. The best friend my son could have. Gentle with women. And your own man. He admires those things. So that's why you got friendly Ned."

Rix smirked. "Gentle with women?"

Jamie returned the smirk. "He didn't need to know that you give Chloe shit every chance you can."

Rix was relieved to have a real reason to laugh.

"Though, you'd throw yourself in front of a bullet for her or Dru, and I might have mentioned that," Jamie continued.

Rix grinned at him.

Jamie also returned that but then he got serious again.

"I remember Alexandra as a quiet kid. Bright. Very active. But shy. I've seen her more than once, Rix, but I didn't want to say it that way because I knew she wouldn't remember me, and I didn't want to make things awkward. She was always in another world, or maybe trying very hard to pretend she wasn't in the one she was in."

"That hasn't changed."

"You two okay?"

Rix didn't fuck around.

"We're falling in love."

Jamie's head ticked to the side, but he let show he was happy for Rix.

"She doesn't like crowds," Rix told him. "Her family has treated her like shit. You're not wrong in your take. She's learned to retreat into a shell where she feels safe, so right now, she's exposed. And she doesn't like it so I *really* don't like it."

Jamie dipped his chin again. "So, in the end, you're here to protect your woman, and I'm telling you how to shore your resources. Because Helena is not a warm person and Blake is a goddamn mess."

"Tell me about her. Blake."

"I don't know much about her either, except being aware of some of her shenanigans. That said, my daughter is a lovely, good, kind-hearted young woman who captures spiders and carefully lets them free outside. And she hates Blake Sharp."

Incoming…outgoing.

Rix looked to where the women disappeared.

"You need a car while you're here," Jamie went on and Rix turned back to him. "A driver. A shelter from the storm. An escape plan. Dru or I'll make it happen for you."

"Thanks, Jamie," Rix muttered.

"You've been holding that beer for ten minutes and not drinking it. You want something else?"

Rix shook his head and took a sip.

It was a good ale, still cold.

Jamie clapped him on the arm and left his hand there. "You two'll get through. Sunday will be here before you know it. And tomorrow, you'll be with us, so she'll be safe."

It was deeper when he repeated, "Thanks, Jamie."

A flash exploded.

Rix growled.

Jamie dropped his hand and smiled.

"You'll get used to it," he remarked.

"Maybe, but I still won't like it," Rix replied.

"Sadly, no," Jamie agreed.

Another flash popped.

Yeah.

They'd make it through.

But maybe by the skin of their teeth.

SHE'D BEEN GONE TOO LONG.

The only thing okay about that was that Dru hadn't returned either.

And clocking the mean girls (all five of them, including the brides-maids, Blake and Helena), Alex and Dru weren't in their clutches.

Still, Rix didn't like it.

He texted, she didn't reply.

Jamie noticed, Dru wasn't returning his texts either, he was also getting concerned, so they made a plan to separate and search.

Rix had gone inside, was walking down a hall, heard a woman's voice behind a door, it was muffled, didn't sound like Alex or Dru, but since it could be part of the crush of the party, he knocked and opened it anyway.

To see Chad plowing a brunette that was not Blake.

They both looked to him.

He shut the door and stepped away from it.

He wanted to be far from there, but his phone sounded with a text.

Then it sounded with three more.

He stopped and looked down at it.

Four texts had come in from Alex.

He was in New York on a fucking roof and apparently, his reception sucked.

We're down at the lobby bar. Come meet us. We'll order some food.

Coming to the bar?

Dru can't get hold of Jamie, is everything okay?

His text went through then, *Baby, where are you?*

And her latest, *We're downstairs at the bar! Aren't you getting my texts?*

The door he was standing several feet from flew open.

The woman went scurrying.

Chad was frantically tucking in his shirt.

"Hey, bro—"

Rix lifted his hand up an inch from the guy's face.

"Don't."

Chad shut up.

Rix dropped his hand.

"I'm not your bro."

Chad swallowed and nodded.

Rix strolled away to find Jamie and get to the bar.

He did this texting, *We're coming down.*

And thinking, *Well...fuck.*

CHAPTER 21

THE PICKLE

Alex

"*N*ow I'm in a pickle," I groused, sitting on the side of our bed in one of Dad's guest bedrooms, bent fully forward, tugging at the thin strap on my sandal.

Rix had told me about Chad.

I was not surprised about Chad.

Because he was *Chad*.

But I was annoyed.

"There's a good chance she's not going to believe me if I tell her," I continued complaining. "There's also a good chance she won't care. And I honestly think those are the only two options."

I tipped my head to look up at him.

He'd shrugged off his jacket and was unbuttoning his shirt, his eyes to my feet.

Sadly, I had my thoughts on a variety of other things, not only Chad, so I could not focus entirely on how hot my beautiful man looked, unbuttoning his shirt.

Though I did focus (alas, just not entirely), and he was *hot*.

"They're never going to forgive me for the torture I'm putting them through this week," I remarked. "In other words, we're day one, and my feet are already killing me."

His shirt open to his navel, he came to stand in front of me and muttered, "Give it."

He had his hand out, cupped in front of him.

For a second, I didn't understand.

Then I lifted my foot and rested it in his cupped hand.

With a couple of expert tugs, the strap was released and then the six hundred dollar shoe (the other one was another six hundred dollars) went sailing, landing with a thud on the floor.

Rix then covered my foot with the fingers of both his hands, digging the pads of his thumbs into the arch.

Ohmigod.

Heaven.

"Don't know your sister much, babe. What I do know, I'm not impressed. But I don't care who it is, or if they're an asshole. They deserve to know shit like that's going down. Especially right before they legally commit to a punk-ass cheat," he advised.

He was now holding my foot in one hand, digging his knuckles into my heel.

It felt awesome.

But my sigh wasn't about that (or, not all about that).

"Was getting off on how you're stealing her thunder without even trying," Rix went on. "Considering what you've told me about her, and the little I've seen which confirms it. But no one deserves to walk into a life of that."

He was right.

Far too soon, he bent to set my foot down, but lucky for me, he picked up the other one.

Tug, tug, shoe was flying, and he was kneading.

"Suggestion?" he offered.

I looked from his long-fingered hands doing their magic up to his face.

And it did its magic.

"Yes," I agreed.

"Maybe talk to your dad about it. The Helena and Edward show is fucked up, baby, and I gotta admit, Blake may be a bitch, but I've never seen a dad act so shitty to his kid. But even with that, he seems the most level-headed and functional of the bunch."

"He wasn't always that way with her," I muttered.

"Yeah. Jamie clued me into some shit. Same thing you told me. Said she'd act up not in good ways."

I nodded. "I'm not surprised Jamie shared, seeing as maybe I downplayed it when I was mentioning it before. The truth is, Blake was beginning to get a serious reputation."

"Yeah?" he prompted.

I felt my face get soft at that one word.

Always.

Always interested.

Interested in everything about me.

My Rix.

My Rix

Really mine.

And my face got even softer.

His face did the same as mine did, and for a second, I focused entirely on how gorgeous my man was.

When his lips quirked, and I knew he knew I was focusing on that, I pulled myself out of it and began the Tales of the Dread Adventures of Blake Sharp.

"She's been arrested. Twice. Little stuff, but it took Dad's time to deal with. The scariest part of all her devilries was that, for a while, she got caught up with some drug people. Not like, dealers or anything. Just a crew of debutants and dandies who liked cocaine too much. And when I say that, I mean *way* too much. While she was using that stuff, she wasn't just acting like she ruled the world, because she kinda always acted like that, it was just pronounced when she was high. She also acted sometimes like she could leap from tall buildings. It could be pretty terrifying. We were all worried, in our ways. I talked to her a couple of times; she blew me off that couple of times. Dad eventually sat her down. Apparently, cocaine costs a lot of money. And the Bernhard-Sharp-Coddingtons haven't stayed rich by blowing money on stupid stuff. I also think he told her she wouldn't stay rich if she kept up with that shit. So she gave it up."

Rix nodded.

Thus I kept sharing.

"One of that group went on to get seriously into heroin. Another had a really bad car accident when she was under the influence. One's been married and divorced twice, and she's only thirty years old. Blake never talked about it, but I think she was glad she got out when she did."

"Have to have no brain in her head if she sees what that shit does to your life, and she wasn't grateful she pulled herself out of it," Rix commented.

"Yeah," I agreed, and then kept going, because, sadly, there was more to share. "She got into a habit of playing some uncool games with a number of exclusive stores. To the point she isn't allowed into them anymore. Still. Buying expensive clothes and shoes and handbags, using them, even damaging them, then demanding they take them back for return. Doing this not because she needed the money back, obviously she didn't. But because she's a Coddington-Sharp and was throwing her weight around. Though, once beleaguered store managers started calling Dad to intervene, and he told them to treat her like they would anyone else, that eventually stopped."

"Chloe tells stories about how some folks behave in her store. People can suck. But that's another level," Rix remarked.

I nodded my agreement.

And sadly, since there was more, kept going.

"And she had some family sue, because apparently she messed up their boathouse pretty badly. In the end, with all her larking about, Dad's spent a lot of time and money smoothing things over for her."

Since it seemed he thought he'd paid short shrift to it, Rix put that foot down, and went back to the other one.

I was very okay with that.

I went back to talking.

"Which is a thing with her. Damage and destruction. She had a party here once when Dad was out of town, and I guess the results were extreme. To the point there was graffiti spray-painted on the walls, and Dad had to hire some experts to restore and clean some pieces that had been vandalized. And we're not talking this happening when she was sixteen. She was twenty-six."

"Jesus," Rix muttered.

"Yeah," I said. "She'd had other get-togethers, and those weren't good either. But that one was the last. I think that's one of the reasons he tends to be precious about his space, definitely with Blake. I don't think she's ever here without Dad here. She doesn't even have keys to get in anymore."

I rolled this around in my mind while Rix dug his thumbs into my sole.

And then I noted, "I also think he might be kinda like me. He never seemed really comfortable in big social settings, and he likes his space to be just his. So when she did what she did to his home, that was kind of a last straw deal for Dad."

"Mm," he hummed, that sound getting my full attention.

That meaning Rix had my full attention.

And I didn't want to think of Blake anymore.

Or Dad.

Or any of them.

I wanted to think of Rix.

Here.

With me.

How handsome he'd looked that night.

How he made it fun, being all he was.

The preposterously beautiful ring he'd chosen for me.

So that part was pretend.

Still, that ring was gorgeous.

How we were now…us.

No end.

No limits.

Exploring this.

Together.

"Want to see something?" I asked.

He didn't miss my change in tone, his gaze growing more attentive on me, and he nodded.

I pulled my foot from his hand, got up, which put me close to him, and I took his hand.

On bare feet, I led us out of the crisp and impersonal creams and whites with the elegant flash of De Gournay wallpaper on the wall behind the bed and minimal accents of chartreuse green of the guest room.

Then I led him up the stairs to the third floor, down the hall to the middle room at the back with a view to the garden.

We walked in, and I flipped the switch.

The personal touches were gone, and impersonal ones were put in their places in order the room could be ready for the guests who were never invited who would never use this space.

But the queen-size bed still had the filmy canopy gathering and draping around its head, fit for a princess. The satin bed linens were elegant, but just that shade or two beyond simply feminine to being girlie.

And the walls had been refreshed, but that paint had always been the same ballet pink.

"My room," I told him, "*sans* the piles of books and CDs and smelly tennis shoes and reset, so if anyone ever used it, though no one does, Dad wouldn't expose a single thing about me. And I'm not talking about him hiding me. He's just private that way."

Rix wandered in.

"No Rage Against the Machine posters. I was allotted the Degas that was moved to the library," I said. "Though I had a couple of their CDs."

I stood in the door and watched as he stopped at the window. He pulled the curtain aside, looked down.

He then turned, his eyes moving around, taking in the space, before he went to the bed and sat at the foot.

Shirt open. Dark slacks. Shoes that would remain on his feet once he removed his legs.

He seemed just like what he'd teased me he liked to pretend to be.

The invading marauder, a slash of alluringly sinister against an ivory satin duvet.

"I used to lie in that bed," I started, and his caramel eyes came to me, "and dream about being a pirate." I pushed from the door and began making my way to him. "Or living in a gunslinger town, drafted into a posse, riding my horse fast, chasing the bad guy."

He opened his legs, and I came to a stop between them.

He put his hands on my waist and stared at my middle.

I put my hands on his shoulders and kept talking.

"I was quite a swashbuckler," I whispered.

His head dropped back to look up at me as his hands went down, under my skirt, and hit bare skin.

My body welcomed that with a surge of wet.

I felt pressure on the back of one knee and got the message.

I welcomed that and climbed on his lap.

Rix spent some time under my skirt, arranging it just so over his lap and legs and the bed and even up his chest.

There was something tender about that.

Tender and excruciatingly sexy.

I slid my hands to his jaw and recaptured his attention.

"After all my adventures on the high seas, or bringing order to the Wild West, why is it not a bummer I ended up the damsel-in-distress sex slave?" I asked.

His answer was simple and so Rix.

"Your captor's got a big dick."

I laughed softly and murmured, "Oh yeah. Right."

"He needs that dick in you, wearing this dress," he murmured back.

"As his sex slave, I'm powerless to stop him."

Rix grinned, and his hand worked under my skirt again until what I felt straining against my damp panties was freed.

He slid the gusset of those panties aside and rubbed the head of his cock against me.

I bit my lip.

He positioned, wrapped his fingers around my hips, and agonizingly slowly, he took me.

And he kept doing it. I did none of the work, his strong hands guided me.

I watched the heat build in his eyes, my heart tripping faster, corresponding to his breath coming more and more heavily.

No noise. No grunts. No mews. No whispers. No kisses.

Just labored breaths.

Breathing into each other.

Breathing each other.

Our eyes remained locked as Rix made me make love to him on my bed, where I'd spent hours while growing up, absolutely dreaming of the shadowed, dark, strong, protective savior who would love me for me and sweep me away into a world of adventure.

I knew he was almost there when his thumb shifted to my clit.

My orgasm was massive.

But it came out as a sigh.

I watched and saw his was powerful.

But it exposed itself only as the cords of his neck tightening.

When we were done, he again took pains to keep my skirt as it was even as he pulled his hands out from under to wrap his arms around me.

I rested my cheek on his shoulder, my face in his neck, and whispered, "You really like this dress."

"I really like this girl who can sleep under the stars and glide along lakes and show kids the beauty of trees and then command every man's attention in a bar in the big city and be the only one in her entire high-class family who's lousy with grace."

I closed my eyes in order to fully feel all that his words meant to me.

But I said, "I didn't command every man's attention."

He gave me a squeeze. "I've changed my mind. I'm okay you think that, baby, even though you did. It's all sorts of good for me you don't notice that shit."

I loved that moment, with Rix, in that room.

But I'd come hard, so had he, we'd gotten up really early, and our trials and tribulations had just begun.

In other words, I needed some rest, and I needed to take care of my guy, who probably needed some too.

So as much as we could be in that room, in that mood, and I could sit on his cock forever, I actually couldn't.

"Do you want to sleep here?" I offered.

"No. I want my only memory of this room to be you on my cock in that dress on your bed."

Again tender.

And sexy.

Though, a little strange, because it didn't have the personality of his, but I thought my room was kind of neat.

"Okay," I agreed.

He pulled me off him and set me on my feet. He held me until I was steady then he tucked himself away, zipped and got up.

And holding hands, we walked back to our room.

Elsa Cohen

"The Elsa Exchange"
Celebrity News and Interviews
YouTube Channel

"Oh, my wonderful watchers, things are always interesting in the world's most thriving metropolis, but I *must tell you* I am veritably *agog* with how *exciting* things are going to be *this week!*"

Picture on screen, full-body of Alexandra Sharp in an elegant, Grace Kelly-esque dress, magnificent earrings and stunning strappy sandals gazing up at John "Rix" Hendrix who's wearing an impeccably tailored charcoal gray suit and an open-necked black shirt as they stride into a fabu-

lous hotel on which, everyone who is anyone knows, the rooftop terrace is to-die-for.

Cut to picture of Alexandra and Hendrix tucked close together, gazes aimed at the camera, Hendrix looking brooding and protective, Alexandra smiling a Cheshire cat smile.

Cut to another picture of Alexandra and Hendrix, she has her hands up in front of her, he has his on her waist. She's leaned into him, head tipped back, the skirt of her remarkable dress is tangled with his legs. His mouth is on hers.

Cut back to Elsa.

"That's right, my wonderful watchers, our current favorite couple have winged their way to the busy, bustling city, and don't they clean up *good?*" Elsa fans herself. "Oh my. If they weren't so… impeccably…*fabulous* it would be embarrassing how they're showing up the locals."

Photo on screen of Chad Head standing alone, tie askew, holding two glasses of champagne and looking like he doesn't know where he is.

Cut to picture of Blake Sharp, leaning too far forward, mouth too far open, her bodice at her inside breast gaping a little too much and showing nipple.

Cut back to Elsa.

"Whoops! I forgot the spoiler alert! It isn't a PG rating today, my wonderful watchers. Please, someone in the Blake camp, share the wonders of double-sided tape. Wardrobe disaster at your own pre-wedding cocktail party? I can't. Fortunately, eventually, class arrived to tip the night in the right direction."

Picture on screen of Alexandra and Drusilla Lynch, sitting at a bar, heads close, chatting, while the men around them watch.

Cut to photo on screen of Hendrix and Jamie Oakley, Oakley has his hand on Hendrix's arm in a friendly/fatherly fashion, they're smiling at each other while several women stand close, watching.

Cut to photo of Hendrix and Oakley standing while Alexandra and Drusilla continue in their seats at the bar. They've now ordered food, and it's clear Hendrix has said something amusing, for they're all laughing.

Cut back to Elsa.

"Oh me! I *do* play my favorites, don't I? But seriously, they just make it *so easy*. Jamie Oakley is the *sheer definition* of getting better with age. And his daughter Drusilla, the apple of his eye, indeed, she's the red shine on the entire Big Apple, is such a stunner, she'll be snapped up in a trice. And I cannot *wait* to see who claims that blazing beauty. But, what's this I see?"

Close-up grainy photo of an unusual but stunning diamond ring surrounded by a surfeit of the same resting on a left ring finger.

Cut back to Elsa.

"*Yes*. That's on Alexandra's finger. And yes, it's *uh*-may-*zing*. And yes, I've never seen a ring like that used for that very particular purpose, but how marvelous *someone* knows how to buck tradition at the same time following it and *enhancing* it. And *yes*, rumor has it this means it's official. But boo! We don't have that official news officially. Once we do, guess who'll be the first to know?"

Elsa points at the camera.

"You! Now, I'm sorry to report that today's exchange is so very short."

Elsa frowns.

"Though the good news is, we have *days* ahead of us of the ostentatious dragging out of the Sharp/Head wedding, so my exchanges will probably be more frequent."

Elsa claps in front of herself twice.

Then she does a forward-flapping wave.

"Now, until our next exchange, keep it positive. Elsa is signing off."

The branded Elsa wink and blowing of kiss.

Sign off.

CHAPTER 22

THE LINE

Alex

*R*ix's ringtone woke us.

He grunted and took me with him when he rolled to his back and reached to the nightstand.

I lifted my head from his chest to see him looking at his phone.

I looked at it too.

And saw it said MAGS CALLING.

I also saw the time, which was six-twelve in New York.

Though in Flagstaff, it was a lot earlier.

We both pushed up at the same time, Rix yanking the charger out of his phone and taking a call that could not be good, coming at that time in Flag.

"Mom, all good?" he answered.

He listened.

I watched, tense.

He relaxed.

Automatically, I relaxed with him.

"Yes," he said. "Yeah, Mom." Pause and, "Yeah and no. It's a diamond ring. It's from me. It means something. But it doesn't mean that," Pause again, his sleepy-alert eyes coming to me. "Yet."

Oh.

My.

God.

His attention went back to the call.

"Alex's family is kinda fucked up." Pause and, "Mom, you meet them, you'll understand that using the words 'fucked up' is the only way to go."

I started laughing.

Rix smiled at me and kept speaking to his mother.

"So, we're kinda messing with their heads, mostly her sister's, who's seriously uncool with Alexandra." Pause and, "Yeah." Pause and, "No one ever said that. It's not official. But *we're* official. Though you already knew that." A further pause and, "I should have warned you. But how could I know that woman would broadcast an exchange maybe hours after that shit went down, and she'd see the ring?" Another pause and, "No. Yeah. It's good. We're good. I'm good. New York has good pizza. And we gotta get up and get ready for some uppity-ass brunch that's gonna suck." One last pause and, "Get some sleep. Love you. Love to Dad. And totally. We'll come up again soon when we're back. Later."

He tossed the phone on the nightstand.

Then he shared unnecessarily, "Mom saw the ring."

"Elsa?"

He nodded.

"Wow," I mumbled, impressed in spite of myself. "She's fast."

"She's a pain in the ass."

"She's that too."

Rix was done with this.

He communicated that with, "Wanna fuck or you want me to eat you out?"

My legs shifted.

He gave me another option. "Or sixty-nine?"

"I wanna suck you," I told him.

"Then sixty-nine," he decided. "Because I dig your mouth on my dick, but I want your cunt on my tongue."

Well then.

We had a plan for the start of the day.

And it was promising.

Regrettably, however, as such things had a way of going when my family was around, this promise wouldn't continue.

WE WERE AT THE BREAKFAST TABLE.

Which shouldn't be misconstrued as the dining room table.

The breakfast room was smaller, the table more intimate, and there were a lot of big potted plants.

We were here because we were instructed to be here after Rix answered a knock on our door and got this news from Dad's housekeeper, Cassandra, who shouldn't be confused with Dad's cleaner. Nor should she be confused with Dad's personal assistant who was not his work personal assistant (of which, there were two), but his home and life and social personal assistant. And she shouldn't be confused with Dad's handyman, maintenance man, groundskeeper. Who obviously would not be confused with Dad's personal chef.

Honestly?

Outside of serving him on the rare occasion he was home and answering the door, I had no idea what Cassandra did.

But I didn't have to do anything but adhere to her orders from Dad as communicated through her that we were to meet him at the breakfast table for "coffee and a light meal prior to the brunch."

Brunch was at eleven-thirty.

We were to be at the breakfast table at eight-thirty.

It would be good to have something to tide us over.

And definitely good to have coffee.

Therefore, that was where we were.

The breakfast table.

And we were ready for the most part for brunch (which meant Rix was looking handsome in his cashmere pullover, his sports jacket still in our room, I was in a gray pencil skirt with a green, ribbed, cross-over-front sweater and green suede pumps with a string tie at the front of the ankle, my matching green shawl-style cardigan also back in our room).

I was pouring coffee from a silver service while Rix watched like I was performing brain surgery.

The table was set and tendered beautifully presented croissants and breakfast pastries, half-cut grapefruits with fanned slivers of strawberry in the middle, a bowl of prepared melon, an arrangement of cheeses and cured meats, rolls, a filled toast caddy, molded butter in the shape of fall leaves and acorns, and pots of different jams and marmalades.

All of this was positioned around an elegant, squat arrangement of mums, dahlias and winterberries.

"I see there's an art to that," he remarked.

"Sorry?" I asked, finishing with his china cup and moving the pot over mine.

"Just sayin', baby," he said softly, "you're the shit."

This was nice, though I was confused by it, thus giving him a puzzled smile when Dad strolled in.

"Good. You're here," he said, rather than good morning.

Rix shot me a look which I interpreted and understood, considering it wasn't us who wasn't turning up to stuff.

"Morning, Dad," I replied.

"Darling," he said, bending in and touching his lips to my cheek.

He then rounded Rix, slapping him heartily on the back, as if the fifteen minutes they spent in each other's presence made them best buds, and he was entitled to touch Rix physically.

This made Rix's jaw twist.

I pressed my lips together.

"Rix, sleep well?" Dad asked, taking his seat and shaking out his napkin with a snap, like the man he was, born heir to the throne he currently inhabited.

"Yeah, Edward," Rix answered.

"Ned, Rix, call me Ned," Dad murmured. "Alex, my love, please pour for me."

I poured Dad's coffee.

The second I put the pot down, whether to make a point, or just Rix being Rix, he picked up the plate of pastries that was sitting between him and Dad and offered it to me.

I took a chocolate croissant.

Rix took an almond one and set the plate down.

"I'm delighted you managed to escape the tedium of last night, for the most part. Though tedious, I'm also glad you made an appearance, for your sister's sake. She's a difficult woman, but family is family," Dad announced.

There was nothing to say to that, so no one said anything.

Then Dad turned to Rix, "How's Jamie?"

This seemed more of an important question than that question would normally seem to be.

"He's fine," Rix answered cautiously.

Dad nodded, reaching for the toast caddy. "It's good you'll have time with them." His attention shifted to me. "Darling, especially you and Dru. Her intentions are kind and noble. Her actions are detrimental to the goal."

"What are you talking about?" Rix asked my question.

However I just didn't know what Dad was talking about, but Rix's tone bordered on surly.

Dad looked to him. "She's twenty-one years old and lives with Jamie."

Before Rix could comment on that, Dad turned to me.

"She's clever, an exceptionally talented flautist and pianist. It's my understanding, even if she's still in school, she works with some recording artists. I've no idea her financial situation, though I do know Jamie can and would purchase a flat for her so she didn't have to concern herself with the ridiculous rent required by this city to live anywhere decent. I understand why she won't leave. She's still in school, perhaps she shouldn't. You stayed home with me when you were in school. But she's by his side at every event. And she's his daughter, not his date."

I felt Rix's mood shift alarmingly and therefore said quickly to Dad, "It's my understanding that family is close."

Dad looked right at me. "What the understanding is, darling, for *everyone* is that those two suffered the torment of watching a wonderful wife, loving mother and a just plain fine woman battle heroically, and die anyway."

I stared at Dad.

"There's all sorts of trauma, Alexandra," Dad continued, swiping butter on his toast. "They've shared their own personal one, together. And now they've bonded over that, which is unsurprising. Also unsurprising is that bond is difficult to break. However, it must. Drusilla must live her life and Jamie's his best with a woman at his side. As much as it quite literally makes me ill to think of him with anyone other than Rosalind, who, outside of you, is the finest woman I've ever known, life goes on. He needs to find someone. She needs to enjoy being young with people her age. Neither of those things will happen if Drusilla doesn't break free."

At first, I was dealing with the "outside of you" remark.

Then, I looked to Rix.

Rix was studying Dad.

"You disagree?" Dad demanded.

I turned to Dad to see this was aimed at Rix.

"No," Rix replied. "Everything you said concerns Judge too."

Dad nodded, now spreading marmalade on his toast, murmuring, "I've no doubt."

Rix caught me watching him and shared, "I've seen it, sweetheart. It's beautiful what they have. But the longer it goes on, it may be not healthy."

Oh dear.

I turned again to my father.

"I just met her last night. Not sure I can wade into her family functioning."

And again, he looked me dead in the eye, before he stated, "You're my Alexandra. You've proved you can do anything."

My mouth dropped open.

I felt something burning into my face and forced my gaze to Rix.

He was watching me so intently, if Superman laser beams shot from his eyes, I wouldn't blink.

"*Father!*"

"*Fuck,*" Dad clipped, immediately collapsing back in his chair.

And now I was alarmed, because Blake could be a lot, but that seemed like a rather dramatically defeatist response.

I didn't get a second with this thought before Blake showed in the room.

Her torso wheeled back after she stopped and got a look at us, and that was unsurprisingly dramatic.

"Look how fucking *cozy,*" she sniped, taking us all in. "Did anyone think to invite *me,* the firstborn *daughter,* this week's person of *honor* to this breakfast soiree?"

I was further not surprised she woke up on the wrong side of the bed considering she might not know whose bed her fiancé woke up in.

And I was also kinda understanding Dad's reaction to the news she was there.

"Alex and Rix are staying with me, and you are not," Dad pointed out.

Blake ignored him.

"I mean, do you *pay her?*" she asked me.

"Sorry?" I asked back.

"*Elsa Cohen!*" she shrieked. "She *adores you.* Why on *earth* would she adore *you?*"

"Right, this is the thing," Rix started.

Uh-oh.

He also threw his napkin down and stood up.

Uh-oh.

Dad looked up at him.

Blake looked up at him.

I looked up at him.

He only had eyes for Blake.

"I don't know what your damage is, but you see your sister, you say hello. You ask how she's doing. You have some issue, you rein it in and speak to her like you're both adults. What you *don't* fucking do is say snide shit or get in her face. *Ever.*"

No one said a word.

Which was good, because Rix wasn't done.

"She's got no control over what that vulture does or says. If the woman said something you don't like, either suck it up or find some way to shut her up. Do *not* take it out on Alexandra."

"She showed a picture of me on her show where I looked *horrible* and you could see my *nipple.*"

Annnnnnd, *again.*

I pressed my lips together.

"So what?" Rix asked.

"So what?" she asked back. "*It's my wedding week!*" she screeched. "And all the pictures of *you two*"—her finger jabbed at him then sliced to me—"*and there were many of them*, look like Steven Meisel took up society photography as a hobby."

Dad cut in at this juncture.

Unhelpfully.

"That damned dress was inappropriate. I couldn't believe my eyes when I saw you wearing that."

"We're not living in the fifties, *Dad*, where Alex got *her* dress."

Oh boy.

Mistake.

"Do not say another goddamn word about Alexandra's dress," Rix growled, so low and ominous, even Blake paled.

Fortunately, though it'd turn out to be unfortunately, it was then Dad's housekeeper showed at the door.

"Mr. Sharp, Mr. Head is here to see..." Cassandra hesitated in order to convey her confusion at her next words, "Mr. Hendrix."

Now it was Rix that was clipping, "*Fuck.*"

But I was thinking it.

"Chad's here to see you? Why is Chad here to see you?" Blake asked.

And now Dad was standing, a lot slower than Rix did, saying, "Yes. Why Rix?"

So I stood. "Okay, now, let's—"

"Invite him in, Cassandra," Dad ordered.

Shit!

Cassandra disappeared.

"What's going on?" Blake demanded.

Rix looked to me.

I sat back down.

His head tipped to the side to say, *No help from you? Really?*

I wanted to help. Really.

But I was at a loss of how to do that.

"Oh, wow, babe, hey. You're here. A surprise."

Chad was in the room.

He was rushing to Blake, ignoring her stiff body, kissing her cheek, and acting so completely guilty of something, it would have been hilarious if this whole thing wasn't so terrifying.

"Uh, Mr. Sharp," he greeted Dad.

Okay, it was then I realized that I'd known Chad a while. Chad had been dating Blake a while. Chad (maybe?) was marrying Blake in three days. And Dad had invited Rix to call him Ned.

But Chad still called him Mr. Sharp.

Suddenly, I had to fight smiling.

Dad didn't mess about.

"Chad, what brings you here to see Rix?"

Chad spoke like a little boy would clasp his hands behind him, look at his feet and swing his body, telling tales giving no eye contact.

"Well, uh…I just thought, us guys, you know…"

Like that did it, he trailed off and spoke no more.

Since it didn't do it, Dad remarked, "No, I don't know."

Suddenly, I worried Chad had swallowed down the wrong pipe, because he looked like he was silently choking.

"Maybe Rix and Chad and Blake and I could go to another room," I suggested.

"Maybe you couldn't," Dad contradicted.

I gave big eyes to Rix.

Rix now had his arms crossed on his chest and was simply watching Chad.

Chad gulped and abruptly turned to Blake.

"Okay, babe, you know I love you, but…"

His eyes darted to Rix.

"But what?" Dad demanded.

"Yes," Blake said suspiciously. "But what?"

Chad turned back to Blake. "Can we talk privately?"

Blake was looking uncertain.

"Sure," she said.

"No. Here. Right here. Now. Right now," Dad declared.

"Sir—" Chad started.

"What the fuck is going on, Chad?" Dad bit out.

"Can I please talk to Blake—?"

"Rix?" Dad pushed.

"His to own up to," Rix grunted.

This was true.

But maybe not the right thing to say to Dad.

"What?" Blake asked.

"You little fucking slither of *slime*," Dad said quietly to Chad.

That right there was why what Rix said wasn't right.

Dad might not have been an attentive father.

But he was far from stupid.

"Sir—" Chad.

"Dad!" Blake.

"Tell her." Dad.

"Please." Chad.

"What…is…*happening*?" Blake.

Dad's voice was ice cold, and his eyes were shards as they gazed at Chad. "Stand in my home and tell my daughter who you are."

Chad swung to Blake. "She didn't mean anything, I swear to God."

Blake's eyes got huge.

The room existed in suspended animation for long, tense moments.

Then she jumped Chad.

I jumped up from my chair to race around the table.

But Rix caught her with two arms, one at her chest, one at her ribs, and pulled her back.

"You *motherfucker!*" she shrieked, striking out with fingers set to claws.

"Blakey, baby," Chad whined.

Blake went stiff as a board and screamed, *"Pencil-dick motherfucker!"*

I knew I was right about his manhood.

"Leave now, Chad," Dad ordered.

"But, Mr. Sha—"

"Leave!"

Chad went ramrod straight, turned stiffly to Blake, and said, "We'll talk, honey. We will. We'll talk. We'll sort this out."

And then he quickly took his leave.

Rix held on to Blake long enough for Chad to get a head start that she couldn't possibly catch up to him on her heels, and then he let her go.

She whirled on him instantly. "And how did *you* know this?"

Rix didn't sugarcoat it, and it was bad (for Blake) but good, because she needed to understand what was happening.

"I walked in on him when he was inside her."

Blake blanched and whispered, "At our cocktail party?"

Ugh.

I felt sorry for her.

Then I stopped doing that when she turned to me and accused, "You knew this and didn't tell me?"

"Hup." Rix used that sound to call her attention, which he got. "Remember? We don't blame your sister for shit that's *your* problem?"

Blake's face scrunched in anger.

"I'll call your mother and tell her to cancel the brunch," Dad murmured.

"Don't you do that, Dad," Blake snapped.

Dad stilled. "Why not?"

"We're not canceling the brunch," Blake decreed.

"Have you lost your mind?" Dad asked.

"I can't...I have to think. *Let me think!*" she screeched.

Dad didn't let her think. "You cannot possibly be entertaining the notion you'll carry on with this wedding."

"I should talk to Chad," she told the table.

"Blake, look at me," Dad demanded.

Her eyes coasted to him.

"You are not marrying that pathetic, worthless pile of shit," Dad proclaimed. "I've never liked him. You know this. I've told you often enough. I'd say he hasn't had a single original thought, but I'm not even certain he's actually even had a single *thought*."

"We've been together for years," she returned.

"Who fucking cares?" Dad asked. "He was *inside another woman just last night*."

"Oh my *God*! Everyone stop saying that!" Blake yelled.

"I am not paying another dime on this wedding, Blake Charlotte. And the final bills have not come in," Dad warned.

Blake lifted her chin. "I have to talk to Chad."

"And I'm freezing your fund if you marry that vast waste of space," Dad threatened.

Blake's face flamed.

"Daddy!"

He sat and put his napkin back in his lap, stating, "You take time. Gather yourself. And for once in your goddamned life, make good decisions."

Dad reached to his coffee.

Rix and I glanced at each other.

"Alex, Rix, please, join me," Dad urged. "Blake, do I need to ask Cassandra to bring you a plate?"

"*Gah!*" Blake cried and raced out.

Dad sighed.

"Should I go after her?" I asked.

"I wouldn't, she'll not thank you and she won't make it worth your time," Dad declared, and bit into toast.

Rix sat.

So I sat.

Dad set his toast on his plate, chewed, swallowed, dotted his lips with his napkin, and for the third time that morning, looked me in the eye.

"Welcome home, my darling," he drawled wryly.

Never.

Not in my life did what happened next happen with me and my father.

But it did then.

I burst out laughing.

BREAKFAST WENT WITHOUT FURTHER INCIDENT.

And after we'd finished eating, Dad hung around, we found, because he was working from home that morning due to the fact that he was meant to be at a brunch at eleven-thirty.

Also, because I was home.

We chatted over a fresh pot of coffee that Cassandra brought in, discussing things Rix and I could do in New York now that all the wedding festivities were sure to be canceled.

In that time, Dad had been on his phone once.

To talk to his home/social/life assistant and tell her to contact his work assistants, and Cathy, not to mention the wedding planner, to put them on call to deal with all the possible cancelations.

"I'm taking charge of Cathy," he said as he slid the phone face down on the table. "Your sister has no idea how to handle an employee. The only reason Cathy has stayed is the exaggerated salary I pay her to cope with being managed by Blake. I honest to God don't know how the poor woman has succeeded in not murdering your sister with the numerous and contradictory demands."

I had a sinking feeling Dad's hopeful thoughts about the demise of Chad and Blake would be dashed, but I didn't say anything.

Instead, I sat back and kinda marveled about how well he seemed to be getting on with Rix.

There was definitely a hint of We're Both Men! going on from Dad's side.

But Dad hadn't even inferred he was going to test or challenge Rix, cerebrally or physically. No invitations for a squash game or a round of golf or request for a verbal dissertation on Santiago. And I wasn't sure Dad knew Rix had lost his legs, so that wasn't the reason why Dad refrained.

He was himself: not-so-subtly arrogant, plainspoken, unabashedly privileged and elitist.

But there was something…changed about him.

More relaxed.

Outside his behavior last night when he was around Mom and Blake, which was no different than usual, the only concerning thing I'd noted was how he'd slumped in his chair when Blake showed.

Until the second concerning thing happened in the middle of Rix and Dad discussing the pros and cons of the learning experiences found in foreign travel.

And how Dad felt (and I couldn't rebut this) kids would get a great deal out of understanding there was a whole wide world out there with different cultures, languages, religions, customs, and how, in all these places, they, too, were doing good—or bad—things that affected the planet.

Dad was pro this idea (he'd always been big into travel, and I wasn't just talking about skiing in Gstaad or visiting Capri (though, he did those too), he was an adventurer, traveling to some hard-to-get-to village in Thailand because there was a local dish that had to be tasted, or to tour a remote facility in Iceland that produced energy from the earth's heat).

He was arguing using Hale's money to significantly expand exchange programs or offering camps in different countries and shuffling where kids would go.

Rix wasn't con. But, outside hitting beaches in Mexico and the Caribbean, and to go camping in Canada, he'd never left the country.

So it was *Rix* quizzing *Dad* about the value of this.

And they both looked like they were enjoying it.

And I was enjoying watching them enjoy it.

Rix had just said, "It's expensive, and because of that, the reach would be limited."

"Yes, Rix," Dad replied, "but in history, it was never the masses that changed the world. It was the visionaries that changed the thinking of the masses. You reach that one child who will grow to be a visionary, he or she will lead in the charge to change the world."

This was a good point, and I could tell Rix was pondering it (I sure was), when another feminine shout was heard.

"God! You dare! Let me in! Where is he?"

Mum.

And the second thing that concerned me that morning happened.

Dad reached out and grabbed the edge of the table.

It was so *not Dad* to hold on to anything, and I didn't know if he did it because his first inclination was to upend the table in a fit of fury, or if his blood pressure had just spiked one too many times, and he was about to have a stroke.

But whatever reason, it served to steady him.

Which was good.

Because we then heard Mum yell, *"Don't you touch me!"*

At that, Dad was up swiftly.

Rix got up too.

I followed.

We found Mum in the hallway just off the foyer, Cassandra behind her looking stricken.

"Your staff leaves a lot to be desired, Ned," Mum decreed.

Dad had stopped and was looking beyond Mum to Cassandra.

"I didn't try to touch her, Mr. Sharp," she said, sounding distressed. "She...well, she forced her way in."

"That's a lie," Mum sniffed.

"I just told her what you told me and tried to keep the door—" Cassandra attempted to explain.

"That's fine, Cassandra. Thank you for trying. It's fine," Dad said. "We're done in the breakfast room, I think."

She nodded, and relieved to have something to do that was actually listed on her job description, because it was clear she didn't double as a security guard, she took off.

"It's fine your housekeeper bars the door to me?" Mum asked.

"Yes, because that was the directive I gave her," Dad answered. "Though, I did it never once imagining you'd force your way into my home."

"I cannot believe—" Mum began.

Dad's shoulders drooped. "Helena, it's been a difficult morning. I'm not doing this."

As usual, Mum ignored him.

"Yes, it is a difficult morning, as you're well aware we have a situation. It's my understanding that it has not escaped you that an issue has arisen between Blake and Chad, because that issue arose in this very house."

"Would you care to say hello to your daughter?" Dad invited.

Mum looked to me, glanced up at Rix, then back to me, and she took in my outfit.

Then she came in, and we did non-cheek touches while she murmured, "You look lovely, dear. Chloe Pierce has such good taste."

I'd picked this outfit.

And my dress for last night.

But I didn't share that.

I said, "Thanks, Mum."

"John," she said to Rix.

"Rix," I corrected.

She did a demure grimace and returned, "Such an odd thing, that. What kind of name is Rix? That isn't even short for Richard."

"His last name is Hendrix," I explained.

"I know, dear, it still seems baffling to me."

I decided I wasn't talking about that anymore.

Rix decided not even to say "hey."

Mum was done with us too.

She turned to Dad. "Now, this brunch is on."

Again, I knew it.

Dad shouldn't have gotten his hopes up.

He straightened his shoulders. "Hel—"

She charged on. "And you and I are hosting. Obviously, Chad and Blake have things to chat about. They won't be attending. We'll cover for them."

"Having a wedding brunch for a couple who doesn't attend is asinine," Dad said. "And I'm not going. I've already made myself clear about this to Blake."

She looked horrified. "But Ned, if you don't go, people will whisper about you and I not getting along again."

"Helena, they won't. They know we don't get along. They know we haven't gotten along since you dropped all pretense about a year after *our* wedding."

Uh.

What?

What pretense?

"There was no pretense," Mum hissed.

"You were not the woman I married."

"Drivel," she bit.

Dad sighed. "I'm not doing this either. And I'm not going to that fucking brunch."

She gave up on him and turned to me.

When she did, I knew what was coming.

Thus my heart sank, my palms started sweating, and I honest to God felt a little dizzy.

"Then it's you and me, Alexandra," she declared. "You must stand in for Blake."

Yes.

That was what I knew was coming.

Now I felt sick.

"No fucking way."

That was implacable.

That was Rix.

Mum's gaze shot up to him.

"I beg your pardon?" Mum demanded.

"You know that'd be torture for her," Rix returned.

My mother shook her hair. "It's high time she developed a stiff upper lip."

Yes.

She knew it'd be torture.

She just didn't care.

"My woman owns her own home, keeps it, pays her own bills, goes to a job every day that offers things to people and even makes a difference in their lives," Rix retorted. "I've seen her, very literally, stand on the edge of a cliff and look right into the abyss without flinching. If you don't know she's already got one of those, then you don't pay much attention to your daughter."

Wow.

How sweet.

And he wasn't done.

"She doesn't like parties. Just like about half a billion other people on the planet. It's not a big deal. It's not something to get over or force yourself to do. Though, someone's gotta get over something, and that's you."

Mum looked insulted.

"Well said, Rix," Dad enthused.

My mother recovered swiftly.

"Of course," she sneered. "The man is here a day and he's on your side."

"This is a family, Helena, there are no sides," Dad shot back.

Oh boy.

I could tell by the shift in Dad's tone.

Here we go.

As ever, Mum was there for it.

"If that's the case, why don't you take your daughter's and attend this brunch?"

"Because I never liked Chad Head, but my daughter wanted him, so I put up with him. Now he's proven himself to be what I thought he was all along, and I'm not going to toe the line simply for the sake of appearances."

Toe the line.

Mum's voice was rising. "It's not for the sake of appearances, Ned. It's for *your daughter*."

Dad collapsing back in his chair.

"For God's sake, explain to me how it helps Blake that I pretend I think that brainless twat is worth my time, or hers. I'm not surprised Rix saw him fucking another woman. He's barely above an unneutered lapdog, rutting against the furniture."

Dad holding the table.

"I cannot *believe* you said that about Chad. He's a Head!"

Toe the line.

"Good God, woman, listen to yourself!"

The Helena and Edward Show is fucked up, baby.

Mum was opening her mouth.

"Stop it!" I shouted.

Both of them looked to me.

Rix crowded me.

I stared at my parents.

"Just stop it. Can you *not* see how *awful* this is? How *ugly* it is?"

I focused on my mother.

And kept going.

"Mum, *enough*. I cannot even *begin* to imagine how it would be helpful for *any* of us to pretend we're okay with Blake settling for a man who would betray her that way *ever*, much less on the eve of their wedding. It's lunacy not only that you expect Dad and me to show, but that you'd have any part of it. Dad's not going. Rix is not going. I'm not going. And frankly, *you* should not go. The united front this family should make is that we're behind Blake, and we don't think it's all right for a *second* that someone treat her so unconscionably. Honestly, take Dad up on using his assistants to cancel. There's still time."

"If we cancel, people will know Blake and Chad are having issues," Mum retorted.

"They are!" I cried. "Just last night, he was caught fucking another woman!"

"Baby," Rix murmured, his hand flat and pressing on the small of my back.

That felt comforting, but I shook my head to him.

"Rix, no." I turned to Mum. "And while I'm sharing my truth, you and Blake have got to stop dumping all your garbage on Dad."

I heard Dad make a noise.

I ignored it because Mum's eyes were dangerously narrow.

"If you still love him and want his attention, then tell him and see where he's at with that and maybe see a counselor. If you don't love him, and this is for spite, please, God, for all of us, especially Dad, *get a life.*"

A rod slammed right down her spine, and she snapped, "I do not still love your father."

"Then leave him alone. For God's sake. Live your life. Let him live his. Can you think for one second what it's like to be your daughter, the product of both of you, and watch you be so incredibly nasty to each other *all the time?*"

"Alex," Dad murmured.

I turned on him. "You too. You try to avoid it, but it doesn't take long for you to fall right in. What's it going to take for you to stop doing it, Dad? A heart attack?"

"I'm in perfect health, darling," he said quietly.

"Well I'm not, mentally," I returned. "I'm fed up with all this tired, regurgitated *shit.*"

"Alexandra, you—" Mum began.

Rix cut her off.

"Alex said a lot you need to process. How about you all let things lie as they are and take some time to do that?"

"I barely know who you are," Mum sniffed. "Why on earth would I do what you say?"

"Because you love your daughter?" Rix asked by way of answer.

Mum's chin clicked down.

"Why don't we all take a moment, move this out of the hall, perhaps have another cup of coffee...Helena, I have tea, and discuss how we're going to support Blake through this," Dad suggested.

"I have one hundred and fifty people coming to brunch in less than two hours, Ned. I don't have *time* for tea," Mum bit.

Dad sighed.

Mum looked among us and remarked acidly, "I can't believe you're all abandoning me like this."

"Mum," I whispered.

She homed in on me. "Especially you, Alexandra. This is your *sister.*"

Rix pressed closer, and I knew he was going to say something.

Dad got there first.

"Helena, go."

"Ned—"

"Enough, just go."

"Blake will not thank any of you," she bit out.

The defeat came back for Dad.

In his tone.

"Of course she won't. And it saddens me how obvious it is how we managed to raise a girl with such abysmal manners, a failure that I fully participated in it, but you still don't see it."

"Always the last word," she sniped.

Dad looked to his shoes.

She glared at him, at me, at Rix, back at me, then she twirled and marched out.

She was in such a tizzy, the winterberries in the enormous dahlia, mum and winterberry arrangement that sat on the grand table in the middle of the even grander foyer trembled as she stormed by.

I turned to my father.

"Dad—"

His head came up. "I do. You are correct. I let her push my buttons. I'm so furious with her for...for everything, I hang on to that and argue with her to remind myself of what an excellent decision it was for me to finish things with her. Did it occur to me once what you girls would think? How you would absorb that? It is impossible that my answer to that is no. But until you mentioned it just moments ago, it was no. And I will admit to you, I feel that like a blow. And now that it does occur to me, as your fiancé suggested, I need to ponder that."

"Okay, but I'm here for a visit. I'm not home very often. Maybe you can do that later, and we can spend the morning together," I suggested.

And for the last time that day, he looked me in the eyes.

"I'm very glad you spoke your truth, Alex, but this is mine. I was a terrible father. I know that. I live with that every day. Even as I was being that when you needed me, as my mother warned me to have a better mind to my children, I was torn between family obligation and just simply family. I chose poorly. Even so, all three of the most important women in my life at one point abandoned me. You did it when you were a little girl, and I've missed you since the moment I lost you."

My frame locked and my throat closed.

Rix growled unintelligibly.

I knew Dad heard it, but he ignored it, turned…

And walked away.

CHAPTER 23

THE AGREEMENT

Elsa Cohen

"The Elsa Exchange"
Celebrity News and Interviews
YouTube Channel

"Oh, my wonderful watchers, we have a special report! As ever, I wanted to get the news to you as quickly as I could, though as yet I cannot say what's causing these unusual happenings. However, under not one single hat could be found the head of the bride who will be a Head in but a few days. Yes, I'm talking about the most anticipated brunch of the autumn season, given by the Marchioness of Norton for her daughter Blake as part of the festivities leading to the big event this weekend, Blake Sharp marrying Chad Head."

Zoom in on Elsa.

"Or should that sentence end in a question mark?"

Zoom out from Elsa.

"I ask because the blushing bride was not there. The towheaded

groom was nowhere to be seen. The bride's father was not in atten-
dance. And the maid of honor, Blake's sister and her fiancé, well..."

*Picture on screen of Alexandra Sharp in gray cords, a cross-front, ribbed
green sweater with matching shawl-style cardigan and side-notched,
D'Orsay styled, low-rise black booties standing next to John "Rix" Hendrix in
a black cashmere sweater over which was a weathered canvas jacket atop
dark-wash jeans. They're at the 9/11 Memorial looking solemn.*

Cut back to Elsa.

"They seemed to have better things to do. Though, this isn't a surprise,
considering Mr. Hendrix's former occupation. And if I had been invited
to this brunch, which sadly I was not, and I'd known that neither bride
nor groom would show, I might also find something else to do that better
serves my time. Thus miss the twittering of the guests wondering what
could possibly cause the happy couple to be no-shows at their own gathering. Or perhaps, I wouldn't miss the twittering. Because, of course..."

*Photo on screen of Chad Head at a party with a party girl in his lap.
Chad is ogling her breasts.*

*Cut to photo on screen of Chad Head pouring a bottle of clear liquor on
the mostly naked body of a woman laid out on a bar. Chad's face is very red,
his eyes are very bloodshot, and his mouth is wide open, appearing like he's
shouting.*

*Cut to picture on screen of Chad Head looking quite sweaty, sloppy and
disheveled while grinding against a woman on a dance floor.*

Cut back to Elsa, who is now leaned toward the camera.

"We all know, twittering is one of my favorite things to listen to."

Elsa leans back.

"Now, do tigers change their stripes? Do little boys ever grow up? I
can promise you, wonderful watchers, I will keep my ear to ground
and let you know the answers to those questions the moment I find
out."

Elsa hops in her seat and claps.

"I just *knew* this week would be interesting. Now, until our next
exchange, keep it positive. Elsa is signing off."

The branded Elsa wink and blowing of kiss.

Sign off.

———————

Rix

THEY WERE IN YET ANOTHER LIMO.

This one, though, was sent by Jamie to pick them up for dinner.

Alex was being quiet, and it wasn't her usual quiet, nor was it the reflective quiet they'd both lapsed into after going to the Memorial.

Rix had wanted to make a pilgrimage there since he knew he was going to New York, and thought he could step out some time during their visit, maybe when Alex was getting ready for one of the events.

But with their time freed up, he'd told her that was what he wanted to see, and although, being a native New Yorker, it was a pilgrimage she'd already taken, she took him.

Once there, he wished they hadn't gone.

Not that the Memorial wasn't thoughtful. Fitting. Moving.

It was.

It was just that there were too many people and the majority of them acted like it was a tourist attraction, hustling around, elbowing in, posing for pictures and smiling for selfies.

Doing all of this standing on a site of unimaginable tragedy.

He was physically sickened by it.

Alex noticed and took him to the museum, which had a more appropriate somber feel.

But they didn't linger after they left the museum.

No, now she had something on her mind that was making her quiet and Rix knew what it was.

"Don't take on his shit," he ordered.

She turned her head to look at him.

"Sorry?"

"Your dad and that horseshit about abandoning him. Don't take on his shit."

"Rix—"

"Give him time, then ask him what he meant. Don't sit on that. Don't try to figure out what was behind it. The only way you can know is for him to explain it."

"That's easier said than done," she pointed out.

"I know, but it's still horseshit, Al. He should never have laid that on you then walked away. What the fuck was that?" Rix shook his head. "Christ, your family is all about drama."

"I have to admit, with the morning we had, I cannot deny that," she mumbled.

The morning they had?

Try the life her family lived.

"The morning we had and a rooftop terrace in October and a brunch with fucking hats," he reminded her. "It's fucked up."

In the muted city lights coming through the darkened limousine windows, he saw her lips twitch.

But he didn't get a full smile.

It disappeared fast, and she asked, "Did you catch that thing about Mum dropping all pretense?"

Oh yeah.

He did.

He also caught Alex catching it.

"Don't sit on that either, sweetheart. Give him time"—he leaned toward her—"*then ask him about it.*"

She nodded.

He leaned in more and brushed his lips to hers.

He then sat back, took her hand and turned his head to look out the window at the city gliding by.

That was, until the limo stopped, then started moving again.

Christ, he didn't get it. Why so many people lived there.

Rix had traveled a lot. Though he'd never been to NYC, he'd been to a number of cities. Phoenix. LA. San Fran. Seattle. Denver. Dallas. Nashville. New Orleans. Miami. Boston. But he never stayed long in a city. He'd go to do something specific or see something specific, staying a couple days, and then getting the fuck out.

Usually when he went somewhere, the spaces were wide open, and the population was sparse.

He felt the vibe in New York. It was cool. He saw the bustle. That was cool too.

But he was understanding his girl way more with each passing second in this fucking place.

The crowds…*everywhere*, which sucked. Lines to get in. Lines to get seated. Lines to get served.

You looked up, and what little you could see of the sky, it didn't look like a sky.

It was a gray-white canopy of nothing.

When he'd see a tree, or any green, his eyes would unconsciously latch onto it, like it was proof that the forests and the plains and the mountains and the valleys and the farmland were still out there. No need to panic. The earth was still doing the things it was meant to be doing.

Rix had never found it surprising, considering Alex's habits and hobbies, that she got out of the city.

But being here, it all clicked into place in a way that was unexpected.

Especially with that house.

The room she grew up in.

The way she poured coffee.

Oh yeah, he got off on Society Alex in her tight skirt and stiletto heels.

Her grandmother had taught her well. She was so good with camouflage, she was a goddamned chameleon.

And fucking that Alex in a dress that was stunning, but still totally her, how she had a lock on who she was even in an entirely different element, was hot.

But he was glad in a few days they were going home.

They stopped and started a good twenty more times before they stopped for good.

He knew that when their driver said, "We've arrived."

"Thank you," Alex replied.

But the driver was making a move to get out so he could come around and open their door for them.

"Stay put. We got it, man," Rix assured. "Thanks. We gonna see you on the return?"

"Yes, Mr. Hendrix. Mr. Oakley has arranged for me to be available to take you back."

"Great, then see you in a while," Rix said, pushing across the seat to follow Alex, who was already out and standing on the sidewalk.

He took her hand, they started up the steps to another brownstone, and a flash popped.

Rix looked left, saw the guy with the camera, noted his angle, turned his head away and positioned his body to block Alex as another two flashes popped, and he hustled her up the steps.

They hit the brass-plated bell.

Luckily, the door opened in seconds.

And Chloe stood there.

"Well, hello, you two," she drawled.

"Chloe," Alex said, surprised, and clearly happy.

Rix just smiled at her.

Another flash popped.

Chloe fully opened the door and ushered them in, only for them to see Judge and Dru standing in the foyer.

"What the fuck, bud?" Rix asked, grinning and lifting his hand to Judge.

They clasped, bumped chests, but no back pounding this time before they broke away.

"It was killing Coco. She had to be closer to the action," Judge answered.

Rix started laughing as Chloe finished her greeting to Alex, moved in for a kiss on the cheek from Rix, he gave the same to Dru, Alex was hugging Judge, then Jamie strode in and there were more hand clasps and cheek kisses.

"Come into the kitchen," Jamie invited. "Let's get you some drinks."

Rix took hold of Alex again and began to follow the others.

It was then he noticed it.

Something he'd never normally notice, mostly because it was normal, but after the time spent at her dad's place, he did.

The foyer was about half the size of Ned's, but it was still impressive.

In it, as well as the center table, there were narrow tables on the walls on each side of the door with vases that did not have fresh flowers. Just the vases. And on one, a silver tray on which were a couple sets of keys.

There were also velvet covered benches on each side further into the foyer, and tossed on one was a trench coat and on top of that, a sweater.

They moved through the house, and it was posh. Total luxury. In some ways even lavish, though never losing the overall sense of refined elegance.

But there was more.

Rix saw a book upended on an ottoman.

There were picture frames everywhere filled with photos of a beautiful redheaded woman, with and without Jamie. Lots of Dru. Lots of Judge.

There were also artfully thrown toss blankets, handy to grab if you got cold.

On the floor in one room, Rix saw a pair of Dru's shoes she'd obviously flipped off before she'd curled up in front of the TV.

This pad probably cost millions of dollars, the taxes on it were likely crippling, and what was in it probably cost millions more.

But it was a home.

They hit an enormous kitchen, its complete back wall being black, square-paned windows with a view to the garden. The sink and a counter had been set freestanding in front of that window.

There was a massive island in the middle, on which was the range, as well as a black-tiled wall to the side that almost made Rix laugh because it had a fucking wood-fired stove built in it.

Beyond that, a counter-to-ceiling wall of shelves with carefully stacked white bowls and plates and shit. Another wall that was filled with light gray cupboards, among those, a restaurant quality fridge and freezer.

All of that was there, with some nice décor, and top-of-the-line counter appliances.

And it was still a family kitchen.

It smelled good and it was warm and there was light rock playing and there were filled wineglasses and beer bottles scattering the counters. And even though there were six of them, the island had been set, close but comfortable, and apparently that was where they were eating.

Not in a dining room that was not actually the dining room.

No silver or china to be seen or butter formed into acorns.

Rix looked down to Alex, to see her nodding her head to Dru, who was offering her some wine.

What she wasn't doing was looking around in wonder.

Seeing this was in the city.

This was money.

But this was a home.

And *this* was what she'd been missing while she was growing up.

What she should have had.

He didn't have time to point that out, and if he did, he wouldn't know how, when, a little later, he was leaning against the island with a beer. Alex and Chloe were on stools with their wine. Jamie was at another counter, watching the action.

And Judge was doing annoying big-brother shit, messing with Dru's mojo while she was preparing homemade garlic bread.

Chloe launched in.

"Obviously, Elsa reported about half an hour after the brunch was over. Therefore, you must spill. What's going on?"

Alex didn't hedge.

"Rix caught Chad *in flagrante delicto*," Alex shared.

Chloe's eyes widened.

Rix felt Jamie, Judge, and Dru's attention on him.

Alex gave them the rest.

"Therefore, Chad showed at breakfast this morning, probably to invoke the Bro Clause to keep him quiet. The problem was, Blake was already there to have a tantrum about Elsa's report. Dad has Chad's number. He forced him to confess. And now, we're in limbo. Will they, or won't they?"

"There's a will they?" Jamie asked.

Alex nodded.

Jamie turned startled eyes to Rix.

Rix shrugged.

"Jesus," Jamie muttered.

"Okay, Judge!" Dru suddenly exclaimed. "I've made this garlic bread, like, a gazillion, trillion times! You can back off!"

"I can also help brush olive oil," Judge returned, grinning unrelentingly at her, knowing he was bugging her, also not budging.

"I'm making enough for six, not six hundred," Dru shot back.

"You have sauce to look after."

"The sauce doesn't need my attention. It's simmering."

"You haven't started the pasta."

"Because we're not ready for pasta," Dru retorted. She then turned to her father. "Dad, that reminds me. Can you get out the antipasto platters?"

"Sure thing, sweetheart," Jamie murmured calmly, and headed to the fridge.

"Give me something to do," Judge urged.

"There's nothing to do. Just go sit and drink your—"

"Dru," Chloe said softly.

Dru looked to Chloe.

Then she looked to Judge.

"Do you want cheese on top of the garlic bread?" she asked.

"Is that what you want?" Judge asked in return.

"Maybe, half and half?" Dru suggested.

"Sure," Judge agreed.

"You can grate cheese, then," Dru allowed.

"Cool," Judge muttered, bent to kiss her head, then headed to where their father had vacated, the fridge.

Rix didn't need an interpretation of this story.

Dru was not Jamie's blood daughter, but she grew up that way.

Judge was Jamie's blood son, but he'd been kept from his father, something that harmed them both.

Now, they finally had the chance to be a family.

Dru had always had the good stuff.

Judge had had none of it.

And Chloe was seeing to Judge getting it.

Including giving him opportunities to be the big brother to his little sister.

Wisely, Jamie didn't get involved.

But Chloe never kept her nose out of shit.

Dru had her way of doing things in the kitchen.

More importantly, though, Dru adored Judge.

And...

The end.

Chloe picked up the thread.

"Have you talked to your sister?" she asked Alex.

"I called, she didn't pick up, but I left a message that if she wanted to talk, I was there. I texted the same," Alex answered. "She hasn't contacted me."

"Why did your mother carry on with the brunch?" Chloe asked.

"I honestly have no idea," Alex told her.

Rix felt Judge's gaze, he met it and gave another shrug.

Chloe took a sip of her wine and noted, "It'd be a shame that Marchesa gown is wasted. You look lovely in it."

"Coco!" Dru cried. "You can't think Blake should go through with it."

"Of course not," Chloe replied. "It'd still be a shame. No matter how Blake is, she has excellent taste in bridesmaid gowns."

Dru laughed, and Alex's dimple came out.

From there, they segued into Chloe and Judge's engagement. Thoughts on their wedding. Chloe opening another boutique, this one in Prescott. How well Genny's new series was being received, and that she was now in Boston, filming her latest movie. After which there would be Duncan and Genny's wedding.

Then came updates on Sully, Chloe's soon-to-be stepbrother, who was at a new job in Texas. And Gage, Chloe's other soon-to-be step-brother, who was finally getting serious about his degree. Meaning he'd fallen on a major for his coursework. He'd decided it was natural resources with an emphasis on ecology and management and restoration of rangelands.

So Sul was an environmental engineer.

Gage was getting into ecology.

And there was proof those apples didn't fall far from the tree.

They finished their group discussion with everyone getting in on the act of sharing what they thought should be done with Hale Wheeler's half a billion dollars.

The conversation was free flowing, easy, constant and animated. There was laughter. Dru's spaghetti was awesome. Rix tried both, but he liked the garlic bread with the cheese better. And they were all stuffed, even if Dru warned them not to be because she'd made a homemade spumoni ice cream terrine.

So they were giving it time for the food to settle and had moved into a large room that ran the front to the back of the house. It had paneled walls of glossy wood and lots of leather seating.

The women were curled into the corner of a sectional in front of the fire.

The men were across the room in a cluster of chairs where the paneled walls gave way to an angle of floor-to-ceiling bookshelves.

And Judge got into it.

"You caught the man fucking someone else?" he asked low.

Rix jerked up his chin.

"The mother has no soul. The sister is a nightmare. You're right," Rix said to Jamie. "Ned is waking up to shit."

Judge glanced between his father and friend, not having been in on this, but not interrupting.

Rix kept going.

"And Chad is a waste of space. It's all dicked up. I don't know how Alex came to be Alex, except maybe her grandmother was more of a force of nature than she said. She sounded awesome. But we're talking miracle worker. Alex showed me the room she grew up in last night. It had been cleared out, but the bones of it were there. It didn't take much imagination to see it was always bones. Or trappings. Nothing fertile. No imagination. She told me she didn't have posters, but she did have a Degas."

Jamie, a father, flinched.

Judge just stared at him.

"I couldn't even keep my feet in that room," Rix told them. "I had to sit down, that shit was so heavy. I hated it so much she grew up in what really was kind of an actual ivory tower. Nothing for her roots to push into. No nourishment to be found. Her bed has this stuff at the top, like a curtain, you see them in movies. The beds the princesses sleep in. And straight up, she was that. A princess, stuck there, waiting for the chance to get free."

"And how is she handling all of this, being back?" Judge asked.

"She laid into her mom and dad today. Tore them up. Helena was insulted at the time, but she's probably forgotten it happened by now because she's probably forgotten Alex exists by now. Ned's thinking on things."

"Well, that's good," Jamie remarked.

"Would be," Rix told him, "if he hadn't told Alex she abandoned him when she was a little girl. Then he just motors. Drops that bomb, and he's gone." Rix shook his head. "The drama is fuckin' madness. You wouldn't believe the extremes. But he got what he wanted. Alex has no idea what he was talking about, and it's been eating her up all day."

"Abandoned him?" Judge asked.

"Your guess is as good as mine," Rix told him.

"He's a grown man and he's a father," Jamie said in a steely way. "That's not on. If he has something to discuss with his daughter, he discusses it. Fully."

"You know that. I do too," Rix agreed. "But you've been to his place. Probably don't think of it. Cool place. Really something. But compare it to what you have. Which is a cool place. Really something. But Dru doesn't pour your coffee in the morning from a silver pitcher with a hella long swooped spout, that if I tried to use it, I'd pour coffee all over the table."

"Ned doesn't strike me as that traditional," Jamie noted, looking mildly freaked.

"You were right about something else," Rix told him. "Ned fell into a life of who he was supposed to be and forgot to figure out who he actually is. When she's with him, like she slips into a second skin, Alex is in that life too."

"It's good this is over in a few days," Judge put in.

"My thoughts, man," Rix returned. "And now you're here. That's good. Al likes it when my people are around."

Judge sounded vaguely offended. "We're her people too."

Rix grinned at him. "Right. Yeah." His grin died. "And again, that's good. Alex hasn't talked about a single friend she wants to visit while she's here. She was full of ideas of places she wanted me to see. We hit up Battery Park today after the Memorial. Took a walk and a selfie with the Statue of Liberty in the background. She's told me about bookstores she digs. Cool buildings she thinks I'd like. But no friends."

"Okay, so tomorrow, if the sister doesn't call it off, it's what? The rehearsal?" Judge asked.

Rix nodded. "Yup. Rehearsal five to six-thirty. Dinner at seven-thirty."

"Right. I got time to show you some of the good New York. I'll swing by and get you in the morning. We'll take a run in Central Park. No way Chloe's gonna be up then, but if Alex doesn't come with us, we can come back, get showered. Chloe and I can grab you and Alex. Dru's in class tomorrow. But maybe she can meet us for lunch. We'll go to the first Shake Shack in Madison Square Park. It's next to the Flatiron building, which is kickass. We can decide over lunch what's next."

"Sounds like a plan," Rix replied. "Alex will be with us when we go in the morning. She's not a runner, but she'll wanna be out. Maybe we can pick a loop where we can meet back with her?"

"Absolutely," Judge finished.

Jamie shifted. "You men want another beer? Or is it time for bourbon? Scotch?"

"You're pouring, I'm not gonna say no," Rix replied.

"Which?" Jamie asked.

"I trust you," Rix said.

He grinned at Rix and looked to his son.

"Same, Dad."

Jamie clasped Judge's shoulder warmly before he took off.

They watched the guy go.

Then Rix looked right at Judge.

"He good?"

Judge drew breath into his nose before answering, "She goes to class. He goes to work. She does a few things with her friends. *A few.* He works too much, but when he gets home, he's home. That's it. Outside that, they're attached at the fucking hip."

Rix grimaced.

"Yeah," Judge agreed. "Chloe's ready to hatch a plot the minute I give her the go ahead. Her dreams and schemes scare the fuck out of me. But I'm thinking it's almost time to give her the go ahead."

"Yeah, a plot like when she *accidentally* told me weeks ago I was gonna be here with Alexandra?" Rix asked.

Judge's lips went up on one end.

Rix couldn't say he'd clued in at the time.

But since, he'd clued in.

"Seems like she's got it goin' on to me," Rix noted.

That was when Judge grinned, but there was a different emotion in his voice when he said, "She loves you a lot, Rix."

"She doesn't hide it, Judge. Never thought I'd be one with my bud's woman sticking her nose in my love life, but I find I got no complaints."

They shared a look.

Then they got back to it.

"Ned likes him," Rix shared. "Lots of respect there. Thought the world of Rosalind."

"She was fantastic," Judge confirmed.

"Maybe get him involved in the wedding. Pull him somehow into Trail Blazer. Give him something to do so Dru knows you got him, and she can do her thing. And Jamie isn't just existing on nothing but the time he gets to look after his girl, and the less time he gets to be with his boy."

"Good idea," Judge muttered.

Judge then looked right to Rix.

"She really okay?"

Rix nodded.

"I think so. Proud as fuck she ripped them a new one, bud. Her father made a noise when her blade struck true, I know he's spent all day with her words in his head too. The mom is a wash. But as pissed as I am Ned's parting shot left Alex with something to worry about, I think she misses a dynamic that's always been there. Ned is proud of her. Straight up, doesn't hide it. He isn't crawling up her ass. It rolls out of him like he's done it a million times before. Even in front of her sister, or maybe especially. But Helena gives shades of the same thing. Their expectations of her are high, not just that she act like a rational adult. Maybe because Alexandra always exceeded them. And they haven't missed it. Though I think the fact is they haven't, but she's missed that they haven't."

"You gonna talk to her about that?"

"If Ned doesn't sit down with her soon, I'll be talking to Ned about talking to her about that."

"Good call," Judge agreed.

"Oh my God!" Dru cried.

They looked to the couches.

Dru looked surprised.

Chloe was shaking her head in disgust at the same time she was staring at the fire and sipping her wine.

Alex was looking over the back of the couch at Rix.

"Just got a text from Mum," she called.

Shit.

"The wedding's still on," she finished.

And...

Fuck.

———————

RIX WAS SITTING ON THE SIDE OF THEIR BED, ROLLING THE LINER OFF HIS left leg when he sensed her.

He looked up.

Alex was leaning against the door to the bathroom, watching him.

Her pajama pants had a drawstring at the waist. She had a thin thermal on. He could see one of the little bras she wore to bed through it.

She'd had a shit day and she seemed zoned out, her gaze aimed to his legs.

"All good?" he asked.

Her eyes came to him.

"I've timed you," she said.

"What?" he asked.

"The first time was the day before we left to come here."

She wasn't making any sense.

"Baby...*what?*"

"When you're doing it by rote, it takes you just over a minute and a half to put on your legs. And the first time you didn't hide it from me was when you took them off the night before we left to come here."

He sat still.

"You'd always gone to the bathroom second, so you could turn your back on me, and I couldn't see. That night, I came in the room later. And I looked it up. That neoprene thing is called the liner. The cuff you put your leg in is called the socket. That thing you roll up your thigh at the end is called a sleeve."

"I could have told you that," he said quietly.

"You hid it. I was giving you time. And I wanted to know." She didn't move when she went on, "Did you know you switch up? When you put them on, you do left then right. When you take off, you do right then left."

Rix did know that, but that wasn't the only reason he had no reply.

"You're trained to keep your head in an emergency. Even should that be personal, I have no doubt you'd have your legs on in under a minute, maybe a little over one. If there's an intruder, we're calling nine one one anyway, but in a minute, you'd be ready."

"Alexandra," he whispered.

"You played left field on your fire crew's softball team and batted clean up. At your party, your friend Drake told me they missed you in the lineup. You can run and you can hike and you can fuck me on your knees, but you can't play softball?"

"Come here."

"I have never in my life seen my father approve of anybody. Not without years and batteries of his tests. You introduce yourself to him by agreeing that I'm perfect, and he immediately accepts you. But it's the man you are. You saw him with Chad today. He's no dummy. He read who you were the minute he saw you."

"Got my legs off, baby, come here."

"Thanks for standing up for me today, repeatedly, and once, literally."

"Baby."

"I couldn't have done this without you."

"Get your ass over here," he growled.

She got over there, crawling right into his lap, where he liked her, but he fell back, twisted and rolled, so her head was to the pillows, and he was on top of her.

She had his face in her hands.

"You take care of me."

"Yeah," he grunted.

"I don't ever want you to doubt it again. I don't."

Fuck.

Fuck.

Fuck.

"Quiet," he ordered.

"Okay," she whispered.

"The day you had, I'm supposed to be looking after you, and you're all over seeing to me," he grumbled.

"Rix, if you don't think I know you're looking after me. If you think I missed the trench coat and the grown-up sibling squabbling and the man huddle, whispering about how you're all worried about me, you're crazy."

She hadn't missed the trench coat.

"We're right now in a glorified hotel room that's in a home and you gave that to me tonight," she continued. "I didn't miss it, honey."

"This is fucking with my head, not the drama, knowing you grew up in this mausoleum," he admitted.

"I know. I'm sorry."

"Not yours to be sorry for."

"I'm still sorry."

"You saw what Jamie and Rosalind gave Dru. You saw what I had."

"Yes."

"That's what we're giving our kids."

Her eyes closed. Then they opened.

It wasn't a blink. It was more like a surprise seizure.

He grinned.

And teased, "Gimme a break."

"Give you a break?"

"Babe, you're wearing my ring."

"It's fake."

"It's unofficial," he corrected.

"Rix!" she snapped. "This is huge. What's with you acting all blasé about it?"

"Because it is what it is. You're giving it back when we get home so I can give it to you again when I ask you to marry me."

"I'm not giving it back," she retorted. "I love it. I'm keeping it. You can do the deed with the question whenever, but I'm not giving up this ring."

He gave her more of his weight and replied, "No way in fuck, baby. You're not wearing that ring after you put it on yourself which was after I tossed the box with it inside across a room to you. I'm gonna figure out something memorable and slide it on your finger my own fucking self when it's official."

"That's totally a waste. We know what this is," she bitched.

"Then why the surprise seizure when I start talking about our kids?"

Her eyes narrowed. "Surprise seizure?"

"Told my mom it isn't what it is…yet, and you're all big eyes and bullshit surprise."

She shoved at him. "I *am* surprised."

"Baby, *we know what this is.*"

She started bitching again. "This is maybe the least romantic proposal-non-proposal, future-children discussion in history."

"I made no promises about romance. I promised sexual slavery and excellent grill skills."

"Ohmigod! You're the worst."

He dipped his head, and against her neck, he murmured. "Now, time for the sexual slavery part."

"Ugh!"

He slid a hand under her thermal at her belly.

"Two kids," she snapped at the ceiling.

He lifted his head and looked down at her. "Three."

"Okay, three," she agreed grouchily.

"Better give me a Kinsley, baby," he warned.

"We *must* have a boy with your caramel eyes or we're going to keep going until I have one."

"Caramel eyes?" he teased.

"Just shut up, Rix, and fuck me."

He was him, so he had to take a beat to shoot her a cocky smile.

Alex lifted her head.

And kissed it off his mouth.

CHAPTER 24

THE CONVERSATION

Alex

I didn't know what woke me.

I was not typically a sound sleeper. But when I was in bed beside Rix, my sleep had been the best I'd had in my life.

But I woke.

And when I did, I saw through the dark that Rix was sitting on the side of the bed.

This didn't seem strange to me at first.

But then he didn't move.

I got worried, and as it goes when that happens, a number of possibilities washed through my mind.

Such as, he needed to go to the bathroom, and we hadn't put his chair close enough to the bed.

Or the chair was close enough, but he needed to go to the bathroom, and although we'd brought a portable bench for the shower, there were no handrails anywhere, and this made everything in the bathroom harder to maneuver from his chair.

I'd fretted about this when we'd gone in and checked that night we'd arrived.

Rix's bathroom at his house had been completely modified to his needs.

We'd put a bench in the shower at my house, and he had his old foldable walker that he'd used in the beginning when he was getting used to his legs in there so he could use it to swing in and out until we had the mods done around the shower and toilet areas.

But the en suite bathroom for this room was not accessible.

Rix had said not to worry. It had a handheld showerhead, which was helpful, and he'd been a lot of places where he had to get creative. He had specifically built up his upper body strength and worked with his therapists and mentor on these strategies so, as much as possible, he could resume the active life he'd had, no matter what unexpected challenges he might face.

Still, in the middle of the night in a strange room when you needed to go to the loo, it could be disorienting.

"You okay?" I called.

His body seemed to jolt, and he turned his head to look at me.

"Yeah, baby," he murmured. "Go back to sleep."

I wasn't very hip on that body jolt.

Therefore, I asked, "You need anything?"

"No. All good."

Did I let this go?

No, this was Rix.

I didn't let this go.

"Then why are you awake in the early hours of the morning and sitting on the side of the bed?" I asked.

"My foot hurts."

I got up on my elbow, not comprehending this answer.

Was he sleep sitting?

"Your foot hurts," I said carefully.

"Yeah. My brain consciously knows they're gone. But my brain physically hasn't gotten with that program. It doesn't know what to do with the fact that my feet aren't there to give it signals, so sometimes it decides to tell me something's up. When it happens, I try to get in the zone to talk it down."

He was referring to phantom limb pain.

"Get in the zone?" I queried.

"Meditate. I've got some guided meditations I usually use, but I left my earbuds in my bag and I'm too lazy to go get 'em. So I was trying to go it alone."

"I can get them," I offered.

"That'd be good, honey," he murmured. "They're in the side pocket."

I rolled out, went to his duffel that was sitting on a chair across the room, and dug out his buds.

I also made a mental note of this, so I could be sure these were where Rix needed them, even if he forgot.

I walked to him.

He took them from me and reached for his phone on the night-stand, saying, "Thanks, sweetheart."

I crawled in bed at his side, sitting on my hip. "Has this happened since we've been together?"

Rix shook his head. "No. Happened a lot in the beginning, after they took my feet. That's a serious mindfuck. You're grieving some-thing you lost that you used every day of your life and totally took for granted, and your brain's stabbing pain up your feet that are no longer there. But it's a lot better now."

"And it's hurting right now?"

"It's hurting right now," he confirmed.

I kissed his shoulder and said, "I'll let you get on with it."

"Mouth," he ordered.

I pushed in and kissed his mouth.

Then he put his earbuds in, and I crawled to my side of the bed and got settled.

I didn't sleep until I heard him put his stuff back on the nightstand, and he curled into me.

"It gone?" I whispered.

"Mm," he hummed.

I didn't know if that was an affirmative.

I did know he sounded sleepy.

Then I got proof he was sleepy because his weight fell into me, telling me he was asleep.

That was when I fell asleep.

***

LATER THAT MORNING, AFTER THE LYFT DROPPED US OFF IN FRONT OF Dad's house, I used my key to let us in.

Rix was sweaty from his run in Central Park, but mostly he was drenched because it was misty outside, there'd been a light rain a couple of times while we were out, and he, unlike I, hadn't worn a slicker.

I felt bouncy because I'd been outside, but also it was nice to be in the cool and mist and rain. Unlike Phoenix, Prescott could be cool and even cold. But there weren't any mists and not a lot of rain.

Oh, and because Rix was sexy when he was sweaty and damp and exhilarated after having a run.

I was looking forward to whatever was about to happen in our room pre- or post-shower.

I was looking forward to the Shake Shack.

I was looking forward to taking Rix to see Rockefeller Center and Times Square, just because everyone had to see both in person.

While we waited for the Lyft, Judge, Rix and I had decided on a whirlwind NYC tour. Thus, after lunch, we were hitting those two then going to the top of the Empire State Building. And then we'd see what else we could do if we had time.

I liked this. It was fun and kitschy, and I enjoyed spending time with Chloe and Judge.

And I could use the distraction from all that was in my head.

At present, the fact my sister, who I might not be close to, but she was still my sister, was marrying a total loser the next day.

We got halfway to the stairs when my father showed in the foyer.

Okay, at the *present* present, my mind was on my dad.

I hadn't seen him since he'd walked away from us the morning before.

My step faltered, and I stopped.

Rix's did the same, and his hand in mine squeezed.

"Morning, Dad," I greeted.

"Good morning, Alex," he replied, then he looked up at my side. "Rix."

"Ned," Rix grunted.

Dad interpreted that correctly that he wasn't Rix's favorite person right then, but he was Dad. He had Bernhard-Sharp blood in him. He got what he wanted, and not much fazed him.

"Can I steal Alex for a while?" Dad asked Rix.

Why he did that, I didn't know, since Rix didn't set my schedule for me.

Rix informed him of that. "Not me you gotta ask. Though, we got less than two hours before Judge and Chloe are swinging by to pick us up. We got a full day planned."

Dad looked to me. "I can't promise to make this quick, darling. I can promise it's important."

Rix's hand squeezed mine harder.

But this had to happen, and one of the myriad awesome things about Chloe and Judge was that they'd get it if we had to be late because of it.

"Okay," I said to Dad and looked up to Rix, saying it quieter, "Okay."

He studied my face.

And with another squeeze of my hand, he let me go, bent down to touch his mouth to mine, and then muttered, "Slicker."

I nodded, took off my damp rain slicker and handed it to Rix.

I didn't know if it was to communicate something to Dad or me (or both) that Rix didn't move from his spot as he watched us walk to the hall that led to such rooms as Dad's study and the library.

I just knew he didn't move a muscle until we were out of sight.

I thought for sure Dad would take me to his study.

He didn't.

He took me to the library, to the two armchairs with ottomans that sat at angles to each other and were positioned to face the room from the far corner.

Chairs where I'd spent a lot of time growing up, because if I couldn't be out in the city doing something to escape my life, I was going to be in a book, escaping my life.

And that was where I was.

Before I sat, I noticed the Degas that used to be in my bedroom but now was on the wall hanging over the chair I'd always favored.

I knew it was there, but something about that caught my attention just then.

Maybe because I'd mentioned it to Rix.

Maybe because I was having this sit down with Dad after an emotional few days.

I hadn't decided by the time I'd taken that chair, Dad sat beside me and asked, "Judge Oakley is in town?"

"Yes, he and Chloe arrived yesterday."

I didn't add to that, like sharing with him our friends came all the way across the country because they thought we needed moral support.

I left it there.

"That's lovely for you," Dad remarked.

"Yes," I agreed.

He pulled in breath through his nose.

"I like him," he declared. "Rix. He's good. Solid. I didn't know what I'd get, him being handicapped."

So Dad did know Rix had lost his legs.

"It isn't handicapped, Dad. He lives with a disability."

"Right," Dad murmured. "I meant no offense."

"Now, you know," I stated.

Dad gave me a curt nod. "My point is, he's impressive. And not just with that."

"I know," I agreed.

"He suits you. You make a good couple. You're both highly attractive. You have a great deal in common. In other words, Alexandra, you have my blessing. And obviously, so does he. I'd like a chat with him.

I'd like to meet his family. But we'll discuss your budget for the wedding and the plans you're making. Obviously, I'd like it to be here. Though, my assumption is, that won't happen."

Though currently it was "unofficial," I now knew it was going to happen and how many children we were going to have, even though neither of us had said the words "I love you."

I didn't have an issue with this. Rix and I hadn't done things normally from the beginning.

Why start now?

"No, it won't."

Another nod, less curt, more understanding. "Perhaps, after the honeymoon, you can come home for a small reception with family friends."

"I'll talk to Rix about it," I murmured.

"A small one, Alex," he said quietly. "And I mean friends like Jamie."

"It's likely Jamie will come out to Arizona for the actual event," I pointed out.

"What I'm trying to say is, people who I respect. Who mean something to me. To you. To this family. Not one hundred and fifty people you nor I know very well sitting for a brunch wearing hats. I wouldn't put you through that. But I'm proud of my daughter. She's accomplished and part of that is to be intelligent enough to find a good, decent man who knows his own mind, has his own ambitions and looks after my girl."

I stared at him, an odd feeling simmering inside me.

"You must know, it pains me you're looking at me like that," he stated tersely. "In the world you built around yourself, Alexandra, did you convince yourself I showed you no love?"

I was unprepared for the attack.

"Dad—"

"Do you not understand why I chose this room to have this talk?"

And now he sounded hurt.

The Degas.

My hands were on my lap, but they went to the armrests to hold on.

Dad didn't miss it.

"You don't," he whispered.

"Because I was in here a lot, and you know it's my favorite place in the house."

"Yes, because of that, and because of that desk over there."

I looked across the room at the writing desk.

The writing desk that had not, when I was much younger, been there.

The writing desk that Dad had purchased at auction at Sotheby's. It had some important lineage, like George Washington or Ben Franklin used it at some point. It was gorgeous and worked perfectly in the room. And around the time I started spending a lot of it in that room with my books, that desk showed up.

And sometimes, not often, but sometimes, when I was sitting right where I was right now reading, Dad would come in and work at that desk.

Not in his study that was just across the hall.

At that desk.

In the library.

With me.

Oh my God.

"This is our room, Alexandra."

I felt them trembling at the edge of my eyes when I turned my attention from the desk to him.

"By the time I lost you," he said in a voice that was nearly a whisper, "I didn't know how to reach you. So I settled for being close to you."

I struggled with holding back a sob.

Dad cleared his throat.

"I shouldn't have said what I said yesterday," he announced. "I'm a grown man. I was wounded by your words, regardless that I deserved them, and because of that, I behaved like a child."

He shifted in his seat uncomfortably, cleared his throat again.

And then continued.

"I was also feeling vulnerable. Your defense of me was unexpected.

Welcome, my darling. But unexpected. It has not escaped me that we all have felt cast adrift in our own ways in this family, me included. However, it was my responsibility to reel each of us in. I failed in that. But I had always thought that you and I…"

He trailed off, but instead of finishing, caught another thread.

"Your sister does have her charms. She doesn't allow them to be seen very often, but they're there. But I was close with my mother. You were close with her. We shared that. We had a bond. You were like her. A quieter version of her, but very like her. I loved her. And I love you."

"Dad," I whispered.

He held my gaze.

And even lower, he kept talking.

"When you were a little girl, you were mine. Your mother hated it. Detested it. She had no interest in you or your sister, but she didn't like I had interest in you. The both of you. I got lost in the disintegration of my marriage. Your grandfather got ill, and more responsibility fell to me. He died, and then all of it fell to me. And I lost you in the meantime. It wasn't that we were inseparable, but you'd wake up and your nanny knew to bring you directly to me. You crawled in my lap and sat there while I had breakfast. I read to you before you fell asleep. That stopped because you got older. It stopped because I wasn't around for us to allow that to shift naturally to something else. And it stopped because you pulled away from me."

"Dad, I'm so sorry. I don't remember any of that from when I was young. I just remember you not being around very much," I told him, saw something unhappy shift in his eyes, and quickly went on, "But I didn't…I can't imagine it was conscious that I—"

His head bobbed as he cut me off.

"Your mother and I fought, and it was ugly. Of course you'd find places to be where you felt safe, because that was not safe. I was dealing with other things. I lost both my girls in all of that, Alex. I don't blame you. You were not the adult in that situation. You were not parent to my child. I was your father. It was up to me. But that said, I missed you."

"I...I...Dad, this means a lot. So much. But I don't know what to say."

"I don't mean for you to say anything. I'm not defending myself, but explaining. I don't know why it is. You'd left home, went so far away. All the mischief your sister's been up to. I don't know why this wedding has shaken something in me. Perhaps it's that she's marrying a man so completely unworthy of *anybody*."

I couldn't help but to press my lips together so I wouldn't smile at that.

"It's amusing even if it very much isn't," Dad murmured.

"I'm not laughing at Blake. It's just...*Chad*," I explained.

"Yes. It is just...*Chad*," he agreed.

We shared a look, and I felt that look straight to the heart of me.

Having that moment with my dad.

His expression shifted again, and he said, "And it could be that you came home with a handsome gent on your arm who so very much loves you and now I know I have to give up both of my girls when I don't even really have them in the first place."

So very much loves you.

Give up both of my girls.

I reached out and grabbed his hand. "You have me, Dad."

He wrapped his other hand around mine so he was holding me with both. "I knew that, yesterday, when you had words with your mother, and it meant the world to me, Alex."

"Maybe I didn't try either. I'm an adult now too," I noted.

"You won't be taking that on," he decreed.

"Dad—"

"Let's just begin from here, shall we?"

I stared into his eyes.

They were the green of mine, not the brown.

The green.

He was part of me.

I didn't remember crawling into his lap.

But I did remember him sitting at that writing desk. I remembered him buying it. I remembered it being set up. I remembered him being across the room from me, him doing his work, me reading.

No, he didn't reach out.

But he didn't desert me.

"We shall," I agreed.

And another shift.

Gratitude. Relief.

And something a lot deeper.

What was simmering inside me warmed and settled.

God, I had a dad.

No.

I'd always had one.

"To that end, I must ask your advice about your sister," he announced.

I blinked.

He kept going.

"My kneejerk reaction is to refuse to pay for what's left of this debacle and donate what's left of her trust fund to your Trail Blazer organization."

I blinked again.

"Though my conscience is not following along with this thought," he concluded.

There was a reason for that.

"You need to pay the bills," I informed him. "You need to walk her down the aisle. You need to stand by her side. You need to keep a tight rein on her funds so she doesn't squander them. And if she doesn't pull it together, you need to shift them to a trust where she'll never have full control of them, you'll either manage them, or someone you trust will. But the next time she makes a mistake, you need to let her dig herself out from under it, Dad. No matter how embarrassing it is to her or the family."

He knew I spoke truth, which was why his lips tightened and his nod again was curt.

"Can I ask you something?" I requested.

"Anything, love," he answered.

"What did you mean when you told Mum she dropped all pretense yesterday?"

With both of his, he gave my hands a squeeze, let me go and sat back.

I wasn't sure what to make of this as a preamble.

"I sense there's no love lost for either of us with your mother, which upsets me in your case, but nevertheless, it's true."

I stretched out my lips.

He watched and his twitched.

"Even so," he continued, "it makes me uncomfortable to speak ill of her directly to you. However, I very much understand why you'd wish to understand."

It was my turn to nod.

And that was when Dad told me the story.

A story I'd always wanted to know and buried that desire, but that wasn't the reason why I never asked.

"Your grandfather, your mother's father, who we were all very fortunate lived an ocean away so that he could not interfere with our lives very much before he passed…" Dad paused and assured, "I'm not being unkind. He was truly a callous, autocratic man, and there would come a time when I would realize I should have paid much closer attention to him."

This preamble was even worse.

Dad continued sharing.

"However, he was also both a very modern man and a very old-fashioned one. He understood that American money was what it was. Money. That bloodlines need to be diversified. That the world was getting smaller and smaller. As such, he decided who your mother would marry, and that would be me. She was given her directive, and she set her sights. She was immensely beautiful, had wonderful manners, and although I'd traveled quite a bit, and an English rose isn't exactly mysterious, she seemed that to me. I was hoodwinked. However, I wouldn't know this until she was carrying Blake. It wouldn't do for me to discover it before the stake was thoroughly claimed. Although the woman I married was well-traveled, cultured, stylish, all the things she still is today, she was also affectionate and adventurous. She was a good listener, or so I thought. She had a sense of humor."

He sighed.

I waited, entirely unable to try such things as affectionate, a good listener, and having a sense of humor on my mother.

None of them fit.

He carried on.

"It was all a ruse. She was as she is now. Cold. And back then, calculating. She did her duty to her family. She carried on the line. And then, frankly, she wanted nothing to do with any of us. Sadly, I was impossibly in love with her by this time and felt in my heart she couldn't be so thoroughly the woman I married without that woman being somewhere in her. I thought marriage counseling would help, she flatly refused. I suggested therapy to her, she laughed at the thought. I worried something horrible had happened to her that she hadn't shared, like she'd been assaulted, and that was why her personality changed so completely. But it eventually proved that fortunately, that hadn't happened, but the rest would be no help. She is who she is. There will be another Marchioness of Norton, and through Blake, or you, the title will sit directly in the bloodline. Her duty was done, and her life was her own."

"So in the end, for you, all the fighting was because you loved her," I guessed.

Another nod from Dad, but he said, "Though, not only. My pride was stung. I lost my wife, but in truth, I never had her to begin with. I'd been played. I fancy myself an intelligent man, Alexandra. That was a blow to my ego that was difficult to sustain." He leaned toward me. "But I should have let it go long ago. Not just for myself, but for you girls." He tipped his head to the side and his voice was gentler when he asked, "Do you suffer?"

I knew what he was asking.

"Not really," I replied.

"A girl needs her mother."

"Dad, I found coping mechanisms ages ago. And I had Grandmother Brooke." I smiled at him. "I had a father who made it so he could work close to where I escaped, and I figure somehow, that penetrated for me. I made my own life, and I love my life."

I leaned deeper into him and curled the fingers of both hands on his forearm on the arm of the chair.

Then I finished, "I'm happy."

"Good," he whispered.

"Do you have a sense why she fights with you?" I asked.

Unlike the rest of our conversation, he didn't readily answer.

"Dad?"

"As I said, I don't like to speak ill of her directly at you."

My tone was lower when I prompted, "Dad."

His chest expanded with the heave of this sigh.

Then he said, "It pains me. I've considered it quite a bit, especially recently, dealing with your mother and your sister and this wedding. And yesterday, for reasons I'm sure you understand, thoughts of it consumed me. My mind tried other avenues, but I was always directed back to the fact that the truth of it is, your mother is not a nice woman. She is wholly selfish. She is wholly surface. And she isn't very intelligent. How I was deceived by her for so long I'm afraid has quite a bit to do with my manhood and ego."

I started chuckling.

He smiled at me.

But he finished, "And my greatest worry is that your sister is quite like her."

"Yeah," I agreed and scrunched my nose.

He in turn smiled at me giving him that look, before he chided, "Though, they will always be your mother and sister."

"Yes, of course."

"And I will warn you now that she will wish to interfere in whatever festivities you and Rix are thinking about for your wedding."

Oh no.

I hadn't thought of that.

"This current affair went well because Blake enjoyed the attention, and Helena enjoyed spending my money. However, we'll both need to firmly put our foot down so you'll have what you want."

"Rix will put his foot down too," I reminded him.

"That might actually work."

That was when I started laughing.

When I was getting control of it, I saw Dad was doing it with me.

Really, truly...

That felt *so good*.

"And that doesn't even count Mags drawing the line," I shared.

"Mags?"

"Mags, Rix's mom. His dad is named Garrison. He's called Gare."

"Ah."

From there, we talked.

We kept doing it even though, eventually, Dad took my hand and pulled me up from my chair.

We continued to do it as he walked me to the door of Rix and my room.

We only stopped doing it when he kissed my cheek and said, "We'll ride together to the rehearsal, yes?"

"Yes, Dad."

He pressed his four fingers flat on my cheek in a gesture of affection he'd never made with me before.

And that didn't feel good.

It felt beautiful.

Then he said, "Enjoy your day, my darling," and walked away.

I walked into a room that had a boyfriend that was unofficially a fiancé in it who had his hair still wet from his shower and was wearing a sweater over a T-shirt and faded jeans.

Oh, and his eyes were sharp on me, and his bearing was almost primal. Like, if he saw I'd sustained a single wound from my conversation with Dad, he was going to chase him down and tackle him.

He didn't see that.

As such.

He watched the tear drop from my eye and fall down my cheek.

And then I said, "Dad's wrong. I'm twenty-eight. And he's still my daddy."

That was when I was in Rix's arms.

And I was weeping.

Quietly.

And happily.

I EXPECTED IT TO BE PRETTY BAD.

But it was worse.

Bride-idorah would have been welcome.

Blake was so past Bride-idorah, it was full-on scary.

In other words, during the rehearsal, Blake was in amped-to-the-max ball-busting mode.

Which meant Chad was deep in groveling mode.

And for some reason, Mum was in fawning mode, that being all over Chad's parents, which made me have to stop myself from checking the Peerage to see if, somehow, they were closer to the throne than we were.

Dad was clearly plumbing new depths of his patience.

And I'd discovered almost immediately Blake's bridesmaids were what Dru said they were.

Irredeemable bitches.

First case in point, the minute Rix, Dad and I showed, Rix had caught me with an arm around my neck, pulled me close, put his lips to my ear, and said, "Jesus, baby, the brunette at the end was who Chad was plowing."

So that was one bridesmaid down.

And apparently during their talk, Chad had not shared who his indiscretion was with, even though that person would be standing up with his bride.

Second case in point, after we were introduced and were standing out in the vestibule, waiting to practice walking down the aisle, another attendant, named Chelsea (who, not-so-incidentally, was the one who, the instant she laid eyes on him, drank in Rix like he was a cool glass of water and she'd just run a marathon) asked, "What's it like to be with a guy with no legs? Does it feel kinky?"

To which I'd replied, "What's it like to have no soul? Do you feel empty?"

Her eyes went squinty.

But she got my point, or more accurately, realized she couldn't toy with me and avoided me from then on.

Then again, she got busy with other things.

This being that the other two, not including the brunette Chad had been plowing (her name was Brea), began huddling with Chelsea and commenced whispering, snickering and throwing looks Brea's way anytime Blake wasn't paying attention. This making it very clear they knew what Brea had done.

Though why they were friends of Blake's and hadn't told her, I didn't know.

But now I did know about Brea, so I had to decide whether to tell Blake myself.

Though, I had no shot since she was so busy making Chad feel like the piece of shit he was.

Of course, Rix was not missing any of this, so the entire time, he looked like he was in pain from trying to stop himself from laughing.

When there was a lull in the action, I hightailed it to Rix's pew and collapsed against him in it.

"Is it as fun as it looks?" he joked.

I fought punching him in the stomach and instead threw him a look. "You should never have told me about Brea. Now what do I do?"

Rix brows went up. "Does it matter who he fucked?"

"Rix, we're in a church," I said low.

He smirked. "Does it matter who he drilled? She decided to marry him anyway."

"But it's clear she doesn't know it was Brea."

"Babe, tomorrow, she's gonna stand by that guy in this church knowing he's a punk and a cheat and legally tie herself to him in front of God. It's not your problem that, down that line, a friend who is not a friend is standing there. These are all Blake's choices. They are not your damage. Let it go."

He was right.

"In your life, you got in trouble for what she did, Alexandra," he went on, not sounding amused now. "Her shit isn't yours anymore. It never was. But it one hundred percent isn't now."

He was right again.

I nodded and said, "I'm okay, honey. You're right. It isn't my deal."

"You didn't even agree to be in this wedding," he reminded me. "Even though you offered to talk, she didn't ask your opinion. This is not yours."

I turned fully to him and put my hand on his chest, repeating, "You're right. I'm good, Rix."

"Christ, I'll be glad when we're outta here," he muttered.

"Again, church," I reminded him, pressing into his chest and smiling.

Watching me closely, he asked, "You got some friends in town you wanna see tomorrow?"

I was still smiling when I asked back, "Trying to get out of going to the Russian Tea Room?"

Chloe had put up with the sightseeing that day.

So she was planning tomorrow.

And that was our plan for tomorrow.

"No, I wanna know if you've got some friends in town you wanna see," he replied.

He was slipping this in now, but asking a different question.

I answered that different question.

"I was inseparable from a girl name Aderonke. Until we were forced, with a lot of teenage angst that was very real, to be separated. She's Nigerian and her dad was a diplomat. My world ended when she had to go back to Nigeria. We're still friends. We talk occasionally, and I saw her in New York at Christmas last year, and earlier, in the summer, when I was visiting Mum in England, she was in London, and we met for lunch that lasted through dinner."

"Right," he grunted.

"Aderonke was my bestest bestie from sixth through tenth grade. Our posse, though, also included Yael and Shelby, who remained my posse until I left New York. Yael's now a systems engineer for Google and lives in California. Shelby's in Austin. She restores old furniture."

"Right," he murmured.

"I'm still tight with those two too," I assured him. "Though I had other friends, I didn't keep in touch as much. But we do hook up when I'm back. I just didn't think it was in the cards this time so I didn't reach out."

"Okay, honey," he said.

"As for when I was at Columbia, none of my friends were local, but me. They all scattered to the winds after graduation. But a lot of them, I keep in touch with too." I got closer and finished, "I wasn't alone, honey."

Mollified, he bent even closer and touched his mouth to mine.

"Alexandra!" Blake shouted. "If you don't mind, we're going again! Can it be about *me* for maybe a *minute?*"

Ulk.

"What did your dad say about being the better man?" I groused to Rix.

"Brian didn't mean to blow up my life. Your sister fully understands her reason for being is to suck the joy out of everybody around her so they can be as miserable as she is. There's a difference. Keep your joy. Let her have her misery."

He was so smart.

And protective.

And funny.

Love you, I thought as I stared in his eyes.

They flared, then the caramel melted.

I said nothing.

But he heard me.

"Darling?" Dad called.

I turned and saw he was standing at the end of the pew, offering his arm.

I took it, and he walked me to the vestibule, where Blake and the rest of her attendants were waiting.

"Dad," she snapped, taking his arm from my hold and marching him away.

I sighed.

"Again and…music!" Mum called.

Pachelbel's Canon began.

I took my place in line.

And as I practiced the difficult maneuver of walking, Rix was sitting in the pew, smiling at me.

And…

Yes.

Joy.

CHAPTER 25

THE "WEDDING"

Alex

"The two sisters, maid of honor and our bride, closer... please get closer."

The photographer was directing.

We were standing with lighting and screens around us, the bouquets arranged just so in the background, and I was pretending to inspect Blake's veil.

I was also focusing on how fun it was to be at the Tea Room with Rix, Judge, Chloe, Dru and Jamie, the fact my feet had a couple of days respite, so my toes were only pinching a little and that tomorrow, by this time, we'd be on either my back deck, or Rix's.

Last, I was mostly failing at focusing on these things because I was worried about my sister.

"Blake," I called.

"Twitch it, make it look real, *twitch*," she commanded under her breath.

I stopped fake inspecting Blake's veil, walked to stand in front of her, took her hand and got close.

She looked disconcerted.

I ignored that.

"Today, this moment, your day, your moment, I'd like to ask that you give me the gift of listening to me."

She hesitated, then she dipped her chin.

I let out a breath.

Then quietly, I told her, "I want you to be happy."

To that, her jaw slid slightly to the side.

I kept going.

"I really do. I want you to find true happiness," I reiterated. "And I want you to think really hard about if this is going to make you happy."

Her nostrils flared, she looked over my shoulder, then back at me where she clipped, "I know what I'm doing, Alex."

"I hope so. Because we've never been close. We don't get along. We don't share much in common. But you're my sister. I love you. And I want what's best for you. You deserve a good man who loves you for who you are. You're beautiful. You have great style." I wanted to find more, and I should have prepared better for this, but I didn't have it handy right then, so I just concluded, "And you have your charms. So you deserve a lot, Blake." *More than Chad*, I left unsaid.

She just stared at me, saying nothing.

"I'm at your side, no matter what," I told her. "You marry him, I'm there for you. I respect your decision, and I'll hope for the best for you, like always. If you make another decision, I'm there for you too, should you need me to secret you away, or walk out there and make an announcement. Whatever you need. I'm your sister, and on your special day, it would mean everything to me to have the honor of giving it to you."

She held my gaze half a beat before she pulled her hand from mine and repeated, "I told you, I know what I'm doing."

"Okay," I replied.

"Oh ladies," the photographer cooed. "Can we do that again? That was so beautiful. But this time without the bride frowning."

Blake snatched up my hand. We stayed close. We gazed into each other's eyes. Hers were not smiling, but her mouth was. Mine were all the same.

And the photographer snapped away.

I'D DONE IT THE DAY BEFORE.

But still, when I walked down the aisle, holding my extravagant bouquet that not only dangled down my front with long ribbons that, if I wasn't careful to make sure they fluttered off beside me, they might trip me, but also, the flowers draped over my arm (it was huge, and Blake's was three times the size of mine), I saw Rix sitting there.

But he'd never seen the gown.

In fact, after they dropped me off at the hotel where I was to have hair and makeup done with Blake and the rest of the bridal party at two o'clock, he hadn't seen me.

My hair pulled back soft at the nape, trailing tendrils around my face, with a hair piece woven into it at the chignon that was rife with star-like flowers, leaves and pearls that laced into my hair up the back of my head and into the side.

My makeup was subtle and dewy, almost innocent, not a contour in sight (but of course, this was an event, so I had fake eyelashes).

Even I had to say, I looked pretty danged good.

Chloe would approve.

I approved.

And when Rix saw me, his back going straight and his eyes devouring me, he approved.

I smiled at him.

His return grin lit my world so bright, I almost lost track of the trailing ribbon, and I didn't even notice Jamie and Dru sitting with him.

Me and my high heels came to stand in position at the front.

The music changed.

And I watched Dad, very debonair in a tux with a long, blush tie that matched my gown, also looking proud, as he escorted Blake down the aisle.

I didn't agree with my sister's decision.

But she looked beautiful.

Watching her with Dad, I wished I'd told her that and decided I'd find some time that evening to rectify that mistake.

The giving away caused emotion I wasn't expecting to feel, especially after Dad lifted Blake's veil over her head and whispered something in her ear.

And her beautiful face grew startled, then soft.

For the life of me, I would never have expected to gain so much from that trip home, one I didn't want to make at first, one I knew I'd be forever grateful I'd made for so many reasons, it was impossible to fit them all in my head at once.

But that look on her face, it made me think perhaps one day, I'd have even more bounty.

As practiced, we went through the rigmarole of the ceremony commencing, Blake handing me her bouquet, turning to Chad, and taking his hands.

But when the reverend was dispensing with the preliminaries, in my wildest imaginings I would never have guessed what would happen next.

Not even close.

(Nowhere near.)

Precisely, when he asked if anyone objected to the marriage, that they speak now or forever hold their peace.

And Blake said, "Actually…"

My spine locked.

Blake held on to Chad, but twisted toward Brea at the end of the bridal line.

And then she called loudly, "Would you prefer to be standing here, Brea? Since you were having sex with Chad three days ago."

My gaze flew to Rix.

Creases had formed at the sides of his eyes, his broad shoulders were doing slight heaves, and he was biting his lip.

A hum rose up, and in this day and age, it was no surprise, so did a number of cell phones.

"Oh my God," Chelsea, clearly not having been clued in by my sister that this was going to happen, muttered with bitchy glee.

"Right." Blake was now fully turned toward her bridal party.

She had also definitely heard Chelsea.

Because she said, "Then there was you, Chels, who banged his brains out when we were in Aruba." She looked out to the audience and called, "Sorry, Conner. But she did. I know. I've seen their sex tape. When he was pouring his heart out to me, begging me not to dump him, Chad shared he's into that kind of thing. It's also uploaded. Chad has a website for his buds. You have to have a password, though. But maybe he can be persuaded."

I looked to the pews and saw a tall, handsome guy, perhaps one who played rugby, though whatever he did, it left him with a very thick neck, a row back from Rix. He was in a half squat, looking like he was preparing to leap over the pews.

My guess?

Chelsea's beau.

Conner.

"Blake, if you—" the reverend started.

"Blake, honey, maybe—" Chad tried.

Blake whirled on Chad and announced, again loudly, "In fact, the only bridesmaid you *didn't* fuck was my sister."

There were gasps of guilt from behind me.

More from the crowd.

And, um…

Holy freaking *wow*.

I turned squinty eyes on the bitch brigade.

"Blake! Really! I must—" the reverend attempted.

As I turned back, I saw Dad was standing.

Mum looked like she was about to faint.

Blake whirled again, toward me and the others.

"In fact, the only bridesmaid I have, and the only one I didn't want"—her eyes came to me—"because we don't get along."

Oh God.

"We don't have anything in common."

Oh boy.

"And for more reasons than just that, she's the one I treated like shit my whole life, but even so, she showed up. Even so, she flew across the country to stand up for me. Even if she knew, like I know, that marrying this asshole would be the biggest mistake in my life, she's right there, by my side. She's *my sister*, and she at the very least *asked me* if I knew what I was doing when the man I'd decided to spend the rest of my life with proved himself to be a *colossal dick*, because she told me she thinks I deserve *a lot*. I deserve to be *happy*."

Her voice, already loud, was getting louder.

"Blake." I stepped forward. "Hey, let's—"

She turned and took two steps toward the audience. "So let's let it be known how *many* of us *object* to this wedding. What do you say?"

"Blake," Chad bit, getting closer to her.

"Really, Blake—" the reverend tried again.

Blake let it all hang out.

"Conner, obviously, and also obviously there's Rick, Misha and Gerard, but then there's also Robbie, Trev, Ben, Mark and DJ. And the list goes on. You can see them all at w-w-w dot c-h-the-man-tumbles dot com. And I'll throw in, password is basic exclamation point bitches. Capital Bs."

I jumped as her body suddenly jerked, because Chad yanked on her arm, biting out, "*Stop it.*"

And immediately, I dropped her ridiculously heavy bouquet, kept hold of mine (also heavy), and took two strides while swinging it back.

I did that so, when I was within reach, I could hit Chad with it.

Hard.

Something I did.

Right upside the head.

He careened to the side, blooms, buds, petals and leaves exploded, and I snapped, "Take your hand off my sister or I'll *end you*."

I got those words out before I lost purchase on my bouquet, was crying out and going up.

Rix had an arm around my back and one under my knees and he was stalking down the altar steps.

Commotions were breaking out when he dropped me to my feet close to Mum and Dad, pivoted, and then he jogged back up the steps.

Up went Blake, and he carried her down.

Which was good.

Because Conner and about four other guys were bearing down on the pulpit.

Or bearing down on a certain someone who was standing there.

Women were crying out to men (I was guessing the men were Robbie, Trev, Ben, Mark, and DJ), who were angrily shrugging them off.

Groomsmen were trying to hold Conner's crew back.

The reverend was calling for calm.

Some people were up, filming.

Others were up, just watching.

Still others were down, heads bent to their phones, likely looking up www.chthemantumbles.com.

Still others were attempting to leave.

The bridesmaids were shoving each other or being shoved aside by Conner's crew.

And Rix said to Dad, "You got her?"

Dad took hold of Blake. "Certainly." He looked down at Mum. "Are you coming?"

She stared up at Blake and screeched, *"What is the matter with you? Are you insane?"*

That was answer enough for Rix.

He grasped my hand, and we motored.

Down the side aisle, Rix shouldering people out of the way, me, Dad and Blake using his opened wake to get through (I would have made it though, seeing as I had his hand, so I reached out to Dad, who took mine, and he had Blake, so, powered by Rix, we became an unstoppable train).

Out the doors we blew, down the steps, where Rix ripped open the door to the bridal limo and used my hand to shove me in.

I essentially landed on my ass inside, then quickly scooted out of the way when he did the same to Blake.

Gathering and shoving her long train at the same time he ducked in, Dad landed, sitting opposite us then scooting.

Rix got in, sitting beside Dad, and slammed the door.

"*Drive*," he growled.

The chauffeur started up and glided out.

There was silence.

I reached and grabbed Blake's hand.

It was slack in mine for a second, then tentatively, her fingers curled around mine.

"Blake," Rix called.

I watched her look from gazing forlornly out the side window to him.

Oh man.

She'd actually really loved Chad.

I tightened my hold on her and looked to Rix.

He grinned at her. "That...was...fucking...*epic*."

Again tentatively, she smiled.

I failed at biting back a giggle.

Dad started chuckling.

And then we all burst out laughing.

Until Dad and I had to switch seats.

Because he was intent to catch her in his arms, a goal he achieved, when Blake dissolved into tears.

———

"THEN SHIT GETS EVEN MORE REAL BECAUSE IT LOOKS LIKE THE offensive line of the Giants is about to rush the pulpit, so I gotta get there before them and get the women outta there, when Alex walks right up to Chad, beans him with her bouquet, flowers flying everywhere, and says, 'Touch her again, *I will end you*,'" Rix related.

Chloe, Judge, Jamie, and Dru roared with laughter, with Dru chortling through her, "Best wedding I've ever been to!"

Dad sighed, but he was smiling.

"It was really a shame to leave those bouquets behind," Blake drawled. "They were stunning."

Everyone started laughing again.

But with my attention on my sister, I only chuckled before I agreed, "They really were."

Blake caught my eyes.

I smiled at her.

She didn't exactly smile back. But she didn't...*not*.

Progress.

We were in Dad's kitchen.

It had never been warm and welcoming, like Jamie's.

But now, it felt that way.

Dad had popped a couple of bottles of Veuve and had ordered Cathy to instruct the caterers to redirect a goodly amount of the canapés and the top of the wedding cake to his house.

This, Cathy did.

Therefore, the black marble countertop of his island was covered in food, and we were all gathered around it.

I'd kicked off my shoes, but was still in my bridesmaid's dress.

Blake, who could likely play golf in heels, was still in hers, as well as her dress, but the veil was on the table in the foyer, and Dru, Chloe and I had figured out how to pin up her train.

The women were on stools, and the men were standing because we only had four stools.

"That was inspired," Chloe purred Blake's way. "Allow me to speak for womankind when I say, *brava*."

I wasn't sure, but it looked like my sister might be blushing.

When the conversation turned from her, I caught her gaze and mouthed *You okay?*

She tipped her head to the side and shrugged.

Since it worked on me when Rix did it, I winked at her.

She rolled her eyes.

There she was.

There was my sister Blake.

I turned from her and saw Dad watching us.

He looked happy.

Rix leaned into my back from behind. I could feel his chest pressed into me as he nabbed a perfectly toasted petite square of bread on which a sliver of beef tenderloin had been formed into a rose, embedded in some herbed cream cheese, and hugged by a sprig of spring greens.

He popped it into his mouth and listened to Judge saying something.

And it wasn't (just) the canapé that made him, too, look happy.

I sipped champagne.

And I sat with a group of people who I sensed I'd always be comfortable with, and I didn't say a lot as the evening progressed.

But still.

I had an excellent time.

Elsa Cohen

"The Elsa Exchange"
Celebrity News and Interviews
YouTube Channel

"My wonderful watchers...I can't...it's just...the level of deliciousness...I'll simply show you."

Video onscreen of Blake Sharp standing at an altar in a stunning bridal gown beside her groom, saying, "...Chels, who banged his brains out when we were in Aruba."

Video carries on through Blake's speech. And through her maid of honor, Alexandra Sharp, belting the groom with her bouquet and threatening him. And also through John "Rix" Hendrix carrying Alexandra and Blake free right before a brawl begins.

And it carries on through quite a bit of that altar-wide brawl that included the slender groom, his groomsmen, a number of rather beefy members of the congregation, with a couple of bridesmaids falling into it because they weren't smart enough to get out of the way.

Cut back to Elsa.

"Suffice it to say, my wonderful watchers, Blake Sharp, who is quite the dark horse, is back on the market. I sense that, considering it seems she got smart, and quick, that raven-haired, violet-eyed beauty will take some time to lick her wounds before she soldiers back into the dating game."

Camera closes in on Elsa.

"But I, for one, offer her my hearty congratulations on this special day. And I wish her all the luck in the world. Now, until our next exchange, keep it positive. Elsa is signing off."

The branded Elsa wink and blowing of kiss.

Sign off.

Alex

Sunday afternoon, I sat next to Rix on my deck.

He had a beer.

I had some wine.

He also had something on his mind.

"This place, we don't have any room for kids, 'cept we could finish the storage space in the bottom level."

I turned to him.

"Or build on," he told the trees.

"We're living at your house," I told him.

He looked to me. "You're happy here."

"I'm happy in your house."

"Al, you love your forest."

"My deck is cool, but your deck is awesome."

"I'll agree. Your deck isn't as cool as my deck. But I can make your deck as cool as my deck."

"We can also just use your deck."

"Alexandra." Oh boy…my full name. "You're not giving up your trees."

We went into a staring contest.

I broke it saying, "There's too many stairs here."

He twisted in his seat to better face me, starting, "Babe—"

"Honey, it'll mess with your head. And I can't have that. If you're set on giving me my trees, we'll find another cabin that works for now and future or we'll find some land and build something. Hey?"

His lips quirked and he agreed, "Hey."

"Now, do you need another beer?"

"If I need another beer, I'll get another beer. Do you need more wine?"

"If I need more wine, I'll get more wine."

His heavy black brows snapped together.

"We've played," he said low. "But you haven't been spanked and I'm feeling that coming on."

My legs suddenly were restless.

This was not lost on him.

Thus, he turned back to the trees, threw back a tug of beer, and muttered, "Totally my mountain fuck bunny."

"Oh my God," I said to the trees. "You're *the worst*."

The next came supremely cocky.

"I know, but you love it."

Oh yes.

I did.

I really, really did.

EPILOGUE

THE HOUSE

Alex

C *rack!*
        I no longer tensed when Judge threw up the softball and hit it with his bat toward left field.

Because what happened next was what had been happening for the last fifteen minutes.

Rix jogged, got under it, and caught it.

It was just the two of them out there.

Now.

I'd been out there before, when Judge was pitching, and Rix was hitting. Obviously, I had a lot of ground to cover. Mostly, I just chased after balls rolling toward the fence that had flown over my head. I hadn't caught any, but I'd scooped up a couple of grounders.

Now, I was in the bleachers with Chloe.

Because Rix was fielding.

Crack!

"I can't even begin to understand my visceral response to this," Chloe began, sitting beside me, lounging back into the bleacher seat behind us with sunglasses on her nose, a chunky mohair sweater covering her upper body, skinny jeans, and booties on her lower.

It was a crisp late autumn day in Prescott, and she looked like a What to Wear picture.

Her focus was on Judge.

And her mouth was still moving.

"But it's safe to say that Judge is going to get thoroughly ravished when we get home."

I chuckled, watching Rix wing the ball under arm so it'd roll back to Judge after he'd fielded it. Then he got back into position. Feet apart. Knee slightly bent. Arms half loose, half tense, ready to help propel him where he needed to go to tag the ball.

And, yes.

He was going to get thoroughly ravished tonight too.

Though, I'd never tell him I was "ravishing" him. He'd be laughing too hard for me to concentrate on the ravishing.

"The guys are pretty excited Rix is going to come back to the team next season," I noted.

"I'm sure they are. I know nothing of this, but I think it's good practically every pitch Judge threw ended up in the grass."

This was true, though it had started out frustrating, with Rix needing to come out of the batter's box to go to the back stop to nab the ball and throw it back to Judge after he'd missed it. It hurt so much to watch, I almost jogged in so I could play catcher.

But Rix's shoulders always stayed straight. His chin up. His concentration focused. And a couple of times, Judge jogged in to talk to him about things he was seeing that Rix was doing but wasn't catching.

Eventually, he pulled it together, and when he did, boy, did he do it.

I figured he might have been more of a powerhouse before he'd lost his legs, but he was no slouch now.

He was going to be a ringer.

Crack!

"I know you saw it," I said to Chloe.

"Saw what?" she asked.

"Saw it the first time you met me." I gave it a beat and then explained, "How into Rix I was."

I was watching Rix field.

But I was feeling Chloe's attention turn to me.

"I also figured out you knew I hadn't asked him to be my fake boyfriend when you called to talk to us about him being my fake boyfriend," I continued.

Chloe said nothing.

Crack!

It was a line drive.

Those were harder to field. You needed to be more nimble on your feet.

I tensed.

Rix couldn't get to it, but he reached for it anyway. My heart slid up in my throat, but when it passed him by, he just started jogging after it.

"He's the best guy I've ever met," I finished.

"Fortunately, my life is such that he's in my top ten," Chloe replied. "But he's *high* up in that top ten."

Happy she had that, and for other reasons besides, I felt my lips curl up.

Crack!

I watched Rix field.

Then I noted, "You were never going to throw us in front of Peri."

"Mm…no," she confirmed.

"That was about getting me motivated," I went on.

Crack!

"Did it motivate you?" she asked.

I turned to Chloe.

She wasn't watching Rix or Judge.

She was watching me.

"Yes," I stated the obvious.

She smiled.

"Thank you," I said quietly.

"I love him. He deserves the best."

Ohmigod.

That was *so* nice.

"Can I hug you?" I asked.

Her face behind her shades grew soft. "Of course."

We hugged. Chloe made a move to let go, but I held on.

Just for another couple of seconds.

When we broke apart and looked back to the field, Judge was turned to us, and Rix had his hands on his hips, flipped to rest on their backs because of his ball glove, and he was watching us.

"We're bonding. You're bonding," Chloe called out. "No need to stare."

We got two male smirks.

Then Rix got into position.

Judge turned and threw up the ball.

And...

Crack!

"So," I began. "Who's next?"

And that was when Chloe busted out laughing.

WE WERE IN THAT GLASS TENT THING AMONG THE JOSHUA TREES.

It was the dark of night.

Rix had just finished fucking me while I was on my belly. As I took his cock, I'd been twisted at the waist to the side just a little so my view could be unobstructed of the shadowed trees off the foot of the bed. As I felt our connection, the power of him up on his arms, one hand planted above my left shoulder, the other hand lower, planted in the bed by my upper arm, his hips driving, his thighs straddling the outsides of my own.

I was contained under him, receiving.

He was surrounding me, giving.

He liked that position. We did it often, even if it was just one of several he pulled me into.

As for me...

I loved it.

I knew what I enjoyed with sex, and if I felt comfortable with a partner, I wasn't timid about getting it.

But this was us.

This was me letting go what I didn't need in order to give him what he did.

He needed to dominate.

He needed to be my shelter.

He needed to find every opportunity to let me be just who I was.

In other words, sex was no different than the rest of what he gave me.

It just came with the bonus of world-rocking orgasms.

Now, he was on his back, and I was on my side, tucked tight to him, head to his shoulder, eyes to the stars.

The truth?

I'd forgotten about it.

We were off on a quick weekend glamp.

We'd been home just a couple of weeks after New York, and not much had happened except the beauty of settling into a life with Rix that didn't have an end looming.

He was my guy.

I was his woman.

I saw him checking out Zillow listings for cabins in the mountains.

We cooked together in the evenings. We slept together in one or the other's bed. We rode to work together in the mornings. I hung out with Katie and Gal. He went out for beers with his buddies on the crew. We spent time with Chloe and Judge. We talked about getting a dog, something he'd avoided at first after he lost his legs, because he had to focus on navigating life. But now, he was ready. I loved animals, so I was ready too. The idea of going hiking with a pooch, Rix taking him or her on a run, weirdly thrilled me.

Like we were starting our family.

So yes.

I was so deep in the zone, I'd forgotten about it.

Until we lay under the stars, pleasantly fatigued from our hike that day, from eating too much food and having a few beers, from Rix making us both orgasm.

Until Rix took my hand on his chest into his.

Regardless of what he'd said, the ring hadn't moved since I put it on.

It moved now, as his other arm that was around me scrunched me tighter to him so he could hold my hand in one of his and slip the ring off with the other.

I was watching this through the moonlit shadows, holding my breath.

Once the ring was off, he lifted my hand and pressed his lips against the back of my engagement ring finger. As he did, I felt the bristles of his mustache and the tuft of hair under his lower lip, and my attention on what was happening was so intense, I could swear in that moment I could account for every whisker brushing my skin.

He then took my hand from his mouth and slid the ring back on.

To finish, he rested it back on his chest, but with his covering it.

And he decreed, "Now, it's official."

I pushed through his hold just enough, curling my fingers around his, so I could see the diamonds twinkling under the stars.

I felt my heart race, my belly flutter, and the beauty of understanding that when you take the leap, you don't hope for a soft landing.

You hope you'll never stop soaring.

And then I announced, "You are such a caveman."

I could tell he was smiling even as he asked, "Are you bitching?"

"I just experienced a modern day, 'You my woman,'" I pointed out.

"No. You experienced that earlier when I was fucking you into the bed."

I burst out laughing.

While I was doing it, Rix rolled us so he was on top.

When I quit doing it, I saw something that glittered more gorgeously than diamonds or stars.

Rix's eyes in the moonlight gazing down at me.

"You my woman," he whispered.

Oh my God.

I loved this man so much, it hurt.

Such a glorious, *glorious* pain.

"You my man," I whispered in return.

He kissed me.

I kissed him back.

After a good deal of time spent in celebratory pursuits, my man and I fell asleep under the stars.

We had not, neither of us, as yet had said the words *I love you*.

But that was all right.

We didn't need to.

Rix

RIX WAS AT HIS DESK IN THE OFFICE WHEN KRISTA SHOWED AT HIS DOOR.

They were all gearing up for Hale's visit next week where they'd be laying out the menu of programs they wanted to launch for Trail Blazer.

In other words, shit was getting real.

The furniture was in.

They'd hired an extra two staff members to take over the continuation of the Kids and Trails program.

Judge was drafting staff designations, organizational charts, job descriptions, strategic plans. Kevin was creating budgets. Alex was designing efforts to recruit volunteers and connect with schools, government services, and others in order to reach the kids. And Rix was polishing the menu of programs they were hoping to launch.

They were all of one mind and excited about what they hoped to achieve, but the fucking-around period was over.

If Hale gave them the green light, all systems would be a go, and it wouldn't be about waiting for furniture.

It'd be about busting their asses to make a difference.

In other words, he was deep in what he was doing, but he didn't miss the notification on the bottom right of his screen telling him he had an email.

And on the heels of it, another one from the same person.

Considering who it was, he went right to his inbox and opened it up.

Rix, only you would land the richest, most gorgeous female on the planet who also kayaks. I mean seriously?

Still smiling after that one, he opened up the next.

You look happy, which means I'm happy for you. We're gonna come down to Phoenix so Sean can golf, and I can get away from the snow and have copious facials in overpriced spas. Probably January. We'll drive up into the mountains and I better meet her.

That was it, likely because she didn't have time for fancy shit, like *later* or *goodbye*.

Both emails were signed, *Rachel Cavill, MD.*

He was smiling at his computer when he sensed movement at his door.

He looked there.

Since Krista was providing support for all of them, not to mention coordinating the finishing touches on the office that would soon have what they estimated to be twenty new staff members, it wasn't unusual she showed at his door.

And now, that was where she was.

He shifted his smile to her and gave a her a chin lift, though his focus grew sharp on her because he couldn't get a take on the expression on her face as he asked, "What's up?"

"Okay, it sounds like her, but I can't be sure. It might be a prank. But some lady who says she's Elsa Cohen is on the phone, asking for you."

Rix's gaze cut from her to the wall that separated him from Alexandra, his mind clicking that Alex was in a meeting with Kevin.

He then went back to Krista when she kept on.

"If it's her, I'd like to tell her to go jump in a lake, or maybe use some other language that isn't appropriate in the workplace. Unless you want to do it."

That earned her another smile.

But he said, "I'll take it."

She faked looking disappointed (or maybe she didn't), nodded, turned and moved swiftly through the open plan work area that they'd designed so the staff wouldn't feel boxed in and separated, which was totally not what they were going for here.

His phone rang, and he picked it up.

"Rix Hendrix."

"How did I know you'd sound like that," an unmistakable female voice said.

It was either her or someone who did a freaking good impression of her.

"You got me, tell me the reason you're taking my time when I've got things to do," he demanded.

"I never do this," she said bizarrely. "Never. Ever. Ever. But you are you. And Alexandra is Alexandra. And you've done the things you've done only to go on and do the things you do. So this once...*just this once*, I'm doing it."

"Doing what?" he asked, his voice tipping the line (further) on unfriendly.

"If you give me your email, I'll send you a link to download a file. And you have my word that file is safe, and I won't use your email again after that."

"A file?"

"I've filmed some interviews with people you know."

Fucking *fuck*.

"And I want you to watch the Exchange that includes them," she continued. "Because you need to watch it. And then I'd like you to let me know if I can air it."

Rix stared at his desk, feeling a lot, including shock she was reaching out for permission.

"John?" she called.

"Rix," he grunted.

Then he didn't let this gesture of good faith slide.

He gave her his email address.

"Got it," she replied, all business. "It'll come through in the next few minutes. Thanks for your time. Take care."

And that was it.

The woman didn't say, *Sorry I made it so, even local, you and your girl can't go out for a beer without at least one person giving you the once-over.* Or, *Sorry for dragging Alexandra's sister when she might not have found her way yet, but she didn't deserve to have her breast exposed to fifty million people and then that exploding to fifty million more.* Or a couple dozen other things she could apologize for.

Just *Thanks for your time. Take care.*

"Christ," he muttered, put the phone back in its cradle, and when his laptop indicated he had a new email and it came from eac@elsaexchange.com, he checked his mail.

He clicked the link, downloaded the massive file, and as the download was rolling, he got up to close his office door.

Then he sat behind his desk, pulled up the .mov file and watched it.

Elsa was in her trademark pastel green velvet chair, and opposite her, in another one, the velvet a peach color, sat Peri.

"God fucking dammit," Rix swore.

"We have with us today," Elsa began to introduce, "a woman who once bore the ring of our current, but very taken crush, John Hendrix, the beau of Alexandra Sharp of the New York Sharps and the Coddingtons of Somerset. Peri Poulson." She twirled her chair to Peri. "Peri. Thank you for reaching out to us."

She'd reached out to Elsa.

Whatever the fuck this was, it was Peri's doing.

Rix clenched his teeth.

"Thank you for having me," Peri replied, looking her normal tan and fit, but he knew she'd had her hair and makeup done professionally and her outfit wasn't the normal active mountain girl gear she wore, and it looked new.

"Now, what do you have to share with my wonderful watchers?" Elsa oozed.

"I just wanted to, you know..." She was off, nervous, maybe intimidated by where she was, maybe some part of her knew she should never in a million fucking years be sitting right there. "I just wanted to say that Rix and I were engaged."

"Rix?" Elsa queried.

"Rix. John Hendrix, but no one calls him John."

"And you were engaged?"

"Yes. Very engaged. At the time he had his accident, we were supposed to be married a few months after that."

Elsa said nothing.

"We...I think it's important to know, you know, I think people out there should know that when something like that happens to someone...I'm talking about when Rix lost his legs, it isn't just the someone it happens to that it happens to."

Elsa eagerly leaned closer to her and noted, "This is interesting. Please explain."

"I mean, Rix lost his legs, but I lost the man I was going to marry."

The camera closed in on Elsa as she appeared confused. "And now you've lost me. Unless I have the identity wrong of our John Hendrix, it's my understanding he's very much alive."

"I don't mean that," Peri said quickly.

"I see, you mean, he was, and I would contend it's justifiable, even if it might not be easy to deal with as a partner, but due to his loss and having to deal with it, his personality changed. For instance, perhaps he lashed out at you?"

Rix tensed, hoping like fuck to make herself look better, Peri wasn't going to lie.

Peri adjusted herself in her chair. "No, what I mean is—"

Elsa cut her off. "He didn't lash out at you?"

"No, what I'm trying to say is—"

"He was cruel to you? Cold to you? Distant? Lost? Recalcitrant?"

Peri shook her head, her shining blonde hair gliding over her shoulders. "No. None of that. What I'm saying is, as his partner—"

Elsa again interrupted.

"He fought treatment? Rehabilitation? He gave up and it was difficult to try to re-engage him in activities that would help him to lead a full life?" Elsa paused, but not long enough for Peri to answer. "Which," she glanced at the camera, "and I'll make it clear, my wonderful watchers, I truly know nothing about this," she turned back to Peri, "however, I would think those would be natural responses. Depression. Grief. And the behavior that comes with both."

"No, he wasn't like that. Rix was never like that. I mean he had his times, but he's always been the kind of man who faces things and then gets on with it. It happened. He faced it and he got on with it."

"So even after he lost his legs, he *was* the man you were going to marry," Elsa remarked.

Peri grew still in her chair.

The air in Rix's lungs grew still in his chest.

So when he whispered, "Shit," it sounded winded.

"Peri, if you would, I'd like you to watch this," Elsa invited.

Before Peri gave her approval, the visual of Elsa and Peri was lost as film of his bud from the crew, Jarrod, standing among a bunch of pines, wearing his blue firefighter tee, a microphone in his face, started rolling.

"Yeah, Rix was home from the rehab hospital exactly two days before she dumped him. And that was after she didn't go to the hospital very much when he was in to be with him. Give him support. Be a part of the process when he was learning what his life was gonna be like and how to negotiate it. He got home, he was still in his chair, they were building his prosthetics and the swelling had to go down and his legs still had to heal from the surgery so he could get into that, and she was outta there. Coupla years later, he's up and got a kickass job, doing cool shit for kids, and she wants him back. Like he's been waiting for her. When he wasn't. He found somebody else. Traded way the hell up. And I gotta tell you what all the guys are thinking, that woman reaching out to you to tell her story is all kinds of fucked up."

Elsa and Peri came back on screen, and Peri looked struck.

"Is this true?" Elsa asked. "Did you wait until John had navigated the difficult journey back to a fully functional life and try to get him back?"

"No one calls him John," Peri whispered.

"But is it true?" Elsa pushed.

Peri straightened her shoulders. "He wasn't the man I agreed to marry. You don't get it. No one thought about me. Everyone thought I was so terrible to take a break from our relationship when I did. But it was like that tree fell on me too."

"No, I don't get it. Because I have been told directly that you didn't"—Elsa lifted her hands and did air quotation marks—"take a break from your relationship. You ended your engagement, returned his ring, moved out of the home the two of you shared, and went on with your life, leaving him to recover from a double amputation and then learn to walk again without the woman he loved there to support him." Elsa's voice turned frosty on her last, "And, let's be very frank here, it is not in the slightest like that tree fell on you."

Peri tried again. "The spouses of people—"

"Yes, the spouses and partners of people who experience traumatic events most assuredly experience their own traumas at watching someone they love have to deal with their circumstances. Have to adjust lives and even let go of dreams to make room to build new ones. And they are intimately involved with all that, doing the same themselves in their own ways." Elsa turned to the camera, which tightened on her. "I think it's important, my watchers, to understand that tragedy has tentacles. Some that may even surprise you. It is rarely only one who suffers."

The visual of Elsa disappeared and onscreen was Nicole, his bud Rob's wife. She was sitting on a bench outside by a beach, the wind blowing her brown hair. A microphone was in her face.

"He pushed Rob out from under that tree," Nic shared. "He knew that tree was going to go, he ran to Rob, and he pushed him out from under. And it fell on him. I wake up at night. Rob wakes up at night. The guilt eats at him. At me. It could have been Rob. It should have been him. It wasn't him because of Rix. I'm not telling you this so Rix will see it and feel bad. We love him, and not just because of this. He's still tight with Rob, even though we don't live close anymore. They text each other. They talk. They still give each other a ton of shit." Nic busted out a smile. "That's Rix and Rob. Always the same. That never changed." Her smile died. "I'm just telling you this because that woman wants to make this about her. And it's about a lot of things. It'll always be about a lot of things. For me, it's about how deep my gratitude goes that Rix gave what he gave so my husband didn't have to give anything. So yeah, it's about a lot of things. The only thing I know for sure it's not about. It's not about her."

The onscreen visual went back to Elsa and Peri.

"Do you have anything to say to that?" Elsa asked.

"You told me I could tell my story," Peri accused. "I flew all the way out here to tell my story. Rix won't listen to me, his buddies are messing with me, and you told me I could share my side."

"I think what you don't understand, Peri, is that your side doesn't have very many dimensions. You've already shared it."

Peri started to look pissed.

Elsa turned to the camera, and it closed in on her.

"Now, with that, my wonderful watchers, I think we've all learned so, *so* much that is *very* important. So I think for now we'll call it a wrap. Until our next exchange, keep it positive. Elsa is signing off."

She then winked, blew a kiss, and the video ended.

Rix sat with it for a second, then he went back to the email, hit reply and typed, *Don't air it.*

And he hit send.

After that, he picked up his phone and sent two texts.

The first, to Jarrod: *You're an asshole, but you look good on camera. It's not gonna air. Leave P alone. It's done for me. Tell the guys to lay off. Sorry to kill your bid to score pussy through a gossip show. Fuck off but let's get a beer.*

The second, to Nic: *It's not gonna air. Love you, beautiful. Tell that*

*ugly mug you married he's safe. You won't leave him for me now that I've
found my own woman. And stop it. Both of you sleep. I'm happy.*

He'd just put his phone down when he got a three-word email
reply from Elsa.

Understood. It's dead.

At that, Rix had to sit for a minute because he had a feeling all of
what he just saw was not about Elsa developing a conscience but
giving something to Rix she thought he needed.

And he did not want to like that woman.

But there it was.

The first text back was Nic.

Love you too.

The second was Jarrod.

*I don't need a gossip show to score pussy. I'm a way bigger stud than you
ever were. Brats and beer at my house Saturday. Fuck off until then and
bring Alex.*

Rix smiled.

Got up.

Opened his door.

Returned to his big, important desk.

And with the only thought in his head being a mental note to
remember to tell Alex they had plans on Saturday, Rix got back to
work.

"IT'S CRAZY," SHE DECLARED.

They were sitting in line behind two cars at the window at Scooter's, waiting to roll up and get their coffee. It was Saturday morning,
and they were heading to Cottonwood to hike the Jail Trail.

Well, they'd be doing that, just not right after coffee, like Alex
thought they were.

"It isn't crazy," Rix replied. "I know you don't have a lot of experience with shit like this, but this is normal."

"It's normal for someone's father and sister to show the week of

Thanksgiving, commence occupation of the six thousand square foot, five-bedroom, six-bath monstrosity they've rented, and do that until the first week of January?"

He grinned at her. "Six thousand square feet for two people, no. Family wanting to be around family for holidays. Yes. Your sister doesn't have a job, so she can be anywhere she wants to be for seven weeks. And your dad needs a break."

Because she knew he was right, she did a visible if not auditory huff and looked forward.

Then she mumbled, "Go, honey."

Rix looked forward too, saw the car at the window had taken off, the next one was up, so he inched up a car length.

"Blake insists on making Thanksgiving dinner, and that terrifies me," Alex went on complaining.

It terrified him too, especially since this was Blake's new thing. Alex had told him she'd never cooked before. Now she'd thrown herself into learning and had decided to show off her new skills on the most important cooking day of the year.

"We'll keep an eye on it, we'll make sure there's plenty of snacks stocked and backup shit we can do if things go south, and who cares if it sucks? It's just a meal," Rix returned.

"A meal your mom, dad, brother, sister-in-law, *you* and *me* will be eating," she retorted.

He turned and grinned at her. "Yes, that's what's happening next Thursday, Thanksgiving, where family gets together and stuffs their faces."

"Ohmigod, it's gonna be a disaster," she grumbled to the windshield.

He stopped teasing her, getting the feeling she was actually concerned about this regardless that Blake was getting her shit tight. And regardless her dad was doing this because he was far from stupid, he saw his opportunity to have a deeper bond with both of his girls, so he was taking his shot. And regardless that Rix's family liked every-one, especially Alex. Which meant, even if they didn't get along with her dad or Blake, they'd still love Alex and make the most of whatever they could build with Alex's family.

But they'd get along.

"Babe, it's gonna be awesome," he assured. "You're worried your people aren't gonna jive with my people. That Blake's gonna be Blake. That my folks are going to be intimidated by dinner in a mansion with an unrestricted view of Thumb Butte."

He wasn't finished when she said, "Your parents are down to earth and have a really awesome house, they won't get intimidated by that."

"Then okay, what's your issue?"

"I don't know how to be a family," she whispered.

Jesus.

He had no idea how that felt, he still felt that.

"Baby," he called.

She looked his way.

He leaned into an elbow on the console. "I'd put money down on the fact it's gonna be a lot easier learning how to be a family than it was not being one."

Her two-toned eyes roamed his face, they warmed, and she nodded.

He leaned further, across to her, and pressed hard on her lips.

As he was pulling back, the car behind them tooted.

He looked forward, seeing that the car in front was still at the window, so he looked at the rearview mirror, tension hitting his neck at a memory.

He also felt Alex twist to look too.

"Ohmigod. That's Dani," she announced.

The woman who was apparently Dani was a pretty, massively smiling blonde who, for some reason, was pumping two happy thumbs up in front of her.

"Who's Dani?" Rix asked, still watching as the woman shoved her head out of the side window of her Tahoe.

"A…friend," Alex answered, and he heard her window whirring down.

He looked right, and watched Al releasing her seatbelt and pulling her entire body out to sit her ass on the window edge.

"Number, bitch!" Dani shouted. She was now waving her phone out the window. "We need drinks and a very long chat!"

"Okay!" Alex yelled back, shouted her number, Rix watched in the review as Dani entered it into her phone, then Alex yelled. "Text me so I have yours."

"Gotcha, sister. Will do! You rock! You roll! You got it goin' on! I love it!" Dani hollered.

Rix watched her pump more thumbs up as Alex came back into the car.

She buckled up.

Rix pulled up to the window, got out his wallet, and paid.

He waited for the drinks and remarked, "A friend and you don't have her number?"

"When I was giving myself a pep talk to go back out and flirt with you that night at the Raven, she was in the bathroom," Alex began, this share making his gut get tight.

He took the drinks, handed them to her, and she dealt with them as he rolled up his window and rolled out.

She kept talking.

"She helped with the pep talk. She was really cool. I liked her."

Her phone binged, and Rix glanced at her to see she was smiling at it.

Dani had texted.

When she was done programming in the number, she dropped her hands to her lap, and he said gently, "I thought you'd ditched me."

She was quiet right back when she said, "It's okay."

"I wasn't there yet."

She reached out, squeezed his thigh, took her hand away and assured, "I know, Rix, honey. It's okay." When he said nothing, she said, "Look where I am. Do you not think I'm okay?"

He grunted.

But he felt better, and he knew she knew it when Alex didn't reply.

Rix drove.

Alex rode.

He turned left on Mt. Vernon.

"Are we going back to my place? Did we forget something?" she asked.

"No," he answered.

"Then...uh, do you know a different way to Cottonwood?"

"No."

"Then where are we going?"

"Quiet, sweetheart, quick detour."

She grew quiet.

Rix reached for his drink, took a sip, returned it, then went back to the controls so he could pilot them along Senator Highway.

Up they went, past her place, deeper into Groom Creek, then he swung a left onto a dirt road.

They climbed about a hundred feet, swung a right, climbed a hundred feet more, then pulled off into the wide dirt drive next to a semi-sprawling ranch-style log cabin with a blue roof and a full front porch that wrapped around one side and led to a big square deck built suspended over the descent off the back right.

It had a large, blue shed about twenty feet from the house off to the left. It also had a fenced-in area with a greenhouse down the side stairs from the back deck that led to some stone steps in the earth.

There were neighbors, not too close, not too far.

Rix had met them. One elderly year-round couple. Two cabins that were owned by folks in Phoenix and used sporadically, though never in the winter. And the cabin up top that was owned by a park ranger who worked Prescott National Forest, a friend of Rix's. They weren't close, but Rix had put the feelers out. So when that cabin came up for grabs, he arranged it so, in a crazy market where shit was selling within hours of it listing, Rix could have first dibs.

He took them.

The log cabin had also been a weekend getaway house.

Now, it wouldn't be.

The rest of the area around the cabin was just...

Trees.

"Four bedrooms," he stated. "A den. Great room. Master has its own bath and a walk-in. Rest of the rooms share another one, though there's a powder room off the kitchen. Also a small room next to the utility room on the bottom level, could be a playroom or a guest room. There's a three-quarter bath down there." He paused and then said, "Shed is twelve by ten."

She sat next to him, staring at the house, saying nothing.

"Isn't secluded like yours," Rix continued. "Density of trees isn't as much. But whaddaya think? We could raise kids here, hey?"

It took a beat before, slowly, she turned to face him, and from the look on her face, she didn't have to say anything.

But she did.

"Hey," she breathed.

He smiled.

Then he announced, "Good you think so. Because I bought it."

Those beautiful eyes got huge.

"You bought it?"

"I bought it."

"Like, *bought* it, bought it. You own it?"

Christ, she was cute.

"No. *We* will own it once we do some title shit to get your name on it after we get hitched. But yes. Offer accepted. Down payment check has been cashed. And as soon as we close, my name will be on the title of this house."

"You bought us a house," she stated.

"Yup," he affirmed.

"Without me looking at it even on a Zillow listing."

There hadn't been a Zillow listing.

He didn't tell her that.

Still grinning, he repeated, "Yup. We're gonna Airbnb your pad and mine. Be Prescott real estate moguls."

"So you have it all figured out."

"Totally."

"You *are* a caveman."

He didn't quit smiling.

"I was gonna give you your birthday present," she shared.

He felt his smile waver. "Say what?"

"I haven't given you your birthday present yet. You took off that night before I could give it to you. I was waiting until all that wasn't fresh anymore. Which means today. On the hike."

His smile came back. "Cool, honey."

"No, it's not cool," she retorted and threw her hand over the dash. "I can't give you that present after you already one upped me before I even did it by giving me *a house*."

Rix busted out laughing, doing it reaching for her and pulling her to him so he could stop doing it in order to kiss her.

Once he accomplished that, he didn't let her go and he didn't go far.

"I don't need any presents from you," he told her.

"That's good, because I'd brought it with me to Joshua Tree, then you horked in on that action by making us official. So I picked today for my third try, and then you gave me a house. The way you're going, I'll never give it to you."

"I'm sure what you bought me is fantastic, but I'm totally down with that."

"You would be, you're Rix. You can't stop being grotesquely awesome. It'd be annoying if I didn't love you so freaking much."

He was no longer smiling.

He was staring at her, incapable even of giving her shit for calling him "grotesquely awesome."

Then he was kissing her.

Eventually, he had to undo her seatbelt and his to kiss her like he wanted to kiss her.

When it was pull her into his lap and do her in the cab of his truck or get their shit together and go inspect the house they were gonna raise their family in, he stopped kissing her.

"I love you too, baby," he whispered.

"No kidding?" she asked somewhat breathlessly. "You bought me a house."

That made him smile again.

And let her go.

For then.

He opened his door and angled out of the truck.

Alex did the same on her side.

They met at the grill, and he took hold of her, tossing his arm around her neck, tucking her close to his side.

Alex slid her arm around his back, her fingers curling around.

And, holding her tight, Rix walked his woman across the dirt, through the trees, up the steps.

And into their house.

EARLY THE NEXT MORNING, RIX WALKED OUT OF HIS BATHROOM AFTER taking a pit stop from getting Alex and him a fresh cup of joe.

Like he did on the way to the bathroom, he did the same on the way out.

He looked to his nightstand.

Then he looked to his feet and smiled.

He hit the kitchen, made their coffee and carried it out to the front porch, where Alex was where he'd left her. Kicked back in one of the chairs, Uggs on her feet, thick joggers on her legs, one of his sweatshirts up top, knit cap pulled low over her forehead so her thick hair bunched out at the sides, and her eyes to the street.

Rix handed over her mug and got her soft, "Thanks, honey," before he sat beside her and got comfortable.

He sipped his coffee.

They didn't say anything, just sat beside each other in contented silence on a Sunday morning in his quiet 'hood.

They did this as her birthday present sat on his nightstand, and it had a lot to say.

It did, seeing as it was the picture of them out in Cali, the first one they'd taken together.

She'd put in a frame.

So yeah.

In the end…
His woman totally fucking one-upped him.
And Rix didn't mind.
Not even a little bit.

The End

River Rain will continue with the story of Tom Pierce.

DISCUSSION & REFLECTION QUESTIONS

1) Is this the first time you've read a romance with a hero or heroine living with a disability? What did you think? Would you seek out more?

Also, were you as surprised as Rix at the non-issue this was for Alex?

2) The mysterious Dani gives Alex advice about her love life, making it clear life is meant to be lived and risks are meant to be taken, even if the heart is involved. And yet, Rix and Alex are co-workers. Do you feel this was good advice? Or do you think Alex was right to take a step back and think hard about flirting—or taking something further —with a colleague?

3) At first it seems that, due to her shyness, Alex is considered by others as unusual or vulnerable. As the book progresses, however, the reader finds that she's mostly an introvert and in fact knows herself very well and has it together. So much so that, in the end, Rix is quick to defend her as a strong, capable woman who simply doesn't enjoy parties or crowds.

Did you fall into the assumption that Alex has some fragility due to being quiet and/or shy?

Further from this, are you an introvert or an extrovert? Either way, do you feel there are certain expectations put on you because of that trait? For instance, people expecting you to "get over it" and be more social if you're an introvert. Or people expecting you to "carry" a social situation if you're an extrovert. How does that make you feel? Did reading this book help you to realize that introversion is a natural characteristic that doesn't need to be overcome?

4) Those who love him handle Rix with kid gloves due to his change in life circumstances. Judge and Rix have a very open, honest relationship with easy communication, even if what needs to be communicated is difficult. And yet Judge couldn't broach the subject of asking Rix how he's handling living with his disability.

Do you sense that Rix's womanizing might have been alleviated if the ones around him didn't treat this new part of his life as untouchable, and instead he'd had someone to talk to about how he was coping? Or is it your opinion, instead, that Rix should have spoken to those around him and shared what he needed?

5) Onward from this, Peri is set up to be the villain of this book, however, the core of her issue is very true. When life-altering situations happen, like Rix losing his legs, they happen to a person and to those who love them. Everyone needs some level of support and training to learn how to live with the altered circumstances. Peri didn't seek this out, or address it with Rix, but how did you feel when she made her point to Elsa that her life, too, had been changed? Did you feel she had a valid argument?

6) Ned makes the point that the masses don't make change, it's visionaries who change the thinking of the masses. Who are some

visionaries that you admire who brought our society forward? How did they do that?

Further, what kind of programs do you think Trail Blazer should launch that might reach future visionaries? And what real-life programs do you know that help children of any walk of life overcome obstacles and reach their potential?

7) Alex and Rix's families couldn't be more different. Rix has been raised middle class, with a loving, close family, while Alex's family had prestige and wealth, and they barely know one another. Alex only found true happiness when she left those trappings behind and sought a place to be her true self.

With this in mind, what do you think is next for Ned and Blake? Do you think this family will grow closer and face their past remoteness? Do you think Ned will find love after harboring resentment against Helena for so long? Do you think Blake will tackle the superficiality of her world and find something deeper?

8) Alex wears "camouflage" when she's in New York and almost seems to inhabit another life, the one she grew up in and left behind.

Are there times in your life you feel you need camouflage or are in the position to do things you don't normally do in your day-to-day life? What are those? How does that make you feel?

9) What kind of partner do you see for Jamie? Dru? Dani? Ned? Blake?

10) Do you think Rix ever read Alex's binder?

DISCOVER MORE KRISTEN ASHLEY

Gossamer in the Darkness
A Fantasyland Novella
Coming April 19, 2022

Their engagement was set when they were children. Loren Copeland, the rich and handsome Marquess of Remington, would marry Maxine Dawes, the stunning daughter of the Count of Derryman. It's a power match. The perfect alliance for each house.

However, the Count has been keeping secret a childhood injury that means Maxine can never marry. He's done this as he searches for a miracle so this marriage can take place. He needs the influence such an alliance would give him, and he'll stop at nothing to have it.

The time has come. There could be no more excuses. No more delays. The marriage has to happen, or the contract will be broken.

When all seems lost, the Count finds his miracle: There's a parallel universe where his daughter has a twin. He must find her, bring her to his world and force her to make the Marquess fall in love with her.

And this, he does.

Chasing Serenity: A River Rain Novel, Book 2
By Kristen Ashley

From a very young age, Chloe Pierce was trained to look after the ones she loved.

And she was trained by the best.

But when the man who looked after her was no longer there, Chloe is cast adrift—just as the very foundation of her life crumbled to pieces.

Then she runs into tall, lanky, unpretentious Judge Oakley, her exact opposite. She shops. He hikes. She drinks pink ladies. He drinks beer. She's a city girl. He's a mountain guy.

Obviously, this means they have a blowout fight upon meeting. Their second encounter doesn't go a lot better.

Judge is loving the challenge. Chloe is everything he doesn't want in a woman, but he can't stop finding ways to spend time with her. He knows she's dealing with loss and change.

He just doesn't know how deep that goes. Or how ingrained it is for Chloe to care for those who have a place in her heart, how hard it will be to trust anyone to look after her…

And how much harder it is when it's his turn.

Wild Wind: A Chaos Novella
By Kristen Ashley

When he was sixteen years old, Jagger Black laid eyes on the girl who was his. At a cemetery. During her mother's funeral.

For years, their lives cross, they feel the pull of their connection, but then they go their separate ways.

But when Jagger sees that girl chasing someone down the street, he doesn't think twice before he wades right in. And when he gets a full-on dose of the woman she's become, he knows he finally has to decide if he's all in or if it's time to cut her loose.

She's ready to be cut loose.

But Jagger is all in.

Wild Fire: A Chaos Novella
By Kristen Ashley

"You know you can't keep a good brother down."

The Chaos Motorcycle Club has won its war. But not every brother rode into the sunset with his woman on the back of his bike.

Chaos returns with the story of Dutch Black, a man whose father was the moral compass of the Club, until he was murdered. And the man who raised Dutch protected the Club at all costs. That combination is the man Dutch is intent on becoming.

It's also the man that Dutch is going to go all out to give to his woman.

Dream Bites Cookbook
Cooking with the Commandos
Short stories by Kristen Ashley
Recipes from Suzanne M. Johnson

From *New York Times* bestseller Kristen Ashley and *USA Today* bestseller Suzanne M. Johnson…

See what's cooking!

You're invited to Denver and into the kitchens of Hawk Delgado's commandos: Daniel "Mag" Magnusson, Boone Sadler, Axl Pantera and Augustus "Auggie" Hero as they share with you some of the goodness they whip up for their women.

Not only will you get to spend time with the commandos, the Dream Team makes an appearance with their men, *and* there are a number of special guest stars. It doesn't end there, you'll also find some bonus recipes from a surprise source who doesn't like to be left out.

So strap in for a trip to Denver, a few short stories, some reminiscing and a lot of great food.

Welcome to *Dream Bites, Cooking with the Commandos!*

(Half of the proceeds of this cookbook go to the Rock Chick Nation Charities)

Quiet Man: A Dream Man Novella
By Kristen Ashley

Charlotte "Lottie" McAlister is in the zone. She's ready to take on the next chapter of her life, and since she doesn't have a man, she'll do what she's done all along. She'll take care of business on her own. Even if that business means starting a family.

The problem is, Lottie has a stalker. The really bad kind. The kind that means she needs a bodyguard.

Enter Mo Morrison.

Enormous. Scary.

Quiet.

Mo doesn't say much, and Lottie's used to getting attention. And she wants Mo's attention. Badly.

But Mo has a strict rule. If he's guarding your body, that's all he's doing with it.

However, the longer Mo has to keep Lottie safe, the faster he falls for the beautiful blonde who has it so together, she might even be able to tackle the demons he's got in his head that just won't die.

But in the end, Lottie and Mo don't only have to find some way to keep hands off until the threat is over, they have to negotiate the over-protective Hot Bunch, Lottie's crazy stepdad, Tex, Mo's crew of frat-boy commandos, not to mention his nutty sisters.

All before Lottie finally gets her Dream Man.

And Mo can lay claim to his Dream Girl.

Rough Ride: A Chaos Novella
By Kristen Ashley

Rosalie Holloway put it all on the line for the Chaos Motorcycle Club.

Informing to Chaos on their rival club—her man's club, Bounty—Rosalie knows the stakes. And she pays them when her man, who she was hoping to scare straight, finds out she's betrayed him and he delivers her to his brothers to mete out their form of justice.

But really, Rosie has long been denying that, as she drifted away from her Bounty, she's been falling in love with Everett "Snapper" Kavanagh, a Chaos brother. Snap is the biker-boy-next door with the snowy blue eyes, quiet confidence and sweet disposition who was supposed to keep her safe…and fell down on that job.

For Snapper, it's always been Rosalie, from the first time he saw her at the Chaos Compound. He's just been waiting for a clear shot. But he didn't want to get it after his Rosie was left bleeding, beat down and broken by Bounty on a cement warehouse floor.

With Rosalie a casualty of an ongoing war, Snapper has to guide her to trust him, take a shot with him, build a them…

And fold his woman firmly in the family that is Chaos.

Rock Chick Reawakening: A Rock Chick Novella
By Kristen Ashley

From *New York Times* bestselling author, Kristen Ashley, comes the long-awaited story of Daisy and Marcus, *Rock Chick Reawakening*. A prequel to Kristen's *Rock Chick* series, *Rock Chick Reawakening* shares the tale of the devastating event that nearly broke Daisy, an event that set Marcus Sloane—one of Denver's most respected businessmen and one of the Denver underground's most feared crime bosses—into finally making his move to win the heart of the woman who stole his.

Sign up for the Blue Box Press/1001 Dark Nights Newsletter
and be entered to win a Tiffany Lock necklace.

There's a contest every quarter!

Go to www.TheBlueBoxPress.com to subscribe!

As a bonus, all subscribers can download FIVE FREE
exclusive books!

DISCOVER 1001 DARK NIGHTS COLLECTION NINE

DRAGON UNBOUND by Donna Grant
A Dragon Kings Novella

NOTHING BUT INK by Carrie Ann Ryan
A Montgomery Ink: Fort Collins Novella

THE MASTERMIND by Dylan Allen
A Rivers Wilde Novella

JUST ONE WISH by Carly Phillips
A Kingston Family Novella

BEHIND CLOSED DOORS by Skye Warren
A Rochester Novella

GOSSAMER IN THE DARKNESS by Kristen Ashley
A Fantasyland Novella

THE CLOSE-UP by Kennedy Ryan
A Hollywood Renaissance Novella

DELIGHTED by Lexi Blake
A Masters and Mercenaries Novella

THE GRAVESIDE BAR AND GRILL by Darynda Jones
A Charley Davidson Novella

THE ANTI-FAN AND THE IDOL by Rachel Van Dyken
A My Summer In Seoul Novella

A VAMPIRE'S KISS by Rebecca Zanetti
A Dark Protectors/Rebels Novella

CHARMED BY YOU by J. Kenner
A Stark Security Novella

HIDE AND SEEK by Laura Kaye
A Blasphemy Novella

DESCEND TO DARKNESS by Heather Graham
A Krewe of Hunters Novella

BOND OF PASSION by Larissa Ione
A Demonica Novella

JUST WHAT I NEEDED by Kylie Scott
A Stage Dive Novella

Also from Blue Box Press

THE BAIT by C.W. Gortner and M.J. Rose

THE FASHION ORPHANS by Randy Susan Meyers and M.J. Rose

TAKING THE LEAP by Kristen Ashley
A River Rain Novel

SAPPHIRE SUNSET by Christopher Rice writing C. Travis Rice
A Sapphire Cove Novel

THE WAR OF TWO QUEENS by Jennifer L. Armentrout
A Blood and Ash Novel

THE MURDERS AT FLEAT HOUSE by Lucinda Riley

DISCOVER THE WORLD OF BLUE BOX PRESS AND 1001 DARK NIGHTS

Collection One

Collection Two

Collection Three

Collection Four

Collection Five

Collection Six

Collection Seven

Collection Eight

Bundles

Discovery Authors

Blue Box Press

Rising Storm

Liliana Hart's MacKenzie Family

Lexi Blake's Crossover Collection

Kristen Proby's Crossover Collection

ON BEHALF OF BLUE BOX PRESS,

Liz Berry, M.J. Rose, and Jillian Stein would like to thank ~

Steve Berry
Doug Scofield
Benjamin Stein
Kim Guidroz
Social Butterfly PR
Ashley Wells
Asha Hossain
Chris Graham
Chelle Olson
Kasi Alexander
Jessica Saunders
Dylan Stockton
Kate Boggs
Richard Blake
and Simon Lipskar

Made in the USA
Monee, IL
06 January 2023

24690507R00288